As a child, Fiona was constantly teased for two things: having her nose in a book and living in a dream world. Things haven't changed much since then, but at least she's found a career that puts her runaway imagination to use.

Fiona's first book was published in 2006 and she now has twenty-six published books under her belt. She started her career writing heartfelt but humorous romances for Mills & Boon, but now writes romantic comedies and feel-good women's fiction for HQ, including *The Little Shop of Hopes and Dreams*, which was a Kindle bestseller in 2015. She is a previous winner of the Joan Hessayon New Writers' Award, has had five books shortlisted for a RoNA Award and won the 'Best Short Romance' at the Festival of Romance for three consecutive years.

Fiona lives in London with her husband and two daughters (oh, the drama in her house!), and she loves good books, good films and anything cinnamon-flavoured. She also can't help herself if a good tune comes on and she's near a dance floor – you have been warned!

The Memory Collector

Fiona Harper

ONE PLACE. MANY STORIES

HQ
An imprint of HarperCollins*Publishers* Ltd
1 London Bridge Street
London SE1 9GF

This paperback edition 2018

1
First published in Great Britain by
HQ, an imprint of HarperCollins*Publishers* Ltd 2018

Copyright © Fiona Harper 2018

asserts the moral right to be
identified as the author of this work.
A catalogue record for this book is
available from the British Library.

ISBN: 978-0-00-821695-5

Printed and bound in Great Britain by
CPI Group (UK) Ltd, Croydon, CR0 4YY

For Siân and Rose

PROLOGUE

RED COAT

The coat isn't the orangey-red of postboxes, but the crimson of a film star's lipstick. It has boxy shoulders and it nips in at the waist then flares out again, ending just above a pair of shapely calves. Even after all these years, every time I go to the seaside I look for a red coat. I don't think I've ever seen another one like it.

THEN

The lady in the red coat is laughing. She smiles down at the little girl standing beside her. It's windy today and hardly anyone is at the beach but neither of them cares. They race each other along the pier, and their shrieks of mirth blow over the railings and get lost in the vastness of the sea beyond. When they can't run any further, when the sturdy railings stop them leaping onto the flinty waves and sprinting into the horizon, they stand there, panting. Then the woman goes and gets them both an ice cream.

The girl thinks this might be the best ice cream she's ever had, but she doesn't say that out loud, just in case she's wrong. Her mummy has a really bad memory, and sometimes she wonders if hers is the same. There are so many things to keep in her head, you see. So many secrets. It's hard to store all the memories and things for school in there, too. Maybe mint choc chip isn't her favourite after all. Maybe she likes something else better. She really can't remember.

They eat the cones, leaning against the railings and looking out to sea, hair flapping behind them like ribbons.

'I think this is my favourite place in the whole wide world,' the little girl says.

The woman nods. 'Mine too. Whenever I come to the seaside, the first thing I do is walk to the end of the pier. It's a place where land and sea blur into one, a place where you feel anything might be possible.'

'Even flying?' the little girl says, her voice full of awe.

'Even flying,' the woman says, smiling softly at her. 'But maybe not today, eh? I think it's a bit too blustery for that.'

'Can we come back tomorrow, then?'

'Of course,' the woman says, turning to stare out to sea again. 'We've come here every day so far and we can come back every day after if you'd like.'

The little girl thinks about this for a while as she eats her ice cream. Where could they fly to? France or Spain, maybe even Africa? She's not sure she's got the right clothes for hot weather, though, so she turns to ask the woman what she should wear and discovers her companion is no longer smiling.

She's so still, her eyes so empty, that for a moment the little girl is reminded of the dummies in the window of C&A.

'What's the matter, Aunty?' the little girl asks. 'Are you sad?'

For a long time the lady doesn't move, but then she turns to look at the girl. Her mouth bends upwards but her eyes still have the same faraway look they did when she was staring out across the grey, choppy waves.

'A little,' she says and her eyeballs get all shiny.

The girl takes an extra-big slurp of her ice cream and then she reaches out for the woman's free hand. They're very pretty hands. They're clean and she always has such shiny nail polish. Today, it's red to match her coat. 'Why are you sad?'

The woman kneels down so she's at eye level with the girl. 'Only because I know this lovely holiday will have to end soon,' she says, 'but I'm having so much fun with you I don't want it to.'

The girl grins. 'Me neither! Can we just stay here forever, Aunty? Please, please, *please*?'

The seaside is much, much better than home. There's no shouting or shut doors and there's room. Room to run. Room to breathe. Sometimes, when she and Aunty are out together the little girl just spends ages making her chest puff in and out, feeling the salt at the back of her tongue and the clean coldness in her chest.

Before the woman can answer the girl, her scoop of ice cream slides off her cornet and onto the rough planks of the pier. 'Silly me!' she says as she looks at it. 'Raspberry ripple is my favourite, too!' She delves into her shiny black handbag, picks out a tissue and mops the sticky mess from her fingers.

'Don't cry!' the girl says as a tear slides down the woman's face. She holds her cornet out. 'I know it's only mint choc chip, but you can share mine.'

That makes the woman smile properly, but for some reason the tears fall even harder. She takes a tiny lick and then hands the cone back to the girl. 'Thank you, Heather,' she says, and the girl thinks nobody has ever said her name in such a lovely way before, all soft and husky with their eyes full of sunshine.

The little girl hugs the woman, holding her arm out so she doesn't get pale-green ice cream on the smart red coat. 'I love you, Aunty,' she says as she presses her face against the scratchy sleeve.

'I love you too.'

They hold each other for a long time and then they walk back down the pier hand in hand. When they reach the end, the girl starts to turn right, towards the crazy golf. The woman starts to go that way too, but then she stops. The girl tugs her hand but she doesn't move. She's staring at something across the road. The girl can't see what, because a fat man eating a warm doughnut is in her way, but then his friend calls him and he hurries off. Aunty starts walking briskly.

'We're going the wrong way!' the girl says as they trot along. 'We're supposed to be going to the crazy golf!'

'Not this afternoon,' the woman replies. She's looking straight ahead and her voice is all tight. 'We'll go back to the B&B and play cards and eat cheese-and-onion crisps, your favourite. How about that?'

The girl nods, even though that's not what she wants to do. The woman has been very kind bringing her on this holiday and she doesn't want to be ungrateful, but she also doesn't understand. Aunty looks worried, and crazy golf has never made her worried before. The only time she has looked scared on their holiday so far was the moment when the special train that climbs up the cliff lurched as it started its journey. She held tight onto the railing and wouldn't look down when the girl tried to show her how small the people were getting.

The girl has to run a little bit to keep up with the woman as they head back to the B&B. Her head is bobbing up and down, which makes looking over her shoulder difficult, but she eventually manages to do it. There's nothing there to be worried about behind them, though. Only a policeman, and he's giving directions to an old couple with white hair. He's not even looking their way.

CHAPTER ONE

DAISY CHAIN

I pick up a yellowing atlas with a musty-smelling cover. There's something inside, something that pushes the pages apart, inviting investigation. A bookmark, I suppose. I could be contrary and choose a different place to open the book but I let the pages fall where they want to. There's no bookmark, just a circle of crushed flowers, pressed flat and paper thin. Daisies. If I touch them, the petals might crumble. I don't have many memories of my childhood, but I remember putting this here. This is my first daisy chain, the one my sister, Faith, showed me how to make. She taught me to choose the ones with the fattest, hairiest stems, and how to use my fingernail to make a half-moon in the plump green flesh so they didn't break. Yet they were still so fragile, so easy to crush without meaning to.

NOW

Heather shouldn't be there. Everything inside her tells her to turn around, walk briskly out of the shop and run back to her car, but she doesn't. Instead, she stops in front of a display rack of shoes. She imagines the feet that will go inside them – pink and pudgy, with unbelievably small toes that beg to be kissed.

How can something so innocent be so dangerous?

A pair catches her eye. They aren't bright and gaudy like many of the others, shouting their cheerfulness. They are tiny. Delicate. Made of cream corduroy with yellow and white daisies embroidered over the toes and a mother-of-pearl button instead of a buckle. Maybe that's why she reaches out and touches them, even though she knows she shouldn't. Maybe that's why she lets her fingers run over the tiny, furry ridges of the fabric.

As soon as she makes contact, she knows she's crossed a threshold. That's it now. Even though she's telling herself inside her head that she can stop herself this time, she knows she's going to do it. She knows these are the ones.

She pulls her hand back and shoves it in her jacket pocket, anchors it there by making a fist, then browses the adjacent stand: floppy sun hats for doll-sized heads, pastel socks all lined up in pleasing pairs. She tries to forget about the shoes.

She wanders round the ground floor of the Bromley branch of Mothercare, a path she's taken so many times now that she does it automatically. She's been coming here for years, just browsing, just looking at the miniature clothes, all clean and bright and smelling of hope, even though she has no child at home. But it's changed from how it used to be. It's no longer a leisure activity; it's a compulsion.

As she walks she notices the blonde sales assistant – the bossy one with the sharp eyes – is busy serving a small queue at the till. The other one, the new one, is attempting to show a heavily pregnant woman how to collapse one of the prams on display, but she can't work out how to do it. Both sales assistant and customer are totally absorbed in the search for the right button or catch. Heather can't see anyone else on duty.

That's when she does it.

That's when she turns swiftly and walks back to the rack of shoes, her feet making hardly any sound on the vinyl floor. That's when her hands become someone else's, when she slides the plastic hanger holding the daisy shoes off the pole and into her handbag.

She looks around. The sales assistants are still occupied, neither looking her way. No one shouts. No one comes running. So with her heart punching against her ribcage, she heads for the exit, doing her best to pretend this is a normal Saturday afternoon.

When she finally makes it through the doors and the warm spring air hits her, she has to hold back the urge to vomit. She walks down the pedestrianized section of the High Street, blinking furiously, not really caring where she's going.

A little voice in her head tells her to go back, to reverse what she's just done, to slide the shoes back where they belong – no one will ever know! – or even better, she should just surreptitiously pull them out of her bag once she's back inside the shop, go up to the till and hand the cash over.

Heather starts running then, shame, regret and disgust with herself powering her strides, and she doesn't stop until she's at the top of the multi-storey car park, standing outside her car. She doesn't remember pressing the button for the lift, or pushing her ticket into the parking machine and pulling it out again while it spat out her change. She doesn't care, though. She just dives inside her car and yanks the door closed, shutting the world outside, insulating herself from what she's just done.

She throws her handbag onto the passenger seat and braces her hands on the steering wheel. It's the only way she can get them to stop shaking.

CHAPTER TWO

NOW

Heather is tempted to park around the corner from her flat, even though she knows it's a stupid idea. It won't stop the police finding her. They might have tailed her all the way from Bromley High Street and down the hill into the depths of Shortlands. Or they could just look up her registration with the DVLA and find out where her flat is. They have computers in their cars that do that now. She's seen them on TV.

She parks on the drive, as close to the front door as possible, then grabs her handbag and scurries into the large Victorian house. It was probably once the dwelling of a well-to-do middle-class family, but now it has been carved into three flats, nice but not particularly upmarket. Heather has her head down when she arrives in the hallway, her legs working hard to carry her to her front door as fast as possible. It's only when she spots a pair of soft, brown desert boots in her field of vision that she stops and looks up.

'Great,' the owner of the boots says. 'I was hoping I'd run into you.'

Heather tries to say something but her mouth has gone dry. 'R-really?' she stammers.

He smiles and nods. Even that small gesture has the power to cause her stomach to produce an Olympic-worthy somersault. Perfect tens from all the judges.

He runs his hand through hair that probably needs a cut. 'Yeah… I'm having plumbing issues. A guy has been round to take a look, and it's sorted for now, but he told Carlton the whole house might need seeing to, so don't be surprised if he gets in contact.'

Heather nods. She doesn't like Carlton, their landlord, much – he's nosy, always wanting an excuse to get inside her flat and poke around – but she hasn't had any issues with her water supply, so she reckons she's probably safe for now. 'Thanks for letting me know,' she says quietly.

Jason puts a foot on the bottom stair, preparing to return to his first-floor flat. As he does, it breaks Heather's trance and she remembers why she's hurrying towards her front door, why her handbag is burning underneath her arm. She starts to move but he turns and smiles that smile again. She has to try very hard not to reach out for the cool, solid wall for support.

'We never did get a raincheck on that coffee,' he says, looking straight into her eyes. Usually, she finds it hard to maintain eye contact with other people, but with Jason it's not as difficult. 'My sisters clubbed together and bought me one of those fancy pod machines for my birthday. Don't suppose you want to help me christen it?'

She feels as if everything inside her is straining towards him, even as she grips her handbag tighter against her body with her elbow. He must see her hesitation, because then he adds, 'Or there's always good old instant. I make a mean cup of instant, even if I do say so myself.'

The contents of the handbag burn hotter against her torso and she looks helplessly at him. 'I'm sorry,' she whispers, 'I can't today…' and then, before he can begin to unpick her shabby excuse, she turns and heads for her door. It's only when it's closed safely again and she's leaning against it that she feels her pulse start to slow.

She exhales loudly. Jason Blake. He's been living here for a few months now, and every time she bumps into him she feels like this. She thought it would wear off after a while, but if anything it's getting worse.

She shakes her head, trying to dislodge the image of him, his long limbs relaxed and easy, his brown eyes smiling at her, and then she opens her eyes, pushes herself up so she's bearing her whole weight on her feet again, and walks down the hallway to her living room.

Just being in here makes it easy to breathe again.

The living room of her flat is at the back of the house, leading onto a long, narrow garden that all the tenants share. She walks over to the large bay window with the French doors and stares outside. Jason moans that the garden is stuck in the 1950s. He hates the two thin flowerbeds flanking each fence, with the concrete path down one side, but Heather quite likes it. It's soothing.

Also soothing is this room, her oasis. It has the minimum of furniture – a sofa, one armchair and a bookcase. A TV and a small dining table with a vase on it. She doesn't believe in owning things that don't get used regularly. They're a waste of space and energy and emotion.

She likes the way she can stand in the middle of the room, close her eyes, and know that nothing is within touching distance. She does that now – closes her eyes – and the feeling of space, of knowing the walls are white and unmarked, that all of the books in the bookcase are perfectly lined up, that the fake hydrangea in the vase on the table will never drop a dry, dead petal, helps her to feel more like herself.

But then the handbag under her arm begins to burn again and she remembers she has one last thing to do. She walks back through the hallway (more white walls, no photos or prints to break up the space) and past the kitchen (sides swept clean of every crumb, all the teaspoons curled up behind each other in the cutlery draw), and stops outside a door.

Heather doesn't think of this room as her second bedroom. It's the flat's second bedroom, foreign territory in her little kingdom. She stares at the brass knob for a few seconds. She can feel the calm she generated only a few moments ago in the living room starting to slip and slide, but she knows she has to do this. It's the only way.

The long key sits waiting in the lock and she turns it, bracing herself against what she is about to see, against what she will try very hard not to look at before she shuts the door again, and then her hand closes around the doorknob, cold and slick, and she twists it open.

It feels as if the contents of the room are rushing towards her, as if they're all fighting, climbing, spilling, falling over each other to reach her first. It takes all her willpower not to stagger back and run away.

From floor to ceiling, all she can see is stuff. Her mother's stuff, crammed into the room in teetering piles. Stuff that came from her old family home, a house that Heather had not been allowed inside for years and never wanted to visit any more anyway. All this clutter is hers now, left to her in a will she didn't even know existed and was shocked anyone was able to find. The cardboard boxes, the old suitcases, the plastic containers and carrier bags. All of it.

All those things filled with stuff she doesn't want and doesn't care about. Just looking at it makes her want to go and take a shower.

She looks to the front of the hoard, to where there is a two-metre-square patch of carpet, holding out like a plucky little beach against the tide of belongings surging towards the door. Down on one side is a small chest of drawers. Piles of old newspapers and magazines threaten to slide off it when she tugs open the middle drawer, but she does it quickly, trying to kid herself that she's doing it on automatic, that she's really not taking any of this in.

The drawer is full of her guilt. She quickly pulls the tiny corduroy shoes from her bag and stuffs them inside, pushing down assorted baby hats, rompers, stuffed farm animals and blankets – all with the price tags still attached – to make room for the latest addition. Then she shoves the drawer closed again, backs away into the hallway, and shuts the door so hard her own bedroom door rattles in sympathy.

It stars to ebb away then, the itchy, scratchy feeling she's been having all day, the one that made her go into Mothercare in the first place. She sinks to the floor, her back against the wall, and stares at the brilliant-white gloss of the door she's just closed, trying as hard as she can to let its clean blankness blot out the knowledge of what lies behind it.

CHAPTER THREE

NOW

It's a double-edged experience for Heather as she leaves her flat on Sunday morning and heads off to her sister's in Westerham. On the one hand, it's a relief. Even though she does her best to ignore it, there's a radar-blip deep inside her, always pulsing – the awareness of all the *stuff* lurking behind the faceless door of her spare room – but its intermittent throb lessens in intensity and frequency as she joins the A21 and heads out into north Kent. On the other hand, she's out there. Exposed. And the locks on her doors, the ones keeping all that stuff safe and secret, seem flimsier with each mile she travels from home.

It only takes half an hour to get to Faith's. The red-brick Victorian houses, pre-war semis, and chunky blocks of flats of Bromley slowly give way to fields and hedgerows, country pubs and rows of flint cottages. Faith says Mum and Dad used to bring them to the little commuter village when they were kids. Before the divorce, obviously. Before things got so crowded in their mother's head. But Heather doesn't remember that. She doesn't remember very much of her childhood at all.

She used to think everyone was like that, that anything before the age of thirteen was just smudges of sound and scent and colour in people's memories, like the inkling of a dream after waking, but she's since discovered that some people have crystal-clear memories of their early years: who their first teacher was, what kind of cake they had for their best-ever birthday, stories their parents used to tell them before they went to sleep.

She doesn't worry about this, though. Mostly because she doesn't want to remember any of it anyway. The tiny snatches that do try and poke through the fog aren't that pleasant.

All except one. The holiday with Aunt Kathy at the seaside. Lovely Aunt Kathy with her dark curls and her red coat. Heather doesn't mind letting that one come.

She's smiling when she pulls up outside Faith's house, thinking of candyfloss, jeans rolled up over pale calves, and icy water on her toes, of running out of reach of the waves and then back again, just to tease them into catching her once more.

Faith's front door opens before Heather is fully out of the car, and her sister stands there, waiting. She isn't smiling but she isn't cross either. Just neutral, accepting the monthly visit as she always does.

Faith is three years older than Heather. She has the same gradually darkening blonde hair that won't keep a wave, no matter how deft she is with the curling tongs, the same grey eyes. They are exactly the same height, but her sister has always seemed taller. Heather has never quite been able to work out why.

Heather follows Faith inside. Her brother-in-law, Matthew, wanders into the hallway from the kitchen, wiping his hands on a tea towel, and gives Heather a proper smile. 'I keep wanting to do a roast, but there's never enough time after church, so I'm afraid you're stuck with slow-cooker casserole again,' he says with a smile.

Heather nods and smiles back. She likes Matthew. He always treats her as if she's just another one of the family. Normal, in other words. Lots of people would shrug off that label, thinking it boring, but Heather would love to embrace it. For a couple of hours a month, Matthew makes it seem as if that might be possible.

But then Heather thinks of the chest of drawers in her spare room, the one containing all her dirty secrets in pastel colours, and she starts to doubt herself again. She doesn't let Faith or Matthew see it, though. She keeps smiling, she says the right greetings and asks after the children, whom she can hear stampeding in another part of the house. They're the only reason she keeps this monthly 'duty' date with her sister. She can feel her heart thudding in anticipation of seeing them again.

As if on cue, they come thundering down the stairs at the sound of an unfamiliar voice in the hall and then stop short, staring at her shyly, as they always do at the beginning of a visit. Alice is six and Barney is three. She wants to go and hug them so much. She yearns to feel their tiny arms around her. She wants to rest her chin on their soft hair and just breathe them in, but now they're all standing there staring at each other and the moment to lean in naturally for a cuddle has passed.

Thankfully, Alice saves Heather with one of her usual blunt questions. 'Did you bring any presents for us? Aunty Sarah always brings presents.'

Barney nods seriously as his sister watches on.

'Barney wants to know if you've brought chocolate,' Alice adds, translating her little brother's gesture.

Heather shakes her head, silently disgruntled with Matthew's beneficent sister. 'Sorry, no chocolate today, or toys.' She risks a glance at Faith. 'Mummy says you already have lots and lots of toys.'

It happens then – one of those moments that rarely flashes between the two sisters. Just like Alice, Heather is able to translate the look her sibling gives her, an expression on Faith's face, both knowing and grateful, that for once acknowledges their shared past, their shared hatred of extraneous *stuff*.

'But I will play any game you want after dinner,' Heather adds, hoping that the gift of quality time – something she would have killed for when she was younger – has not gone out of fashion in this era of brightly coloured electronic worlds accessed with the swipe of a chubby finger.

Barney looks blank, but Alice pipes up. 'I get to pick what game?' she asks brightly, and Heather nods. Alice is pleased with this response. She smiles to herself and skips off towards the living room, leaving Heather to wonder if it's right that a six-year-old should look quite so much as if she's cooking up a plan.

Heather follows her sister and brother-in-law into the kitchen, where pans are boiling on the hob and delicious smells are wafting from a large slow cooker. She watches her sister as she and Matthew bustle round each other, putting the finishing touches to the meal. When he puts an easy hand on Faith's hip as he reaches past her for a wooden spoon, Heather looks away. It seems too intimate. Too much. Too much to watch, anyway. It's been so long since someone of the opposite sex touched Heather that she can't even remember if a man's fingers have ever rested on her hip that way.

Faith doesn't even notice the affectionate touch, and that makes Heather sad. And maybe a little bit angry. She's reminded of her mother, who amassed so much stuff that even her treasures were lost in the sheer volume of her possessions. This seems to be the same kind of wastefulness. Faith has also amassed much – but it comes in the shape of love and people, not things, so now the moments that would be treasured by Heather if she were in Faith's place are buried and lost in the fullness of her sister's life.

Once again, it causes Heather to wonder how they turned out so differently. Is it just that she's broken, damaged, in a way that Faith never was? And how could that be, after the childhood that they both endured?

She waits for Faith's mask to slip, prods the robustness of her sister's smile each time it appears. But either Faith is much, much better at this game than Heather is, or her sister has attained the thing that has eluded Heather all her life: she's moved on. She's over it.

If that's the case, Heather isn't sure whether to worship her or hate her. Faith knows, you see. She knows what's behind Heather's façade. She has an understanding that can never be gained from a distance, by studying and logical analysis. This is knowledge that comes from experience, from being flung in the mess and the chaos and struggling through it to come out the other side. Even though they frequently think to themselves that they would rather just cut each other loose so they no longer have to deal with each other, it is this shared struggle that binds the two sisters together. Another thing to blame their mother for.

As the aroma of the cooking chicken intensifies, wrapping the country kitchen in a herby fog, Faith marshals her troops. 'Come on, you lot! Time to lay the table.' They snap to attention and set to work without a word of communication. Matthew grabs the crockery out of the cupboard and Alice helps with the knives and forks, although Matthew has to switch them all around when she's finished. Even Barney has been given a job, and he carefully puts coasters next to each setting.

The table looks lovely, with Faith's blue and white Calico china and a jug full of flowers from the garden in the centre. Faith's family are lovely too – the kids are just naughty enough to still be adorable as they whine about the casserole having mushrooms and refuse to eat their peas, and Matthew sometimes looks across at his wife and smiles. Not for any reason that Heather can see. Just because.

It makes her feel as if there's a gaping hole in her chest, one that is only lightly papered over by her summer blouse and, as she eats the buttery mashed potatoes and creamy sauce, she imagines what it would be like if this were her dining table, if it were her husband sitting at the head, smiling at her. She wants it so much it almost makes her gasp.

Unbidden, a picture of Jason pops into her head. She wants to swipe it away again, because it feels foolish to have him there, even though it's only within the private confines of her own mind, but she can't quite bring herself to do it when she sees the way he's smiling at her. However, her imagination falls down when it comes to filling Alice and Barney's seats. It seems, even in her fantasies, she can't allow herself to hope quite that much. She snaps back into the real world to find Faith looking at her, weighing her up, and Heather starts to resent her sister just a little bit more.

How did you do it? she wants to yell. *How did you manage all this? It's just not fair.*

And why hasn't she whispered her secrets to Heather? Why has she guarded them so closely, so jealously? Surely sisters are supposed to share? *Only maybe they don't,* Heather thinks bitterly, *when you grew up in a home where everything was defined by what you possessed.*

When they've finished the main course, Heather tells Matthew to sit as she clears and stacks the plates and takes them into the kitchen. Heather always finds this part of the afternoon wearying. Faith will be cross if she doesn't offer to help, but when she does, Faith just shoos her back into the dining room.

Alice is showing off a bracelet made of neon plastic beads she made at a friend's party, and is insisting her aunt has a better look, so Heather slides into her sister's empty seat to do just that. It's nice, being there, Matthew on one side, Alice next to her and Barney opposite and, as she listens to her niece chattering away, a warm feeling spreads through her chest.

But then Faith returns with the apple crumble to place in the centre of the table. She stops short and shoots her sister a territorial look. Heather slides off the chair and skulks back to her seat next to Barney, and Faith is reinstalled upon her fashionably distressed oak throne.

When dessert is finished, they all tramp dutifully in the direction of the study. It's time for Faith's weekly Skype call with their father, who currently lives in Spain, and when Heather is here she's expected to show some family spirit and join in.

Heather hates it. Not that she doesn't love her father – she does – but it feels like she's playing a part for the black pinhole at the top of the computer monitor. Say 'cheese', everyone. Pretend you're one big happy family!

Matthew sets up the connection and moments later Heather sees her father's smiling face, while Shirley, their stepmother of more than fifteen years, bustles around in the background, leaning in for a wave, but then discreetly disappearing. Probably to dust something. *From the sublime to the ridiculous,* Heather thinks, although she understands why Shirley's military cleanliness must be soothing for her father.

'Hey, there!' their father says, and Faith gets the kids to tell him what they've been doing at school and pre-school respectively. They have some finger painting and spellings to show him, all prepared and laying ready on the desk. Faith fills him in on the wonderfulness of her domestic life, turning the taste of the custard that accompanied the apple crumble a little sour in Heather's mouth, and then, before Heather can think of anything to say or plan an escape route, it's her turn. She smiles weakly at the camera.

'Hi, Dad,' she says, feeling her sister's eyes on her, monitoring her levels of family participation and judging her accordingly.

'Hey, Sweetpea,' he replies, using the nickname he gave her that everyone else has forgotten. 'How's work?'

Heather breathes out. Work is a safe subject. Work is good.

'Going well. I've only got about four months left of this contract now, though, so I'm on the lookout for another post.'

'Anything on the horizon?'

She shrugs. 'There's a senior archivist position in Eltham I'm interested in, but I'm not sure I've got enough experience yet, so we'll see. In the meantime, I'm enjoying the work at Sandwood Park.'

'Ah,' her father says, nodding, then goes on to quote the first line of a novel. 'That's one of his, isn't it?' he adds brightly.

Heather nods. Sandwood Park used to be the home of the celebrated author Cameron Linford. His widow died recently and donated the house to a private trust. It's due to be opened to the public in a month or two, and it's Heather's job to sort and catalogue the masses of documents chronicling the couple's life: diaries, letters, financial ledgers, and photographs.

'Found any missing literary masterpieces?' her father asks with a twinkle in his eye. He always makes this joke and Heather always gives him the same response.

'Not yet. But I'll keep hunting.'

The shared moment of humour doesn't do its job, though. Instead of connecting father and daughter, it only highlights the distance between them. Maybe it would be better if Heather did this when she was on her own – video chatted from the safety of her own flat without Faith scrutinizing her every word – but she never does that. She's pulled the app up on her iPad a few times but always stops short of pressing the screen to connect.

Thankfully, the kids are eager to show off to their grandpa again, allowing Heather to relinquish centre stage. Alice conducts her little brother in a rendition of 'Twinkle, Twinkle, Little Star', bringing the call to a dazzling finale.

When the monitor is blank again, Matthew goes off to settle the kids in front of the TV, but Faith hangs back.

'Are we going to join the others?' Heather asks. Even though she comes here every month, she's never sure what to do, what the right or natural thing is.

'If I have to watch even one more episode of *Peppa Pig* I might just shoot myself,' Faith says drily, but then she turns to look at Heather. 'We'll go through in a second. Before that I have something I need to discuss with you…'

Heather's stomach swoops. She and Faith never 'discuss' stuff. They're polite, cordial, and matter-of-fact with each other, none of which involves sharing anything of any depth. After all the rows they had both before and after their mother died, they've allowed a crust of civility to harden over their relationship, and they both like it that way. 'Ok-ay…' she says warily.

'Do you still have Mum's things?'

A flash of cold runs through Heather, as if she's just sprinted full-pelt into a wall of ice. Faith has blindsided her and being forced to think about 'that room' without her carefully constructed mental defences in place pulls her chest tight and her jaw even tighter. 'W-what?'

'Mum's stuff,' Faith repeats, frowning slightly. 'You have some old family photos, right?'

Heather can't speak. Her mouth has gone dry. Thinking specifically about what sits in her spare room has a tendency to do that to her. She nods.

'Well, Alice has a school project. She needs photos of both Matthew and me as children, and I wondered if you could root one out?'

It would be odd for most people not to have photographs of themselves when they were young, ones passed on by parents, maybe when they moved out of home for the first time or started a family. Heather wishes she could play that card now, just tell her sister to go and hunt through the storage boxes in her vast attic, but she knows she can't. It's not that the photos don't exist, just that they're lost. Buried. At least, that's what she assumes.

'I... I don't even know if I have them,' she stammers, hoping against hope that Faith will let this drop.

Faith gives her a sideways look. A 'Heather's being difficult again' kind of look that only a big sister can bestow. 'Well, can you at least have a rummage around, see if you can lay your hands on any? After all, Mum didn't leave any to me, just to you.'

Ah, there it is. The dig. She knew this was coming. Faith always wheels this out when she wants to guilt Heather into doing something, even though they both know being left out of the will was an act of kindness. If anything, Heather should be using that to hold Faith to ransom.

The thought of going through her mother's possessions makes

Heather feel physically sick. She wants to yell at Faith, tell her to do it herself, but she can't let Faith see inside that room. She'd be even more disappointed with Heather than she already is. But Heather can't rummage (just thinking the word makes her stomach churn) in there either. She's stuck.

Faith sees the war going on behind Heather's carefully schooled features and snorts. 'You're always so precious about Mum's stuff, although God only knows why!'

Heather flinches. *Not precious,* she thinks, *anything but.* She'd rather let dust balls grow to the size of watermelons under her sofa than go in that room and *really* look around. It holds too many secrets. Too many horrible, horrible things.

Faith puts her hands on her hips. 'It's for Alice!' she says, exasperated. 'I know it's a stretch to get you to do anything for me, but I thought, since it was for the niece you supposedly adore, that maybe just for once you'd act like you were part of this family and show some loyalty.'

It stabs Heather in the heart to hear this. She does adore Alice, even though she suspects the six-year-old is on the verge of mastering her mother's disapproving look every time her aunt steps over the threshold. She so badly wants the kids to love her, for them to be able to come for days out and sleepovers, but once again that stupid room is getting in the way of anything good happening.

'You don't understand,' she mutters.

Faith's voice is silky smooth. 'No, of course I don't. How could I? Because Heather is special, Heather is different, no one understands her.' She shakes her head. 'It's probably my fault,' she says more to herself than to her sister. 'I should have been tougher, shouldn't have let you play the victim for so long, but I just...' She trails off, shaking her head again.

Heather glares at her sister. She's always known that the blame lies at her own door. She doesn't need Faith to remind her.

Faith breathes out, regains some of her usual composure. It's unlike her to lash out like this, to actually put words to the resentment Heather knows simmers under the surface. Pointed looks and a here-she-goes-again attitude usually describe Faith's demeanour when dealing with her younger sibling.

'Look…' she begins, softening slightly. 'I know you have… issues. But you don't have to let them define you. I haven't! Mainly because I got help, talked to people. There's a really good person at our church. I'm sure she could fit you in if I asked her nicely.'

'No.' Heather's response is firm and low.

Faith just stares at her. 'Fine,' she eventually says, her eyes narrowing. 'But I'm starting to suspect you actually enjoy being this way, because you won't get help, you won't let anyone close.'

Seeing no change in Heather's shut-down expression, Faith gives up and heads for the living room, obviously preferring the hated *Peppa Pig* instead of the company of her one and only sister. 'Just find a bloody photo for Alice,' she says over her shoulder as she walks away. 'Because if you don't, I'm going to come and dig one out myself. It's the least you can do for this family.'

Heather shivers and wraps her arms around her middle. *That can't happen,* she thinks. *It just can't.* She'll find some way of putting Faith off, maybe even scour the internet for old pictures that *could* have been Faith when she was younger and print them off.

She slopes into the living room and perches on a chair in the corner, more there for decoration than because it's comfortable to sit on. Faith steadily ignores her as the children jump up and down, acting out parts of Peppa's story as it unfolds brightly on the screen. The cartoon shows a made-up world where everyone fits in, where every story has a happy ending, and every child gets kissed goodnight before they fall soundly asleep in their own bed.

After four episodes, Matthew clicks the TV off. The children moan in unison, then Alice turns round and spies her aunt. Heather has been trying to blend into the wallpaper, just counting down the minutes until she can leave without Faith throwing another hissy fit.

'Aunty Heather, you promised you'd play a game with us!'

Heather nods. Thank goodness. One shining moment in an otherwise crappy afternoon. Anything to distract herself from looking at the back of Faith's head, when she knows her older sister is just sitting there, stewing. She smiles warmly as Alice comes running towards her, trailed by her little brother.

'What do you want to play? Snap? That Disney-princess board game I got you for Christmas?'

Alice shakes her head and then glances at Barney, who is grinning, her obvious accomplice.

'We want to play hide-and-seek,' she says firmly.

The smile freezes on Heather's face. 'What?'

Alice rolls her eyes, a perfect reproduction of her mother. 'Hide-and-seek, silly! You know, one person counts while the others hide? And then you have to try and find us. Only, I'm counting first because it was my idea, which means it's my game.'

Heather shakes her head, her neck so stiff that the side-to-side movement is only barely perceptible. 'I can't play hide-and-seek,' she whispers.

Alice folds her arms. 'You promised,' she says, with the air of someone producing a winning card.

Heather shakes her head again. 'Sorry, darling. It's just that I hate… I just can't…' She looks helplessly at Faith, who has now turned her head and is watching the exchange, frowning. Her sister just tightens her jaw and says nothing. 'I'll play anything else you want,' Heather adds. 'As many times as you like. For hours and hours!'

It's then that Alice's eyes fill with tears. Her bottom lip wobbles impressively. 'But you *promised*!'

Heather's eyes threaten to fill too, but she manages to squeeze the tears away. Who knows what Faith will say if she has a total meltdown this afternoon, on top of everything else? 'Sorry,' she whispers.

Alice runs off crying, followed by a bemused-looking Barney. Heather catches Faith's eye. 'Everything has to be on your terms, doesn't it?' she says in a low voice, thick with disapproval. 'Always by your rules and within your boundaries.'

'That's not true!' Heather blurts out, surprising herself.

Faith just looks back at her. 'Then go and tell the little girl who's sobbing her heart out on her bed you've changed your mind.'

Heather stares back at her, unable to respond.

Faith huffs and stands up. 'Exactly,' she says. 'Like I said: on your terms or not at all. I honestly don't know why you bother coming to these Sunday dinners if you're going to be like this.'

One tear slides down Heather's face, but it doesn't melt her sister's frosty expression at all. Faith marches towards the door and, just before she leaves the room, she rests a hand on the jamb and turns round, shaking her head in both disgust and pity. 'You know, sometimes you're just like Mum.'

CHAPTER FOUR

CASSANDRA

The doll is queen of this house. She stands on the corner of the highest bookshelf, surveying her kingdom. The stuff climbs like a mountain towards her, a worshipper reaching for its god. Her eyes are clear and blue, haughty, her glossy brown ringlets perfect, her miniature faux-Victorian dress pink and delicate. Who can compete with the cold porcelain skin of her face and arms? Who can match the rosy cheeks and coral painted lips?

THEN

'One… Two… Three… Four…'

Heather runs as Faith starts counting, her heart jumping in her chest. She has to find the best hiding place this time, one her sister will never guess, because Faith always wins at hide-and-seek. She always catches Heather quickly, shaking her head and telling her younger sister she's an 'amateur', even though Heather isn't really sure what that is. Someone who's really bad at playing hide-and-seek, she supposes. She just hopes she knows as many big words as Faith does when she's ten years old.

Heather thinks hard about a hiding place as she runs away. She can't just race around giggling, like she did last time. She makes herself slow down. It's not hard, though, because no one can run really fast in their house. There's too much stuff in the way.

As soon as Faith started counting, Heather set off down one of the 'rabbit trails'. Heather's not quite sure why her sister calls them that – she's never seen any bunnies in their house.

The trails are the paths between the stuff. They have lots of stuff. There are books and papers, plastic containers full of things Heather's mummy doesn't like her to touch. There are clothes, lots and lots of clothes. They're piled high on the armchair and the table where the family used to eat their dinner. There are toys too, some old and broken, which Heather's mummy says she'll fix one day, and some still with tags on that Heather couldn't play with even if she wanted to, because they're so high up she can't reach them. Some of the piles of stuff are so big that sometimes, when she looks up, they seem to lean over and look at her, trying to decide whether they should fall on her or not. She doesn't like it when they do that.

There are also lots of things Heather's mummy says she's going to get around to throwing away when she's not so tired. Maybe that will be when Heather's daddy stops working so much and spends more time in the house. She overheard her parents arguing about that the other night. She also once overheard Aunty Kathy joke their house was like an Aladdin's cave, only full of crap instead of treasure.

Heather's not allowed to say that word Aunty Kathy said. Patrick Hull said it once at school and Miss Perrins made him sit in the corner then had to have a quiet word with his mum when she came to collect him.

Miss Perrins has had quiet words with Heather's mummy quite a few times too, but not because she says anything naughty. Heather's not exactly sure what the quiet words were, because Mummy and Miss Perrins were talking in the hallway, but it looked important and Miss Perrins' face wasn't smiley like usual.

She thinks it was about her school uniform one time (Mummy lost it under all the other clothes in the house and Heather had to wear her denim pinafore dress to school instead), and another time was when Heather was really itchy and the little insects from Fluffy the cat kept biting her tummy so she kept scratching instead of doing her spellings. Sometimes they hid in her jumper and came to school with her, and then they bit the other children too. Faith called them 'bloody little hitchhikers' but her teacher didn't hear her say that so she didn't have to sit in the corner. There were more quiet words after that, because the boys started calling her 'Hobo Heather' at playtime and wouldn't stop chasing her.

Heather's mummy has never been cross with her about the quiet words, though. Afterwards, she just comes home, lies on the sofa in front of the TV, and cries. She hugs Heather and tells her she's a good girl, that it's not Heather's fault and that she's going to do better from now on.

Heather is trying her hardest to move silently through the dining room when she hears Faith stop counting. It's difficult to stay completely quiet, because of all the old plastic cartons and scrunchy cellophane that seem to collect on the floor in their house, and her feet slip on bits of paper and clothes that fall off the top of the piles.

'Hea-ther!' Faith calls in a sing-song voice. 'I'm coming to *get* you!'

Heather starts to move faster. She's not even thinking about giggling now and her heart is beating extra-hard. She's got to find somewhere, somewhere small, somewhere Faith won't expect.

Heather turns and heads up the stairs. Her feet are smaller than Faith's and she finds the gaps in the piles of books and papers lining each step without making them fall over. When her foot hits the clear patch of carpet where the stairs meet the landing, she turns left and darts into the room there. This used to be her bedroom until the stuff filled it up. Once upon a time, the stuff was only downstairs and in her parents' room, but it started to spread. Somehow the piles just kept getting bigger and bigger. Heather wonders if the big piles have babies. She asked Faith this once and her sister told her not to be stupid, but it makes sense to Heather. How else do new ones keep appearing?

So now the pile babies sleep in her room and Heather sleeps on the armchair downstairs.

She looks around the room for a good spot. She remembers that Daddy took his guitar out from under the bed and sold it to a man down the street. There's a hole where it used to be that's just big enough for her to climb into. Once inside, she pulls a bit of blanket down from the edge of the bed to cover herself.

Something on top of the blanket, maybe one of the piles balancing on the bed, comes crashing down and Heather freezes. Faith goes quiet too, and Heather hears footsteps coming closer and closer. Faith's coming up the stairs! Heather holds her breath and closes her eyes, wishing she could turn herself invisible.

'Hea-ther,' Faith sings again. 'You know I'm going to find you, don't you?'

Heather wants to giggle so badly. She presses a hand over her mouth to hold it in. She can see Faith's feet. She can just about make them out from under the edge of the blanket. Her sister is standing in the doorway.

Go away, go away, go away, she wishes inside her head.

Just as Heather thinks Faith is going to yank up the blanket and say, 'Ha! Found you!' her sister's feet move. They turn and walk away. Heather's so surprised she doesn't breathe out again for ages, not until her chest starts to feel funny and then she gulps in air.

She can hear Faith walking around, calling her name, but her voice sounds different now. Not so pleased with herself. More fed up. Heather smiles to herself and curls up even tighter under the bed. Today she will win hide-and-seek and Faith will be the amateur!

Heather stays there for ages. Faith looks in all the other rooms upstairs and then she goes back down to the ground floor. Even when Mummy calls to say lunch is ready, Heather doesn't move. It could be a trick and, even if it isn't, she doesn't want Faith saying she gave up. She's not coming out again until Faith does what she makes Heather do when she can't find her: stand in the middle of the house and shout that Heather is the queen of hide-and-seek and Faith is the loser. Heather wants that way more than a ham sandwich, even if her tummy is starting to rumble.

A long time later, Heather starts to feel cold and she opens her eyes. Did she fall asleep? The sounds of the bedroom, and then the rest of the house, come back slowly. She strains her ears. Somewhere downstairs, someone is crying and someone else is shouting.

'Heather! Heather? Where are you?' Faith's voice has lost its taunting tone. Heather wonders if it is a trick to make her come out.

'Oh, my God! Oh, my God!' their mummy is saying in between sobs. 'I can't lose my baby! I can't lose my baby! It can't be happening again!' There's a pause and she hears her mother shout at Faith. 'You were supposed to be watching her!'

There is thunder on the staircase after that and lots of shouting. Heather starts to feel scared. Something tells her this isn't a game any more, that she needs to come out, but she's too scared to move. She can't even open her mouth to shout out.

Eventually, she manages to shuffle forward a bit. At the same time, feet appear behind the blanket. Heather tries to say 'I'm here!' but her voice comes out all croaky and quiet, like she's forgotten how to use it.

The pounding feet and loud voices stop. The air goes very still.

'Here,' she squeaks, and then the blanket is wrenched away from the entrance to her hiding place and, at the same time, everything else that was on top of the bed comes crashing to the floor, sealing her in. That's when she starts to panic. She pushes at the things trapping her with her hands and feet, and starts to shout 'Mummy', over and over and over again.

There's more crashing, and she can't hear what the others are saying, but eventually she hears her mother yelling, 'Stop! Stop, Heather! *Stop*!'

Heather goes still.

After a few moments, air comes rushing into her hiding place and she sees her mother's face. 'Are you okay?' she asks shakily.

Heather nods, but then when her mother starts to look worried, Heather realises it's too dark under the bed for her to see her properly so she adds, 'I'm okay. This is my hide-and-seek spot. Did I win?'

From behind Mummy, there's a huff. A Faith kind of huff. Heather smiles to herself.

Her mother laughs but when she speaks her voice sounds like it does when she's been crying. 'Yes, darling. I think you won. I also think you scared us quite badly. Are you sure you're okay?'

Her mother reaches for her, and Heather finally pops free from under the bed. She looks around the room. It's worse than ever. The landslide from the top of the mattress has made the path disappear. Not even the tiniest bunny could hop down that trail now.

'Your foot!' Faith says and Heather looks down. There's blood coming through her sock. She must have hurt it on the stuff when she was kicking it away.

Her mummy lets out a noise that reminds Heather of how Fluffy sounds when he's hungry. At first Heather thinks she's upset about the blood – now Heather knows it's there, her toe is starting to sting – but then she realises her mother isn't even looking at her. She's looking at something on the floor. 'Oh no, oh no, oh no...' she says, and then she kneels down to pick it up. 'Cassandra!' she says, and she's properly crying now.

Heather ignores the stinging in her toe and gets up. She puts her arms around her mother's neck and whispers 'I'm sorry' into the skin behind her ear, but maybe Mummy doesn't hear her, because she's looking down at a doll she's holding. She has lots of curly hair, a pretty pink dress and a smooth face and limbs. Two of her tiny cold fingers are missing. Her mother is holding them in her other hand.

Heather feels a dark, empty hole opening up inside of her. This was her fault. Hers. *She* made her mummy sad.

Heather suspects her mother must be thinking this too, because she doesn't look at Heather, she doesn't ask about her poorly foot. She just stares at the dolly and cries, saying something about the doll being her favourite, her very, very special girl.

A hand rests on Heather's shoulder and she looks up to find Faith staring down at her. Her sister doesn't look cross that she won hide-and-seek any more. 'Come on,' she says. 'Come downstairs and I'll find a plaster for your foot.'

CHAPTER FIVE

NOW

Heather bangs the front door when she gets back to her flat. Although she was careful to keep her expression neutral as she said farewell to her sister and her family, she is now scowling. Faith just hadn't been able to resist getting another lecture in, especially after they'd abandoned the idea of hide-and-seek in favour of KerPlunk.

'It's time you stopped floating around the edges of this family and plugged yourself in properly,' Faith said, arms crossed, as she walked Heather to her car. 'I don't know why you come, honestly I don't. You obviously don't want to be here.'

Heather mumbled something about that not being true.

Faith let out a snort of laughter. 'Really? You really think that?' she said, then listed all of Heather's shortcomings over the visit – the way she'd let the kids down, the lack of any effort at conversation – before landing on the topic Heather had most wanted to avoid: the photograph.

'I'm only asking one thing of you, and it's not even a big thing. I'm not asking you to go to family counselling, or to phone me occasionally just to chat or ask something about my life. I'm not even asking that you have us over one month, instead of us entertaining you. All I'm asking for is one photograph. Is that really too much?'

Yes, Heather wanted to say. *It is. Because you don't know what you're asking.*

Faith has no right to back her into a corner over this. No right at all.

Heather almost runs into her living room to complete her ritual: standing in the middle, arms outstretched, eyes closed. It's only then that the anger at her sister starts to fade. But just as she is beginning to breathe properly again, there is a loud rap on the glass of her French doors. Her eyes snap open and her heart starts to gallop. And not just because Jason is standing there smiling softly at her from the other side of the glass.

What must he think she was doing, standing in the middle of her living room like a cross between a scarecrow and a zombie? She smiles weakly back.

He makes a motion to indicate she should open the door. Heather has to look for the key. While she likes looking at the neat, orderly garden, she doesn't often go out there. Opening the door would let insects and grass clippings in. She'd be worried she'd missed something that blew under the sofa and it would sit there for days undetected, slowly contaminating.

Heart still pounding, she opens the door and steps outside, closing it behind her to keep not just the bugs and dandelion heads out, but Jason too. No one else has set foot in her flat (except nosy old Carlton) since she moved in three years ago.

Before that, she hadn't lived in Bromley for a long time, but her mother's declining health and a maternity-cover job had brought her back. She knew she was lucky to have found another post close enough to stay here. Her job was competitive and, at her age, permanent positions were scarce. Usually, she lived from contract to contract and had to go where the work took her.

'Yes?' she says to Jason, who's still got the hint of a smile on his lips, and she knows her tone has added bite because of her lousy afternoon. Another thing that's Faith's fault.

'Thought I'd mow the grass and give the borders a bit of a weed,' he says cheerfully. 'Now the weather's turned nicer, I was also thinking about having a barbecue – you know, the housewarming I didn't get round to organizing – just a few friends over to have some burgers and sausages.'

Heather nods. Oh, so that's it. While it's a shared garden and Jason is perfectly within his rights to mow, cook or even turn cartwheels in it, he's being polite. He's asking if she minds. 'Go ahead,' she says. 'Although it'd be nice to know the date and time when you've arranged it.' That way she can make sure she keeps to the bedroom and the kitchen that afternoon, then there's no chance of her being mistaken for an undead scarecrow again or having people peering into her space like she's an exhibit in the reptile house at London Zoo. She might even go out.

His smile gets wider. 'Well, I thought maybe you'd like to join us? It seems rude not to ask, especially as we'll be hanging out right in front of your living room.'

Heather checks his face for the usual telltale signs of a pity invite: the tightness around the edges of the mouth, the narrow pupils and fixed jaw (she's thinking of Faith's face as she does this), but finds none of them. However, she can't believe he's asking because he actually *wants* her there, so that leaves her standing in her garden, worrying whether aphids from the nearby roses are attaching themselves to her hair, and not knowing quite what to do.

'Okay?' he says as if it's the most natural thing in the world to offer invitations to strangers, bring them into your world, your stuff.

There's no excuse she can give. Not yet, anyway. So she just nods and says, 'Okay.' And then she turns and goes back inside her flat without looking round. She desperately wants to, though. She wants to know if he's still smiling or if his brows are drawn together in a deep frown of confusion.

Heather heads for her bedroom, but as she passes the spare room she pauses.

It's in there. The photo. The thing Faith wants. She doesn't know exactly where, but it's in there somewhere. Probably. Heather stares at the blank door for a full minute, and then she thinks to herself, *Not today. I've had as much as I can handle today. I'll do it soon, though. Maybe tomorrow.*

CHAPTER SIX

NOW

'She's in tears, Heather! Everyone else in her class has brought their family-history projects in already. The teacher has given her until Monday, but that's absolutely her last chance! I am driving over to you Sunday afternoon and picking a bloody photo up. Have you got that?'

Somehow, looking for a photograph 'tomorrow' had turned into the day after that, and the day after that had turned into a week, and then that week had become two. There have been texts from her sister, hard, barking little questions fired into her phone like missiles. Heather hasn't exactly ignored them, not really, not when each one has lit a fire of shame and guilt inside her, but she hasn't exactly replied to them either. And now it's Friday evening, almost two weeks later, and Faith is on the warpath.

'Yes, got it,' Heather whispers penitently. What else can she do?

There is a relieved sigh on the other end of the line.

'Okay.' Mamma-Bear Faith is standing down. Heather exhales, mirroring her sister.

There is so much Heather wants to say to her: that she truly does love Alice and Barney; that she knows her sister doesn't believe that because Heather's just so useless at acting normal around them. But that is only because she wants so desperately to see that love reflected back in their eyes that she second-guesses every move, every word. She wants to tell Faith that she's gutted she's made Alice cry and feel 'the odd one out' with the kids at school because she knows how awful that is. But Heather says none of this. It's as if, when it comes to Faith, her mouth is perpetually glued shut.

'Right. I'll give you a bell on Sunday morning to let you know what time. Matthew has a meeting after church, so it'll depend on whether he can take the kids too or not.'

'Okay,' Heather says meekly, but a chill is unfurling inside her. They say their goodbyes and she puts the phone down slowly. Then, before she can chicken out, she turns and walks down the hallway and stops in front of the innocent-looking closed white door. Blood rushes so loudly in her ears that it drowns out the sound of traffic on the main road outside.

She doesn't move for the longest time, just stares at the door, and then, when it feels as if she has almost hypnotized herself into a catatonic state by staring at the blank white paint, she reaches out and her palm closes around the door handle.

This is how to do it, she tells herself. *Like it's not real. Like it's a dream.*

She has a vague memory of something that looked like photograph albums in the left corner of the room, in a box on top of a bookcase, next to piles of her mother's old clothes, still bagged up in black sacks. She pulls up a mental image of that box and fixes it at the front of her brain.

She inhales deeply, resists the urge to hold her breath, and twists the creaky old brass knob. The door swings open.

Don't look. Don't look. Just move.

She's fine at first, as she's crossing the bare patch of carpet near the door, even as she treads carefully down the narrow path between the boxes and bags on that side, but there's obviously been a landslide at the back of the room. One of the storage boxes containing some bric-a-brac that was sitting atop a pile of newspapers has toppled, spilling itself gleefully over the space. She needs to go forward, but she doesn't want to bend and clear the mess up. She doesn't want to touch it. She doesn't want to touch any of it.

So she doesn't. She just keeps moving, walks over the top of the contents of the spilled box. It was what her mother did when she was alive, after all. When the 'rabbit trails' were devoured by the growing hoard, she'd just walk over the top, changing the topography of the house from flat carpeted floors into hills and mountains of rubbish. In her later years, they'd grown so huge that in some places they were four or five feet deep, and spaces that should have been doorways had turned into crawl spaces.

However, when Heather's foot crunches on one of the photo frames, one that's just a wooden surround, already having lost its glass, memories come flooding back, things that have nothing to do with this room, this hoard – the lack of light, the perpetual twilight caused by the skyscraper piles, the sting of cat urine in her nostrils and the particular smell of dirt that's built up over years not months. A sob escapes her, but she thinks of Alice and pushes forward.

Blindly, she throws the black sacks full of clothes out of the way until she spots a ragged cardboard box, one so weak and old it might disintegrate if she tried to lift it. So she grabs the forest-green spine of what looks like a photo album, clutches it to her chest and retreats as fast as possible. It's only when the door is safely shut behind her, the key turned in the lock, that the swirling feeling in her head stops.

She takes the photo album into her living room and lays it on the desk – a coffee table would have been the perfect spot, except Heather has no coffee table. What's wrong with a shelf or a side table to put your mug on? A coffee table would fill up the centre of the room, rob her of that perfect, precious space in the centre of the rug. She leaves the album there, then goes back to the spare room, removes the key and carefully places it in her desk drawer. For some reason, it just doesn't feel safe leaving it in the door any more. She then makes herself a cup of camomile tea.

When that is done, she fetches the album and sits down on one end of her sofa. As Heather turns the first few pages, the sense of uncleanness at having been in the spare room fades. When she tries to think back to her childhood, which isn't often, most of it is just a big white fog, yet here it is – all the things she can't remember – in colour prints, yellowing a little with age. They come rushing up off the page to meet her.

There's her mum and dad together, actually looking happy. She'd seen her dad smile like that when he'd met Shirley, but she'd forgotten he must have looked at her mother that way too once upon a time.

How odd. The only thing that drifts through the fog when she dares to look into it are raised voices and soft male sobbing. He left when she was still in primary school, and he had just got to a place where he couldn't take it any more. She doesn't blame him for leaving. Who in their right mind would have wanted to stay?

She looks at the photos on the opposite page. One draws her curiosity enough for her to peel back the protective layer and prise it from the gluey lines holding it down. On the back, hastily scrawled in biro, it says 'Kathy and Heather, Eastbourne (1994)'. Heather places it back down and smooths the cellophane over the top. They're standing against some metal railings at the seafront. It's sunny, but obviously windy. Aunt Kathy is smiling brightly at the person behind the lens, and so is the little girl next to her, but her hair is being blown forwards over her face so Heather can't even see her own features. She's holding a mint-choc-chip ice cream, though, so she doesn't seem to care about the wind.

Mint choc chip. I used to love that, she thinks. *How did I forget?*

That holiday with her aunt is the one bright oasis in the pearly fog of her childhood, the one thing that stands out, bold and colourful. She remembers those two weeks as if they were yesterday – except she doesn't remember this photo being taken. Never mind. The rest is still clear: building sandcastles with complex moats on the beach, fish and chips under one of the shelters on the pier after a sudden cloudburst, crazy golf... Oh, how she'd loved the crazy golf, even if it took fifteen attempts to get each ball in the hole. But Aunty Kathy hadn't minded, she'd been patient and encouraging and had never once hurried her along.

The little girl in the photo looks happy. Heather knows it must be her, but she doesn't recognize herself. This girl looks as if she might grow up to be someone nice, someone with a good job and maybe a decent man to love. Not a freak who can't even go into her spare bedroom without having an epic meltdown.

Heather's eyes go dull and she stops smiling. Aunty Kathy. She hasn't seen her favourite aunt since her childhood. Yet another casualty of her mother's addiction. Heather closes her eyes. Her mother had been selfish, so selfish. Driving everyone who loved her away. Sometimes it had seemed as if she was on a mission to make everyone hate her.

Heather shakes her head and opens her eyes again. She's not going to think about that now, because far from recoiling from the other memories leaping up at her from the pages, she's actually enjoying this. She doesn't remember seeing any of these photos before. Probably because this album had been buried under two tons of crap in her mother's house for most of her formative years, and since Heather had taken custody of the belongings... Well, let's just say she hadn't wanted to go there.

But these photos are safe. They're two-dimensional, stored behind cellophane so they've stayed clean and nice. Not like the rest of her mother's stuff, which is too rich with memories, too immediate. Her mother always said she had to keep most of her stuff because the objects were her memory keepers. She'd pick up something – an ornament or a book, even a piece of Tupperware for the kitchen – and she'd be able to reel off all sorts of details about the item: when she'd bought it or who had given it to her, along with a story. There were always stories.

But Heather doesn't want those memories; she doesn't want that talent. On some level, she misses her mother, grieves for her, but that is obscured by the overriding sense of fury that engulfs her every time she thinks about her. *So selfish.* And then to leave things so Heather had to inherit what was left of her crap, had to take responsibility for it. She never asked for that burden and she doesn't want it, and she can't even go and shout at her mother for her final self-absorbed act, for once more protecting her *stuff* more than caring about what was good for her own flesh and blood.

Heather takes a deep breath and refocuses on the photograph album. *Not thinking about that, remember?* It only ever makes her miserable, and it's a wonderful revelation that there were some happy things that happened in her childhood, evidenced in the smiles and laughter caught on these pages.

There's a snap of a few older people at what looks like a birthday party. She thinks two of them might be her grandparents – her father's parents – but she's not sure. They both died when she was very little. And thinking of little… the next page reveals a picture of her and Faith taken at Christmas. They're wearing matching woollen jumpers in a horrible shade of orange, but they are hugging onto each other and doing their cheesiest grins for the camera so their faces are all teeth and hardly any eyes. It makes her smile.

But then she notices something, and the joy slides from her face.

The room behind them… It's empty.

Well, not actually empty, but… normal. She can see a wall painted in magnolia. An actual wall. Heather's not even sure she knew what colour the walls were in some parts of her family home because, as far as she could remember, they'd always had things stacked against them.

Heather stares at the picture, unable to tear her eyes away. It's a shock to realize her mother's house hadn't always been that way, although, if Heather didn't studiously avoid thinking about her mother in every waking moment, maybe she'd have worked this out by now. After all, she can't have been a hoarder from birth. It had to have started somewhere. For the first time, Heather asks herself when.

The problem is that she hadn't been able to talk to her mother about her hoarding. Even as an adult, if she'd tried to raise the subject, her mother would get defensive and cross. 'There's nothing wrong with a bit of clutter,' she used to say. 'I'm a collector, that's all.' And Christine Lucas had been right about that. She'd collected *everything* as far as Heather could remember: newspapers, old plastic pots, clothes – lots and lots of clothes – every toy Heather and Faith had ever owned, even though many were broken and unwanted by their owners.

There had been the china ornaments, cutesy little things – unicorns and fairies, covered in glitter – that had made Heather want to gag. Worst of all were the dolls. Even now, when Heather thinks of the frilly dresses, the porcelain faces with staring blue eyes, it makes her shiver.

But there seems to be none of that in this photo. From the outside, and at a distance of more than twenty years, these two girls look as if they come from a normal, happy family.

She can't resist pulling the cellophane back, even though it tears a little in the corner, to check if there's writing on the back of the print. There is: 'Faith and Heather, Christmas 1991.' Heather does the maths: Faith would have been eight, just about to turn nine, and she would have been five.

She turns the page. This one is close enough to the back of the album that the spine creaks and shifts, pulling the pages behind it open, and some things fall out the back of the book: more photographs and a couple of hand-drawn birthday cards from her and Faith to their mum. This makes an odd warm feeling flare in Heather's chest. Normally, she hates the idea of her mother keeping anything, especially if it had sentimental value – because *everything* she owned had sentimental value, even the bags of rubbish that had filled the kitchen so they could no longer cook in it, let alone eat at the table – but this is something she can understand. Somehow, it helps her breathe out.

The other crap in the pile quickly erodes the sensation: grocery receipts from fifteen years ago, a pizza-delivery flyer that must have come through the letterbox, and numerous newspaper cuttings, carefully clipped and folded in half. Heather prepares to tuck it all back inside the cover of the photo album, but before she does so she checks the newspaper articles, just in case something of more value is hiding inside. She'd like to feel that warm feeling again, even if it confuses her a little.

One article is about the discovery of Roman ruins in nearby Orpington, another about the opening of the massive shopping mall that now takes up most of Bromley town centre. Heather refolds and discards them. Maybe these were saved in the earlier days of her mother's hoarding? Later on, she didn't bother being this organized, cutting things out and folding them; she'd just kept the whole newspaper.

The last one is yet another clipping from the *Bromley and Chislehurst News Shopper,* the free local paper that used to come through the door. Sadder, though. 'Hunt For Missing Bromley Girl Continues,' the headline reads. Heather takes a moment to look at the child in the photograph taking up a quarter of the report. It's a school picture with a mottled blue background. The girl has a uniform on – a white shirt with a green and blue striped tie – that looks too big for her, as if she's still trying to grow into it.

Something flashes in the back of Heather's brain. She recognizes these colours, this uniform. St Michael's Primary. That was the school she and Faith had gone to. Maybe that's why her mum had kept this clipping, because of that sense of connection? Something about the story had made it personal. Maybe Heather had known her, been at St Michael's at the same time?

She looks more closely at the girl and decides that if they had been in the same year, maybe they would have been friends. The girl has neat long, blonde plaits. Her fringe is a little too long but there's a mischievous twinkle in the eyes peering from underneath the silky strands. Heather smiles. *I hope they found her,* she silently wishes, *I hope she was okay.*

She gets ready to fold the article up and store it away with the other ones, but as she moves the paper, something catches her eye:

Police are asking for anyone local who might have been in the Fossington Road area on Friday, 3rd July, around three in the afternoon, to contact them, in case they saw something relevant to the enquiry.

Heather wonders what she was doing on 3 July. She checks the date at the top of the page. The report is from 15 July 1992, almost two weeks later. Yes, she would have been six then, and at St Michael's. Just finishing the summer term of her second year.

A chill runs through her. She was probably running around in the playground, or reading a book under one of the big horse chestnuts, completely unaware.

Hooked now, she carries on reading:

Her mother is begging anyone who knows anything to come forward. 'We just want our little Heather back safe and sound,' she says.

Heather.

Heather?

Deep down inside, she begins to quiver. It has to be a coincidence, right? Even though her name wasn't massively popular at that time. But it was possible there was another Heather at the school. There had to have been.

Heather frantically tries to focus her eyes on the print at the top of the article, but she can't seem to make her brain stay still enough to interpret what she's reading. She closes her eyes and opens them again, resetting them, to see if that helps, and the opening paragraph slams into focus.

Heather Lucas, aged 6, has been missing for the past twelve days...

CHAPTER SEVEN

NOW

'Did you know about this?'

As her sister enters the communal hallway of her flat, Heather flies towards Faith waving the newspaper clipping wildly. Faith has arrived to collect Alice's photograph. She backs up, tripping slightly over the threshold, and ends up on the porch.

Heather has been sitting inside all morning, holding the scrap of newsprint in her hands. Obsessing. When the door buzzer sounded, it had the same effect as a starter's pistol. Heather knows she's acting like a complete lunatic, but on one level it's quite pleasing to see the look of shock and confusion on her sister's face, rather than the well-worn eye roll and look of saintly forbearance. It's an admission that something really, truly is wrong.

'Did you? Did you know?'

Heather finally stops moving enough for her sister to see what she's waving around. Faith's eyes fall on the grainy photograph in the newspaper cutting and she goes pale. 'Why don't we go inside?'

Heather stares at her. She's whipped herself up into such a

tornado of fury that she hasn't thought about how she'll react if Faith actually answers in the affirmative. It's only because she's so flabbergasted that Faith manages to grab her by the arm and manoeuvre her inside.

'Hey, Heather,' a voice calls from the stairs. It's Jason. But Faith bustles her past him and into her flat, glancing up at him with her mouth set in a thin line. Heather can't unscramble her brain enough to say something sensible to him at the best of times, so maybe it's a blessing in disguise.

She regains her language skills as Faith steers her into the kitchen. 'You did, didn't you?' she asks, surprised at how calm and rational she sounds after her outburst only moments before.

Faith looks at her for a few seconds, then nods.

'Why didn't you tell me?' Heather says, her volume rising again. 'Why didn't anyone ever tell me?' A rush of pure hatred for her mother leaps through her like a flame. She wants to throw things, to scream so loud that Mrs Rowe in the top flat will get worried and call the police. She picks up a mug, feeling the smoothness of the china under her fingers, and imagines hurling it towards the kitchen units. It's only the fact that this was precisely the sort of thing her mother used to do that stops her.

Faith is looking confused. 'You don't remember?'

Heather's fingers grip the mug tighter. The urge to launch it towards the opposite wall is almost overwhelming now. 'I was six!'

'But I remember things from when I was that age, and less traumatic things, too. I always thought those sorts of memories – the ones accompanied by strong emotion – were supposed to be the clearest.'

Heather makes an incredulous little cough of a laugh. 'Wasn't the fact I've never once in my life mentioned it a bit of a giveaway?'

Faith eyes the mug in Heather's hand with a concerned expression, which only makes Heather want to fling it all the more. 'I suppose I assumed you just didn't want to talk about it. You've got to admit, you're not big on sharing, are you?'

Heather slumps into one of the chairs surrounding her tiny, two-seater dining set. The mug falls from her fingers and totters for a second before making contact with the tabletop, landing gracefully on its base.

'Why?' she whispers, more to herself than to her sister. 'Why would you think that? Why would you never even think to mention it?'

Faith looks helpless. Heather realizes she's never seen her sister look helpless before. 'Well, none of us talked about it. We just... didn't.' She pauses and frowns before carrying on. 'Okay, maybe that's not true. I remember Dad and Aunt Kathy talking about it a couple of times after it happened, but if they ever mentioned it to Mum she just shut down or got hysterical. I learned very quickly not to raise the subject.' Faith looks long and hard at the table before raising her eyes to meet Heather's again. 'I loved Mum, despite all her flaws, but she was a very controlling person.'

Heather can't help laughing. Is her sister living in a parallel universe? 'What are you talking about? She had no control over anything! Do you not remember how we lived? It was chaos!'

'The freaking out, the meltdowns. That was her way of avoiding things she didn't want to face, and making sure we didn't bring them up again. If that's not being manipulative, I don't know what is. She might have seemed weak, but she controlled us all.' Faith lets out a long, memory-laden sigh. 'She was a master at it.'

Heather stares at her sister. What she has said is shocking, something Heather had never considered, but even more shocking is the expression on her face. It's calm. Not serene and at peace, but accepting. If Faith really feels that way, why isn't she shouting and screaming with the unfairness of it? That's what Heather wants to do.

This is all Mum's fault, she thinks, feeling venom pulse through her veins. *How things are between me and Faith, the shoplifting, everything… And now I find she's landed me in this mess, too.*

She turns to her sister. She only has one point, but she's going to keep hammering it in until Faith understands. 'It doesn't matter what Mum was like. We've been grown up and out of that house for years now. You should have told me.'

Faith sits down on a chair and pulls her hand through her hair. 'I was only nine myself,' she says quietly. 'And all I know is what I remember from back then. To be honest, I haven't thought about it in years.'

This makes Heather's spine stiffen. 'The most horrible, momentous thing that's ever happened to your little sister and you don't even think about it? How very telling.'

'Don't be like that.' Faith sighs wearily. 'I did used to consider mentioning it, but I really wasn't sure if it would help. I mean, help you, if it was all dredged up again. Sometimes you just seem so…' Her expression softens, begs forgiveness for what she's about to say. 'Fragile. And I suppose, to some extent, I did block it out, bury it. I don't know if you've realized it, but our family is very good at that kind of stuff.'

Heather sits down across from her sister. *Yes. Very good,* she thinks, and all the energizing adrenaline begins to leak away. 'So what do you know? I went missing… Did I wander off and get lost? What?'

Faith takes a moment. Heather can see her eyes making tiny movements, as if she's pulling up memories and facts from a dusty drawer in the back of her brain. 'You were taken.'

Heather breathes the word, echoing her sister. 'Taken.'

Faith looks worried. She nods.

'You mean… kidnapped?'

'Sort of.' Faith's voice is scratchy and dry. '"Snatched" is what I remember hearing people say. I don't think there was a ransom or anything. Nothing like that.'

'But I was obviously found. Returned home. How… how long was I gone?'

Her sister looks pained. Heather suspects she's not 100 per cent sure of the facts any more. 'It seemed like forever at the time, but I think it was only a week or two.'

Heather swallows. Long enough. For exactly what she doesn't want to think about.

Faith leans forward, looks genuinely distressed. 'Mum was such a mess afterwards. She just… fell apart. Everyone was walking on eggshells. Even one mention could set her off and send her into a downward spiral for days.'

Heather nods. She knows what their mother was like.

'I was cross with her at the time, but now I understand totally.' Faith's eyes fill. 'If anything were to happen to Barney or Alice…' she trails off, unable to finish.

Heather finds a lump in her throat, too. Losing a child, whichever way it happens…

'You don't know anything more than that?'

Faith shakes her head. 'I'm sorry it's come as such a shock. I would have said something if I'd known you had no memory of it, believe me.'

Unfortunately, Heather does, which leaves her with a ball of anger, curled up in the slingshot of her chest, with no one to fire it at. No one alive, anyway.

Faith looks at Heather. 'What are you going to do?'

Heather just looks wordlessly back at her. She really has no idea.

CHAPTER EIGHT

NOW

The following Saturday, Heather gets into her car and drives to Bickley, an affluent area just a couple of miles away on the other side of Bromley town centre. It's full of leafy streets, nice schools and even nicer houses. She drives down Southborough Road, then turns into a side road and stops her car halfway down.

She gets out and, not having parked at her exact destination, walks a little farther down the street. She stops opposite an Edwardian detached house but doesn't cross the road. She doesn't walk up the path and knock on the door; she just stares, arms hanging limply by her sides.

This is her childhood home, the house her mother lived in until just two years ago. She hasn't been back down Hawksbury Road since shortly after that, and before her mother's death, not for almost five years.

It's a shock to see the overgrown rhododendrons stripped back at the front, cleared to make way for a driveway, she guesses, from the neat row of stone blocks lining the perimeter of a bed of flattened sand and the paving slabs piled up on the adjacent lawn. The house looks naked this way.

The ground floor is aged red brick, and the upper floors are covered in the original pebble-dash, now painted a gleaming white instead of mottled cream with pocks and holes in its render. The roof tiles are all uniform and lined in neat rows, with no cracks or mossy patches to be seen, and the satisfyingly heavy original front door is now a stylish dove grey with frosted panels at the top.

She and Faith had inherited the house, but they'd sold it as speedily as possible, probably forfeiting tens of thousands each because they hadn't spruced it up at all. The only person willing to snap it up had been a developer. He'd boasted about building a block of flats, carving the spacious garden up into numbered parking spaces. Heather had happily pocketed the money, glad to be rid of the property, and had thought no more about it. But it must have niggled Faith because she'd kept tabs on the progress, done a bit of digging, and had eventually informed Heather that planning permission had been refused. The shark-like developer (the only thing Heather can remember about him was his teeth: overcrowded and slightly pointed) had put it straight back on the market without even mowing the lawn.

She supposes she must have known someone would buy it eventually, given the desirable location, despite the state it had been in.

It almost looks like a different house now, as if their life there has been erased, like a computer drive reformatted and written over. It will be as if her past, her childhood, never occurred. A new family will lay down their memories here now. From the quality of the work done so far, she guesses they'll be bright, happy ones, and she silently hates them for it.

She isn't quite sure why she drove here, only that she thought there might be clues, something ghostly left behind that would silence the questions that have been running round her brain since her discovery last week, but this is just a blank canvas.

But then Heather remembers that, even if you erase a hard drive, little telltale fragments are left behind, and as she continues to stare, the air around the house starts to shift and shimmer until she can almost see the Virginia creeper crawling back up the house, suffocating each window as it goes. The overgrown shrubs that almost obliterated the path and obscured the plastic storage crates and junk from passers-by begin to form like ghostly shapes in the garden.

She can imagine her mother sitting on the only seat in the house: one end of the sofa where she'd made a nest for herself, where she sat to watch the TV, slept and even ate. Heather takes a step forward until she is right on the very edge of the kerb, but she goes no further.

Why? It is a question she has never asked of this house before. In the past, she didn't want to know. Recently she's been so focused on the immediacy of her anger and hurt that she hasn't looked for the root beneath it.

Why did things get this way, Mum? How did you come to do this to yourself? To us?

And why did she never ask these questions of her mother while she still had the chance?

CHAPTER NINE

DOORBELL

The doorbell is old. Not horrible old, like one of those plastic boxes with a flat, round button that fools you into thinking it's working but never produces any sound. No, nothing as cheap and deceitful as that. This bell was installed in the 1920s. It has a creamy domed Bakelite button set in a decorative brass surround. Even now it works, heralding the arrival of every visitor with a clear, self-confident ring. The sound can be heard in every dark and shadowy corner of our house.

THEN

'Mummy, can I have Megan round for tea?'

Heather's mother looks up from where she is digging in a pile of clothes. She's trying to find Heather's PE kit. Heather brought it home to be washed before the Easter holidays, but she's been back at school for three weeks now and nobody can find it. Miss Perrins has said she's very sorry, but she's going to have to give Heather a red mark on her behaviour chart if she doesn't have it for her next lesson. Heather really doesn't want to get a red mark. She hasn't had one yet, because she tries super-extra-hard to be good at school.

'What?' her mother says.

'Can Megan come for tea one day?' Heather hops from foot to foot because she's really excited about the idea. 'I've been round to hers loads.'

Her mother sighs and looks around the living room. 'I don't think so, darling. Sorry. Maybe when I get the house straight.'

Heather looks down at her shoes. Ever since the hide-and-seek incident, the whole family wears shoes indoors all the time. 'But you said the same thing after the summer holidays…'

Her mother stops rummaging in a pile of clothes that has just come back from the launderette. The washing machine is broken, but her mum gets cross if her dad mentions getting someone round to fix it.

'I said "no", Heather. Now run along. It's teatime soon.'

Heather crosses her arms. 'It's not fair! Megan says that proper best friends go round each other's houses, and Katie Matthews asks her to tea nearly every week. If we don't let her come here, she might just end up being Katie's friend instead and I'll be left out.'

'Heather! Just go and find something to do! I'm trying to find your PE kit, and you know you'll be upset if I don't, so you need to let me do this now and we'll talk about it later. Understood?'

'Understood,' Heather mumbles, reversing back through the rabbit trail and going to find Faith, who's in the kitchen cooking their tea. Now Faith's eleven, she's allowed to do things like that.

Heather climbs over some plastic bags tied at the top when she gets to the hallway. They weren't there yesterday. They're full of dollies. But these dollies aren't pretty ones like Cassandra. A Barbie with no clothes on is sticking out the top of one bag and her hair has been cut funny. It looks rough and fluffy, not smooth and silky like it does when they come out the box. She's also missing one arm. Heather guesses her mother must have been to the charity shop again on one of her 'rescue missions'. She gets the dollies so she can fix them and make them better, then she'll be able to give them to the hospital or to poor children.

Heather thinks her mummy must be a very good person to do something like that; she just wishes there weren't so many of them. There are bags and bags now, lining the hallway and the landing. Some even creep into Faith's room, but Faith keeps putting them back outside again. Not where anyone will notice they've reappeared, of course. She finds a spot somewhere else and hides them so their mother won't get upset she moved them.

Faith is cooking chicken nuggets and chips in the oven. They have to do everything in the oven at the moment because the bit on top doesn't work.

'Go and find the ketchup,' Faith says when she sees her younger sister. She's looking a bit cross, but Faith always seems to be cross these days. Their mother says it's because she's almost a teenager. Faith says it's from living in a dump like this.

Heather climbs on top of some boxes full of pots and pans to reach the cupboard where the ketchup lives. She pulls the bottle out, but it's empty apart from some red sludge at the bottom. 'It's all gone,' she calls to Faith.

Her sister sighs dramatically. 'Keep looking. There'll be another one back there. You know how mum likes to stock up.'

Heather throws the empty bottle on the floor with the rest of the rubbish, then stands on tiptoes to reach further into the cupboard. The box wobbles a little but she manages to stop herself from falling by holding onto the cupboard door. There's another bottle in there, and it's half-full with ketchup, but round the top it's green and fluffy. 'Shall I throw this one away too?' she asks.

Faith shakes her head. 'Put it back for now. Mum will want to check it if it's not properly finished.'

'But it's yucky!'

'I said she'd want to check it. I didn't say it'd make sense,' Faith says. 'There's only one thing for it – we'll have to break into the emergency rations.'

Heather jumps down from the boxes, smiling. 'Cool! I know where Mummy keeps them!' She goes to the drawer by the back door and opens it. Inside are hundreds and hundreds of tiny packets – sugar, salt, pepper, salad cream, vinegar – just about anything you can find in a café or a restaurant. Mum always puts loads in her handbag when they go out to eat (which is getting to be more and more, with the top of the oven being broken) because she says it's part of what they pay for when they pay for the food, and you never know when they'll come in handy. When Heather got up this morning, she didn't know today was going to be that day. It's kind of exciting!

She reaches into the drawer, feeling the sachets slide through her fingers, enjoying the shifting colours as she searches for the ketchup ones. It's kind of like looking for buried treasure. By the time Faith gets the nuggets and chips out of the oven Heather has six sachets clutched in each hand. Faith serves up their food and carries the plates through to the living room. They have to squish up together to fit into the space on the end of the sofa, but they don't mind. At least this way they can watch cartoons while they eat.

The best bit is opening up the little packets and squeezing out the ketchup from the inside. It feels like they're being fancy. There are still two or three each left over when they've finished eating.

Faith grins at Heather as she rips open another one. 'Look,

Heather! It's like blood.' She says the last bit in a creepy voice that makes Heather's spine feel all tickly, and when Faith presses on the packet so the ketchup oozes out, she does a laugh that goes *mwah-hah-hah!* and makes Heather giggle, so Heather tears open one of her packets and does the same.

After that they can't stop. They both keep ripping and *mwah-hah-hah-ing* until they're laughing so hard they're in danger of missing their plates and decorating their legs instead.

But then the air in the room goes instantly cold. Heather and Faith freeze.

'Girls! What on earth do you think you're doing?'

Heather drops her last unsqueezed ketchup packet onto her plate, where it lands in the big blob of pretend blood she's been collecting.

'Just eating our tea,' Faith says. 'I cooked chips and nuggets for me and Heather.'

Heather's mother hasn't got time to be impressed by that; she's too busy staring at the twisted and torn wrappers littering the girls' plates. 'Where did you get those?' she says, and her voice sounds all quiet and quivery.

'From the 'mergency draw,' Heather says helpfully. 'The other ketchup was fluffy.'

Their mother's expression changes to the one she wears when she's trying to explain something and keep her temper at the same time. 'Those... those... They're not for you to use! They're to be kept there. Just in case.'

'But it *was* "just in case", Mummy!' Heather explains.

Their mother shakes her head, closes her eyes. 'You don't understand.' And then her eyes snap open again and she looks at Heather. 'How many did you take? How many?'

'I... I...'

'How many, Heather!' She's shouting now and Heather can't seem to make the counting bit of her brain work.

Faith stands up. 'Don't shout at her! It's not her fault. I told her to get them. And there were twelve, okay? Just twelve. And there are hundreds left in there!'

Their mother runs down the hall. The sisters put their plates down on the sofa and follow. Inside the kitchen, their mother wrenches the drawer open. The packets rustle and slide over each other as she sticks her hands inside and moves them around, counting softly.

She goes still and lifts her head up. 'Right. Girls, get your coats on. We're going to the Harvester for tea.'

The girls look at each other, big grins on their faces. That's *really* fancy! But then Faith stops smiling. 'But we've just eaten our tea,' she says, looking confused.

'Don't get cheeky with me, young lady!' Mum yells. 'I need to get a dozen more and then it'll all be okay again. You did say it was twelve, right?'

They both nod, but neither moves, and then their mother's expression stops being hard and angry and she starts to look as if she's about to cry.

'Sorry, girls. Sorry, my babies.'

She comes and puts her arms round them and pulls them to her, one in each arm. 'I tell you what, you don't need to eat more tea – just dessert. How about that? An absolutely giant ice-cream sundae if you like. With sprinkles! And I can pick up more sachets to replace the ones we're missing.'

She lets go of the girls, and all three of them are excited now.

'Is Daddy coming?' Heather asks.

'No, poppet. He's working late again tonight.'

Faith sighs. 'He's always working late,' she grumbles.

Their mother's eyes get that shiny look again, but then she smiles and says, 'All the more for us, then! Go on, go and get your coats!'

Heather starts to run towards the piles near the front door. She *thinks* that's where she left hers, but then the doorbell goes and everyone freezes. Both sisters turn and look at their mother. She puts her finger to her lips and motions for them to come towards her. Quietly. It's hard to do, because everything underneath their feet is crunchy, but they've had plenty of practice.

'Hello?' a voice calls through the front door. 'Mrs Lucas?' The man knocks loudly. Heather starts to feel scared.

Her mother points at the next room, near the big table that's always full of all her important papers. There's a space down the side and both girls instinctively head for it and crouch there.

The letterbox clatters. The man must be peeping through it. 'Mrs Lucas? I'm just here to read the electric meter… Are you there?'

But Mrs Lucas doesn't answer him. Instead, she runs to where her daughters are hiding and squats down beside them, holding them tight. As they all close their eyes and wait for the man to go away, Heather realizes there probably isn't going to be any ice-cream sundae tonight after all, and probably no chocolate sprinkles either.

CHAPTER TEN

NOW

It's much later in the afternoon when Heather gets back to her flat after visiting her old house in Bickley. She goes into town for a cappuccino, sits outside her favourite café and watches the people march up and down the pedestrianized section of the High Street.

This is a mistake.

Because eventually she joins them, and then Mothercare pulls her inside, and by the time she's feeding pound coins into the parking machine in The Glades shopping centre a squashy toy giraffe is tucked securely in the side pocket of her bag.

She's really glad to get back to her flat, her sanctuary. She stows her contraband in the forbidden drawer and hurries into the living room, ready to perform her breathing ritual, but when she finds her usual spot in the middle of the rug and looks up she gets a shock.

Instead of flat, green grass and regimented borders, she's met with a garden full of people. And there's Jason in the middle of them, flipping burgers on a barbecue and swigging Coke from a bottle. He looks completely at ease as he smiles and chats with a group of guys.

Heather is completely infuriated, but she knows she has no right to be. When they'd bumped into each other in the hallway a couple of days ago, he'd told her he was having his housewarming thing this afternoon. The weather forecast was good for once, he'd said, so he'd decided to go for it. It's not Jason's fault her thoughts have been so tangled lately that the information got lost inside her head.

As if he knows she's staring at him, he turns and looks at her, meets her gaze and smiles. She waves back. His smile grows wider and he makes a beckoning motion. She has no choice but to follow his tractor beam, to unlock the French doors and walk outside. She doesn't look to the left or the right, doesn't pay attention to the other bodies or the curious glances she's getting. She just walks straight towards him.

'Hi,' he says softly, once she is standing in front of him.

'Hi,' she says back.

'Want a burger?'

She nods, even though she has no idea if she's hungry or not. It's not a fancy affair, no lettuce or pickle, just a charred piece of meat stuck inside a floury white roll with a blob of ketchup. It tastes like heaven.

'Glad you could make it,' he says as Heather takes another bite. 'I wasn't entirely sure you were going to put in an appearance.' And before Heather can say neither was she, he steers her towards a group of people. 'Here, let me introduce you to the gang.' Her mouth is too full of burger to object.

'This is Damien, my partner in crime from my university days, and this is his girlfriend Tola.' More names fill Heather's head as he goes round the group, all instantly rejected and lost – her brain's storage drive is too full – but she pulls her cheek muscles into what she hopes is a smile and nods with each introduction.

'So,' says Damien (the one name she can remember), 'you're Jay's mysterious girl downstairs.'

Heather's eyebrows rise. She's mysterious? That sounds a lot more interesting and romantic than the truth: that she is Jason's terminally damaged girl downstairs, the one who's on the verge of being arrested for petty theft. She doesn't disabuse Jason's friend of the notion, though. She learned right from childhood that most people don't look too far below the surface and anything they superimpose on you is invariably better than the reality. These assumptions create a useful shield, one she does her best not to dislodge.

'Put on a good face,' her mother always said when they left the house. So no one would guess, so no one would know. Even social services hadn't guessed the horror that lay inside the detached house in a 'nice' area for years. And Heather has cultivated this approach in her adult life, carefully painting a veneer of Perfectly Normal on top of her real self.

'Oh, I'm not mysterious at all,' she says.

'How long have you been living here?' Damien's girlfriend asks.

'A couple of years,' Heather replies, feeling as if she's giving something away she shouldn't. Her mother taught her that information was to be hoarded just as much as belongings. It wasn't until Heather was almost a teenager that she realized not everyone shared this mindset, that some people live their whole lives spilling everything out of their mouths with no thought for the consequences.

'Oh well, don't let Jason here keep you awake late at night when he gets maudlin and decides to play his Smiths albums back to back,' Tola adds, sticking her tongue out at their host.

'Oh, no, I don't... I mean... he doesn't. Not that I've heard anyway. He's a good neighbour.' And she shoots a look across at him and is rewarded by a burning sensation in her cheeks.

Thankfully, the rest of the group are in an ebullient mood and the conversation quickly sweeps by Heather. She stands there on the fringes of the group, sipping a beer that someone handed her, and smiling shyly every now and then when someone says something funny. She doesn't mind that she doesn't know any of the people they're referring to or that she doesn't get the in-jokes. It's nice to stand out here in the sunshine and feel… well, as a thirty-two-year-old woman ought to feel. Just for a moment, she forgets about the faceless house in Hawksbury Road with the new driveway. She forgets about the toy giraffe that rode all the way home in her handbag.

'So, what do you do, Heather?' the guy with the ginger beard in the stripy T-shirt asks. She wants to call him Isaac, but she's not sure that's right.

'I'm an archivist.'

'You work in a library?'

'Yes, well, sort of, I've moved all over the country since I qualified, but I'm from this area originally. I moved back when I got a job covering maternity leave for someone at the V&A. Now I work at a stately home.'

'Cool,' Tola says. 'I love that museum. Which bit do you work in?'

'Um, I'm not…' Okay, maybe this isn't as easy as she'd first thought, but Tola and T-shirt Man have open, enquiring looks on their faces. They don't look as if they're scanning the garden for someone more interesting to talk to, so she carries on. 'I finished there about a year ago and was lucky enough to find another contract within commuting distance, so I didn't have to pack up and move away.'

Jason comes up behind her. She knows it's him from the smell of hickory smoke and the way the whole of her back warms up as he gets closer. 'What's this I'm overhearing about packing up and moving away?'

She turns to look at him. He's frowning instead of looking hopeful, which surely has to be a good thing. 'Oh, no one!' she says quickly. 'I was telling…' – there's a pause where she realizes she still doesn't know T-shirt Man's name – 'your friends about my job.'

'Which is?'

'I work at Sandwood Park in East Sussex. It used to belong to a famous author but his widow died recently and the whole estate was left to a private trust.'

'They didn't have any kids to leave the house to?' Tola asks.

Heather smiles. This is nice, having people interested in what she's saying. Slightly giddying, in fact. She can't resist keeping it going by sharing a bit of gossip. 'Well, yes, actually, they did, but the wife decided not to leave her beautiful Arts and Crafts home to any of her two remaining children or five grandchildren. She left specific instructions to her solicitor to that effect, saying she didn't trust her offspring not to rip out half the walls, replace the grand conservatory with sliding glass doors that fold up like a concertina, or make a swimming pool out of the rose garden. So she left them nothing but the ashes of their dearly beloved family pets: three dogs, two cats, and a guinea pig.'

'Ouch!' Tola says, laughing.

Heather feels as if she's floating inside. She made another person laugh; she had no idea she could do that.

This leads to some bantering back and forth about jobs, during which Heather learns that Jason is an 'heir hunter' like that programme on daytime TV. His firm, based in central London, tracks down the beneficiaries of unclaimed estates and reunites them with their inheritances. For a commission, of course.

Someone new saunters up. 'Hey, Jason. Great barbecue,' the guy says. 'Is Alex coming? I haven't seen him in ages.'

Something odd happens then. Jason's normally affable and friendly demeanour cools to freezing point and he gives the intruder a stony look. 'No. Alex isn't here.' And then he just walks off, leaving the rest of the group looking awkwardly at each other.

'Well done, Jack,' Damien mutters.

'What?' the new guy says, looking most perplexed. 'He and Alex have been best mates for years. I thought they'd have patched things up by now.'

Tola shakes her head and rolls her eyes. 'Really? What parallel universe are you living in? I know Alex was caught between a rock and a hard place, but once you break Jason's trust like that, there's no coming back from it. Don't you remember what he was like about Caleb and the whole bike incident?'

Jack's eyes widen. 'Oh,' he says. 'It's as bad as that? I didn't know.'

Heather feels as if she's eavesdropping, even though she is not. She should really walk away, but she's too hungry for information about Jason to do that.

'Well, when you factor in there was a woman involved…' Tola adds darkly.

All of them glance over at the barbecue, where Jason is now flipping burgers so hard that one falls on the ground.

Damien sighs. 'He's a great bloke, but he's got to get over his knight-in-shining-armour complex. It might work in the storybooks, but in real life those girls he keeps trying to rescue are the kind of women who'll really do a number on you.'

Tola flips her long braids over her shoulder. 'Are you saying you're not the rescuing type? What if I needed you to rescue me?'

Damien pulls her to him with one arm and plants a kiss on her lips. 'You're much too feisty to be anyone's damsel in distress,' he tells her, and Tola obviously approves of his answer because she grins at him.

'You'd better believe it!'

The whole group laughs, which causes the cluster of people nearby to turn and join in. Heather merges into the group with them and listens to the stories about other people's lives – what they do, who they love, who they don't love any more and would, therefore, love to shame on Twitter, if it wasn't beneath them.

The group are all in stitches about someone's tale of a drunken-holiday tattoo when Jason calls her over to the barbecue. 'Sausage?' he says, brandishing a plump offering with a pair of giant tongs. She nods. She even smiles. 'We could do this again some time over the summer,' he adds. Heather must look a bit panicked because he laughs and adds, 'Don't worry! I'm not going to be filling the garden with people every weekend. I meant, now that I've got this barbecue, I might as well use it. You could join me for burgers and sausages one evening. Or if I get really adventurous, maybe even a chicken drumstick or two?'

Heather flushes. 'I couldn't let you do that—'

'Yes, you could,' he replies, interrupting her so cheerfully that she can't seem to mind. 'Because I'm hoping you might be able to bring a salad or something. I'm good with meat but hopeless with vegetables. It's not that I can't cook them, just that everything ends up looking… well, not very pretty. I don't have that artistic touch.'

Heather lets out a little laugh. 'And you think I do?'

He smiles, and this one isn't a full-on grin like the other ones, more of a playful one, like they're sharing a secret. 'I think you look like the creative sort – a girl who has a bit more going on under the surface than anyone else knows.'

Damian's words from earlier flash into her brain: *Jason's mysterious girl.*

Her smile doesn't dim, but she feels something deflate inside. *If only you knew,* she thinks, but she's glad he doesn't know because, if he did, he wouldn't be inviting her for burgers and drumsticks in the garden, and she thinks she might rather like that.

He looks away as he searches the plastic table set up next to the barbecue for something. 'Gah!' he says, frowning. 'Run out of plates.' He glances back up towards his flat and then back at Heather. 'Think I brought down every one I owned. Don't suppose I could borrow a few off you, could I? I'll even wash them up afterwards!'

'Um…' Heather stutters. 'I'm not sure—'

He places her sausage back on the edge of the grill rack, as far away from the heat as possible. 'I'll come and get them, if you like? Save you lugging them all the way out here.' And he heads off towards the French doors before Heather can say anything.

Panic mode snaps in. That same thing that always thumps in Heather's chest when anyone gets too close to her flat. She doesn't even like the postman pushing things in through the letterbox, and is always relieved when she sees his red fleece strolling back down the driveway, even though she knows her territorial reaction is stupid.

She runs after Jason, neatly intercepting him and standing at the threshold of her living room, barring his way. She stretches one arm across the open doorway. 'It's fine. I'll get them. You need to keep an eye on the barbecue anyway.'

Jason smiles at her. A slightly perplexed one this time. 'I'm here now. No problem at all.'

But Heather doesn't give in. She doesn't back down. Jason can't see it, but she's bracing her hand even harder against the doorframe. She shakes her head.

You can't come in, she tells him silently. *No one can ever come in.* Even though she knows her kitchen is spotless and her set of lovely white plates with the broad grey border are neatly stacked in a clean, white cupboard. She can't have him this close to That Room. It's making her feel sick just thinking about it. Her blood starts to pound in her ears.

'You know what?' she says suddenly. 'I'm not sure about that sausage anyway. I hadn't planned on…' She stops, gathers herself a little, pulls herself tall and looks him in the chin because that's as far north as she can manage. 'Thank you, but I think I'd better be going now.' And she steps back and closes the doors in his face, then turns and runs to the kitchen where she throws open the cupboard and stares at her plates, all neatly stacked and in pristine condition. For the first time ever, she gains no solace in that.

CHAPTER ELEVEN

NOW

Heather stays in her flat for hours. She doesn't even go into the living room. She stays in the kitchen, caught between wanting to turn the radio up loud to block out the sounds of the barbecue outside and not wanting to turn it on at all, in case Jason hears it and it reminds him what a nutjob she is.

Sometimes, she goes to the window in the far corner of the kitchen. If she leans over the counter, just to the point where her stomach starts hurting, and presses her face against the cabinet above the kettle, she can see him standing near the barbecue, tongs in hand.

He's still smiling, still chatting to his friends, but every now and then he glances over towards her French doors and his expression darkens.

He must think she's a freak.

Only when it's dark and the last stragglers have shouted their goodbyes from the driveway as they saunter back to their cars or nearby Shortlands station does Heather creep back into her living room. She closes the curtains then switches on a single lamp.

She reaches for the TV remote and the screen leaps into life. Football is on, highlights from a match earlier that day, so she hits the button over and over, searching for something to watch – through the comedy and drama channels, through the 'plus ones' of the terrestrials, until she ends up in the nature, reality and crime section of the channel list. It's there that an image freezes her thumb mid-air.

It's one of those awful programmes about compulsive hoarders. Not the jaunty, pretend-it's-comedy kind where they make neat freaks go and clean their houses, but the kind that interviews people, sends in crews of trained professionals to help. Usually, Heather doesn't venture this far up the channel list, precisely because she doesn't want to see this sort of thing, but until a moment ago she was caught in a trance of button-pushing, rhythmically pressing to soothe herself instead of tapping in the number of her favourite movie channel and jumping straight over this section of programming.

She makes herself put down the remote and crosses her arms to stop herself picking it up again. *You deserve to watch this,* she tells herself, *because this is what you came from. This is who you are.*

The episode features a man who's car obsession has raged out of control. His whole two-acre property is filled with rusting wrecks, some of them so far gone they're not even recognizable as vehicles, yet he still refuses to let the TV helpers cart them away, just in case some part in the depths of their bellies might be useful to him some day.

The other subject of the programme – she didn't realize there'd be two – is a young mother. Yes, this looks much more familiar: clothes stacked to the ceiling, piled so high they've created mountains of fabric; papers and books stuffed in every available hole, and rubbish filling in the gaps. Apart from the fact the voices are American, when Heather looks at the shots where they show the house and not the people, it could have been their family home on Hawksbury Road twenty years ago.

There's a kid in the family, a daughter with wiry brown hair and glasses. Heather pauses the TV as the camera zooms in on the girl and takes in the haunted look in her eyes, the silent plea for someone to help, to get her out of there.

They might come, she tells the girl inside her head. *They might take you away to somewhere clean and uncluttered, but you'll never be free. Sorry, kid. No happy-ever-after for you.*

Even the Dad reminds her of her own father. He has that same trapped expression, the one that says he stopped fighting about the mess long ago. The professionals buzz around, offering advice. Don't they know it's hopeless? That even if they get the place spotless, it'll be just as bad in a couple of years?

Heather reaches for the remote in disgust. She can't watch any more of this fairy story.

But then the TV shrink asks the husband where it all started, why he thinks his wife is driven to this. Pain crosses his features and he shrugs. 'I guess it was when we lost our son, Cody. Sudden Infant Death Syndrome. It was nobody's fault but Selena blamed herself.'

A picture of a cute little baby with chubby cheeks and a gummy smile pops up on the screen.

'She started buying things, getting ready for the new baby,' he continues. 'We'd been trying for a second one for five years by then and she was so excited. I knew she was going a little overboard, but I couldn't begrudge her. I really couldn't. And then, somehow, after... we lost him... she didn't stop. She just kept buying more and more baby stuff. At first she would say we were going to try again, but after a couple of years it became obvious that was just an excuse.' He sighs heavily. 'I just don't know how to help her, and I don't know if I can take any more.'

Heather's stomach has been sinking ever since the man started talking about babies. She doesn't want this. She doesn't want to feel this rush of empathy for the woman, to share in her pain for the child that will be forever missing from her life, so when the mother has a meltdown because someone wants to throw away a ratty baby blanket covered in cobwebs and mouse droppings, Heather grabs at the opportunity to turn the warm feeling sour.

'You have a child!' she shouts at the screen. 'You have one left that didn't die and you're losing her in a pile of junk! Why don't you think of her for a change? Think about what this is doing to her?'

It feels strangely good to hurl the words at these stupid people who can't hear her, people who are flushing their lives down the toilet and won't get off their sorry backsides to do anything about it. So instead of switching over, she suspends her disbelief as the house is cleared and the families are shown happy and smiling at the end of the episode, and she watches the episode after that too. Apparently, the channel is having a bit of a marathon this weekend.

The next one features an older lady who started hoarding after her beloved father died, and a waste-of-space woman who can't see that seventy cats in one cluttered house is too many. Heather shouts at her, too. Why not? There's no one here to see, and she's really starting to enjoy herself. It's two in the morning before she crawls into bed.

She lies there, her duvet tucked neatly under her arms and her pillows arranged just so under her head, and she stares at the high ceiling of her bedroom. As much as she doesn't want to, she can't stop thinking about those people on the television, particularly that baby.

That was the common thread in a lot of cases, wasn't it? Loss. At least five of the eight people in the episodes she watched had lost someone, either through death or divorce, even children being given up for adoption. Someone had been taken away from them, without them expecting it and without their permission, and to fill the hole they'd started to shop and store and collect.

Is that what her mother had done? If you'd have asked Heather a month ago what her mother could have lost that would make her start behaving that way, she would have shaken her head and said there was nothing, no rhyme or reason to it. But now she knows better.

It was me, she thinks. *The thing she lost was me.* But somehow, even though she came back, her mother behaved as if Heather had never returned and she never threw another thing away for the rest of her life.

Heather thinks of the photo she gave to Faith for Alice, of how everything looked normal and clean. Christmas 1991. Only seven months before the date on the newspaper report. Is that the key, then? Is her being 'snatched' what started it all?

She closes her eyes, not so much to welcome sleep but because she's stemming the tears that are pooling there, and lets out a long, ragged sigh.

Even when she was little, she'd always been afraid, from the way her mother talked to her, sometimes even the way she looked at her, that maybe everything had been her fault. Now she knows she was right.

CHAPTER TWELVE

HORSE CHESTNUT

The bark twists round, spiralling upwards, holding the tree in like a corset, then when it gets so high it can't contain itself any more, it explodes into leaves, showering them out like a firework, only they never fall and reach the ground. Tall white flowers balance on the ends of the branches like fluffy candles, even though it's the height of summer. When the breeze stirs the leaves, I can hear them whisper, 'Just you wait until autumn. Just you wait until I drop my prickly fruit on the grass.' For the intrepid hunter, prepared to part the flesh, there is a reward of hard, shiny treasure. I stare up into the branches, wishing the months away, because I know good things are on their way.

THEN

Heather is running around the garden because her mummy has told her she needs fresh air. But the air doesn't feel very fresh today. It feels a bit hot and sticky and if Heather runs around too much it makes her head wet and then her hair sticks to her face. But the air is even hotter indoors, so she keeps running, trying to make her own breeze. Every now and then she gets tired so she flops down on the grass, and then when she feels better again she jumps up and carries on.

But she can't be looking where she's going properly. Her mummy says she does that a lot, because she's always bumping into things in the house and knocking them on the floor. She thought it'd be okay out here because there aren't any piles, but when she runs under the big tree near the fence one of its roots pops up from underneath the ground and trips her up.

Heather lands flat on her face and her nose hits the grass and she gets mud in her mouth. At first, she doesn't think she needs to cry, but she realizes she does after all and tears begin to run down her face. She doesn't move; all her attention is taken up with the crying. Nobody comes. Nobody pops their head outside the back door to check on her or see what all the noise is about. When there are bigger gaps between her wet, snuffling sobs, she pushes herself up onto all fours and gets up. There is blood on her knee from where the tree tripped her up. She starts crying again. Loudly.

'Are you okay?'

Heather hears the voice but she can't see anybody. She quietens, swallowing her tears.

'Hello?' the voice says again. It sounds worried. 'Is anyone there? Are you hurt?'

Heather nods. Her lip wobbles. She turns to where the voice came from. It sounded like it came from near the fence. She takes a few steps then stops because she still can't see anyone. All she can see is the tree.

'You tripped me up!' she says, putting her hands on her hips. 'With one of your long underground fingers!'

There's a laugh. 'I don't think I did!' the voice says, but it doesn't sound like it's making fun of her. She stares at the tree, trying to catch it out, but it doesn't move. She knows it doesn't really have eyes, but she gets the feeling it's staring straight ahead, ignoring her.

'Hello?' says the voice.

Heather turns to see a face appear over the top of the fence. It isn't the tree talking, after all. It's a lady. 'Hello,' Heather says. 'Who are you?'

'I'm Lydia,' she says. 'I'm your next-door neighbour. I just moved in a month ago. I hear you playing in the garden sometimes.'

Heather starts to run away. Her mother is always telling her off for being too noisy. She says Heather chatters too much and sometimes she tells Heather to go out into the garden because she just can't think. Heather didn't realize she might get in trouble for being noisy out here as well.

'Wait!' the lady shouts after her. 'It's okay. I like hearing you singing away and talking to your imaginary friends.'

Heather stops and turns round. 'You do?'

Lydia nods and then she looks down and spots the blood on Heather's knee. 'Did you hurt yourself?'

'Yes. The naughty tree tripped me up!'

Lydia laughs again. 'So you believe me now?'

Heather nods. 'You seem like a nice lady. I don't think you'd go round tripping little girls up on purpose.'

'Thank you,' Lydia says, and her voice is a little bit scratchy like Heather's is sometimes when she catches a cold. 'Where's your mother?'

Heather jerks her head in the direction of the house. 'In there.'

Her mother is always in there, but she doesn't tell Lydia that because her mother says what happens inside their house is secret and they mustn't tell anyone about what it's like inside. Especially strangers.

'Well, it's been lovely talking to you. What's your name?'

'Heather.'

She smiles. 'That's a pretty name for a pretty girl. Well, Heather, I think you'd better go and find your mother. That cut looks as if it needs cleaning.'

Heather looks down. There's a fat red dribble running down her shin and there are smears of earth on her knees. She runs off and calls out for her mother.

She calls and calls, but Mummy doesn't shout back. She tries to get in the back door but it's shut tight. She runs back to the tree in the corner of the garden. 'Lady? I mean, Lydia? Are you there?'

The lady's face appears over the top of the fence again.

'I can't find my mummy,' Heather says tearfully.

'Do you want me to come and help you look?'

Heather nods.

'Come to the front of the garden, then,' Lydia says, 'but don't go out the gate, okay?'

Heather nods again and then does what she's told.

A few moments later she opens the gate and Lydia appears from behind the overgrown hedge that separates Heather's garden from the street. She's wearing a lovely yellow and white shirt with daisies on and her hair is tied back in a headscarf. She takes a pair of big, thick, leathery gloves off and holds them in one hand. 'Right. Shall we try the front door first?'

'Okay!' Heather runs up to the door and pulls at the handle, but it won't open.

'What's your last name?' Lydia says, coming up behind her.

Heather pushes her fringe out of her eyes and looks over her shoulder. 'Lucas.'

Lydia presses the doorbell, but when no one comes she raps on the door loudly. The knocker falls off in her hand. 'Oh,' she says, and puts it down on the little ledge next to the door, then she curls up her hand and knocks with her knuckles. 'Mrs Lucas?' she calls out. 'Mrs Lucas?'

Nothing.

Lydia tries the door, but it doesn't open for her either. 'It seems to be locked. Do you have a back door?'

Heather shows her the way. She likes being helpful. Lydia calls and knocks there, too, but nobody answers. 'How odd!'

'She's probably just gone shopping,' Heather says with a shrug. The lure of new treasures is the only thing that'll make her mother leave the house, so that's where she must be.

Lydia's forehead creases up and her lips press together. 'Well,' she says and holds out her hand. 'Maybe you'd better come over to my house until she gets back. We'll see if we can get that knee cleaned up. How long is your mother gone when she goes shopping?'

'Oh, ages. It's her favourite thing. Sometimes she visits all three charity shops on Chatterton Road on her way to the Co-op and then goes in them again on the way back.'

Lydia holds out her hand and Heather takes it. They go out of Heather's front gate and into the garden next door. It's so beautiful that Heather stops in her tracks when she sees it. Everything is neat and tidy and there are hundreds and hundreds of roses. It's almost a shame to go inside.

Lydia takes Heather into her kitchen and sits her on a wooden chair, then she gets a cloth and cleans up her knee. The red dribble has grown and grown until it went all the way down to Heather's sock, and Lydia dabs at it until it's just a pink smudge.

'You're very brave,' she says. 'You didn't make a squeak.'

Heather looks at her. She doesn't know what to say to that. It did hurt, but she kept all her squeaks inside, the way she always does. She looks around Lydia's kitchen. It's very nice. The cabinets are soft yellow and there's lots of wood and the floor is ever so clean. There's not a plastic bottle or an empty food carton in sight. Heather wonders where she keeps all her rubbish. Maybe she has one big room for it instead of spreading it out all over the house?

'Would you like an ice cream?' Lydia asks.

Heather's head bobs up and down furiously. Lydia goes to her fridge and fetches her an ice cream with chocolate round the outside and a stick to hold it with.

'Do you want to eat it out in the garden?'

Heather's mouth is full so she shakes her head. As much as she'd like to smell the lovely roses again, she prefers being in the pretty kitchen. She sits on the chair and swings her legs while she eats her ice cream. Lydia just moves around, putting things in cupboards, washing things in the sink. Every now and then she looks over her shoulder to check on Heather, and smiles. Every time Heather smiles back.

When Heather is finished she licks the stick as hard as she can to get all the chocolate off, and then she throws it on the floor and stands up.

Lydia frowns. 'Lolly sticks don't go on the floor,' she says. 'You have to put them in the bin.'

Heather stares back at her.

'My bin is by the back door. You pop open the top by putting your foot on the pedal.'

Heather's not really sure what Lydia's talking about, so she just blinks and keeps looking at her. Standing on a pedal that makes something pop up sounds like fun, though.

'Heather, I would really like it if you put your lolly stick in the bin.' Lydia says, and then she pauses, thinking. 'Would you like me to show you how to do that?'

Heather nods again. She enjoys being helpful, after all, and this is her second chance this afternoon.

After Lydia has shown her, she asks if there's anything else to throw away – stepping on the pedal was fun!

Slowly, the sun goes down and it starts to get darker. They go and check Heather's house again and Lydia knocks on the door with her fist really loudly. Just as she's about to give up, a car pulls up outside.

Heather runs to her father when he gets out of the car, and he gives her a big hug, lifting her off the ground, but then he sees the lady from next door and he walks up the path towards her. She smiles, introduces herself and tells him all about the tree and the ice cream and all the knocking on the door.

'Thank you so much,' Heather's daddy says. He puts his key in the door and lets it swing open just enough for Heather to squeeze through but not enough for Lydia to see what's inside. 'Run along, Heather, and I'll get you some tea.'

Heather hesitates for a moment then squeezes through the gap in the door. Before she gets all the way through she turns. 'Thank you for the ice cream,' she says to Lydia, 'and for letting me play with the pedal.'

They look at each other, smiles in their eyes, just for a moment, but then Heather's daddy follows her inside and closes the door so Heather can't see the nice neighbour lady any more.

CHAPTER THIRTEEN

NOW

All this time Heather thought there weren't any answers. Maybe that's why she never bothered to ask any questions in the first place. But now she knows the answers she's seeking are hunkering down in her spare room, tucked into the back of another photograph album, or stuffed inside a coffee tin, or possibly even stored in the sort of folder that's actually meant for organizing important papers.

There must be more newspaper clippings, more information in there. Her mother's philosophy had definitely been: why have one of something when you can have fifty? Why on earth would the one exception to that habit be something to do with her daughter's disappearance? It wouldn't. The information is in there; Heather just knows it.

The only problem is, even though the answers are whispering to her from behind the closed door, even though they are calling her name, she's not sure she wants to listen to them. What if something truly awful happened to her while she was missing? Things she can't even bring herself to name or imagine? Does she really want to know? Would it make her life any better? And even if she's curious, having to open that door and hunt through the shameful hoard is something she really doesn't want to do.

So Heather does nothing. For two whole weeks. She's very good at putting things off when they're too painful to deal with, or stuffing them down and closing the lid on them.

After work one evening, she pops into the Waitrose by Bromley South station to grab some vegetables for dinner. It's busier than normal in there, full of people like her, grabbing a few bits they need before heading home. Maybe that's why the urge hits. Because she knows there's less chance of being caught, that she won't be a lone figure in the wide aisles, and many of the staff will have been called to the tills.

Heather goes down the toiletries aisle to grab a bottle of shampoo, but once that's in her basket she looks up and spies the section at the end of the row. Nappies, wipes, brightly coloured sippy cups and jars of food. She starts walking towards it.

No, no, no! She shouts inside her head. *Not now. Not here. Besides, it's too soon. It shouldn't be happening again yet. Walk away. Walk away!*

But her compulsion is a contrary and angry god requiring sacrifice; asking for mercy is too much. Her inner protestations are heard and discarded.

She walks up to the display and browses, against her own will, taking on the guise of a busy working mother just off the train from central London about to pick up a few essentials before she heads off to pick her little darlings up from the childminder.

Her eyes fix themselves on the jars of organic baby food. They're small enough to slide into a pocket quite easily, aren't they? She could just pick one up and turn it over, pretending to look at the list of ingredients, then palm it like a magician, hiding it up her sleeve then dropping it into a pocket.

And before she's even finished that thought, she's done it. The jar is weighing her jacket down on one side.

She pays for the things in her basket, smiles at the girl on the till, then walks out of the shop and into the warm summer evening. The trains are pulling in and out of the station on the other side of the car park, the people spilling out of them and carrying on about their business as if nothing has just happened. She jumps in her car and drives away, refusing to look back.

When she gets home, she runs into the kitchen and unpacks her shopping, putting each item away neatly, and then she reluctantly pulls the jar of baby food from her pocket. She puts it on the centre of the kitchen table and looks at it.

She doesn't know what to do. Usually, she'd creep into the spare room and hide her ill-gotten gains in the chest of drawers. But this is baby food. It can't go in there. Chests of drawers are for clothes and accessories, maybe even other miscellaneous items, but not food.

Oh, my God, she thinks. *I just stole baby food! What's wrong with me?*

She still can't bring herself to go and hide it with the other stuff, though. Putting things where they aren't supposed to go is what her mother used to do. She can't take even one step down that path. But she can't leave it standing in the middle of her kitchen table, either. It has to go. Out of sight, where it can't torment her.

There's only one other option.

Heather walks over to the cutlery drawer and pulls out a tea-spoon, then she twists off the lid of the jar, sits down, and begins to eat.

CHAPTER FOURTEEN

NOW

Heather washes the jar carefully once she's finished eating. It made her want to gag a couple of times, but she managed to get it down. She's not sure why it had that effect on her. It was a pudding – apple and cinnamon – so it should have been quite pleasant.

The following morning she hides the jar in the recycling bin and tries to pretend it never happened. It doesn't work, though, because she can't stop thinking about how hard she's tried not to turn into her mother. Despite all her efforts, she's sliding down that same path, faster and faster, and there's nothing she can do to stop herself.

She described her mother's life as miserable, isolated, driven by her compulsions. Is hers really any better? Different location. Different compulsion. But it all feels horribly familiar.

Heather inhales slowly then lets the breath out again, measuring it, keeping it calm and long. There's only one thing to do. She can't hide from the past any longer.

She gets up, retrieves the spare-room key from the desk and stops in front of the blank white door. Then, slowly, carefully, she slides the key into the lock, turns it, twists the doorknob, and walks inside.

The only way to do this is to not think of the contents of the room as a whole, but to mentally break them down into chunks, so that's what Heather does: she focuses on the bookshelf where she found the first photo album, fixes her gaze on it and gingerly walks through the mess towards it.

There are two more albums there, along with a big cardboard concertina folder. Just those three things. She can manage those, surely?

And it seems to be going well at first. She picks up the folder and tucks it under one arm and then reaches for the first album, intending to hold it flat in her upturned hands so that she can balance the second one on top, but when she pulls it out, the second album topples over.

It's like the first crack in a dam.

The rest of the items on that shelf start to slide, piece by piece, onto the mess below, then a cardboard box balanced on top goes, vomiting its contents into the growing chaos. Lying on it is a tacky unicorn figurine that was one of her mother's favourites. Heather's heart starts to pound. She holds out a hand to stop a second box going, dropping the concertinaed folder as she does so. Now the peaceful equilibrium of the hoard has been altered, it's like a beast awakened, and this one is roaring, demanding appeasement, demanding sacrifice.

Heather has nothing to give it. Only herself. And the beast reaches for her. She feels the dread creeping into her bones, starting at her toes and working its way up. Her heart begins to drum and her skin becomes cold and clammy. There's a weird tingling in her knees as her stomach rolls over three times in succession.

It's coming. Coming to get her. She can feel it. The glittery uni-corn stares back up at her, nostrils flared, teeth bared. She can't stand to look at it any more, to hear its hollow laughter in her head. She has to get out of there. Now.

She pulls her hand from the pile of boxes, and gravity stakes its claim immediately. It seems as if the whole left-hand side of the room is about to slide and fall. She grabs for the folder, managing to nab it by the corner of its cover, clutches the first of the two photo albums to her chest, and bolts.

But even when the door is slammed shut behind her, when she's standing in her living room, the two rescued items clamped to her chest by arms whose muscles have locked into place, she can't seem to calm down. The terror comes in waves, blocking everything else out. Her heart is beating so hard she's sure it's going to burst out of its fragile membrane and decorate the inside of her chest cavity. And her breath... It's gone. She can't find it. It won't come.

Eventually, the lack of oxygen releases her frozen muscles. She drops the folder and album, letting them clatter to the floor, and her knees give way underneath her. She ends up kneeling on one of the items – she isn't sure which – and it digs painfully into the side of her kneecap, but all she can think about is the next breath: sucking it in through her nose and mouth, trying to trap as much of it as she can before the tightness in her chest steals it away again.

It feels like hours before everything returns to normal. Even her living room seems weird for a while – distorted, unfamiliar – but eventually her pulse slows to something approaching normal and her breathing steadies. She places her palms on the floor and pushes herself up. There's a deep red mark in the side of her knee, and the tiniest of scratches where the corner of the photo album has broken the skin.

She picks up the offending item. The corner is dented now, no longer sharp and square. That's going to bother her. She places it on one end of the sofa and sits on the opposite end. The folder can wait until later.

What just happened? She tries to remember it objectively, as if she was an observer on the outside, but her memory is blank and useless – like one of those dummy security cameras that's all for show and doesn't actually record anything.

The panic. She remembers the panic.

Her mother used to have episodes like this sometimes, often brought on when anyone tried to 'help' – which usually meant cleaning or decluttering or moving any of her stuff around in the slightest. It had all seemed so melodramatic at the time, but was this how it had felt on the inside? As if she was going to die? And not even just that, because a plain and simple end to the feeling would have been welcome, but instead it was a feeling that doom itself was pursuing her, wouldn't be content until it swallowed her whole and kept her churning in its belly for the rest of eternity. It hadn't felt nice. It hadn't felt nice at all.

Heather's almost scared of opening the photo album now or of peering in the pockets of the folder, but she knows she has to. Taking a deep breath, she pulls the album towards her and flips open the front page.

This one is much like the other one – photos missing here and there, yellowing edges where the lines of glue under the cellophane are ageing – but this one contains pictures from when she and Faith are older. Heather flips through, mentally reminding herself to come back and have a good look another time, but for now she's hunting for two things: one, any other newspaper reports tucked inside the pages and, two, any photo taken inside the house in Hawksbury Road.

She gets to the last page without finding any of either item. Nothing is tucked inside the back cover of this album and there are no photographs at all taken inside the house. Family holidays, yes. Christmas day at Aunt Kathy's, yes. Even outings to Crystal Palace Park and Broadstairs. But nothing else. Heather doesn't even have to guess why. She knows. It must have been bad by then. Bad enough to be ashamed of it, bad enough to want to hide it.

She looks at a photo of her and Faith on the beach in Broadstairs with her father. Heather thinks she looks about eight in the picture, which means Faith would have been eleven. This must have been the last family holiday they had all together. How sad she can't remember it. She doesn't remember wearing that T-shirt with the glittery rainbow on it, or making that sandcastle with the four turrets. Nothing.

She can see a difference in herself from the earlier photo album, though. Not the blonde hair and the big eyes – those are still there – but something about her expression, as if she's having too much of a good time. That seems strange, doesn't it? But, while Heather can't remember this holiday, she can remember that feeling when they went away from the house for more than a few hours: that feeling of freedom and release. She remembers the dark underside, too – both the desperation to enjoy the time wildly and the sadness that it wouldn't last. She can see it in her eight-year-old eyes. It's there behind all their smiles, although, in her father's case, it's less frenzied delight at the escape and more broken-down tiredness. Heather wonders if he knew when the shutter was clicked that he was planning to go.

She's never really thought about that much before. It was such a shock at the time, so devastating, it had always felt as cataclysmic as a natural disaster: sudden and unanticipated. It was odd to think about it brewing under the surface for weeks, maybe even months. But the more she thinks about it, the more she realizes this must have been the case.

She closes the album and turns her attention to the folder. There are important things in here – a copy of her parents' wedding invitation, and records of her and Faith being christened – but along with them are smoothed-out chocolate wrappers, flyers for window cleaners and Chinese takeaway places, and with it all is a folded-up square of newsprint.

Heather flushes hot and cold when she sees it, and for a moment she thinks the panic is going to engulf her again, but then it subsides. She unfolds the paper carefully, reverently – this is what she went in the spare room to find, after all, what she'd endured all that turmoil for – and is horribly, horribly disappointed to discover it's the same as the first report she found. Exactly the same. Same date, same reporter, same newspaper. The same grey eyes laughing at her from under the blonde fringe. She folds it up and puts it back, frustrated.

And then she frowns. What is she going to do with the junk that was in there? The receipts and sweet wrappers and flyers? She probably ought to throw them away.

Still, now the folder is closed again, she feels as if she's had as much as she can handle for tonight. It's too exhausting to consider opening it up again. She bought a plastic container with a lid to store these items in. She feels a rushing sense of relief when they're put away neatly inside. Her own belongings are safe now, uncontaminated from what has been retrieved from the room. But the pleasant feeling only lasts for a few seconds before she realizes the sealed plastic tub holds no answers and there's only one place she's going to find them. Just thinking about going back into that room makes her feel jumpy again.

She stands in the middle of her living-room rug and begins to breathe slowly, trying to recover a fragment of peace, when the doorbell rings and makes her jump.

Jason? She has no idea why that's her first thought. He's never rung her doorbell before now, and he's hardly likely to after the way she snubbed him at his barbecue, is he? He probably thinks she's a cold bitch who's far too precious about her crockery.

But there's also a part of her that can't quite give up hope. Over the last few years, her life has become smaller and smaller. The number of people she interacts with on a daily basis has shrunk considerably, and those who actually have a kind word and a smile are even rarer. Jason was one of those people. Just the fact he took the time to greet her, to not rush past her in the hallway as if she was invisible, made her feel a little more alive.

But it's not Jason and his lovely twinkling eyes standing at her front door. It's her sister.

'Faith!' Heather exclaims, and her volume isn't right. It's too loud. The words echo round the tiled hallway. 'What are you doing here?'

It's 6.30 on a Thursday evening. Faith never comes here during the week, and she never arrives at Heather's looking as if she's ready for a night out. Her hair has been swept off her face and tied in a loose up-do, and she's wearing black jeans, heels, an embroidered kimono, and bright lipstick.

'Can I come in?' Faith asks. 'Just for a little bit?'

Heather can hardly slam the door in her sister's face, so she nods and lets Faith pass, then follows her closely as she heads for the living room. Heather is relieved that her sister doesn't even glance at the door to the spare room as she passes. It's not even on her radar, thank goodness.

'I'm off for a girls' night out in Bromley – you remember Helena and Emily from school, don't you? – and I thought I'd pop round first, just to… just to make sure you're okay.'

Heather folds her arms. 'Why wouldn't I be?'

How does her sister do this? How does she always manage to show up when Heather is at her shakiest? It's just not fair. It paints entirely the wrong picture, reinforcing all the bad things Faith thinks about her.

'Don't be like that,' Faith replies, more gently than Heather would have expected. 'I know you think I'm always hounding you, always checking up on you – and okay, maybe sometimes I am – but this is different. It must have been…' She breaks off, searching the ceiling for the right word, 'devastating to find out about… you know… what happened when you were little. Is there anything I can do?'

Heather stares at her sister. It's nice that Faith dropped by, but her presence really isn't wanted, and Heather wishes her sister would stop trying to fix her as if she's a damaged toy that just needs a bit of glue or sticky tape. It just makes her feel even more pathetic and broken.

'Not really. I mean, what can anyone do? It happened. I can't change that.'

'Have you found out any more?'

Heather shakes her head. 'I found that first article tucked away in the album I got that photo for Alice from. Who knows if there's anything else or what illogical hiding place it has amid Mum's stuff?'

'Do you want me to help you look?' She checks her watch. 'I've got about forty-five minutes. Maybe it would be better to have someone with you if you actually did find something?'

Heather stands up abruptly. 'I've already searched,' she says, maybe a little too loudly.

Faith gives her an odd look. 'Ok-ay... You've gone through all of it? I mean, I know Mum had a lot of stuff. You've finally thrown all the crap away and kept the treasures?'

Heather nods, realizing for the first time that a gesture – even a silent one – can be a lie. 'I've got it here!' She scrabbles to pull the plastic-lidded box from the bookcase.

Faith looks at it incredulously. 'That's *it*?'

Heather nods again. Another lie.

The truth is she has no idea what else could be buried in her spare room. There could be more photos, birth certificates they've already had to replace, even her mother's engagement ring, but the thought of going back in there is making her want to hyperventilate again, and the thought of Faith going in there...

She peels the lid off the box and pulls out a photo album, hoping to distract her sister with its shiny pages full of memories.

Like a starving woman, Faith pounces on it. Heather doesn't think she's ever seen her sister so animated. She looks over Faith's shoulder at a picture of herself at the seaside, all blonde fringe and hot-pink flip-flops. 'When was this taken?' she asks, pointing at it.

Faith takes a look. 'Hmm, difficult to tell. Is there any writing on the back?'

'No.' Heather's already checked this one at least three times, which is stupid. It's not as if some ghostly handwriting from the past will magically appear after a certain number of tries. Dead end, then. She thinks for a moment. 'Do you remember me going on holiday with Aunty Kathy?'

'Of course. There were a couple of times just you and I went away with Kathy and Uncle Mike. I reckon they enjoyed it and it gave Mum and Dad a break. Pity they never had kids.'

'Did I ever go on my own?'

Faith frowns. 'Maybe. I do remember one summer when my friend Carly invited me to go with her family to their villa in Brittany. I was only there for four weeks, but I came back convinced I could speak fluent French, even though most of it was gobbledegook.' She turns her attention back to the album. 'Can I take this home so I can scan some of these in?'

Faith continues to pore over every page, stopping every few seconds to jabber on about events and people Heather has absolutely no memory of. Heather would like to join in, would even be happy to fake it, to laugh at family in-jokes she can't recall, or make up stories about the strangers in the pictures, but all she can think about is that Faith is only approximately twenty feet from all her secrets and lies, and she feels the door must be burning, glowing bright, betraying her.

'When did you say you were meeting Helena and Emily?' she asks innocently.

Faith looks up, confused for a second, then checks her watch. 'Oh my goodness! In five minutes! I must get going.'

Her sister hurries out the door, promising to be in touch about the upcoming Sunday dinner – maybe they'll go out? There's a nice gastro-pub in the village that's just got a new chef and Matthew's heard it's very good – and then she's gone. Heather leans on the door to check it has shut properly, double-locks it and then slumps to the floor, exhausted. Her mind is full of sea breezes and Aunty Kathy's red coat.

CHAPTER FIFTEEN

NOW

Heather can't sleep. Her head is too full of beaches and Christmases and smiling blonde-haired girls. It's as if the static, two-dimensional pictures from the album she looked through earlier that evening are burrowing through her skull in an effort to graft themselves in as proper memories. The only problem is that the recollections they correspond to – their living, moving, three-dimensional counterparts – are missing, and without an anchor the images just swirl around, spinning on a carousel that won't stop.

In the end, Heather decides to get up and go to the toilet, and then maybe she'll go and sit in the living room and read a book. It would be better to be either properly awake or properly asleep. She's had enough of this surreal slide show. So she throws back the duvet, swings her legs out of the bed and, barefooted, heads for the bathroom.

She's only three steps down the hallway when she treads in something cold. Something liquid. She's instantly awake. She turns and reaches for the light switch.

Her hallway is full of water, only a few millimetres deep, but it's stretching from outside the kitchen to where she's standing just by her bedroom door.

She sloshes through it, grabs a couple of towels from the laundry hamper and throws them on the hall floor, then goes back to find more. It takes a good ten minutes to mop everything up. She deposits the soaking towels directly in the washing machine and turns it on. She's properly exhausted now, and the knowledge brings a flush of relief; she wasn't looking forward to sitting in her living room and staring out into the darkened garden. The blankness of sleep is much more welcome.

Only, as she heads back to her bedroom, she notices there's a sheen on the hall floor again. She reaches down and her fingers come away wet. Damn.

Adrenalin wipes away any traces of sleepiness as she remembers Jason saying something about plumbing problems, about workmen maybe needing to check the pipes out.

She snaps into fight-or-flight mode, runs out of her front door and up the stairs, and hammers on Jason's door before she thinks properly about what she's doing, noticing too late that she's wearing only a pair of shortie pyjamas and a cardigan grabbed from the hook near her front door.

She's on the verge of running away again, leaving him to think it was a cruel, nocturnal version of Knock Down Ginger, when he opens the door, messy-headed and smothering a yawn with his hand. 'There's… there's water!' she stammers.

Jason looks just as confused as she does. He also looks utterly delectable, in a dressing gown thrown over a low-slung pair of pyjama bottoms. 'Water?' he mutters.

'In my hallway! You said something about plumbing problems…?' She starts to back away towards the top of the stairs, her eyes begging him to follow her. Jason blinks a few times, ties his dressing gown, and nods. By the time they're back down in Heather's hallway, it's almost as bad as when she first discovered it.

'I don't understand,' Jason says, yawning again as he squints at the long puddle snaking down the hallway. 'Carlton sent a plumber round. It was something to do with a dodgy pipe under my shower, but he said it was all fixed.'

Heather looks at him.

'You're right,' he says. 'This doesn't look very fixed to me either.'

Heather wraps her arms around herself. She's starting to shiver. 'What are we going to do?'

She's surprised when he pulls a mobile phone from his dressing-gown pocket. He must see her eyes widen because he gives her a lopsided smile just as she's trying not to wonder who he might have been texting late at night.

'Best mate having a crisis called just before I went to bed,' he says. 'I'm not sad enough to sleep with my phone – honest!'

He dials a number and starts talking to someone whom Heather assumes must be the emergency plumber, leaving her to wonder about the friend who called him seeking support, and if she's the kind of person people would call in the middle of the night if they were having a crisis. If she had any close friends, of course.

Probably not.

She always seems to *be* the problem. Her admiration for Jason grows as he chats effortlessly to the person on the other end of the line – a stranger, someone he's woken in the middle of the night. When he's finished he puts his phone back in his pocket.

'He says he'll be here in about fifteen minutes. While we wait, we may as well try and find out where it's all coming from. Have you got anything we can mop this lot up with?'

Heather runs to get her few remaining towels from the airing cupboard and they set about soaking up the water. *At least it's clean,* she thinks, as she crawls around on the floor, trying to keep the corners of her cardigan from draping into the mess. At least it's not sewage. She definitely wouldn't have been able to cope with that.

When they've finished, they bundle up the towels and wait. But it's only a minute or two before the water starts to pool again. Jason frowns and walks up and down the corridor, Heather watching him silently.

'I think it's coming from under here,' he says, stopping in front of the door to the spare room, and before she can prevent him, he tries the handle. Heather leaps forward. Sure enough, she can see clear water seeping from underneath the door, spreading in every direction once it meets the cheap laminate flooring of the hall. He turns to look at her. 'Have you got the key?'

Her mouth moves and no sound comes out.

'Because if you've got anything of value in there, we really ought to move it.'

Heather is about to say there's nothing she wants from that room, that she'd be happy if it was all swept away on the tide and never seen again, but then an icy feeling spikes through her. Her mother's papers. The newspaper clippings she knows must be in there but hasn't found yet – they're her only hope for answers. She nods, so far past the point of panic that she's reached an eerie state of numbness, and runs to get the key from the desk.

She pauses as she slides it into the lock, her hands shaking. Her voice shakes too when she speaks. 'There are important family papers in here, in… um, storage,' and because she can't think of any other explanation for what he's about to see, because she can already imagine the water sneaking in and turning the secrets of her past to soggy mush, she turns the key and opens the door, knowing that this will be the last time she'll ever be able to day-dream about her upstairs neighbour, that after this the engulfing shame will prevent even that. Maybe she'll move, find a studio flat closer to work.

But Jason doesn't say anything, doesn't react at all. He doesn't move either, scanning the room before he dives in. He points to the left-hand side of the room, where the painted lining paper is glistening slightly. 'It's coming down the wall over there,' he says, and glances at her apologetically. 'Must be my dodgy shower after all. Sorry.'

Heather just shakes her head and dives for the nearest box of stuff. For the first time in her life, she's grateful for her mother's addiction to plastic storage containers. Not all the stuff is stored that way – some is in cardboard boxes and bin liners – but a lot of it is. Switching herself onto automatic, she grabs a crate from the left-hand side of the room and places it against the far wall in the hallway, and then another and another, trying to clear a path as quickly as she can to the more vulnerable items.

It's only when she becomes aware that Jason is following her lead, that he's silently collecting crates and boxes and adding them to the stack against the wall, that 'coping mode' begins to subside and the reality of the situation seeps back in.

'This… This isn't my stuff,' she says breathlessly as she picks up another item and clutches it to her chest. 'It's my mother's.'

Jason just nods. Either he's concentrating on the job in hand or he's so appalled that he's speechless, but his phone beeps before she can explain any further or tell him this stuff has nothing to do with her. Absolutely nothing at all.

'The plumber's outside,' he says, glancing up at her. 'I'll go and let him in.'

Heather keeps working when the plumber comes in. She doesn't look at him. It seems one stranger in her flat this evening is as much as she can handle. Thankfully, they don't stay long. Once Jason has shown him her spare bedroom and the steady glistening waterfall down the wall, they both plod upstairs to his flat, presumably to deal with the source of the problem.

Now she's alone again, Heather ventures deeper into the room, to the bit where the water came in and, as sod's law would have it, where the most chaotic section of the hoard is.

The two men don't return for ages, giving her a chance to deal with the worst of the soggy mess, the most shameful area. Deep in the corner she finds a cardboard box so wet it's barely holding together. She removes the top layer and finds a collection of framed prints of big-eyed children she presumes her mother rescued from a charity shop or a car-boot fair, but underneath she hits pay dirt.

There are scores of newspaper clippings in the bottom of the box. She picks the top one up. Even though it's so wet that the tiny black words on the front are merging into those on the back, she can still read the headline: LOCAL GIRL FOUND. Maybe she can dry it out? With a hairdryer or maybe on the radiator? The flat will boil if she turns the central heating on, given the fact that June is actually behaving like June and not October for once, but she doesn't care about that.

However, as she tries to unfold it, revealing the same school photograph of herself that was used in the first report, the paper starts to disintegrate. 'No, no, no!' she chants, frantically trying to hold it in such a way as to prevent any further damage, but the newsprint is too fragile now, stretched to its limit by the weight of the invading water, and her younger self starts to melt into her fingers.

'Everything okay in there?'

Heather jumps, destroying the clipping further. She turns to find Jason standing in the doorway and she nods. He goes on to explain that the plumber has done a stopgap fix she doesn't really understand, involving pipes and connections, and adds that he'll be back on Monday to do a proper job. Jason then looks down at the grey mush in her hands. 'Is that important?'

She looks down. It's all gone, all that information, that possibility of working out why her mother did what she did and how Heather can stop herself turning out the same way. She feels like crying but instead she just shakes her head, her expression neutral, revealing nothing. She drops the soggy article into the cardboard box and picks it up. 'It's just old newspapers... Stuff my mum saved.'

'Well, there's no use stacking these with the rest and making them damp too. I'll put it out by the bin if you like?'

He holds out his hands. Heather can't seem to make herself pass him the box.

'The whole lot is ruined, right?'

She nods. It can't be anything but. The bottom of the box, which is pressing against her midriff and making a damp circle on her pyjamas, is wetter than the top. The pages of newsprint are practically floating in there.

She wants to tell him to leave it, to let her keep this one thing, even if he doesn't understand – causing her to sound more like her mother than she'd ever wish to – but how can she? She has no sane explanation for doing so, not unless she spills the whole sorry story of her family from the time she was small, and that idea is even more abhorrent than discarding the box of what now looks like papier-mâché ready for pasting.

He gently eases it from her hands and disappears out of the front door. With nothing to clutch onto any longer, Heather hugs her arms around her middle, pressing the cold wet patch the box has left on her pyjama top against the goose pimples on her stomach. When Jason comes back, he finds her shivering, still in the same spot.

'Oh, my God, you're freezing!' he says. 'Come on, I'm making you a cup of tea.' He places his hands on her shoulders and steers her towards her kitchen. She's about to ask how he knows where it is, but then guesses it's probably because his flat has a similar layout. He makes her sit down at the table then notices she's trembling and so peels off his dressing gown and rests it on her shoulders – which leaves him in only the pyjama bottoms, revealing a toned and slightly tanned chest. Heather swallows and looks away, trying to hide the rising heat in her cheeks. If you'd have asked her yesterday to bet on the likelihood of there being a half-naked man in her kitchen, she'd have laughed so hard she'd have probably run out of oxygen and died.

He places two steaming mugs on the table, then sits down across from her. 'Okay?' he asks.

'Yes,' she says quietly. 'Thank you so much for your help. I don't know what I'd have done...'

'Well, the fault did kind of arise in my flat,' he says, giving her a rueful smile. 'I could hardly do otherwise.' He pauses for a moment then glances towards the hallway. 'Do you think your stuff is going to be alright?'

'It's not mine!' Heather says before remembering she doesn't need to snap. 'I mean, it belongs to my mother.'

'That makes sense.' Heather frowns, which he must spot because he adds: 'Well, the room was so… What I mean is, the rest of your flat is spotless.' He grimaces at her, apologizing for the implication of his words, and steers himself in a safer direction. 'Did you say something about storing it for her?'

She shakes her head. 'She died two years ago. It was… what was left in her house…' She looks across the table at him. There's a question in his eyes. She shrugs. 'I just haven't been able to face going through any of it.'

His mouth curves into the smallest of smiles. Not a happy one, or even a sympathetic one, but one of recognition. He nods. 'It's weird, isn't it? How things connect you to people, to memories?'

Heather smiles back. What else can she do? He thinks he's understood her but he hasn't. He thinks she's just like her mother. 'I suppose I'd better try and mop up some more of that mess,' she says, pushing her chair back. Just the thought of walking past the stuff in the hallway is making her feel jittery, but the sooner it goes back in there, the better.

Jason stands too. 'Leave it,' he says. 'I spoke to Carlton. He's arranging for a couple of his lads to come round and sort it out. There's not much more we can do to make it any better at the moment. Besides, after all the drama, I'm starving. Do you want to grab some breakfast?'

'Breakfast?'

He nods at the window. Heather's been so busy focusing on the inside of her flat that she hasn't thought to look outside. The sky is no longer dark; it's a washed-out grey with a hint of blue. 'I know a truckers' café down on the A2 that'll be open at this time of morning. How does a bacon sandwich sound?'

Heather's stomach takes the opportunity to answer for her. Loudly.

Jason laughs. 'Well, that's agreed then. I'll nip upstairs and get dressed and I'll be back down here in ten.'

It's only when he mentions clothes that Heather remembers he's wearing next to nothing. Somehow, between him boiling the kettle and making breakfast plans, that must have slipped her mind.

CHAPTER SIXTEEN

SUITCASE

It's large and grey, big enough to climb inside and hide, but only if you're little. At first glance, it looks like mottled grey leather, but closer inspection reveals it's just imitation: thick, spongey plastic that tears more easily than it should. There are no wheels, just one handle at the top for carrying and two large buckled straps, but they're more for show than anything else. If you need to depart quickly, you can leave them undone.

THEN

Heather is walking along the landing to the bathroom when she hears a noise in her mum and dad's bedroom that makes her jump. She knows it's not her mother in there because she's watching TV downstairs. Heather can hear her shouting at Ian and Cindy in *EastEnders* for being such idiots. And it can't be her dad because he's at the office again, and Faith has gone up to London to see a play with her English class. That means someone else is in there. A stranger or a robber.

She glances towards the stairs. She's the only person here to keep her mother safe, so even though she's scared, she creeps along the landing, making hardly any noise.

The door to the bedroom is open, but instead of peeking round it, Heather sneaks up to where it joins the wall, and looks through the crack. There is a suitcase open on the bed and someone is piling things into it. Someone is stealing their stuff!

Heather jumps out from behind the door to confront them, preparing to scream the house down, but when she sees who it is, she stops. 'Daddy?'

Her father is holding a carefully folded pair of trousers in his hands. He looks up as he places them gently into the case, where there is already a thin layer of clothes. 'Hey, Sweetpea,' he says with that sad look in his eyes.

'I thought you were at work tonight,' Heather says, then launches herself onto the bed and crawls up to the suitcase so she can see inside better.

'I was,' he says as he walks over to one of the big piles of clothes on top of the chest of drawers that almost reach the ceiling. He pulls a couple of shirts from somewhere near the middle. Even though they're horribly creased, he lays them out on the bed and folds them. To Heather, it seems as if he's performing the task in slow motion.

'What are you doing?' she asks, pushing herself onto all fours and bouncing so the mattress wobbles.

His hands are in the case, and he stops and looks up at his daughter. Only his eyes move. His hands grip the edges of the shirt. 'I'm going away for a little while,' he says quietly. 'Don't bounce on the bed, darling. It's making it quite hard to pack.'

Heather tries her best to stay still. 'For work?

He turns and reaches for a T-shirt from another pile, but this time he doesn't do the slow-motion folding and just shoves it in any old how. 'Heather, I—'

'Oh, there you are.'

Heather turns to see her mother standing in the doorway.

'Stephen? What are you doing?'

Heather jumps up, excited. 'That's what I said!'

Her mother's head spins round. It's as if she's only just noticed her there. 'Heather,' she says, frowning. 'Go and do your homework.'

'I can't,' Heather replies. 'I don't get homework on weekdays. I'm too little.'

'Well, then go and play in Faith's room!'

Heather shakes her head. No way. Faith will kill her if she goes in there without permission. It says so on a sign she put on the door with BluTack. Heather turns to her father, hoping he'll understand, but he sighs and says, 'I think your mum and I could do with a little time to ourselves, Sweetpea.'

Heather scowls at them both. Not fair. She's always being told to go away while people talk about secret things. She's starting to get really fed up with it. She folds her arms and jumps off the bed with a thump and then stomps all the way along the landing and down the first part of the stairs, but when she reaches the little halfway landing, she stops, thinks for a moment, and turns round. Carefully and quietly she creeps back up the way she came, stopping just short of the bedroom door, and tucks herself into a narrow gap in the row of piles that lines the landing, hiding just like a super-secret spy would do.

Her mother is crying. 'No, no, no,' she says in between sobs. 'Please. I'll do better. I'll try really, really hard!'

Her father sighs. 'You've been saying that every month for the last few years.'

'I know. I know I have, but this time I mean it, Stephen. I just let things get out of control for a while. You know things got harder for me after that thing with Heather.'

At the mention of her name, Heather's stomach goes cold. A good spy would stay hidden, but she can't resist getting closer. She can see her mother's hand palm down on the mattress, but the rest of her is blocked by the door. Her father is standing by the suitcase. He hasn't moved. It's as if he's guarding it.

'I know,' he says softly, 'and that's why I haven't pushed it for so long but, seriously, Chris…' His voice starts to crack. 'I just don't think I can take it any more. I can't live like this. No one should have to.'

The only reply is a strangled little sob. Heather's father disappears from view, and there is a squeak of springs as the mattress dips. Heather guesses her father has sat down next to her mother and has put his arm around her.

Heather holds her breath. It's just dawned on her what all this is about, why her daddy is filling a suitcase. Tears roll down her cheeks. She wants to run back into the bedroom and cling onto him, to both of them, but now she knows she should move, but she can't.

No one says anything for the longest time, and then her father lets out a shaky breath. 'Okay,' he says. He sounds weary – the kind of heavy-lidded tiredness Heather feels when she tries to stay up until midnight on New Year's Eve. 'But only if we all work to get the house cleared out – and I mean properly cleared out.'

Her mother starts crying again, but this time they sound like happier tears.

Faith told Heather once that where we only have one word for snow in English, in Inuit there are fifteen. Her sister says it's because they live with snow so much they have names for all the different kinds, from big fat wet flakes to the dusty powder that flies in your face when you try to walk to school. Heather wonders if somebody should come up with some more English words for tears. There's definitely a difference between the happy, sticky kind that come with a smile, like these ones, and the fat, silent ones that mean their mother is going to lie on the sofa for days and days and not get up.

'I will!' her mum says, and there's a squishy kind of sound that makes Heather think her mother is kissing her father over and over on his face. 'I'll put in extra time, starting tomorrow—'

'Chris. Chris…?'

'What?'

'You just trying harder isn't going to work,' Heather's dad says seriously. 'We've gone down that path before, haven't we? Many, many times. I think I should take a couple of weeks off work and we'll do the whole house together. It has to be gone, all of it, or I'm not staying.' He pauses for a moment. 'And I can't leave the girls here either.'

There's a long, thick silence then, the kind that only happens when people are talking to each other with their eyes. Heather's feet finally unglue themselves from the landing carpet and she runs into the room and throws her arms around her parents. 'I'll help,' she says, tears flowing down her face too. 'I'll be the best tidying helper ever!'

Arms come round her and squeeze her tight and, for once, no one tells her off for listening when she shouldn't have been.

CHAPTER SEVENTEEN

NOW

Jason has a motorbike he keeps in the garage, but they don't go out to breakfast on that. Instead, he opens the door of his little white MG sports car for Heather. He calls it 'vintage'; she thinks it could probably be more accurately labelled 'rusty'. He's doing it up, he tells her. By the summer it'll look as good as new. Heather smiles but doesn't believe him. Her mother used to say that sort of thing all the time.

Despite the fact a section of the A2 has been moved and widened and now has a couple of Costas and M&S Food shops at the petrol stations, the little truckers' café that Jason takes Heather to on the old road is bustling. Burly men in thick jackets tuck into full English breakfasts and massive mugs of tea. The smell of frying bacon when they walk through the door is incredible.

'What do you fancy?' Jason says, smiling at her as they nab a table and sit down.

She finds it very hard to come up with a sensible answer, but eventually she manages to tear her eyes off him and fix them on the menu. She picks the first thing she sees. 'Sausage butty.'

'Good choice,' he says. 'Fred is famous for his sausages.'

'Fred? You know the owner? Do you come here a lot?'

'Yep. My grandpa used to bring me here when I was little. Kind of became a habit on a Saturday morning.'

He smiles at the scrawny-looking waitress as she approaches. *She must be seventy if she's a day,* Heather thinks. 'Usual?' the waitress asks Jason.

Jason nods. 'And a sausage sarnie for the lady, and two large teas.'

Her stomach gurgles in anticipation of breakfast. She had no idea that staying up half the night and battling floods could make a person so hungry. Jason is leaning back in his chair and his eyelids are growing heavy.

'Thank you again for rushing to my rescue last night,' she says, and sees him jolt upright and refocus on her.

He shrugs, looking a little embarrassed. 'It's what good neighbours do.'

She nods.

'It's what friends do,' he adds.

Heather's eyebrows rise. They're friends? She hasn't had one of those in a while. Work colleagues, yes. Acquaintances, sort of. But no proper friends. The girls at school made sure of that. And by the time she'd finished school and moved on to university, she'd just got out of practice. She can't help smiling softly to herself. This feels nice. A little bit scary, but nice.

The waitress brings their food and Heather peels the thick, white bread back so she can add sauce. The ketchup is in little packets, so she avoids those, preferring the HP anyway. As she's dolloping it over her sausages, Jason puts down his knife and fork and grins. 'We have to stop meeting like this,' he says and takes a great glug of tea.

Heather frowns, puts the sauce bottle back down and carefully reassembles her sandwich. 'What do you mean? I've never been here before.'

'I mean…' He swallows a mouthful of fried egg so he can talk properly. 'I mean that sausages seem to be a common theme.'

She stares down at her breakfast then looks back up at him. She doesn't get why that's significant. He just shakes his head and looks a bit goofy. 'Don't mind me. Sleep deprivation. It's a killer. I was trying to be funny.'

'Oh.'

He chuckles softly. 'That bad, huh?'

Heather takes a bite of her sandwich and chews thoughtfully. When she's finished, she says, 'We'll just have to find another way to ketch-up.' Jason stares at her. She looks away. Oh hell. That was the wrong thing to say. She starts to try and dig herself back out of the hole she's created. 'Ketchup… Catch up?'

He doesn't say anything, and she's afraid to turn back and look at him, but when she can bear the silence no longer, she does, mainly because the brown sauce is starting to run down her finger and she needs to put her sandwich back on her plate so she can wipe it with a paper napkin.

'Eggs-actly,' he says and his mouth twitches.

Her eyes widen and she makes a soft huffing sound, a laugh cut short by surprise.

Jason is smiling as he continues to dig into his breakfast, eyes on his plate, and Heather watches him as she makes short work of her sandwich. Every time a bit of the peppery, soft sausage hits her taste buds she wants to smile.

Don't get too carried away, a little voice in her head warns. *He said 'friends', nothing more.*

Heather does her best to absorb that fact, not to hope for more than she could ever have, but it's surprisingly difficult. She feels warm, light. Not alone. And those things are very hard to feel sensible about.

When Jason has wiped the last of the egg from his plate with his toast, he pushes it away and leans back. 'Time to get bac-on the road,' he says, smiling most unapologetically at his awful pun.

'What in your old banger?' she shoots back, surprised at how fast she's getting the hang of it.

'Ouch!' Jason chuckles. 'Muffin's wrong with my car, I'll have you know.'

Heather opens her mouth to say muffins aren't even on the menu for breakfast here, but instead of arguing, she just tries to give him a tenner from the purse tucked in her jeans pocket. He won't hear of it.

When he's put his wallet away, he says, 'Time to go ham!'

Heather groans. 'That's not even a breakfast food!'

'Yes it is!'

They argue whether continental breakfasts can really be included in this pun-fest all the way out to the car. She climbs inside, aware she is close enough to smell the fabric conditioner on his clean T-shirt as he drops into the driver's seat and folds his long legs into the car.

'We'd better curry up,' he says. 'I had a text from Carlton saying he was going to get there bright and early to check the damage.' He pulls out of the car park and heads for home.

Heather thinks about the mess in her hallway, the fact her land-lord will see it, and her sausage sandwich rolls in her stomach, but before the panic has a chance to settle in, another thought hits her. 'Hang on… Curry? For breakfast?'

Jason just smiles as he keeps his eyes on the road. 'Of course. Straight out of the foil container after a takeaway the night before. Breakfast of champions.'

Heather shudders. 'Cold curry?'

'Don't tell me you've never had takeaway for breakfast?' Now it's his turn to sound astonished.

'No,' she replies seriously. 'I have. Plenty of times.' She thinks of the empty pizza boxes and plastic containers with snap-on lids that had littered her mother's kitchen. After the oven had broken down completely, sometimes scavenging for leftovers from the takeaway meal the night before was the only breakfast available. 'Just not for a very long time.' She'd promised herself she'd never live like that again. It just hadn't occurred to her that normal people did it by choice.

Neither of them can think of any more puns after that, and Heather's eyes are feeling gritty and tired, the lack of sleep catching up with her. The two of them slip into silence as the pale grey sky turns peachy-yellow and the car rumbles back into the fringes of the city.

When they get back, it's seven o'clock and Carlton is pacing around outside the house, barking into a mobile phone. He ends the call abruptly as Heather and Jason emerge from the car and growls at his now-silent phone. 'Bloody cowboy!' he remarks as they approach the front door. 'Wants to charge me a ton for coming out last night, even though it was his shoddy work that failed in the first place! Well, if he expects me to pay him more, he's got another think coming!'

Heather tries to keep as far away from Carlton as she can as she heads inside. He reminds her of a pit bull – round-headed, meaty and almost always snarling. The only time he doesn't talk that way is when he knocks on her door for what always seems to be an invented reason; then he's all syrupy sweet and calls her luv and darlin'. She's not sure which side of him she dislikes more. She's not scared of him, but she would rather limit her interactions with him as much as possible.

This time, though, she is not going to be able to make her escape so easily. 'Alright, angel,' he says as she attempts to slide past him. 'Had a look in your flat. Carpet in your spare room's gonna have to go, I'm afraid.'

'You've been in my flat?' Heather stammers. 'Without me there?'

He jangles a bunch of keys at her, one of which she assumes is a duplicate for her flat. She knows he has one, of course, but he's always promised she'd be there if he came in – something in the tenancy agreement. 'Emergency, innit?' he replies. 'Anyway, I'm going to send a couple of my boys round to rip it up, either today or tomorrow.'

'I don't care about the carpet,' Heather says quickly. 'Leave it.' All she cares about is getting that stuff in her hallway back inside the room and shutting the door.

'Nah. Might as well do it now, while we've got the other work to do. Then I won't have to remember to do it if you move out.'

'H-how long do you think it'll take before it's all sorted out?'

He gives her one of those half-huff, half-shrug things builders and plumbers are really good at. 'Dunno. I've got a specialist firm coming with dehumidifiers and what have you to dry it out. No point putting the carpet back down again until the floor underneath is dry. Maybe about a week?'

A week? Suddenly, despite the sun rising above the edges of the valley Shortlands nestles in, Heather shivers. 'Um… I'm…' She looks around wildly, then spots her car. 'I've got to get to work!' she announces.

'Really?' says Jason, who's been listening to the whole exchange.

'Won't your boss let you even have the morning off after something like this? Surely you could ask for special leave?'

She shakes her head, even though she's pretty sure she could get the time off if she wanted to. 'I'm behind. And it's all done with lottery funding. It's not responsible to hang around here when there's nothing I can do.' Her fight-or-flight response seems to have kicked in again, and Heather has never been much of a scrapper. This is the ideal excuse.

'Listen, let me give you my mobile number,' Jason says and holds out a hand for her phone. 'That way you can at least keep me updated.' She pulls it out of her cardigan pocket and hands it to him. A few quick taps and it's done. She resists the urge to check her contacts to see it sitting there next to Faith's number and the details for a few of her current and past colleagues, the only other numbers in there. 'Text me when you get a chance and then I'll have yours too,' he says, obviously taking Heather's jitters for being in hurry.

'Thanks,' she says and then, not being able to think of anything else to say, she slips past Carlton and dashes into her flat.

The first thing she does is get ready for work. The damp-smelling boxes stacked in her hall are neat now, with none of their contents spilling out, but that doesn't mean Heather wants to walk past them. Thankfully, her bedroom is at the front of the flat, opposite the front door, so she puts her head down and heads straight for it. After getting dressed, she pulls a weekend bag out from the shelf in the wardrobe and starts throwing things into it.

She's really not sure if she just lied to Jason or not. All she knows is that she needs to get out of this place, and she needs to do it now.

CHAPTER EIGHTEEN

NOW

Heather arrives at the Central Library in Bromley, a huge concrete monstrosity on the brow of a hill which can be seen for miles around. Built in the Seventies, it is just about old enough to start being 'retro and edgy' instead of 'old-fashioned and ugly' by those who know about such things.

She'd managed to reduce her boss, Cherie, to speechlessness when she phoned from a service station on her way to work that morning and asked for a personal day to deal with the flood. She's never taken a day off before, not even for a holiday. Once Cherie had recovered from the shock, she'd sputtered her commiserations and told her to take as much time as she needed.

Heather reasons to herself that she didn't exactly lie to her boss. While not dealing directly with the flood – she shivers just thinking about those boxes stacked in her hallway, no longer contained and quarantined, like cancer that has spread and started to infect the healthy tissue of her home – she plans to deal with the 'repercussions' of the flood, so that counts.

More has been lost than carpeting and old cardboard boxes.

Precious information was destroyed in the plumbing palaver. Thankfully, after turning round and heading her car back towards Bromley, she had a bolt of inspiration. Given her job, she should have thought of it days ago, but somehow she was just so focused on 'that room' that she didn't see the alternatives.

She heads upstairs to the library's local studies area and pauses in front of the large filing cabinets housing the microfilm collection. There it is. *Bromley and Chislehurst News Shopper 1991–94.* The metal drawer slides open easily and she scans the boxes for the one she wants: June to July 1992. She pauses, just staring at the little cardboard box, before she plucks it out and heads to one of the microfilm readers.

Heather is not a stranger to these machines, so it doesn't take long to load it up. Thankfully, the library has invested in more modern technology: film readers hooked up to a PC rather than the bulky old ones with their own screens. She scrolls horizontally through the pages, fast at first and then more slowly until an image slides by. Even though it shoots past before her finger can react, her brain fires off a signal: this is the one. She clicks the mouse button and the page rolls back into view again.

While this photo is the same as the one on the clipping she found amongst her mother's stuff, the text is different. This is from 8 July, the first issue of the weekly paper since her disappearance. Although she's desperate to gather facts, she's also terrified about what these grainy little words will reveal, so she closes her eyes, pictures Jason smiling at her over the top of a full English, takes a deep breath, and begins reading.

LOCAL GIRL MISSING: Police ask for help from Bromley residents.

Little Heather Lucas, aged 6, has been missing since 3rd July and Bromley police are asking anyone who might know anything about her whereabouts to come forward. The last positive sighting of Heather was by her teacher, Miss Julie Perrins, 25, who describes her as 'an imaginative and sensitive girl' as she left St Michael's Primary School in Bickley at 3.15 p.m. last Friday. One or two parents say they may have noticed a little girl waiting alone in the playground that afternoon, but none can give a positive identification.

Heather's mother, Christine Lucas, aged 36, and her father, Stephen Lucas, aged 40, are beside themselves. 'She's the light of our world,' Mrs Lucas sobbed. 'I don't know how we can carry on without her.'

Heather stops reading then. She can imagine her mother, gluey-eyed and distraught at the doorstep, probably half-loving all the drama. Light of her world? *Give me a break!* Sometimes, her mother could go for days without seeing her in their hoarded house, and it had never seemed to bother her then.

The shaking begins in Heather's hands, the kind she has learned not to ignore, especially as Mothercare is only a minute's walk from the library. She saves the story she has just read to a USB stick, along with a version of the one she found in the photo album, and a third, celebrating her safe return, then bolts out of the library and back to her car.

She drives back towards Swanham, close to work for the next

day, and checks herself into the Park Lodge Hotel, a budget place used by business travellers. Its name makes it sound much nicer than it looks.

Her room is on the corner of the building, at the end of a long corridor, but she sees no one else as she walks down it, keycard in hand. Maybe this is the perfect way to live, she thinks as she unlocks her room's door. It's completely anonymous. Nobody wonders about her because no one even notices her. No one is curious about who she is or what might happen behind the closed door of her room. For a moment she allows herself the luxury of imagining a future where it would just be her, a single suitcase of belongings, and a fresh hotel room with each new month. Bliss.

She puts her bags down, removes her jacket, and breathes out. It's a large room with lots of empty carpet and generic furnishings, but she feels more at peace here than she has anywhere else since she moved back to Bromley.

She digs in her bag for the memory stick she took with her to the library. Now she's feeling calmer, she's ready to face its contents. She pulls her laptop out of her bag and settles herself at the desk, then pushes the USB stick into the slot and opens up a window.

Just three PDF files. That doesn't feel enough for a momentous event like this, does it? For something that changed the course of several lives forever. But then again, Heather has never kidded herself that she was very important in the grand scheme of things. Others may have whole books written about them, but maybe this is all that needs to be said about her.

She re-reads the report from 8 July first, making sure the facts are clear in her head still, and then she gives the one she found in her mother's things the same careful attention. She pauses, and makes herself a coffee with one of the complimentary little sachets of dusty-tasting instant granules and UHT milk. Readying herself, she clicks on the third file and watches it flash up in front of her.

Still the same school photograph and no others. None of the joyful reunion with her parents.

MISSING GIRL FOUND

Missing schoolgirl, Heather Lucas, aged 6, has been reunited with her family after a traumatic and worrying sixteen days.

Heather skips over the rehashed details of her disappearance and heads for the fresh information further down the column.

Police found little Heather in the East Sussex town of Hastings, where she had been taken by her abductor. It is not clear whether they had been there the whole time or had been moving around in an effort to evade capture, but police received a tip-off from a holiday-maker. 'I live in Beckenham,' Mrs June Fallon, aged 67, told our reporter, 'so I'd seen the story about the missing kiddy in the paper. Me and my friend Coral fancied a trip to the ice-cream parlour on the front, and that's where we saw her.'

Police were able to trace a woman and child, who had been eating in Marcello's Ice Cream Heaven, to a B&B in the old town. It was there little Heather was discovered and a woman was taken into custody.

> Police have refused to confirm if this is a suspect,
> simply releasing a statement saying that someone is
> helping them with their enquires...

Heather holds her breath. No, not after all this. Blasted confidentiality! But she reads on, hoping against hope:

> Mr Arthur Horton, proprietor of the Bay View
> Guesthouse on South Street was able to confirm that
> the name of the woman in their register was Patricia
> Waites, also from the Bromley area.

Heather stops reading. She needs to. There's another half a column to go, something about the family wanting privacy at this difficult time, but she'll read it later. For now, she turns those two words, that name, over and over in her head, investigating them from every angle. *Patricia Waites.*

'Patricia Waites.' She says it out loud, wondering if that will help, but there's no recognition. No jolt of memory. Nothing. Just a cerebral and logical processing of the sounds and words. It means nothing to her, both in terms of her lost memory and what she's feeling.

This is disappointing. She was hoping for more. Not a flash of light or a voice from heaven, but... something. However, all she feels as she sits in the bland hotel room and stares at herself in the mirror bolted to the wall is numb.

CHAPTER NINETEEN

FLUFFY

Our cat was beautiful, almost pure white and, as his name suggests, he had a glorious mane of snowy white fur. Sometimes he would wait on the stairs and sting my ankles with his claws when I walked past. I said he was beautiful; I didn't say he was always nice. But sometimes, when he was in a particularly good mood, he would allow me to show my devotion to him by letting me stroke his tummy. He would lie on his back and purr as I rubbed where his coat was softest. I was inconsolable when he ran away.

THEN

It's six o'clock in the evening and the sky is just starting to get dark. The Lucas family are all tired and grimy, but the two girls keep smiling at each other. All day they've been moving things, clearing things, sorting things, and now it is as if a celestial being has pointed down at their house from the clouds and created a miracle. Because that's what it feels like – a miracle.

The house is clean. And not what Heather's mum normally refers to as clean. It's properly clean, like you see in a magazine or on the television.

There are still a few piles of boxes in the dining room and a few more to go up in the eaves, but other than that the stuff is gone. Heather can hardly believe it.

Her dad had to tear up the dining-room carpet because it was no good any more. It left lots of crumbly green rubbery stuff behind, which Heather and Faith had to sweep up, so now there are just floorboards under the dining table and chairs. They also discovered black speckles on the wall in the corner of the living room that aren't supposed to be there, but Heather's dad says he can get someone in to sort that out and just not having all the stuff piled up against the wall will help in future. He even smiled when he said that.

Heather's dad has been smiling a lot today. He's even been whistling. Heather didn't even know he could do that. She asked him to teach her, and he says he will but not today because they're still so busy making the house nice.

Heather has forgotten how lovely it is to have her dad in the house in the daytime. He took the last two weeks off work and every day they've chosen a different room and sorted it out. Best of all is that Heather has her own bedroom again. All her stuff is in there already: her clothes, her shoes, even her PE kit on a special hook so it'll never get lost again.

Heather can't believe how much space there is. She keeps running up and down the hallway and in and out of the rooms until her mum tells her she's giving her a headache and makes her sit down.

Although Heather's mum says she's pleased the house is tidy,

Heather isn't sure she believes her. She isn't smiling like Heather's dad is, and when Heather asked her if she was going to whistle too, her mum told her not to be so cheeky.

It doesn't make sense. For years her mum has moaned on and on about getting the house straight, but as the days of clearing up have gone on, she seems to have been getting smaller and smaller and curling up into herself like one of those funny red cellophane fish you get in a Christmas cracker. She is lying on the sofa at the moment, and she almost looks like a child. Maybe it's because now the piles balanced all around it have gone, the sofa seems much bigger and she seems much smaller?

Maybe it's just a case of getting used to it. Heather thinks she needs to do that too. As much as she likes being able to run around and spin, when she stops it takes her a few moments to remember this is her house and not someone else's.

'I'm hungry,' Faith says after taking one more box up to the bathroom, where the little door to the eaves space is. 'When are we going to get pizza?'

'Soon,' their father says, 'but let's just get these last few boxes put away first, shall we?'

Faith makes a face behind his back and Heather giggles.

'And we'll get a tub of ice cream to celebrate too,' he adds. The girls cheer and grab a box each, grinning, and march up the stairs with them, singing the 'Pizza Hut' song.

They reach the bathroom and head inside. There's always been so much laundry in the way that Heather didn't know there was a little door in the wall until today. It's just the right size for her, but her father has to bend down to get inside. He opens the door, crawls halfway in and then asks the girls to hand him boxes so he can stack them up. This is all the space their mum is allowed from now on, and their dad says he's going to be very cross if the boxes start filling up the bathroom and the hallway again.

He shines his torch into the tiny space. There's just about enough room for one more stack inside. Unfortunately, when he tries to slide the boxes in, he discovers they're a little too big to fit the space. 'Don't worry,' he tells the girls. 'I'll just restack what's there to make room.'

He passes a couple of boxes back out to give himself more space to manoeuvre, but when he tries to push one of the other boxes back it won't go. Eventually, he pulls that out too, to see what the problem is.

'Oh, my God!'

He stumbles back through the little doorway, banging his head on the top. 'Girls, get out! Get back onto the landing!' At first, Heather thinks he's angry, but then she looks at his face and sees his expression is a mix between surprise and fear, so she does what he says. 'Chris!' he yells at the top of his lungs. 'Get up here!'

There's a reply from downstairs, a slightly grumbly one that Heather can't make out. She suspects her mother doesn't want to move off the sofa.

'Now!' he shouts even louder, and a short while later her mum comes running up the stairs, looking worried.

Heather starts to get scared. She wants to hold Faith's hand, but her sister has got her arms folded, hugging herself, and she doesn't look as if she wants to let go.

Before her mum has even got both feet inside the bathroom, Heather's dad is pointing and shouting. 'Look!'

Heather creeps forward until she can see inside the bathroom but not inside the secret space. Her mother pokes her head inside and makes a strange half-scream, half-crying sound and backs away.

Heather knows about secret places in attics and cupboards. A tiny part of her is wishing hard they've found Narnia in there, but a sensible, grown-up kind of voice in her head is telling her not to be so stupid. If it was a nice kind of surprise like that, her mum and dad would seem more excited.

'Grab a towel,' her father says to her mother, and he nods his head towards the two girls, who are now standing either side of the doorway. Her mum digs one out of the airing cupboard and hands it to him, then he disappears into the eaves. A short while later he backs out again, something wrapped up in the towel. He carries it like a baby. 'Out the way, girls,' he says sternly. 'Go to your bedrooms.'

Faith and Heather don't argue. They run off. Heather has never seen her dad's face like that before, not even in all the times he and Mum have shouted at each other. It looks like thunder and lightning is happening behind his eyes.

Heather goes to her new bedroom and walks straight over to the window without turning the light on. She stares out into the twilight, not really looking at anything in particular, but then movement on the lawn catches her eye. Her father walks out there with the towel and a spade. He puts the bundle down and starts to dig a hole.

Heather's tummy is rumbling but she doesn't run to remind her mum about the pizza, even though they're going to deliver it to the house in a box and she's very excited about that. No one has ever delivered food to their house before. It feels as if her family has suddenly become royal, like the Queen.

It gets darker and darker as Heather's dad digs the hole. He has to stop now and then to wipe his forehead with the back of his arm, but eventually he reaches for the towel and picks it up. He's not being as careful to hide the contents now, and as he lowers it into the hole, a corner flops over. Inside there's something white. Something fluffy.

Heather makes a squeak and covers her mouth with her hand. *No!* He ran away. That's what they all thought, anyway. Faith said he'd probably been squashed by a car or eaten by a fox, even though their mum had told them he'd probably just found some lovely cat friends to live with. How could he have ended up in the eaves?

The furry white lump looks strange. Kind of flat, like the cat has been sucked out and just the fluff has been left behind. It doesn't make sense. There aren't any foxes or cars or nice cat families in their attic.

When her dad finishes pulling earth back over the hole, Heather steps back from the window into the darkness of her room. She's trying really hard not to cry and she doesn't want him to see her in case he gets sad too – he's been so much happier lately and she doesn't want that to change. She wants to stay in her bedroom but her mum calls out from downstairs, saying she's about to ring the pizza man and the girls had better come down and help choose because she doesn't want any moaning about mushrooms or olives if they don't.

Heather hears a creak on the landing and she pokes her head out of her door. Faith is standing there. They look at each other, then walk down the stairs side by side. Their father comes back in from the garden as they enter the kitchen. He's not whistling this evening. In fact, he looks as if he never wants to whistle again.

'Girls,' he says solemnly, 'I've got some bad news...'

'No!' their mother shouts. 'You don't have to tell them! They don't have to know!'

He gives her a tired look. 'They do need to know. We talked about this, Chris. It's time to be more honest. And I think that should include the girls.'

He leads his daughters into the living room and sits them down on the sofa, then kneels down in front of them, takes one of their hands each, and looks into their eyes. He tells them Fluffy is dead.

Heather manages not to cry, and she's proud of herself, because even though she'd worked that out already, when he said the words out loud it felt like a punch in the tummy. Faith's face crumples up and big, fat tears slide down her cheeks. Her sister likes to pretend that she's tough, that she knows everything and can handle anything, so Heather is shocked. She hesitates for a moment and then puts her arm around Faith's shoulder and leans in. Then her tears come too.

'H-how did it happen?' Faith hiccups.

Their father presses his lips together and makes a huffing noise as he thinks how to answer. 'We think Fluffy must have run up here – maybe to get some peace and quiet – and that he got stuck behind the boxes.' He swallows, looks over at their mother. She nods.

Heather starts to cry again. 'W-was it my fault?'

'Of course not!' her father says, and shoots an angry look at his wife.

She comes over and puts her arms around Heather. 'Why would you think that, darling?'

'B-because… Because you used to tell me to stop stroking him when he started to wag his tail, that he'd had enough and just wanted some peace and quiet. Maybe he ran away from *me* and got flatted.'

'Flatted?' her dad says, and then he looks out towards the back garden and understands. 'I thought I told you to keep an eye on them while I did it,' he says quietly but not very softly to her mum.

'I… I was…' she says, looking confused. 'But there was one last box I needed to see if I could—'

'Chris!' Her dad holds up his hand and her mum stops talking. He shakes his head. 'It's never going to end, is it?' he says wearily. 'I thought I could do this. I thought this could work. But I can see now I was just kidding myself.' He sighs and walks towards the hallway, turning as he reaches the doorway. 'I'll stay at Dave and Carol's tonight.'

Mum starts shaking her head. 'No, no, no,' she says softly. 'You can't do this. You promised you wouldn't if we cleared up and I've gutted my soul to make that happen. I've given away everything that meant something to me, everything I've ever loved…'

Dad just stares at her. 'Me and the girls are still here. Or have you forgotten about us? This was all about us making room – not just physical space, but space for us to be a family again, but if that's the way you really feel, you've just confirmed everything I've been thinking.'

'You know I didn't mean it that way. You know I—'

'Many a truth slips out in the heat of the moment,' Dad says and his voice is all icy. He holds his hands out, one to Faith and one to Heather. 'Come on, girls. We're going to go and visit Dave and Carol. You remember them, don't you? From the Christmas party last year? Their little girl Nina was just a bit older than you, Heather.'

'No! You promised!' her mum comes flying at her dad, her arms swinging, clawing. She catches him on the cheek and a bright, red line appears.

Heather's dad doesn't hit back, but he blocks her mother's blows with his arms and shouts, 'For God's sake, Chris! Think of the girls!'

Her mum sobs and falls into a heap then. Heather runs over to her, wondering if she's ill, if maybe they need to call an ambulance. Her dad reaches out to her again. 'Come on, Sweetpea.'

Heather looks at his hand. Faith is already clutching the other one. Her mum is crying hard on the floor now, her body jerking in time with her sobs. Heather has never heard anyone cry like that before. Like an animal. Like it's coming from deep inside her.

Her father steps forward. 'Heather? Are you coming?'

All Heather can do is stare at his empty hand.

CHAPTER TWENTY

NOW

Heather is in two minds as to whether she should call off the family lunch with Faith that weekend. She's not sure whether she wants to talk about everything she's found out. The only problem is that if she doesn't go, Faith will want to know why and then she'll be in trouble and she'll still face the inevitable inquisition. In the end she slides into her car, mumbling to herself. At least if she does it this way the kids and Matthew will be there as a buffer. The last thing she wants is for her sister to turn up again at her flat, unannounced.

The car coughs slightly as she turns the key in the ignition and for a moment Heather thinks it isn't going to start, but then it croaks into life and the engine rumbles. She makes a mental note to get the battery checked. When the car was serviced the guy hinted it might need replacing once colder weather hit in the autumn. She'd expected it to last until at least September. But once the car is going, it trundles along as it always does.

Heather reaches Westerham, on what is turning out to be a grey and drizzly summer's afternoon, the smell of warm soil pumping through the car's ventilation system, and Faith greets her as normal then ushers her inside.

Things go smoothly, pleasantly, until they're all seated round the table. Faith's promises that they would go out and try somewhere new had not come to fruition. Still, it's a roast this week: pork with apple sauce and crisp crackling. But Heather knows the pin was pulled from the grenade the moment she stepped inside the front door, and while they're all tucking into their roast potatoes it goes off.

'So... how goes the investigation?' Faith asks innocently while passing the gravy boat down so Heather can help her nephew to a little more. 'Have you found out anything else?'

Matthew gives Faith a look. They've obviously talked about this. Heather loves her brother-in-law just a little bit more for his attempt to reel his wife in, and she shoots him a grateful look. Faith just raises her eyebrows in mock innocence. It's clear she feels she's approaching saintly status for not launching in as soon as Heather walked in the door.

Heather considers her answer as she attempts to trickle gravy on the items Barney's requested in the precise order he's decreed. She takes an extra-long time making sure she's doused potatoes and pork (but leaving both carrots and stuffing gravy-free, which is no mean feat). 'I went to the library. Looked up some old news articles.'

'And...?'

Heather glances across at her niece and nephew. 'Can we talk about this after dinner?'

Faith follows her gaze and nods, but her mouth pulls tight. This is killing her, Heather thinks. Is it wrong that this knowledge warms her a little as she makes her way through her roast dinner, taking extra time, making sure she's mopped up every last smudge of gravy, caught every last pea?

After dinner, Matthew takes the kids into the garden. The rain has stopped now so he fetches a ball for the kids to blow off their pent-up energy, while the two sisters tackle the washing-up.

Heather really doesn't want to have this conversation but there's no escaping it, so she tells Faith about her trip to the library, and gives the bare facts – times and dates and names – as cleanly and swiftly as possible, hoping against hope that this will be an end to it.

Faith sighs as Heather finishes her tale. 'If only we knew where Aunt Kathy was. I'm sure she'd have some answers for us.'

'But we don't.'

Faith nods. 'She disappeared from our lives not long after what happened to you. She and Mum used to argue a lot anyway, but the year after you came back it got a whole lot worse and then one day she was just... gone.'

Heather makes a huffing sound. She's not surprised their lovely Aunt Kathy cut off all contact. Their mother had a gift for driving people away. 'What did they argue about?'

'The hoard, mostly.'

Heather nods. That would make sense. If her mother started hoarding after her disappearance, surely those around her would have challenged her on it. That always created conflict.

'It's a pity we can't find her. I've often wondered if there was something in Mum's background that set the stage for her later behaviour.'

'Maybe.'

'She and Aunty Kathy were taken into care when they were kids, just for a couple of months, but that had to have some impact, didn't it? Maybe we should ask Dad when we Skype him this afternoon?' Faith pipes up.

'No.' Heather's response is firm and low.

'Why not?'

'Because… Because…' Heather stammers.

Because she and her father don't discuss her mother or the house in Hawksbury Road. It's an unwritten rule between them. Even if Heather wanted to talk about that time (which she doesn't), her father would find some way to change the subject. It's as if he wants to erase his life before he met Shirley. Heather understands that. The only problem is that now Heather knows about her disappearance, her abduction, she supposes she's a bigger part of that unwanted period of his history than she ever realized. Maybe that's what causes the distance between them? After all, her sister doesn't seem to struggle in the same way.

'Because…?' Faith prompts.

'Because he's been through enough,' Heather says plainly, looking her sister in the eye. 'Because that time must have been very painful for him too. I don't want to push him about it unless I've exhausted every other avenue.'

Her answer sounds altruistic, which it is. Partly. She does want to spare her father any more distress. He put up with five lifetimes' worth of crap living with her mother. They all did. But a tiny part of her is scared that if she opens that can of worms again, it'll destroy what is left of their relationship. It's hanging by a thread as it is.

It's the right answer for Faith, though, who studiously tries to love her neighbour as herself, as the Good Book commands, even if that amount of care and thoughtfulness is never extended to her sister. 'Okay,' she says. 'I get that.'

When they've put every last plate away and the dishwasher is humming beneath the counter, Faith goes out onto the patio and wipes down the garden furniture with a tea towel. They take their coffee cups out there and stare down the long garden as the kids race around after a pale-blue *Frozen* plastic ball. Heather watches

Elsa's face spinning round and round, over and over, her blonde hair blurring, and knows it's just like the thoughts spinning inside her sister's head.

'Do you think this woman who took you... this Patricia Waites... was mentally ill?' Faith finally blurts out.

'How should I know?' Heather replies.

'Well, haven't you looked further ahead with the newspaper articles? Checked if there was a trial or something?'

'No. Not yet.'

'Are you going to?' Faith says, leaning forward and invading Heather's personal space.

Heather puts her cup down with a clatter, stands up and walks away. 'Oh, my God, Faith! Stop, will you?'

'But I thought you wanted to find out about this woman, about what happened?' Seeing Heather's stony expression, she exhales and looks penitent, which is a surprise in itself. 'Sorry. I know I'm being pushy. It's just that I'm so... so...'

Heather can see fifteen different emotions flitting across her sister's face, but they're travelling so fast she can't pin them down and label them. She's not sure she's ever seen her so worked up before. 'So... what?' she asks, puzzled.

'So *angry*,' Faith replies simply. 'I'm so bloody angry that this woman, this stranger, did this to you. To us.'

Heather sees a familiar fierceness in her sister's expression but it shocks her so much she sits down again. It's the same look she gave Heather the other week when she wouldn't play hide-and-seek, but this time it isn't directed at her; it's felt on her behalf. When Heather looks at Faith she gets that same sense of solidarity she used to feel when it was just the two of them against the hoard.

Faith's arms twitch, as if she wants to step forward and hug

Heather but isn't sure it will be welcomed. Heather wants to give her a little signal that it's okay, but she doesn't know how, so they just stare at each other.

'I'm so sorry this happened to you,' Faith says. 'I know I always knew about it, but revisiting it now we're both grown up... Well, it's made me see it in a new light.' She sighs. 'I know it's not very Christian, but I'd like to punch that woman in the face for what she did to our family.'

'I hate her,' Heather says quietly, aware her teeth are almost grinding together as she talks. 'I don't care who she is or what was going on in her head. I really, really hate her.'

People always say hate is such a destructive thing, but Heather is questioning that prejudice. This burning thing inside her is alive, raw, powerful. It makes her feel like an avenging angel. She downs the rest of the coffee and stands up again, not because she's cross with Faith this time, but because this emotion will not allow stillness.

'How do you wake up one morning and decide: you know what? I'm going to wreck a family today. I'm going to tear it apart so it'll never be the same.' She looks at Faith, needing agreement and sees it. 'And – oh! – poor Mum. No wonder she was such a mess. How do you get over something like that?'

A rush of warmth for her mother fills Heather's chest. She hasn't felt that kind of compassion towards her in decades, and now it's returned it is as if Heather is crushed beneath it. She collapses back into the garden chair and sobs into her hands.

After a few seconds, she feels a palm on her back. It rubs gently. That only makes her cry harder.

'Mummy! Aunty Heather! Oh—' Alice's voice gets nearer then cuts off. Heather hears Matthew's hushed tones as he hurries the children back inside. She can't look up, just cries hot tears until there are no more, then she takes the packet of tissues her sister offers her and blows her nose loudly.

'Have you thought about talking to someone about this?' Faith asks softly when Heather has folded the tissue and shoved it in her back pocket.

'I'm talking to you, aren't I?'

'No,' Faith replies, her voice softer still. 'You know what I mean.'

Heather does one of those weird laughs – the kind that's half disbelief, half offence – and stares at her sister. Hasn't she always known Faith thinks of her as being weak? Damaged? But it's one thing to suspect it and another thing entirely for your sister to confirm it out of her own mouth.

She knew things had been going too well between them. It was inevitable that, after that shining moment of understanding and solidarity, one or other of them would say or do something to send things spiralling back to normal. 'That's what you think I am, is it? A basket case? Thanks a bunch!' She stands up again, mainly because her instinct is to stride away.

'Heather…'

'What? Haven't I got a right to be angry? This is not my fault!'

Faith stands up too, walks towards her. 'I know that. I don't think you're a basket case! Anyone who'd been through what you've been through, who's just found out what you have, would be… struggling.'

Heather crosses her arms. 'I am *not* struggling,' she says through clenched teeth. 'I'm dealing with it fine.'

Faith shakes her head. It begins to rain gently again but neither sister moves. 'Heather…' she says in that same tone she uses on the kids when she knows they're fibbing.

That's it. That's all it takes to blow the lid off Heather's fragile composure. 'Don't!' she says, jerking back as Faith reaches out to lay a sympathetic hand on her arm. 'Don't you dare touch me! You can't understand! How could you?'

Faith pulls her hand back and tucks it into the crook of her opposite elbow. She looks hurt, which is odd because Faith never looks hurt. She never seems to look anything but capable and calm and efficient. But Heather can't think about that now, she's too busy trying not to explode into a million tiny pieces. What a mess that would make of her sister's neat, trimmed garden!

'Can't we talk about this calmly?' Faith begs.

'I can't win with you,' Heather says. 'If I stay calm, I'm bottling it up. If I get angry, I need to see a shrink. Make up your mind, will you?' Faith looks stunned, and well she should do, but it feels wonderfully liberating for Heather to unleash all the things she doesn't usually say for fear of making things worse. But she's not sure things can get any worse now, so she aims and fires. 'Okay, how about this? How about when you discover you were kidnapped and taken from home as a kid, stolen and subjected to goodness-knows-what, only for your return to herald the complete implosion of your family? – Was it so bad to have me back? Was it? – *Then* you can talk to me about staying calm!'

She marches back in through the house, pausing only to snatch up her bag and coat. In the distance she hears her sister call out, 'Heather! Come back! We haven't video chatted with Dad yet!' but Heather ignores her, heading outside, leaving the front door open and getting into her car.

The kids and Matthew are standing there open-mouthed as she pulls away. She sees Faith run up behind them in her rear-view mirror as she exits the driveway and joins the traffic, but she doesn't care. She puts her foot down and drives.

CHAPTER TWENTY-ONE

NOW

Heather moves back into her flat a few days after her horrendous lunch with Faith. The hotel is too expensive and the repair work is finished: the plumbing is fixed, her spare room dried out, complete with new carpet. The men have even moved all the salvaged boxes, crates and bags back in. She can't put it off any longer.

After keeping everybody waiting, summer gets truly underway with one of those bright, unannounced heatwaves that causes the nation to adopt shorts en masse and sport patches of lobster-bright sunburn.

The cheery weather does nothing to stop Heather stealing things. A sun hat, a blue toy elephant, and a packet of two dummies stuffed in her chest of drawers attest to that. Knowing more about the abduction hasn't helped at all. In fact, it may have made everything worse.

Faith doesn't phone. Not that Heather would necessarily expect her to in the days that follow. They don't have that chatty kind of relationship, so it would be unusual for her sister to ring until the next monthly lunch is looming, but every time Heather looks at the handset in the living room she can feel Faith's silence. The phone is deliberately *not* ringing, and it doesn't ring for almost two weeks.

The worst thing is that now she's calmed down, she knows Faith is right. About keeping going with her investigation, anyway. She can't carry on like this. Even though she leaves the door of the spare room locked, she starts digging into the past again. Googling. The information she hopes to find will be her peace offering to her sister next time they see each other.

The only problem with her search for more facts is that her story, while huge and devastating to her, was a minor event in a boring London suburb, overshadowed by much bigger national news stories in those few short weeks. And this was before the internet had come of age and was beamed into every home. It doesn't matter how many times she types 'Patricia Waites' into the search field, she never finds the right person. They're either too old (dead and part of someone's family tree) or too young and posting endless selfies on Instagram, or living in a different country. It's as if the woman she's after has disappeared.

She's mulling this over one evening while sorting through the post on the console table in the hall, sifting her bills from Jason's and Mrs Rowe's upstairs, when she hears a key in the front door. Jason appears, dressed in a suit and looking much less hot and sticky than she is, even though she's had the benefit of air conditioning in her car and he's been stuck on a packed commuter train.

'Hey,' he says, looking for all the world as if he's pleased to see her.

Heather hands him a couple of faceless envelopes and a gas bill. 'Don't say I never give you anything,' she quips.

He folds the letters in half and stuffs them in his suit jacket pocket, then thinks better of it and shrugs the jacket off and loosens his tie. 'That's it,' he says wearily. 'It's officially too hot to do anything this evening. I don't even want to venture inside my flat.'

Heather nods, knowing what he means. In the early part of the summer the building's thick brick-walls and high ceilings keep it cool, so walking through the front door in the evening is blissful, but temperatures have now reached a tipping point, and the inside of her flat is relentlessly stuffy no matter how many windows she opens.

'I'm just going to get changed and go and sit in the garden for the evening,' Jason says. 'I think I'll fire up the barbie and eat out there. Care to join me?'

Heather pictures sitting in one of the garden chairs as the sun dips behind the hills, turning the sky golden, of how the temperature will drop and the breeze will start to curl around her. 'Okay,' she says.

'I've got some steak in my fridge, but only a wilted lettuce and a couple of tomatoes. Don't suppose you could help on that score?' He flashes her a grin that would have had her jogging all the way to the supermarket in the heat if she hadn't got a fully stocked vegetable drawer.

'How does a mixed salad with lemon-and-thyme dressing and jacket potatoes sound?'

'Like heaven.'

She smiles back at him. 'Okay, it's a—' She stops herself from saying the next word. This is not a date. It's just neighbours escaping the suffocating air of their respective flats. 'It's a plan,' she finishes and rushes inside her flat before he can see the blush climbing up her neck.

* * *

Heather's stomach is fluttering when she opens her French doors an hour later and heads out into the garden. Jason has been out there for ages, but she didn't have the confidence to just go and sit with him. Bringing food gives her a purpose, a reason to be there.

He smiles when he sees her and lifts the lid off the barbecue so he can cook the meat. 'Wow!' he says, looking at the colourful salad she's prepared. 'Can't wait!' He gestures towards the steaks sizzling on the grill. 'They won't take long. Do you want something to drink?'

Heather nods, glowing in his appreciation for her food, and he hands her a bottle of coke from a cooler. It's blissfully cold and the sharp, sweet taste quenches her thirst instantly. A few minutes later they load up their plates and tuck in, sitting either side of the wooden table.

'I haven't seen much of you since you moved back in,' Jason says as they eat.

Heather's glad she's chewing so she can't answer straight away. 'Just been busy with work,' she says once she's swallowed her mouthful of food, although that's not strictly true – it's been no more or no less busy than it usually is. The truth is that their break-fast had seemed so special, so intimate, that she's felt awkward about seeing him again. She's been deliberately keeping herself to herself. It was only the fact he caught her off guard this evening that spoiled that plan. 'Anyway, tell me about your work,' she adds quickly, deflecting attention away from herself. '"Heir hunter" sounds a bit like Indiana Jones but looking for people instead of treasure.'

He laughs at her joke, causing her cheeks to flush. 'Technically, I'm a probate genealogist. There's a certain amount of detective work, looking up old birth, death and marriage certificates, trying to make sure you've got the family tree right before you contact the beneficiaries – and a certain amount of competition, as there are often other firms on the same case and who want to sign the relatives up first.'

She asks more questions, and when he starts to talk about the bit where they track down the living relatives, she realizes he might know how she can progress her own stalled investigation. 'So how do you find out where the relatives live so you can let them know they've got an inheritance coming? My brother-in-law did some research on his family tree a few years ago and he said a lot of census records and what have you aren't available until a hundred years have passed.'

'Ah,' he says, taking another sip of his beer. 'We have access to records the general public doesn't. Without them, it'd be much harder to do that part of the job.'

'So, say I wanted to trace someone who's still alive – a long-lost relative or something – it would be much more difficult?'

'Yeah, unfortunately. The rules on data protection are really strict.'

Heather nods. Blast. Back to the drawing board, then.

They talk some more about their jobs, finding connection in their passion for uncovering the truth about people in the past, and about putting that truth to good use – her to provide knowledge and understanding, him to benefit the family still surviving. He has some really interesting stories about working cases both here and abroad and how much you can find out about someone just from looking at the sparse official records that mark their lives.

Only if you know where to start, Heather thinks wistfully. She wonders if she can find a birth certificate for Patricia Waites, if that would give her any leads, but instantly dismisses the idea. From what Jason has said, discovering the woman's parents' names and occupations, where and when she was born, aren't going to answer any of the questions Heather wants to ask.

The conversation trails off as she ponders this, and the sky turns from a pale orange to a silvery mauve. Trees in the neighbouring gardens cast shadows over their garden, drawing the space in and making it seem more intimate even though they are sitting out-doors. Heather can't think of anything else to say, despite racking her brains as hard as she can. She's very relieved when, after at least five minutes' silence, Jason opens his mouth to speak. 'You're very easy to be around, Heather. I like that about you.'

Heather is glad the twilight is masking the look of complete shock on her face. 'Really?'

'Really,' he says, leaning back in his chair and making himself a little more comfy.

Heather frowns. 'I've always thought I'm a bit too shy... not chatty enough to be interesting.'

He turns and looks at her. 'Talkative doesn't always mean inter-esting,' he tells her sagely. 'I have four sisters – I ought to know! Sometimes I couldn't even hear myself think in my house because of the endless chatter. It's nice to know that not all women need to spill every thought out of their heads as soon as it happens, especially if those thoughts mainly consist of boys and nail varnish.'

Heather chuckles. She's sure he's being a bit hard on his siblings. 'I don't even know the last time I thought about nail varnish,' she says, regarding her short, unadorned nails.

'There you go. Knew there was a reason you were easy to be around,' he says with a cheeky glint in his eye. 'And sometimes "interesting" is not in what is said but in what is left unsaid. There's something appealing about a hint of mystery.'

He looks at her directly when he says this, and Heather swallows.

Her heart is hammering again, as it so often does when she's with him. She knows what he's saying – that still waters run deep. The only problem is that she expects he's thinking of coral lagoons or buried treasure hidden in exotic waters. Her depths are murkier, like a canal full of old shopping trolleys and toxic slime.

Faith's words the last time they talked drift through her head. Her sister thinks she's broken. Too broken for this man, certainly. She ought to go back inside, save them both the disappointment of him getting to know her better. Still, it's another half an hour before she manages to make herself get out of the chair, thank him for the steak, and wish him goodnight.

CHAPTER TWENTY-TWO

NOW

Heather's heart is fluttering while she waits for Jason to answer his door. She woke up at 3 a.m. a couple of days ago, her dreams full of night air infused with honeysuckle and roses… and him. She'd sat up and pushed her hair out of her eyes. That's when a thought dropped into her head. A solution. A possible way forward with her search for answers. It's taken her a couple of days to work up to putting it into action, though.

This morning she got up early, went into her kitchen and carefully pulled a selection of ingredients from the cupboards. She mixed and baked her best gooey chocolate brownies, then cut them into precise squares while they were still warm. She hopes Jason isn't the type to lie in bed until mid-afternoon on a Saturday.

He answers the door dressed and looking as if he's not long stepped out of the shower. 'I wondered if you'd christened that coffee machine yet?' Heather asks, reciting her carefully rehearsed opener. 'I was baking… and I thought these would be the perfect accompaniment.'

'Well, yeah… I did.' Her heart sinks. She knew this was a stupid idea. It was just sheer desperation that drove her to it. 'But, you know, they're not a one-use deal. I can always fire it up for a second round.' He smiles and opens the door wider. She follows him inside.

She was right. His flat is almost identical to hers in layout, but it feels very different. More masculine. There is lots of wood and leather, and the hallway is painted a deep red. It should make the space look dark and pokey, but somehow it's warm and inviting. Heather thinks back to her white walls and for the first time wonders if others find them a bit clinical.

They go into the kitchen. The cabinets are arranged differently, probably because of the lack of a back door, and there is a small circular table in one corner. Jason motions for her to sit, while he prepares the compact coffee machine on the counter. A minute later a steaming cup appears in front of her. He makes himself one, sits down opposite her, and immediately reaches for the plate, eyebrows raised in question. Heather nods.

He closes his eyes and moans after the first bite, causing her to glow with pride. She doesn't bake very often, even though she's really good at it. Mainly because there's no one to share it with and it's not healthy to eat a whole pan of brownies by oneself.

'Amazing,' Jason mutters when his mouth is free enough of chocolate to speak. 'If I'd known you could bake like this, I'd have insisted you come up earlier.'

Heather flushes and she hopes it hasn't turned her neck red. 'I… I just wanted to say thank you for all you did regarding the flood.'

He reaches for a second brownie, not bothering with the silent request for permission this time. 'I'd have been a bit of a bastard to leave you to drown on your own. Anyway, that was weeks ago.'

'And for being so nice to me... cooking me dinner the other night.'

He smiles. 'Well, you did half of it – and the complicated half at that. But if this is what a couple of charred steaks gets me, then I'm not going to complain!'

He smiles that gorgeous wonky smile as a third brownie ends up in his mouth. Heather starts to wonder if she's done the right thing coming here, but it's too late to back out now. She doesn't say anything for a while, too caught up with finding the right words to find any at all.

Jason stops smiling and brushes the dark crumbs from around his lips with the back of his hand. 'Are you okay?'

She nods. 'It's just... Just...'

He leans closer. 'Just?'

Heather sighs. Here goes. 'There's someone I need to find – someone connected with my past – and I've run into a brick wall.'

'I presume you've tried Google, Facebook, all that sort of stuff?'

She nods again. 'All I know is their name and that they used to live in this area about twenty years ago. Other than that, all the internet searching I've done has resulted in a big, fat blank.'

'How irritating.'

'Irritating doesn't even begin to describe it.' Heather looks down at her hands and then adds, 'Do you think...? I mean... I was just wondering if...?'

She glances up at Jason. He's looking right into her eyes, waiting. If she ever felt safe enough with someone to ask them a favour this huge, it's him. She doesn't know why. Usually, she runs a mile from guys but she feels she can trust this one. 'Would you be able to help me?'

She waits, her heart thudding unevenly in her chest, and then he grins at her. 'Of course!' He immediately jumps up and leaves the room, only to return with a laptop mere seconds later. Heather feels giddy. She had no idea it was going to be this easy!

He pulls his chair further round the curve of the table and positions the laptop so they can both see the screen. It's already on, so he just has to wake it up with a password, and then they're away. He opens the browser. 'What's the name?'

Heather stares at the screen. 'That's Google. I've already tried Google.'

Jason looks confused. 'But I thought you wanted help?'

She shakes her head. 'No. I mean, I do, but…'

The penny drops then. She sees the light go out of Jason's eyes. 'It's just you want me to use my work access to records to help you find this person.'

The world seems to have gone still. Heather makes herself say the word, but it comes out shaky and breathy, 'Yes.'

He shuts the laptop and pushes his chair away so he can stand up. 'I can't do that,' he says, his expression dark.

Heather feels as if she's dying inside, shrivelling into nothing. But she can't stop now. This is her only hope. 'Not even if it was really, really important? Life-changing, even?'

He gives her a look of exasperation and disbelief – funnily enough, the exact same one Faith wears – and walks to the other side of the kitchen, where he backs up and leans against the counter, his long legs braced in front of him. He looks away and when he turns back he doesn't fix his gaze on her but on the half-demolished plate of brownies in the middle of the table. 'That's what all this was about, wasn't it? The brownies? And there was me thinking you genuinely liked me!'

She swallows. Even if she could talk in this moment, she couldn't deny it. He must read the truth in her eyes because he makes a scoffing sound.

'It's not like that!' Heather manages. She doesn't want him thinking she doesn't like him, because that really would be a lie. It's not her fault he happens to have the perfect job to help her. To be honest, she'd have been much happier if it'd been someone else.

'No?' he says. 'What you're asking me to do is unethical, and even if it wasn't I'm not sure I'd say yes. You're using me, Heather – to find some crummy ex-boyfriend you can't bear to be without, I bet – so I don't care how many bloody cakes you cook, the answer is no.'

Heather's eyes sting but she holds the tears back. She can't humiliate herself further by crying in front of him.

'I think you'd better go.' He walks over and picks up the plate of brownies. 'And you can take these with you.'

She wishes she could tell him he's wrong, but she can't. About the ex-boyfriend, maybe, but not about the rest. So she takes the plate, tucks her head down and hurries from his flat.

CHAPTER TWENTY-THREE

SLIPPERS

I always thought slippers were happy shoes, warm, comforting and safe. I didn't think a slipper was the kind of thing that could make you sad. But then, one day, I saw a lone towelling mule lying in the middle of the street. It looked odd there. Lonely. Bedraggled. I wanted to go and pick it up. I wanted to rescue it.

THEN

Heather's dad is holding out his hand, waiting for her to take it. Heather wants to. She doesn't want to disappoint him, but…

She turns and looks at her mother, who is still on the floor, crying, and shakes her head.

'Sweetpea…'

'No,' Heather says. She doesn't ever think she's interrupted her father before, but this is something she has to do. This is important. 'It's being mean. We can't leave Mummy alone.'

Her mum sniffs, then lifts her head. Sometimes Heather thinks her mother is too busy with all the *stuff* to notice her properly any more, but their eyes meet now. Her mum's are shining with thankfulness and love. It feels as if her mum has come back, even though she didn't go anywhere.

'Heather!' Faith says crossly. 'Don't be idiotic.'

'Don't say that!' Heather shouts back. 'You're always making out you're cleverer than me but you're not! You're just older. It's fair this way. One grown-up and one kid.'

'You're mad! It's a chance to get out of this house!'

Heather looks around at the bare walls and the clear floors. 'But the house is nice now. I like it again. And I want to sleep in my new bedroom.' She glances at her father. He's listening, taking it all in.

'Okay,' he says slowly. 'If you want to stay, I'm not going to make you leave.' He turns to look at Heather's mother. 'Chris? You need to pull yourself together for Heather's sake, okay? As for what happens next...' he shrugs. 'We'll talk tomorrow.'

The reminder that he's leaving sets her mum off again. She drags herself up off the floor and follows him and Faith down the stairs and out of the front door in her slippers. It's getting dark now and a little bit cold, so Heather follows them as far as the front door then stops.

'Please, Stephen! Please?'

Her dad and Faith are in the car now. The engine starts. Her mum's crying gets louder. In fact, it doesn't even sound like crying now, more like howling. Heather creeps down the path, even though she's shivering, because somebody needs to look after her mum, and her dad clearly isn't going to.

The car pulls away and her mum runs after it. Faith is staring through the back window, looking as if she's in pain, but then her lip crumples and she shakes her head, turns around and slumps down in the seat.

Their mum runs off the pavement and into the middle of the street. Her slippers come off, first one and then the other, but she keeps going until the family's red Sierra is a tiny speck in the distance.

A few of the neighbours have come to the bottom of their driveways and are looking this way and that, trying to work out what all the noise is about. Heather is standing at the gate, hugging herself, and she doesn't like the way they're looking at her mum, so she runs along the pavement towards her.

Before she reaches her, Heather spots one of her mother's slippers and hesitates. She knows she's not supposed to go in the road by herself, but it's really quiet down their street – cars hardly ever come down it unless they belong to someone who lives there – so she hops off the kerb and picks it up. The other one is a bit farther along, so she grabs it as well.

She finds her mother flopped down on the ground like a rag doll. Heather can't hear any sound, but her mum's ribcage is juddering. She's got to that bit in crying when the sounds don't come. Heather knows what that's like because she cries that way when Patrick Hull's gang chases her after school.

She goes up to her mother and rubs her back like she's trying to wake her up. Her mum flinches, but it's a few seconds before she looks up.

'Come on,' Heather says. 'It's time to go back inside.'

For a moment it looks as if her mum doesn't understand what Heather's saying, but then she nods and reaches out and hugs her. Heather lets her, even though she's really, really embarrassed that the neighbours are still looking. When her mum releases her,

Heather holds out the slippers to her, trying to smile. That just makes her mum cry again. 'My darling, darling Heather,' she says between sniffs. 'What would I do without you?'

Heather doesn't say anything back. She just helps her up and leads her back inside the house.

CHAPTER TWENTY-FOUR

NOW

Heather can't sleep again that night. She can't stop thinking about Jason. She can't stop seeing the look of disappointment and disgust on his face. She didn't know she had the power to hurt someone that way.

She stews on it until the small hours, when she sinks into a fitful and restless sleep, and then she stews on it all the next day. She's cataloguing letters at work, a job she usually enjoys, but they don't hold her interest. She has to keep reading the date and address on each one several times before logging it, because she keeps forgetting.

That evening, before she can talk herself out of it, she buys a nice bottle of red wine on the way home and thinks about making her way up to Jason's flat and knocking on his door with her peace offering. She thinks about it for two hours and twenty-seven minutes, even picking up the bottle and heading for the front door a couple of times, but she ends up scurrying back to her living room and dumps the bottle down on the little table beside her sofa.

It's as she's sitting there, head in hands, that she hears soft whistling coming from the back garden. She looks up to see Jason himself out there. He's not looking in her direction. The sun set about twenty minutes ago and she hasn't turned the light on yet, so he probably can't see her, but she can just make him out in the twilight, strolling down to the end of the garden, breathing in the mild evening air.

Before she's even decided to move, she's heading outside. She walks out into the garden, the grass cool and soft against her bare feet. Jason's staring out across the valley, so he doesn't spot her at first, but he turns when he hears her coming up behind him. When he sees who it is, he tenses.

'I'm sorry,' she says.

Something behind his eyes flickers. 'Fine. Thanks.' He turns and looks at the view again, dismissing her. Heather digs her heels into the lawn to make herself stay there and takes a deep breath.

'Please... just give me a chance to explain?'

He sighs and answers without turning his head. 'You've got five minutes.'

She nods. It won't be long enough but it's more than she deserves. 'Actually, it'd be easier to show you than to tell you.'

He looks round. He's still annoyed with her, but she's caught his interest.

'Will you come with me?'

He thinks for a moment, then nods, so Heather leads him back down the garden and into her flat. She carefully retrieves the key to the spare bedroom and silently unlocks the door, her hands shaking all the while. She hasn't had a proper look in here since coming back from the hotel, and the sight of the stacked clutter makes her feel dizzy.

'This,' she says, 'all belonged to my mother.' She averts her eyes from the chest of drawers that contains the spoils of her Mother-care trips.

'You said.' Jason is looking at her. She's not great at reading people, but she senses he's not as angry as he was before, that maybe he even wants to understand but he needs more. Heather knows that, but the 'more' he needs is more than she's ever told anyone, ever given anyone before.

'My mother was… mentally ill,' she says quietly. 'She was…' Oh, these words are so hard to get out. It feels as if she's admitting something about herself, not her mother. In the end, she just spits it out fast. 'She was a compulsive hoarder.'

Jason looks surprised but not horrified. He hasn't run away yet. 'And this is…'

'What's left of her hoard. The council had served an order to clean out the house and when she…' She breaks off, and tears burn her eyes. Usually she can turn this around, make them go away, but she has a horrible feeling her usual tactics of deep breathing and willpower aren't going to work this time.

She has to walk away. She heads back down the hall and into the living room, where she stands in the centre of the rug and breathes deeply, not even caring that Jason has followed her, that he can see her performing her ritual.

He comes up behind her but stops just out of reach. When he speaks his voice has lost that hard edge. 'How did she die, Heather?'

Silence, wide and spacious. Heather collects herself and fills it with her words.

'She had high blood pressure. They think she lost her medication in all the clutter and just stopped taking it, and she had a stroke.' That's probably enough information, but now she's started she can't seem to stop. 'When the postman alerted the emergency services, they couldn't get a stretcher inside because of the state of the house. It took them hours to get her out. If they'd been able to go straight in, maybe...' She hiccups, holds her hand briefly over her mouth before carrying on. 'They lost precious time. She died a couple of days later.'

Jason doesn't say anything. He just walks towards her and wraps her in his arms. She lays her head against his shoulder and the tears come. It's such a relief. She feels as if she's been holding herself upright, no one to support her, for most of her life. As her mind starts to drift in the oddest way, she wonders if she could stay like this, warm and safe, forever, but eventually Jason loosens his hold and steps back so he can look at her.

'And that stuff in the room? That's all of it?'

Heather shakes her head. 'The council had an order out for compulsory cleaning, and when my mother died and was no longer blocking their efforts, they enforced it. I didn't know at first, so I didn't get there until they were three days into the clean-up.'

Jason looks shocked. 'You didn't get a chance to go through anything?'

'No. And, to be honest, I really didn't want to. They did me a favour by saving what looked like important papers and family mementoes and anything that hadn't been ruined, and put it all into boxes. I stopped them chucking out any more – my mum would keep precious things in the weirdest of places – then I hired a van and brought it here, intending to go through it, but...' she trails off. Now he knows the real reason she couldn't face going through her mother's stuff.

He nods. 'Hoarding is a kind of addiction, right?'

'I think so. At least, my mother never seemed to be able to stop, even in those rare periods where she could see how destructive it was.'

Jason walks over to the sofa and perches on the arm. 'Well, hoarding I might not have much experience of, but addicts I get. My dad was an alcoholic.'

A long, low breath escapes Heather's body. It's as if she's been on high alert for so many years, and now the threat level has been downgraded to something more manageable. She takes a good look at Jason, really looks at him: past the ruffled dark hair and lean physique. She can't quite marry her idea of him up with what he's just told her. Jason can't have problems. Not real ones. He's too perfect, too normal.

He smiles back at her, a rueful one, a we're-in-this-together one. Heather can't help smiling back, just a little.

'Okay,' he says, shifting his legs so he's more comfortable. 'Things are starting to make a bit more sense to me now – why you were so freaked out the night of the flood, the way you disappeared for what seemed like weeks afterwards.'

'Only six days,' she says, feeling a sudden pang of nostalgia for the Park Lodge Hotel.

'And, yes, I was angry with you the other day, but I'm ready to listen now. The only thing I don't understand is what all of that...' he says, waving a hand in the rough direction of the spare room, 'has to do with what you asked me.'

Heather goes to the bookcase and retrieves the plastic box where the photograph albums and the first newspaper article are stored. She places it carefully on the desk and unsnaps the lid. Her hands shake as she pulls out the folder with the newspaper story, but she keeps going. She slides the flimsy paper from its home and hands it to Jason, lets him read the headline.

'That's me,' she says. 'That girl in the picture is me.'

Jason's head jerks up. He swears. Yup, thinks Heather, that pretty much covers it.

'Hoarding is often triggered by something traumatic,' she adds. 'You think this is what did it for your mother?'

Heather gives him a little half-shrug. He swears again, more colourfully this time, then shakes his head in disbelief. 'Wow. I mean… to grow up knowing this…'

She inhales sharply. 'Well, that's just it. I only just found out.'

Jason's mouth drops open. If he wasn't already perching on the arm of her sofa – bringing his face on a level closer to hers, she notices – she suspects he might have sat down at that revelation. 'No one told you?'

She shakes her head. 'Seems there was a big family secret. I don't know why I'm surprised, though. My family are good at those – secrets. Experts, in fact.'

Even her. Especially her. But she doesn't say that.

Jason looks at her and she knows he understands.

'I need…' she begins, and then wonders what she really does need. More than she can tell him, that's for sure, but she doesn't want to scare him off with her own sordid little compulsions; her mother's are terrifying enough. She breathes out, tries again. 'I need to find out more. There are too many questions cluttering up my head. I need to answer them, sort them and tidy them away. Maybe then I'll be able to move past this.'

Maybe I'll stop turning into my mother before it's too late, she adds silently.

'That's why I came to you… why I asked you…'

He's silent for a few seconds, and his answer when it comes is wary. 'Okay.'

'I found more newspaper stories like this one,' she continues. 'I know the name of the woman who took me.' She walks to the other end of the room and stares out the open French doors into the darkness. 'I just wanted to know who she is, why she did it. I had this idea of trying to find her. It was all I could think of.' She smiles and turns round, even laughs a little. 'Crazy, I know.'

He stands up and walks over to her, looking deadly serious. 'Not at all, under the circumstances. I think I'd be tempted to do the same.'

'You're just saying that.'

'No. My dad upped and left one day when I was sixteen. We didn't see him for years. I know how that uncertainty can eat away at you. I even ditched school one day and caught a train all the way to Bristol to see if he'd gone to visit my uncle. My mum was furious, especially as it was the day of my history GCSE.' He shrugs. 'Like you said – stupid – but sometimes life makes us do stupid things.'

'What happened?'

'Oh, he turned up again after I'd gone to university. Mum wouldn't take him back, thank goodness, so he just drifts around on the fringes of our lives, hiding away when he's drinking heavily and then appearing when he's doing better.'

Heather is silent for a moment. 'I meant about the history exam, but...'

Jason laughs and she marvels at him. How can he do that hot on the heels of telling her something so painful? Something he said as effortlessly as if he'd been telling her the weather forecast.

'Oh, I did resits. Got an A.'

'I'm glad,' she says, and then they go quiet again. This time there's a warmth to the silence that wasn't there before. 'I'm sorry I asked you to break the rules,' she eventually says. 'I was desperate.

I'd tried everything I could think of – internet-based and non-internet-based. But I shouldn't have put you in that position. I'm so sorry.'

'If you'd told me all this right off the bat, I probably wouldn't have said yes, but I wouldn't have got angry.'

Heather nods. It seems so obvious now it's all said and done, but she realizes she's got so used to only giving out the minimum information that it didn't even occur to her to open up a bit more until her own bumbling actions pushed her into it. 'So you'll forgive me?'

He smiles. 'Yeah, we're friends again.'

There's that word again. Friends. *If only you could make words physical, Heather thinks, catch them like butterflies and keep them in a jar. That single word from Jason would be her first specimen.*

His smile grows brighter. 'Is there any reason we're standing here in the dark?'

Heather laughs, and as she walks over to turn on a lamp she spots the bottle of wine she put next to it earlier. She pushes the switch with her thumb, and the living room is filled with gentle yellow light. She holds the bottle up. 'Would you like some?' And then she realizes what they've just been talking about and quickly corrects herself. 'But, obviously, I don't know how you feel about… if you even…' While she remembers other people drinking beer at the barbecue, now she thinks about it, she doesn't remember seeing Jason with one.

Thankfully, Jason rescues her. 'No, it's okay. I drink. I just don't overindulge much. Can't quite cope with the idea of stumbling into the bathroom after a big night out, looking blearily into the mirror and seeing my father staring back at me.'

Heather nods, remembering how much that accusation of Faith's hurt, and goes to fetch a couple of glasses. She returns with a modest amount of Merlot in each and hands one to Jason. She takes the armchair and he settles on one end of the sofa.

They talk about other things for a bit – books, music, TV shows they love and hate – but as Jason drains his glass and stands up, he says, 'Thanks. I'm glad we patched things up.'

'Me too,' Heather says, standing up and walking closer. It seems to be the thing to do.

'And I want to apologize, too – for overreacting the other day.'

Heather waves her hands around. 'No, no, no…' She knows it was all her fault.

'It's just, for a moment, it reminded me of someone else, someone in my past who was just after what she could get.'

'A girlfriend?' Heather asks, and is amazed at her own audacity.

'Yes.' He sighs. 'Wasn't great at the time, but it's for the best. She wasn't who I thought she was. But I shouldn't have taken how I feel about her out on you.' He reaches out and touches her shoulder, just lightly, just momentarily.

When he pulls his hand away she wants to follow it. She wants to walk into the solid mass of his chest and stay there, feel his arms come around her. That hug earlier on has possibly turned her into an addict of a different kind, because she can't stop craving the sensation.

He smiles at her. 'If there *is* something I can do – legally, I mean – just ask. Honestly.'

She nods again. It's an echo of the former gesture, weak and unconvincing – at least to her – because as she follows him to the front door and sees him out, all she can think about is that he's been so nice to her and maybe he shouldn't, because she isn't who she seems to be either.

CHAPTER TWENTY-FIVE

NOW

Jason knocks on Heather's door. She opens it, knowing it's him, because she can recognize his blurry silhouette on the other side of the textured glass. Without saying anything, he hands her a thin folder.

Heather frowns. 'What's this?'

His ever-present smile is missing. 'Take a look.'

She peeks inside. There are only a few lines of writing, but enough to guess what this might be, and she gasps softly. 'You'd better come in.'

He does, shutting the door quickly behind him.

Heather walks towards the kitchen, her heart beating firmly. 'Is this what I think it is?'

Jason nods.

'But... You said...'

'I know, I know. But I couldn't stop thinking about what you told me. Normally I'm pretty much a "play by the rules" kind of guy, but...' He completes the sentence with a shrug. 'You needed my help. It seemed like the right thing to do.'

Heather pulls a single sheet of paper from inside the cardboard folder. Staring at it, she reaches over and absent-mindedly clicks the button down on the kettle, then begins to read out loud, needing to hear the words as well as see them: 'Patricia Waites, 14c Hill Croft Road, Hastings.'

'It's old,' Jason says. 'More than ten years ago.'

Heather is frowning. 'Hastings?'

Jason looks over her shoulder at the piece of paper, even though he already knows what it says. 'Is that a problem?'

'That's where she took me! Why on earth would she go back there? It's creepy!'

Jason nods. 'Yeah, kind of revisiting the scene of the crime.' He pauses for a moment. 'Did she go to prison for what she did?'

'There wasn't much to go on. I did a bit more digging recently and discovered she was arrested and sentenced. The judge ordered a psychiatric evaluation, so I don't know if that meant prison after that or not.'

'Well, there you go,' he replies. 'Obviously not a person who was thinking straight.'

Heather opens a cupboard and takes two perfectly aligned mugs down from the shelf and makes some tea. They sit down at the table, mugs between their hands.

'It's still weird, though,' Jason muses. 'Why would she go back? Did she live there at the time she… you know… did what she did?'

Heather shakes her head and takes a soothing glug of hot tea. 'No. That's the thing. Unless the newspaper was wrong. It said she lived in this area, which makes sense, I suppose. I was taken while I was waiting outside my school – I was in the playground on my own, waiting for my mum to pick me up. It was just one of those fluke things.'

He nods. 'In the wrong place at the wrong time.'

'Yes. Well, that's what I've been thinking since I found out the details, but what if the paper was wrong and she did live in Hastings? It's what… more than fifty miles away and it'd take over an hour to drive from there to here. If that's true, it can't have just been an opportunistic thing. It feels more…'

'Planned,' Jason finishes for her. She's grateful she didn't have to say it out loud; her stomach is churning hard enough as it is.

'Yes,' she whispers and closes her eyes, concentrates on the warmth of the mug against her fingers. She wishes she could remember that time, but whenever she tries to picture Hastings, all that comes to her mind is the holiday with Aunt Kathy, all laughter and fun and sunshine. But that was in Eastbourne, not Hastings. It makes no sense. Her only theory is that she has subconsciously whitewashed the more traumatic events with something nicer. The memory is lost. Buried. Like a forgotten piece of rubbish at the bottom of her mother's hoard.

Jason's voice drifts through her thoughts. 'You're stronger than I am… the way you're dealing with this. Especially finding out after all this time. I think I'd be a mess if I were in your shoes.'

Heather shakes her head. She's not strong. She's not even close.

'Don't sell yourself short,' Jason tells her. 'Deciding to find out the truth – the whole truth – like this is incredibly brave.'

Heather gives him a weak smile in return, but she doesn't feel very brave at all.

'What are you going to do?'

Heather sighs. 'I really don't know. Bow at the altar of Google some more, I suppose. Hope the search gods smile on me now I have something more to go on.'

Jason gets up, puts his mug in the sink, and looks at her. 'Well, if you need any help, just yell.' He glances at the folder on the table and adds, 'Apart from the confidential, work-related kind, that is. Sorry, that's my limit. But if you need someone to talk to…'

Heather releases her mug and stands up too. 'Thank you,' she says hoarsely. She has the stupidest urge to step forward and kiss him on the cheek. She picks the folder up and hugs it to her chest to prevent herself from doing so. *This is a good man,* she thinks to herself. He said they were friends and, unlike others in the past, he's proved it in word and deed. Even so, she hopes this rush of warmth she's feeling towards him is just gratitude.

But then he does that shoulder-touching thing again and she can't help reacting. She raises herself onto her tiptoes and presses her lips softly to his cheek. The instant it's over she feels awkward, sure she's overstepped the mark, so she looks down as she pulls away. She's about to mumble her apologies when something makes her look at him.

He's close. He hasn't backed away. Hasn't pulled a face of disgust. In fact, he's looking the most serious she's ever seen him. She can't stop watching him watching her, especially when he stops looking in her eyes and his gaze drops a fraction lower. Her lips start to tingle. She wants to say something but she's frozen…

And then – *snap!* – the moment is over. Eye contact is back and she can see a million thoughts whirling around behind his eyes. A million reasons, probably, why he shouldn't do what every instinct told her he was about to do.

He nods, as if confirming something with himself. 'Take care,' he says quietly and then he's gone, leaving Heather clutching the folder, both relieved and gutted he made the right call.

CHAPTER TWENTY-SIX

NOW

Halfway down the M25, just as Heather's car crests the North Downs, something starts making a funny whirring noise. She drives on for a bit, hoping it's just something in the air vents, but a few minutes later she pulls onto the hard shoulder, just in case. No warning lights are on, but she turns the engine off anyway and sits there wondering what to do. Perhaps she should double-check before calling roadside assistance?

She turns the key in the ignition but the starter just coughs half-heartedly and gives up. She tries again. Same thing. She turns the key again and again, until all that is left is a wheezing breath.

Fabulous.

She's running late already, thanks to a collision just outside Orpington, and now she'll be lucky if she's at work by lunchtime. Thankfully, it's not raining as the weather forecast had hinted. She's also grateful it's not blazingly sunny as she gets out of the car, pulls her handbag out of the passenger seat, and climbs over the barrier to stand on the verge. At least she's not going to bake like an egg on a hot rock while she waits for roadside assistance.

After calling them, she settles down to wait. The long grass is dry and it tickles the backs of her knees under her navy dress. To pass the time, she opens Google Maps on her phone and types in the name of the town the recovery guy said he was coming from. In the present traffic conditions, it should take half an hour.

Watching cars is boring, so after a while she pulls her phone out again. She stares at Google Maps for a second, then types in a destination. It is exactly forty-seven miles to Hastings from here, straight down the A21 until you reach the sea.

She tries to picture the town again, a favourite haunt of her mum and dad's on a bank-holiday weekend before the divorce. She tries to remember the fish and chips she knows they ate on the promenade as the sun went down, the inevitable weeks of pocket money lost in the penny arcades. Snatches of recollections come, but they're all mixed up with memories of so many other towns like it on the Kent and Sussex coast. Is she really remembering it right, or are images of Eastbourne, Margate and Brighton slipping in there, blurring the truth? It's hard to tell. Even the memories she can pinpoint of the other places are frighteningly similar – wide beaches made up of large, flinty pebbles, weathered groynes and Victorian piers. How is she supposed to know which is which?

She realizes she should have paid more attention to her childhood, that maybe she should have hoarded memories the way her mother hoarded objects. But collecting anything had seemed dangerous and at the time she hadn't known she'd need them. Why would she? Her mother had a million items in her home, each one attached to a bit of family history. She'd kept the memories for them.

Besides, it had been nice to let it all go, let it all fly out of her head. That way she didn't have to think of how pathetic her life had been and how much she'd hated it.

Over the last few days she's been tempted to drop this whole abduction thing and move on, but now a familiar ache begins to throb in her chest. All the things she lost. All the things she never had because of her mother's hoarding. The ache becomes an ember and the ember begins to smoulder. Heather stands up abruptly, even though there's no sign yet of the recovery truck.

That woman shouldn't get away with it.

Okay, on one level Heather knows she didn't. Maybe she paid her debt to society, in whatever way the courts saw fit, but what about the Lucas family? Had that debt been settled? The growing warmth in her belly, the feeling of being too jittery to fit inside her own skin, suggests not. She wants to walk up to Patricia Waites and look her in the eye, to see if she knows what she did. To see if she even cares. For some reason, that's important.

By the time the man in the truck has arrived, declared the noise was indeed something stuck in her ventilation but confirmed her battery is on its last legs, Heather has hatched a plan. She thanks the recovery driver for jump-starting the car and heads for the retail park just outside of Swanham on the way to work. There's one of those places there, the kind that does tyres and exhausts and such like. They should be able to sort her car out.

She hopes so because she's going to need it this weekend. She knows it's probably hopeless, but she's going to go to that address in Hastings and she's going to knock on the door.

Could it have been where Waites took her for those sixteen days?

No, that's not right. The paper had said they were found at a B&B – not one of the ones on the seafront, but one down a back street with no sea view. But still…

Maybe if she sees Hastings again, she'll remember something important.

* * *

At seven o'clock on Saturday morning, she loads up her car with a few essentials – sunblock, a couple of bottles of water – and makes sure her screen wash is topped up. She imagines if she had a significant other, he'd be gently teasing her about this being a trip to Hastings not Outer Mongolia, and it makes her smile. She knows she's making a big thing of this, but it *feels* like a big thing. A scary thing. These small preparations give her a sense of control.

By 7.18 a.m. she's ready. She checks her handbag is on the passenger seat, takes a deep breath, and closes the car door. When she twists the key in the ignition, it turns over but doesn't start. What the heck? It's a brand-new battery! This isn't supposed to happen. She gets out, lifts the bonnet and stares at the silent innards of her hatchback.

'Problems?'

She jumps up, almost banging her head on the underside of the bonnet, to find Jason standing beside her. He's in a T-shirt, shorts and running shoes. Earphones, recently plucked from his ears, are dangling round his neck.

'It won't start.'

He nods, and squints under the bonnet. 'Turn it over?'

Heather obligingly jumps back in the driving seat and turns the key in the ignition, with much the same effect as the last attempt.

'How old's your battery?'

Heather lets out a frustrated groan. 'Four days! I just had it replaced, so I don't think it's that.' She removes the rod holding the bonnet up and lets it slam down. The loud clang is rather satisfying. 'Brilliant. More inconvenience. More expense.'

Jason puts his hands on his hips and stares at the closed bonnet as if he has X-ray vision and can see exactly what's going on inside. 'It could be the starter motor, or even the alternator, but you're going to have to get someone to look at it. I could give you a jump-start, but that will only help for the outward journey.'

He spots the large bag on the back seat. 'Planning on running away?' he asks.

'No.' She's slightly disturbed that he's already pegged her as a bolter. 'Actually, I'm taking a trip to the seaside.'

He smiles at first, taking her words at face value, but then the penny drops. 'Hastings?'

She nods.

'You're going on your own?'

'Yes.' She's so used to doing most things on her own that she hasn't even thought of asking anyone to go with her.

'And you say you're not brave...'

'I don't think I am brave,' Heather says. 'I think I'm just really, really desperate to know the truth.' She looks at the car and sighs. 'I suppose I'll just have to go next weekend.'

'Waiting another seven days would drive me crazy,' he says.

All Heather can do is give him a weak smile and a shrug in return. 'Tell me about it. But what can I do? Like you say, I might not be able to start the car again for the return journey if I risk it, and I don't want to have to pay yet another mechanic to sort me out so I can get back home.'

Jason nods then goes quiet. From the look on his face, he's weighing something up. Finally, he drags a hand through his already-messy hair and says, 'I'll run you down to Hastings if you want. I haven't got anything better to do today – apart from grocery shopping with half the rest of Bromley – and a trip to the seaside sounds like the perfect way to avoid it.'

Heather takes a step back. 'I can't ask you to do that!'

'You're not asking – I'm offering. Besides, I feel a bit responsible. If I hadn't given you that address, you wouldn't be doing this.'

'But…'

'And if I were in your shoes, I'd want someone with me. I mean, the chances are that it'll be a wild-goose chase, but what if it isn't? This is huge, Heather.'

She swallows. She knows it is.

'Besides, who doesn't want to go to the beach on a day like this?'

There is that, Heather thinks. She tries desperately to conjure up more good reasons why she should say no. The only problem is that all the little speech bubbles that pop up inside her head are empty. The truth is, she would like someone with her, and if she had to pick, she'd pick Jason. 'Okay,' she says. 'That would be very nice. Thank you.'

He grins at her. 'Great! Do you mind if we set off in about half an hour? I could really do with a shower first. Shall I come and knock for you about quarter to eight?'

* * *

Twenty-five minutes later, Jason wanders out of the house looking fresh and clean and carrying a crash helmet. Heather stares at it as he walks towards her and hands it to her. 'Here you go.'

'B-but I thought we were going in your car!' is all she can say.

He just smiles at her and dumps something heavy in her arms. 'You can't go to Hastings in a car on a day like this!' he says. 'It'd be positively criminal!'

She looks down and sees that he's wearing the kind of ribbed black leather trousers bikers do, and that the heavy stuff in her

180

arms looks suspiciously similar – a jacket and trousers, she'd guess if she took a closer look.

'They should be okay,' he tells her. 'She was a bit taller than you, but I reckon they're the right size.'

'She?' croaks Heather.

'Long gone,' is all he says. Heather thinks about the woman he mentioned the other day and realizes that, if he'd gone to the trouble of getting her the right gear to join him on his bike, it must have been serious. 'Let's just say she's not likely to be using these again, nor would she want to.'

'What do I, you know, wear...' Heather swallows, 'underneath?'

'What you've got on is fine,' he says, looking her up and down. Heather suddenly feels very self-conscious in her jeans and T-shirt. He motions towards the house, shooing her back inside. 'It'll only take a few minutes to put them on. While you're doing that, I'll get the bike ready.' And he heads towards the garage nestling up against the side of the house.

When she comes back outside she feels a bit weird, as if another person has been painted on top of boring old Heather. Noticing the creak of the leather as she moves, she pauses and looks at the bags dumped on the driveway. Jason is revving up the motorbike. He has a helmet on now too, a black one with a visor, which is presently tipped up, and he's wearing a leather jacket zipped up to his chin, despite the promise of heat this day is bringing. 'What about my stuff?' she yells above the noise of the engine.

Jason pauses and the noise dies away. He glances at the over-stuffed beach bag and handbag. 'What do you actually need?'

Her purse. Her phone. Not much else, really. All the details and directions – even the last known address for Patricia Waites – are stored inside her head. She pulls her purse and phone from her handbag and stows them in the inside pockets of the jacket.

Jason was right. It is a pretty good fit. A little long in the arms, maybe, but otherwise snug without being too tight. Then she shoves the bags in the boot of her car, locking it securely behind her.

'Right,' she says. 'What next?'

His smile is hidden by the chin guard of his helmet, but she can see it in his eyes. 'Now we go. Climb on.' And he snaps the visor down into place.

She hesitates for a moment, then swings one leg over the bike and climbs on behind him. 'You're not going to go too fast, are you?' she asks, wondering what to do with her arms and hands.

He twists round to look at her over his shoulder. 'Nah. This is a Harley. Think of it more like a Rolls Royce than a Ferrari. Is this your first time on a bike?' Heather nods. 'Then I'll be gentle with you,' he adds with a glimmer of mischief in his eyes.

Heather doesn't have to ask what to do with her arms when he turns the throttle and the bike begins to move, because she grabs on tight round his middle, closes her eyes and presses herself against his back.

CHAPTER TWENTY-SEVEN

BAG

It's a pretty ordinary handbag. It's black, and not even real leather. It has three flashy gold zips on the front (mostly for decoration, it has to be said) and no discernibly useful pockets. Even though I've seen at least three other girls at my school with one exactly like it, I love it to bits.

THEN

Heather hitches her bag onto her shoulder and walks purposefully across the playground towards the school gates. When she first started at Highstead Grammar, she had a massive backpack, one her mum had actually gone out and bought for her, saying she was so proud she'd got into Highstead. Heather was pleased too, but not for the same reason as her mother.

Most of the kids from Heather's primary school have moved on to secondary schools in the Bromley area, but grammar schools have a wider catchment area and Highstead is just outside Sidcup town centre. It's even under a different local education authority from her last school. Nobody here knows her.

It doesn't make the kids any less vile if they decide you don't fit in, though. It didn't take Heather long to work out the backpack was a huge mistake, even though it was on the uniform list. The older kids – especially the Year Eights, seeking to establish their dominance – pick on the Year Sevens for having them. Heather has started to get nervous every time she nears a group of older girls because she's seen them hook someone by that little carrying strap at the top of their backpack when they walk past, yanking them backwards and wrenching their shoulders. Then they laugh and say 'sorry' with their eyes narrowed, daring their target to retaliate. It only had to happen to her twice before she told her mum that she'd lost her backpack in the house somewhere. Not a complete lie, because it is in the house – Heather buried it very carefully in what used to be the spare bedroom.

Her dad asks her about the state of the house every weekend when she goes to visit him at his flat, and she just shrugs and says it's pretty much the same. This is also not a lie – she's getting rather good at fudging the truth these days – because if she took a picture of the house in Hawksbury Road each Saturday, it *would* look pretty much the same as it had the previous week. What she doesn't tell her father is that it's almost as bad as it was before he left.

Two years is all it's taken for it to get that way. Two years! Doing that huge clear-out accomplished nothing. If anything, her mother's problem has escalated.

Her mum made her promise not to tell and at the time Heather agreed, but that was more than a year ago, when it was only the dining room and a couple of the bedrooms that had filled up. She wishes she hadn't said it now but a promise is a promise, isn't it?

And if she tells, her father will make her go and live with him. She kind of wants to do that, but how can she leave her mother in that house all by herself? She has nightmares about her mum being buried alive as it is. If Heather wasn't around to secretly tidy up now and then, those dreams might come true and it'd be her fault.

'I can't afford to buy you a new backpack,' her mother had said with no trace of condemnation or, it has to be said, guilt. Heather just shrugged, trying not to let on that she was elated. That had been her plan from the very start. However, it didn't escape Heather that her mother had enough money to buy two crates of celebrity-hairdresser styling products on QVC the very same afternoon.

'Can I use this one?' Heather said, producing a faux-leather handbag with the tags still on that she'd found earlier that morning in the downstairs toilet. She'd deliberately waited to break the sad news about the 'lost' backpack until she'd scoured the house for a suitable replacement.

'Hmm,' her mum had said. She took it from Heather and turned it over, opened the flap and peered inside. 'Are you sure this is suitable?'

'Oh, yes,' Heather said, quickly taking it back before her mum decided to keep it for herself (although it would probably end up back in the downstairs loo and never get used). 'Lots of the girls have bags like this.' And they did. The popular ones, anyway.

So now Heather is walking out of the main school building towards the gate, feeling just that little bit superior to the girls with the sports-shop messenger bags and backpacks, knowing that her oversized handbag with the gold zips looks good. It might even look a little bit cool.

'Hey.' A girl falls into step beside her.

'Hey,' Heather says back, feigning nonchalance when everything inside her is singing. This is Claudia Morris. She's in Heather's English class. Heather has been at Highstead for a month now, and this is the first time someone has willingly started walking with her unless they have been told to pair up by their dictator of a PE teacher.

'Oh, my God, that doodle you did of Miss Adams in English was hilarious!' Claudia says.

Heather smiles. They sit next to each other in that class, and today while their teacher was droning on about Dickens, she'd done a sketch of the headmistress. Miss Adams is tall and thin and she has this funny way of leaning back then sticking her head forward to balance herself out, so Heather just exaggerated it and made it all cartoony. Claudia glanced across just as she was finishing it.

'Can I show it to a friend?' she asks. 'Come on!' And the other girl drags her off towards the edge of the playground. Heather can hardly believe who's standing under the lone tree poking up from the sea of concrete. Tia Paine. She's officially the coolest girl in their year, on account of her uncle being one of the doctors on *Casualty*. She's always talking about the famous people who went round to her house in Blackheath for barbecues over the summer.

Claudia nudges Heather. 'Go on. You've still got it, haven't you?'

Heather nods and digs around in her handbag, thanking someone upstairs that she ditched the backpack yesterday.

'Hey, Tia!' Claudia calls, and Heather remembers that, while not part of the same clique now, they both went to the same private primary school together. 'Look at this.'

Tia turns from her ever-present posse of Charlotte, Summer and Henri – the 'backing singers', as Heather mentally calls them – and arches an eyebrow in their direction.

'Show her,' Claudia says, and Heather pauses a heartbeat before revealing the doodle in the back of her English book. 'Who's that?'

'Oh, my God!' Tia exclaims, her eyes lighting up. 'That's Awful Adams!' At the cue from their leader, the backing singers gather round and make appreciative noises; one of them even giggles. 'Awesome!' she adds. 'Have you got more? Can you do anyone else?'

Heather shakes her head. 'I suppose I can try...'

Tia's smile is white and perfect and dazzling. 'Well, bring them to me when you do,' she says, looking straight at Heather for a whole two seconds, and then she turns her attention to Claudia. 'We're going into town to get McDonald's. You coming, Claudie?'

Claudia practically glows at the attention. 'Sure,' she says, casting a sideways glance at Heather. 'Why not?'

And that's how it happens. That's how Heather ends up strolling down the road into Sidcup like she's one of Tia Paine's gang. Her spine grows taller and she flicks her hair back behind her shoulders the way the others do as they wait at the pedestrian crossing. The backing singers don't even bat an eyelid. Heather can see that Claudia – or Claudie, now Tia seems to have coined that nickname for her – is quietly trying not to burst with glee.

Claudia's using her, she realizes. Heather is her 'in'. But she doesn't mind one bit, because it's her 'in' too. This is what Heather's been waiting for. She's so full of hope and sunshine when the group arrives at McDonald's that she gets flustered and takes ages to tell the guy behind the counter what she wants. She's only got £1.50, so the choice isn't extensive. She ends up with a Sprite and fries, but they could have served her deep-fried floor sweepings and she wouldn't have cared.

The gang sit around a couple of tables, taking up more space than a group of six girls actually need to. Every time a group of boys in school uniform enter for their dose of junk food, the backing singers giggle and silently check with their leader before sighing over them or mocking them. Most of the boys only give the girls a cursory glance, as if they're too cool to be impressed by grammar-school uniforms, but one gang shouts over.

'Give us a chip then, gorgeous!' the ringleader directs at Tia.

She flicks her hair and looks away haughtily. 'Ugh! As if I'd take a second look at anyone from St Joseph's,' she mutters. 'Dream on, comprehensive boys.'

Heather smirks, copying the other girls, and prepares to flick her hair again – she's getting quite good at it now – when she sees this mouthy loser isn't some anonymous boy. It's Patrick Hull from St Michael's. Instead of flicking her hair away from her face, she lets it fall forward like a curtain. She sits silently, shaking and willing him away, dreading the sudden shout of 'Hobo!' when he inevitably spots her. Oh, God. She'd been 'Hobo Heather' throughout the whole of primary school. Moving to Highstead was supposed to free her from that.

But the gods must be smiling down on her, because he just makes a lewd comment and his mates all snort and giggle and then swagger off to get their cheeseburgers. Heather breathes a sigh of relief, and when she's sure they're far enough away she lifts her head again.

The girls tip their chins up and head out back onto the dusty High Street. 'Let's go to Boots and look at the nail varnish,' Tia says and walks off in that direction. Heather hesitates. She doesn't live round here and, unlike Tia, she doesn't have a Mercedes-driving au pair to act as her personal taxi service either. She should have been at the bus stop, waiting for the 269, ten minutes ago.

She doesn't say her goodbyes, though. How can she? This is Tia Paine and her gang! Even the Year Nines and Tens are nice to her because of her uncle. She can't risk doing anything to make Tia think she's uncool.

Walking towards Boots, they spot another Highstead uniform across the road. 'Oh, look! There's Fatty,' Tia sniggers. 'She's in my form. Total loser.'

'Yeah,' Charlotte says. 'She needs liposuction!'

Heather looks across at the girl. She's not fat, not really. Just not as rake-thin as Tia and her gang, who are all as leggy as young show ponies. The girl walking on the other side of the road looks miserable. Lonely. Heather can't say anything to defend her, though. As much as she feels for the girl, she'd do just about anything not to swap sides of the road and be standing there with her while Tia's gang laughed at them both.

'I heard she lives on that housing estate,' Henri says, 'you know, that one with the dirty grey houses in Orpington, the one where the gyppos run riot.'

Summer laughs. 'She probably goes out burning cars on an evening with the rest of them.'

Heather feels like scum as she clamps her lips together and remains silent. It can't be easy coming from a tough background and going to Highstead. While a place at the school is supposed to be based on academic ability, there's an awful lot of posh girls here, probably because their parents can afford the private tutors to hothouse them into passing the notoriously hard entrance exam.

'Hey, Fatty!' Summer calls across the street. 'Why don't you go back to your council house and snog those gyppos you love so much!'

The girl had seemed frozen for a few seconds, but now she turns and runs. She's too far away to see clearly, but somehow Heather knows tears are streaming down her face.

When the girl disappears into the alleyway that leads to

Morrisons' car park, Heather stops watching. She turns to find Tia looking at her, a hardness in her eyes and a question on her lips. 'Heather, is it? Where do you live?'

'Bickley,' Heather manages to stammer.

'Where in Bickley?'

'Do you know Blackbrook Lane? Near there.'

Tia smiles, satisfied with the answer. 'My aunt lives in Bickley. It's nice.'

And by 'nice' Heather guesses she means 'expensive', which a lot of it is, and Heather isn't going to reveal that her house is the one letting the whole neighbourhood down.

She gets home late that night. Really late. It's getting dark by the time she walks through the front door, but her mother doesn't say anything. Heather's not even sure she realized she wasn't in the house. She probably thought her daughter was tucked away in the mess somewhere, doing her homework.

She goes to her dad's the next day and dumps her school bag, along with her bag full of clothes for the weekend, on the top bunk in the bedroom she shares with Faith.

'New bag?' Faith says, looking it over.

'Yes.' Heather can't help smiling to herself.

'What are you looking so smug about?' Faith asks, suspicious.

'Nothing,' Heather says, hugging her secret to her. Pretty soon she'll be one of the popular girls and Faith won't be able to order her around any more. Heather wants to be just like Tia Paine, even though she's a bitch. She wants to not care. She wants to be the one everyone looks up to for a change, and she doesn't care if she has to sell her soul to a pre-teen devil with perfect teeth to accomplish that.

CHAPTER TWENTY-EIGHT

NOW

As they pull into Hastings town centre, pausing at a traffic light, Jason turns to Heather and yells, 'Do you want to go straight to the address?'

'No!' The rumble of the engine is so loud she shakes her head as well. The helmet is heavy. She's ready to be rid of this constricting thing over her face, ready to breathe again. However, she's not ready just yet to ring on Patricia Waites's doorbell.

Jason seems to understand this, because when the light turns green he heads towards the seafront instead of into the curling and climbing streets of the old town. There's a car park at the eastern end of the beach, past the old fishermen's huts huddled together, tall and foreboding with their windowless, black-painted clapboard. He takes Heather's helmet from her and stows it in a lockable box behind the back seat, and without discussing where they are going they both turn towards the town and start walking. When they reach the amusement park, Jason asks, 'What do you want to do first?'

Heather looks around at the dodgems and helter-skelter, then further to the sea beyond. 'Wander round, get a feel for the town?' She sighs. 'I don't remember being here.'

'Not at all?'

'I don't think so.' She starts walking. She wants to see the beach, unobstructed by all the tourist traps. Maybe that will help. Jason falls into step beside her. 'But I don't remember much from when I was little. I always thought it was because I just didn't have the kind of memory that retained things from the past, but since I found out about… Well, I've been wondering if it's because I blocked it all out.' She pauses for a moment, chews on the corner of her lip as a new thought comes her way. 'Maybe this is why. Maybe this place kick-started the habit.'

They've reached a part where the path curves close to the pebble beach, and Jason stops, shoves his hands in his jeans pockets, and stares out to sea. The day is bright, but the water isn't the glaring blue of the postcards – more grey with an underlying hint of green. 'That's hardly surprising. I know there are patches of my childhood I'd quite happily lose in the fog of time.'

Heather comes to stand beside him. Usually he looks at her a lot – an understanding smile here, a glance of concern there – but now he keeps his gaze steadily fixed on the horizon. 'Was it really bad?' she whispers.

'No… Yes.' He exhales heavily. 'It's hard to explain. Not all alcoholics are raging idiots who can't hold down a job and who beat their families up on a nightly basis.'

They start walking again, down onto the stony beach and towards the sea. The tide is out and the pebbles undulate towards the surf in loose terraces. Heather knows she's being nosy, but she can't help herself. She doesn't get to talk to people about their lives much – not the important stuff anyway – and she didn't know how thirsty she was for it. 'What was it like?'

'On the outside, he looked like a pretty normal guy. He had a decent job, although maybe he could have climbed higher if he hadn't been drinking – the fact he often got passed over for promotion was one of the things that used to really set him off. But even with that, even though many of his colleagues must have known he liked a drink or two, I doubt many of them ever guessed the extent of the problem.'

Heather's stomach swirls with pity. She knows that feeling. 'It's horrible, isn't it?' she says. 'As a kid in a family like that? You've got this huge secret: one you didn't ask for, one you would do anything to be free of. It's like your parents have dumped it on you, asked you to carry it for them, then they forget it's there, just leaving you to lug it around for the rest of your life.'

They've reached the shore now. Any closer and Heather's trainers will get wet. Jason watches the surf juggle the smaller pebbles for a moment, then meets her eyes, relief clearly plastered across his features. 'Exactly.'

They spend a moment looking at each other, sharing something neither of them can put into words, then Jason sets off again, strolling parallel to the waves, and Heather catches up with him. The slope of the beach means they're almost at eye level with each other.

'He could be nasty – there's a reason people are called "mean drunks" – but when it boiled down to it, it was the things he didn't do rather than the things he did. After I was about eight, he was never at a football match, never at a concert...'

Heather smiles. 'You sing?' She likes that about him.

Jason coughs. 'Um... let the cat out of the bag there a bit. My next sister up is a dance fanatic, and my mum used to take me along to her lessons with her to keep me out of my dad's way.' He flashes her a winning grin. 'I'll have you know I'm a pretty competent tap-dancer.'

'No way!' Heather is really laughing now, unable to stop herself shaking with it.

'Way,' he says, but he doesn't look embarrassed. In fact, he looks a little bit proud.

'Didn't that just give the kids at school a reason to torture you?'

'I didn't care who knew. I enjoyed it and I was good at it.' Heather's shaking her head as well as laughing now. She doesn't believe him, and Jason knows this, because he grabs her by the hand and runs back up the beach, dragging her along behind him. By the time they reach the path he's laughing too, and they're both so breathless from slipping and sliding on the stones she can hardly believe that he releases her hand, pulls himself up straight and launches straight into a routine, tapping with his thick biker boots and ending with a spin. A couple of old ladies walking past give him a round of applause and he bows, lapping it up.

'Okay, okay, you've convinced me,' Heather gasps, hardly able to get the words out between laughs. When the giggles die out she's left with a sense of wonder. He's like her in some ways, but in others he's so very, very different. 'That was really quite impressive,' she tells him. 'I could never do anything like that.'

'I didn't think I could before I tried. I used to join in at the back while my sister did the class, and eventually my mum said I might as well do it too. Jess still hates me because I got better marks than her in our Grade 2 exam.'

Almost without thinking, they begin walking again. Jason looks around. 'Do you remember any of this?'

Heather looks towards the pier. Normally it's the first place she'd head for on a trip to the seaside. For some reason, piers draw her like a magnet. She always walks right down to the end, leans on the railings, and stares out to sea. She feels a tug inside, prompting her to do just that, but she ignores it. This isn't just a nice day out. She's here for a reason, and this pier isn't going to give her answers because she's never walked on it before. A fire destroyed most of the Victorian structure about ten years ago and the renovated pier is oddly sparse and minimalist. Whatever memories might have been jogged by the pier went up in flames.

'No,' she says, 'I don't remember anything.'

Once again, an image of a red coat pops into her head and she curses herself for not cataloguing and sorting and carefully storing her own memories, as she does for those of others as part of her job. It horrifies her to think that she's like her mother in this respect, discarding them carelessly or leaving them to rot and decay until there are only fragments left. She sighs. 'I think I'm ready now.'

'To go to the address?'

She nods. That's why they've come here, after all. She can't put it off forever.

CHAPTER TWENTY-NINE

NOW

Just as Heather and Jason reach 14 Hill Croft Road she feels a drop of rain on her head, which is odd because the sky, while populated by large puffy clouds, is bright blue directly above them. She has no idea where it can be coming from, but over the next few seconds she feels another couple of drops and, as a cloud wanders in front of the sun, it begins to spit in earnest.

Number 14 is an ordinary-looking Victorian terraced house with bay windows and a slate roof. It's part of a row of four others that are very similar, and all four have been plastered and painted white. There are wrought-iron railings and no garden in the front, just concrete steps leading down to another bay window and another front door. Heather guesses the house has been split into flats. The whole building isn't that large, so each flat must be tiny.

'14c,' Jason says. 'That must be the bottom one. Are you going to knock?'

Heather stares at the door. 'I don't know.'

'Do you want me to?'

'No,' she says sharply, and then immediately apologizes. She's so used to snapping at Faith when she's overwhelmed and irritated that she just does it on automatic. 'I mean, I think I need to do it on my own. I just need... a moment.'

He nods, steps back a little. Heather isn't sure whether it's because he's trying to give her some room or because she was short with him. Cold air rushes in to fill where he was standing and she hugs herself.

'Okay,' she says and starts to move, even though she feels anything other than okay, even though she feels anything other than ready.

She makes her way carefully down the concrete stairs and rings the bell before she freaks herself out. The chime booms out like Big Ben. Heather almost bolts, but the door swings open. She finds herself looking at a young woman in jogging bottoms and a crop top, holding a baby on her hip. 'Yeah?' she says, looking warily at Heather.

'Um... Hello.'

Heather stalls after those first two words. The woman stares back and begins to close the door, her eyes narrowing further. Heather holds out a hand as if to stop her, but she isn't brave enough to actually make contact with the door, so her hand stays aloft and useless, only a hint of her intention.

'I don't suppose you know someone called Patricia Waites?' she says in a rush, the narrowing space between door and frame squeezing the words out of her. 'She used to live here.'

The gap closes further. 'Sorry. Don't know 'er. Only been 'ere six months.'

And then it's shut. Heather turns and walks back up the stairs to where Jason is waiting for her. She shakes her head as she reaches him, even though he must have heard the exchange.

'Are you okay?'

She nods, but she realizes she may be fibbing again. 'This is what we expected, isn't it? We knew it was a long shot. I mean, *I* knew...' She looks away, embarrassed she's inadvertently included him in her thought processes this way.

They turn and walk back towards the seafront. Jason suggests a cup of tea and they sit in a nice little café near the amusements that has bleached wooden walls and colourful prints of boats and the sea hanging above the powder-blue tables. Despite the cheerful décor, Heather doesn't feel her spirits brighten one bit. This feels like defeat.

When their individual teapots are empty, Jason stands up. 'Come on.'

Heather looks up at him. She'd just like to slump a little longer on the table.

'You need cheering up,' he says, 'and I know just the way to do it.'

Heather thinks he's insane, but he's holding out his hand and she's been longing to touch him again ever since the tap-dancing display, so she stands and lets him lead her.

They end up five minutes' walk away, standing outside a little hut. Jason hands over some cash and in return the man inside gives him two putters and two golf balls. Jason passes her one of each, and she turns and looks at the tacky pirate-themed course full of plastic palm trees and even a Spanish galleon about the size of a small van. 'You're not serious,' she says.

He grins cheekily. 'You can't back out now, I've handed over the money.' He turns to the man behind the counter. 'And it's non-refundable, right?'

The man stares at Jason, confused, but then catches on. 'Right.'

Heather doesn't believe either of them, but she's never really developed the skill of fighting her own corner – except maybe with her sister – so she mutely turns and walks to the first hole.

She's irritated with Jason, even though she knows he's trying to be kind, so she decides he needs to pay; she's going to win this round if it kills her. Besides, concentrating on the little yellow ball, using her latent maths and physics skills to weigh up direction and force, keeps her from thinking about the wary look in the young mother's eyes. Heather knows what she was thinking when she knocked on her door, asking about someone she'd never heard of and certainly didn't care about: Freak.

Heather's tenacity pays off. By the time they're halfway round, she's five points ahead. She doesn't even notice that it's started to rain properly. It's hard to tell on this crazy-golf course anyway, because it's full of waterfalls and things that spit at you when you're trying to aim a shot. As they continue round by the galleon – which is playing a tinny recording of cannon fire and growled pirate threats – there is a booming sound and then suddenly, just as she's got one eye closed and her ball is lined up perfectly for the hole, someone tips a bucket of water over her.

'Hey!' She drops her club and looks over at Jason, ready to blame him, but his hands are empty. He's smiling though, the rotter, and it makes her lips twitch too, but then there's another booming sound and she turns towards the galleon, only to be rewarded with a face full of water from a hidden jet inside one of the cannons. Jason can't help himself now, and he starts to laugh.

It's a really lovely sound, low and deep, and she finds herself joining in, even though she's wet through from the crown of her head to the waistband of her jeans. Thankfully, she's still wearing the leather jacket Jason leant her, because she's not sure she's a wet

T-shirt kind of girl, both when it comes to the confidence of wearing one and having the physical assets needed to look good in one.

'Right, that's it!' she tells him. 'You're toast!'

'What?' He's trying to look mock-offended but he can't stop smiling. 'That had nothing to do with me. That was pure bad luck!'

Heather narrows her eyes. 'I'm not sure I believe you,' she tells him, then makes good on her promise. She wins by a clear ten points and Jason accuses her of being a crazy-golf hustler and asks her how she got so good.

'I have no idea,' she says, genuinely bemused at her own genius. 'I must just have a natural knack for it.'

'A likely story,' he says as they head back to the shack and hand in their equipment.

'I want to go and have another look at the sea,' Heather says as they walk away. 'I was too preoccupied before, and it's been ages since I've been on a beach. I used to love them so much, even the stony ones like this.'

'Okay,' he says. 'Your day, your call.'

They fall into step beside each other and head down to the shore. The tide has come in a bit and there's a wide shelf of shingle at the water's edge. Heather stands there, just looking at the lacy froth of the waves as they tumble in one after another, never stopping, never giving up. She can hear Jason moving around beside her but she doesn't turn to look at him until he comes close and says, 'Here…'

She turns her head then drops her gaze to his open palm. A delicate orange shell is sitting there.

'I thought you should have at least one good thing to take home with you today. I'm sorry the trip's been a waste.'

Heather can't answer because there's a ball of something in her throat: all the words she wants to say but probably never will.

She looks down at the shell in his hand. If someone had asked her this morning if she'd bring anything home from the beach – shells, feathers, unusual pebbles – she'd have told them they were mad. That's the sort of thing her mother did, not her. Never her.

Yet she reaches out and takes it from him, her fingertips grazing the soft skin of his palm. She closes her fingers around it, holding it tight, both elated at the thought of having something tangible to tie her to this moment and terrified that the idea appeals to her so much.

When she looks back up at Jason, she notices they're only inches apart. The wind is whipping his hair across his forehead and he is searching her face, waiting for her reaction.

'Thank you...' she begins to whisper, but she doesn't get past the first syllable, because Jason dips his head and kisses her.

CHAPTER THIRTY

NOW

Heather is stunned at first. She doesn't move, doesn't react, doesn't really know what to do, and not just because Jason has taken her completely by surprise. But then he must feel her lack of response and she senses him hesitating. There's only one thing for it – she's going to have to kiss him back.

And she does, reaching up towards him, holding onto the front of his leather jacket and pulling him closer.

Oh, my. It's as if the beach and the surf and the gaudy colours of the seafront fade away and all that exists is her and Jason, the places where they're touching. His hands come up to hold her face, framing it so tenderly that she's afraid she'll just melt into a puddle of nothing and then will be washed away with the tide.

She has no idea how much time has passed when he pulls away. Her eyes stay closed, her face tilted up, the small orange shell still clutched in her right hand.

'Are you okay?' he asks, his voice low and full of concern.

Heather doesn't want to move her lips to speak, afraid she'll wipe the tingling sensation away, so she just nods.

'You're shaking.'

Heather opens her eyes. 'I... Because...' She swallows and tries again. 'Sorry.'

His smile is soft, puzzled. 'What are you apologizing for now?'

'I... I'm just not used to this.'

He smiles. 'Kissing on beaches? I'd say it's pretty much the same as kissing anywhere else.'

She closes her eyes again before admitting the next bit. 'No, I mean just kissing. That was my first...' She trails off, not quite able to say the words. Jason goes still, his eyes wide. She shakes her head. He's misunderstood. 'Not my first ever.' Not quite. 'But my first for a very long time, that's all.' She doesn't tell him about the other kisses, about the other boy. Those ones don't count. They were stolen, not given. Taken under false pretences.

He looks down at her, studies her face, but she feels no sting of judgement, no sense of regret. 'I like you, Heather,' he whispers.

She wills the tears not to come. That might ruin everything. It's just that she's not sure anyone has ever said that to her before, not so clearly and plainly. But instead of warming her heart, his words turn it to ice. It's dangerous to want it this much. She shakes her head, pulls back a little. 'I'm not so sure this is a good idea.'

'Oh, God! I'm so sorry. Here you are, going through this humongous thing, and I'm... I should have thought!'

She grips his jacket tighter with her left hand, stops him stepping away. 'No, it's not that. It's not you. It's...' She knows what she's about to say and she cringes. She's heard it and read it so many times before and has always wondered how people can be so unoriginal. Now she understands. 'It's me. You don't really want someone like me.'

He shuts her up by kissing her again, more decisively this time, communicating his disagreement with actions not words, and something breaks inside of Heather. A dam she didn't even know was there.

She shoves the shell in her pocket and winds both hands around his neck, pulls him as close as she can. It's probably stupid to let him know she wants him this badly, but she's powerless to stop herself. Even though there's a voice whispering in her head, *You did this before, remember? Got lost like this... and look how that ended up.* She ignores it. That was different. This is Jason. He's not like the other one.

* * *

They go and get fish and chips from one of the tacky-looking places along the front and take it away in hot paper parcels. They don't wait to find somewhere to sit before they start eating; they just unwrap and dive in. It's surprisingly good, the tastiest, juiciest scampi Heather has had in a long time.

The renovated pier is calling to her again, and this time Heather gives in. What harm can it do? And it seems the perfect way to end the day, so they start walking in that direction.

The rain has stopped and the sun has come out again. It's as if Hastings can't quite make up its mind what it wants to do with itself today. But the clouds are parting and the sky is both gold and grey in equal measures, reflected on a rumpled, slate sea. They stroll towards the end of the pier, tasting the salt in the air and the sting of vinegar on hot fried potato.

The pier isn't empty but it isn't crowded either. Families have headed home to their hotels for dinner or out to fast-food outlets or family-friendly restaurants, leaving older couples and teenagers.

Jason and Heather head towards an empty patch of railings punctuated by a lone figure, a woman. Heather feels a slight crackle of electricity across her skin as she lays eyes on her, but she ignores it – she's been feeling all sorts of strange things since she climbed onto the back of Jason's motorbike this morning.

The woman braces her hands on the railings, standing straighter, and the crackling sensation intensifies. Heather's fingers remain frozen above the chip she was about to pluck from her paper parcel and she stares at the woman. There's something...

That's when it happens – *bang!* – an image from the depths of her memory so loud and clear and forceful that it stops her dead in her tracks.

The red coat.

There's a strange flickering between the woman standing with her back to them, leaning on the railings, and a similar image of another woman from another time, arranged just the same way. Heather's stomach drops.

She's just about got the real one – the figure in a dark skirt and a turquoise anorak – pinned into place when the woman must sense her standing there, staring, only ten feet away. She turns. Her eyes are empty. Far away. They belong in a shop window, the staring sad eyes of a mannequin.

Heather drops her fish and chips. The packet lands on the wooden boards of the pier with a thump. 'You!' she says, quite loudly, although she has no idea who this person is, only that buried in the shadows deep inside her is a recognition that cannot be denied as she stares into this stranger's eyes.

Jason steps forward. For a moment she'd forgotten he was there. 'Heather?'

The woman's expression had been guarded, quizzical, but now

her jaw goes slack. 'Heather?' she says, almost croaking the name out, and her hand reaches towards the young woman in front of her.

But then it all shuts down. The moment stops being slow motion and is ripped back into real time, real speed. The woman seems to know this, because she turns and flees.

'Who was that?' Jason says behind Heather.

Heather tries to speak but she can't. She has nothing to say. Nothing that makes sense, anyway. How does this woman seem so familiar? And why did she see her wearing Aunt Kathy's red coat?

It clicks into place then. Not by logical deduction or a process of elimination, but by a gut feeling so intense it can't be squashed or ignored because the taste of truth about it is so strong it's almost suffocating.

'It's her,' Heather rasps. 'That woman. It's *her* – the one who took me.'

CHAPTER THIRTY-ONE

NOW

The ride home is nowhere near as joyous as the one out. Heather presses her cheek against Jason's shoulder blades and holds him tight, but the hills and valleys, the quaint villages and stunning views over the chalk downs are all a dark blur.

They tried to chase the woman as she ran off the pier, but she'd got quite a head start on them. There had been tantalizing glimpses of the turquoise waterproof jacket through the tourists milling around the broad space of the pier, but once the woman was back on dry land she had darted off across the main road and down a side street. They'd roamed the area for more than an hour hoping to catch another sight of her, but had eventually given up.

'You're sure that was her?' Jason had said more than once as they'd scoured the streets.

It had been hard to give a definitive answer. On a logical level, Heather knows it's a chance in a million just running into her here, that maybe her mind – and her memory – is playing new and devious tricks on her, but deep down inside, on a more intuitive level, she just knows.

As night falls, Heather finds it hard to get back on the bike and head back up the A21. It feels as if she's leaving a piece of herself behind. But, as the miles increase between herself and Hastings, the weighty sadness gives way to something else, something hotter and fiercer. Patricia Waites – if that's who the woman on the pier was – is a total and utter coward, running away like that. How dare she? How dare she flee, taking all those precious answers with her? It's just so selfish.

By the time they draw up on their driveway in Shortlands, Heather is buzzing. She swings her leg over the bike almost before it's stopped fully and marches towards the house, knowing but not caring that Jason is staring after her. She leaves her front door open so he can follow, peels the crash helmet off and leaves it on the sofa in the living room as she fetches a key from her desk, then she strides back to the spare room.

After taking in a couple of noisy breaths through her nostrils, she shoves the door open with such force it bounces off a pile of junk, springs back and almost hits her in the face. She has to wedge the bottom against a bin liner full of clothes to make it stay open.

And then Heather just starts pulling things towards her – she doesn't care what – and flinging them into the hallway. She needs a skip. Once she's filled the hall, she's going to get on the internet and order one. Hopefully she'll find somewhere that can deliver one on Monday.

A creak on the floorboards further up the corridor reminds her that Jason exists, and that he's followed her into her flat. She glances over her shoulder at him but doesn't stop grabbing and throwing. She can't.

'What's going on?'

'I'm doing something I should have done a long time ago – I'm having a clear-out! It's going. All of it. Right now.'

He sounds infuriatingly calm when he replies. 'This isn't the way to solve it.'

'Oh no?' she snaps back, aware she's taking it out on the wrong person, but if Jason is stupid enough to get in the firing line, so be it. 'What do you suggest instead? Hang around Hastings every weekend, hoping we'll run into her again? Now she knows someone's looking, she's going to be much more careful. We'll never find her again.'

Jason walks over and puts a gentle hand on her arm. The pressure is light, but it's enough to stop her in her tracks. 'I get it,' he says softly.

'Do you?' she replies, on the verge of hysterical laughter. 'Because I certainly don't!'

'You're angry,' he says simply. 'And with good reason.'

And just like that, his sensible words are a pin in the balloon of her rage. But she doesn't want to stop feeling like this – it's the only thing keeping the tears at bay and she doesn't want to be that weak in front of him.

He leads her away from the spare room, carefully stepping over the upturned boxes and crates in the hallway, and takes her into the living room. Somehow he knows to shut the door, blocking all the chaos out.

'It's very satisfying in the moment, the anger,' he says, 'but it's not good in the long term. Believe me.'

She nods, reminded once again that when he says he gets it, maybe he does. He's not just placating her. How awful that she's been on her own for so long that she sometimes forgets that other people have issues too, that it's not just her who's messed up and damaged. 'I don't know what else to do,' she admits shakily.

'There must be a reason you kept all your mum's stuff,' Jason says. 'It'd be a shame to throw out the good things – the memories and family treasures – along with the junk. If you really want to deal with it, maybe you should do what your mum never managed to do and sort through it properly.'

Heather exhales. 'Maybe.' His words make sense, but that still doesn't mean she wants to go rooting around in her mother's belongings, and the alternative – chucking it out wholesale – is just so appealing.

'I thought you'd have been good at that kind of thing, given your job.'

Heather's head jerks up and she looks at him.

'I mean, that's what you do for a living, isn't it? Sort through people's belongings, catalogue and categorize? Maybe it's time to do that for your mum. A fitting way to say goodbye to the hoard.'

Heather stays silent. She's thinking. He might have something here. She's never thought of her mother's things that way – the same way she does the items she comes across in the course of her work – maybe because her mother's stuff feels like dirty junk, whereas the possessions of someone like Cameron Linford feel significant.

To her mother, every item was important in a way Heather could never fathom. It was if she had another range of vision, a hoarder version of ultraviolet or infra-red, that allowed her to see value in things that no one else could.

Heather sits down on the sofa, resting her elbows on her knees as she thinks about this. How odd. She actually wants to do this. And not just to help herself; she wants to do it for her mother. It's as if now the real culprit for her messed-up life has been identified, she can direct the anger in the proper place. She stands up and nods. 'Okay,' she says. 'You're right. Let's do it.'

'Now?'

She gives a helpless sigh. 'I've got to do something or I'll go mad.'

For a moment Jason looks perplexed, but then he shrugs. 'Okay.'

They head back towards the spare room. Although it was only moments ago that Heather was throwing the contents into the hall, she hesitates when she sees the mess of boxes, crates and bin liners.

The closer she gets, the less air there is. Without the lovely, liberating anger to power her on, the old neuroses are creeping back. She gets that heart-fluttery feeling, the one she's starting to recognize now, and clutches onto Jason's arm. She is not going to have a panic attack in front of him. She is not!

'I-I've seen some shows on hoarding,' she says, desperately trying to work out how to breathe and talk at the same time. 'What they do… is… the person, the hoarder, stays in one place, and the team bring things to them so they can say yes or no. I-It's quicker…' She takes a big gulp of air. 'Do… Do you think we could do that?' Suddenly, touching any of it seems an impossibility.

Jason's frowning too. 'Okay,' he says again. She has a horrible feeling he knows what's going on inside her head and is being nice. She's not sure which is worse – this feeling of being as transparent as glass or the fact he must be pitying her. 'Where do you want to start?'

He's looking past the doorway towards the chest of drawers that hides all her worst, pastel-coloured secrets. Heather points to the boxes on the hall floor, forcing him to look in the other direction. 'There. We'll start there.'

She leans against the wall and slides down it until her bottom meets the floor. Jason rights the box nearest him and opens the cardboard flaps. He picks out a sheaf of papers and holds them out for Heather to see. She shakes her head – they're bank statements from her mum's accounts, all closed during the probate process – and Jason starts a pile on the floor to the other side of him.

They keep going like that for a while. The first two boxes are all papers: more statements, insurance certificates (although Heather doubts anyone would have paid more than 20p for her mother's house if it had burned down), endless receipts. She keeps very little, only her mother's birth certificate, which makes her wonder where her own is. She's never seen the original, only a copy that her mother gave her in her twenties when she complained she didn't have one.

By the time the third box is done, her chest is no longer feeling tight and she's started to chat with Jason about the contents. He reaches for a blue plastic crate, snaps the lid off and hands her the first item. It's a toy rabbit with milkshake-pink fur and one floppy ear. 'Was this yours?' he asks.

She stares down at it. 'No. I don't think so.' She hands it back to him. 'It can go.'

'To the charity shop?'

She nods and he starts another pile. 'My mum used to collect things like this. She was mad about toys of all kinds.'

Jason studies the rabbit. 'Any idea why?'

None. It strikes Heather that she has never asked that question before. When she was little, it was just what Mum did, and when she was older she didn't really want to think about it.

They work like this: Jason handing Heather an object, her handling it, experiencing it, and then passing it back to be put on one of the various piles. It's slow work, but as the time creeps towards midnight, they get to the bottom of the last box that Heather threw out into the hallway. She stretches and is rewarded with a creak in her knee joint, then stands up.

'We can't do this all night,' she tells Jason, who also gets up. 'In fact, you didn't need to do this at all. Thank you.'

He smiles at her, but it is hijacked halfway through and turns into a yawn. 'No problem.'

'Why did you?' Heather knows it makes her sound needy and unsure of herself to ask, but she's not going to sleep tonight if she doesn't know the answer.

He steps forward, far too close for comfort of any kind, and looks down at her. 'I don't know if you've noticed this, but I like spending time with you.' And before Heather can say anything his hand cradles her jaw and he leans in for a butterfly-soft kiss.

Why? Heather whispers again inside her head. Not that she's complaining, but it all seems too good to be true. Maybe this is all just a dream and she's going to wake up in her bed soon, sheets tangled around her legs, heart beating hard.

'Get some rest,' Jason says as he turns and heads for the door. Heather nods and he closes it softly behind him and is gone.

She breathes out then turns her attention to the open spare-room door. Her fingers are on the handle, ready to pull it closed, but she stops. And then she lets go and steps inside. She doesn't want to stop, she realizes, even though Jason isn't here any more to hand her the objects.

She's touched at least a hundred now, all without hyperventilating, so maybe she can do a few more on her own? Now she's started scratching this itch, she needs to keep going, to keep chasing it until she gets that lovely 'ah' moment of relief. Itch stopped. Room cleared. So she sits down on the rectangle of clear floor that's been exposed by the evening's work, pulls a box towards her and looks inside.

CHAPTER THIRTY-TWO

NOW

Heather only intends to sort through one more box, to prove to herself she can do it, but somehow she can't stop. The clock marks the hours. One. Two. Three...

It's a slow process, not at all how she'd sort through her own possessions, which she does on a regular basis, discarding with brisk efficiency anything that even hints at being useless. She needs to lift each item out of its box carefully, the same way a bomb-disposal expert might handle a suspicious device, and slowly turn it over, viewing it from all angles.

At first it's more papers: mostly craft magazines, lots of them to do with knitting and crochet, despite the fact her mother never did get around to learning those skills. It's easy for Heather to discard these things. Patterns she saves for the charity shop, the magazines go on a pile for recycling. But down at the bottom of a box she discovers a knitted toy. She stares at it for a moment, puzzled, and then clear as day, a memory pops into her mind. It's so vivid and unexpected that she lets out a gasp.

She remembers someone giving this to her.

She can visualize a hand presenting her with it, a soft voice saying she might like it. It's a little knitted angel that fits in her hand, its dress and wings snowy white and its hair duckling-yellow. There's a loop of wool attached to the back of its head, which suggests it's a Christmas decoration, but now she remembers clutching it to herself and refusing to let it go, insisting that it was a dolly and it was going to live in her pocket. Her teacher at school, Miss.... something... had read them a story about guardian angels, and Heather had got it into her mind that if she could keep this on her person at all times, even tucking it into the elastic at the sides of her knickers while she slept, it would keep her safe.

She looks down at the slightly grubby angel. Her halo is crooked, which is probably fitting. *You didn't do a very good job, did you?* she silently tells the doll, but she hesitates as she reaches for the charity-shop pile. The angel dangles above it by her string for a few seconds, and then Heather snatches her up again and puts her in one of the empty boxes she's saved for the 'keep' stuff that's not paperwork. Up until now it's been empty.

That's the end of that box. She checks the clock: 3.28 a.m. She really should go to bed, she thinks, but she reaches for a plastic crate without a lid. Maybe just one more.

The first item she picks up makes her laugh. It's a framed print, a painting of one of those old-fashioned teddy bears with the jointed limbs sitting on a bed. You can just about see the edge of a frilly pillow behind him. The bear is looking away and down, black eyes staring. It had been one of her mum's favourites. But the thing that makes her laugh is her father's voice in her head: 'Looks like he's constipated!' he'd always said. Her mum had scowled at him when he'd said that.

Heather's still smiling as she puts it in the box along with the angel. She thinks the print is ugly, but she likes the fact she can hear her father when she looks at it. It makes her feel connected to him in a way she never does on those awful Skype calls of Faith's. But then that warm feeling is flushed away with an icy sensation. That's what her mother did, didn't she? She saved things because they connected her to places or people or experiences. Heather almost picks the box up and empties both angel and frame onto the 'discard' pile, but at the last moment she stops herself. *Two things,* she reasons with herself. *That's not going overboard.* There's fifty times that in the piles for recycling, chucking, and giving away. This is what normal people do: they have a few treasured possessions that carry happy memories. It's just her mother's urge for this raged out of control, got way out of balance. She breathes out, puts the 'keep' box down again, and carries on sorting through the crate.

Nothing else prompts a memory, which is kind of disappointing and kind of a relief at the same time. Mostly, it's knick-knacks wrapped in newspaper, and the odd soft toy (because they seem to get everywhere). Nearly all of it ends up on the charity-shop pile.

Down at the bottom of the crate she finds a long rectangular box made of stiff card about half a metre long. A shiver goes through Heather as she turns it over, even before she can properly see its contents through the cellophane on the front.

Cassandra.

Her chestnut curls are still perfect and glossy, baby-blue eyes haughty and unblinking, her porcelain features unblemished by the passing of time. Heather reaches out and touches the doll's cheek. For a moment she thinks the panic is going to come. She feels her chest tighten and her pulse start to trot, but she breathes deeply and closes her eyes, blocks the sight of the little usurper out. *I can do this,* she tells herself. *It's just a doll.*

She's patient with herself, waits until she feels she's got a handle on it, and then slowly opens her eyes and looks into Cassandra's blank, blue stare. 'I hated you,' she says to the doll. 'I think I still do.'

However, she doesn't put her on the 'discard' pile. She starts a new one – eBay. Her mum had always insisted the doll was a collector's item, and now it's time to find out for sure. As well as making a few quid from it, Heather gains a sense of pleasure from the idea of selling Cassandra. Of seeing her formally pass from the ownership of the Lucas family into another, while Heather still remains.

Having put the doll to one side, she reaches in for the last couple of objects. Photo albums! She'd almost given up hope of finding any more. She picks the top one up and opens it. The pictures overlap and there are places where her mother has added in tickets or postcards, giving it a scrapbook kind of feel. Heather stares down at the smiling faces and thinks how talented her mother was, how artistic. It's ironic that the very possessions she hoarded because of their creative possibilities were the same things that stopped her expressing those gifts.

The first album seems to be from about when Heather was eight. Once again, there are hardly any pictures of the house, mainly just holidays and outings, but she supposes that many family albums before digital cameras and selfies must look this way. She remembers using a camera her mother had found at a boot fair as a teenager, and how knowing she only had twenty-four exposures to capture what she wanted made her think extra-hard about what views, what subjects, were worthy of her attention. Now she can snap a million things a day on her phone. It almost seems careless. Wasteful.

She puts the album in the 'keep' box and picks up another. Wow. In this one she barely looks old enough to be at school and there's a picture of Faith in their primary-school uniform. She guesses her sister must have been about eight, which would make her five.

Heather sits up straighter. This would have been *before*, then. Before the abduction. Before the hoarding. She studies the photographs carefully, looking for clues, even though she's not exactly sure what they'd look like. However, there's very little to go on.

She was hoping to find more pictures of inside the house, partly to confirm what she already suspects: that her mother's hoarding was triggered by her disappearance, but partly out of pure curiosity. She'd hated living in that house, thought it ugly and messy and disgusting, but standing across the road from it a few weeks ago has caused her to think differently about it. Once upon a time it must have been lovely. A proper, happy family home.

Another memory pops into her head. It's just as clear and immediate as the previous ones, but not as surprising. This is one of her mother and father laughing together on Christmas morning. She and Faith are on the bottom of their bed, opening their Christmas stockings, and Mum is smiling at Dad because he's put a miniature bottle of Baileys in hers and he's holding an identical one he's just fished from his own.

Heather rests the album on her lap and leans against a stack of crates, smiling, but then tears begin to roll down her face. It isn't long before she's hiccupping and sobbing, unable to stop the tide.

She has no idea why she's crying. Absolutely none. There was just this overriding sense of relief and joy at remembering that, once upon a time, they'd been a normal family.

She continues looking through the photographs, poring over each one, and as she turns the penultimate page, a face catches her eye. She doesn't know why she's drawn to it. It's a group photo taken outside, possibly in their back garden before it got really overgrown, as there are blurs of out-of-focus colour in the background that must be flowers. Her mother and father are in the centre, and she and Faith are in the front. Faith seems to be eating a hot dog and there is a smear of yellow mustard down her white T-shirt, so maybe they were having a barbecue. There are a couple of adults she doesn't recognize: two men and a woman. It's the woman who snags her attention. She's doing one of those open-mouthed smiles at the person behind the camera, as if she's been caught in the middle of a laugh, and one arm is draped over young Heather's shoulders. Heather herself is squinting into the lens and grinning, her fringe long and covering her eyes, and she seems perfectly happy to have this stranger's arm around her.

Heather turns her attention back to the woman, takes in her dark waves, her smiling eyes. She turns the page, the last in the album, and scans the four photos grouped together there, and instantly spots a picture of the same woman outside their house in Hawksbury Road.

She's wearing the red coat.

It's exactly as Heather remembers it, even after all these years. It shocks her that, while her memory has been so lacking in some points, it has been crystal-clear and accurate about this coat.

Well, almost. Because when Heather stops marvelling over her prodigious recall of the red coat and looks carefully at the face sticking out the top, the horrible suspicion that has been floating around in her head since she had that 'flash' of the red coat on the pier in Hastings finally finds somewhere to land.

This isn't her Aunt Kathy. This is her. Patricia Waites. And she's not in faraway Hastings but standing outside Heather's old house in Hawksbury Road, smiling at her from inside her own mother's photo album.

CHAPTER THIRTY-THREE

SKIP

Yellow, battered, ugly. The skip is covered in chipped paint and filled with junk. Someone must be clearing out a house, I think, probably because somebody died. It's sad to see a lovely wooden chair with barley-twist legs upended, one of the struts snapped, showing pale fresh wood beneath the warm varnish, like a broken bone showing through ripped skin. Was it thrown in there because it was smashed or did the act of discarding it do the damage? It must have been picked with care, maybe bought along with others like it, but now it lies upside-down and lonely. While my mother is drawn to skips like a moth to a flame, I don't like them. Too much hope dies in their rusty interiors.

THEN

The next few weeks are like a dream for Heather. Claudie becomes her mentor and guide as they both seek to become part of Tia's core group instead of extras Velcroed on at the sides. Claudie knows when to approach the knot of girls, when to look excited and when to look coolly disdainful. Heather absorbs all of this information like a sponge.

October is blown away and November arrives. Christmas lights start to twinkle in the shops in town. Heather gets a strange, sparkly feeling too, something she's never felt before, and it grows each day with the morning frost, getting thicker and more robust.

She feels hopeful.

Not about Christmas, because her mother has never really celebrated it. Where would they fit a Christmas tree in this house, anyway? And there's never enough money for proper presents, despite the fact her mum spends squillions on TV shopping channels, claiming it means she'll have the right gift for any occasion, should the need arise. Of course, she never actually gives any of them away. But this year Heather doesn't mourn these things, because her life outside the house is bright and shining, making up for all of it.

One Sunday afternoon, she's sitting on her bedroom floor, huddled up next to the radiator with her duvet draped around her like a cloak. The *stuff* usually acts as insulation, especially in the summer when the house is boiling hot, but there's a cold snap at the moment and everywhere else in the house the tall piles are blocking the radiators, stopping the heat from circulating.

'Heather!' her mum calls up the stairs. 'I need you!'

Heather freezes, eyes fixed on her English homework. This is not good news.

Her mum spotted a skip round the corner in Park Road the other day and Heather knew right then that it was only a matter of time before she'd want to go and rummage through it. She also knew her mother would want to haul her along to help. She always does. But this time Heather was especially sure – her mum sprained her ankle a couple of weeks ago. She tripped over a box that had fallen into one of the rabbit trails one afternoon and lay there, half-buried, for almost an hour before Heather came home from school and dug her out.

'Heather!'

The shout is fainter. Heather hunkers down. If she stays quiet there's a good chance she'll escape this dumpster-diving expedition. If there's one good thing about living with a hoarder, it's that they're easily distracted. Hopefully her mum will stumble upon something interesting in the mess and forget all about going out – at least until it's too dark and cold to do anything about it.

She doesn't call again for about twenty minutes and Heather relaxes. She even risks a sortie to retrieve her dictionary from the living room, but as she's creeping back towards the stairs, her mother emerges from the kitchen door and spots her.

'Oh, good! There you are! I need you to come with me.' She pulls a coat from the pile in the hallway and starts to head out the door. When Heather doesn't move, she looks over her shoulder. 'Come on. We need to get out before the light goes.'

'I'm supposed to be writing a poem for English.'

'It'll only take ten minutes.'

Heather's shoulders slump and she grabs her coat from under a bundle of carrier bags. There's no point fighting. Her mother will cry and plead and beg until she gives in. At least if she goes now it'll be over and done with – in much more than ten minutes, she expects; but at least she'll be back inside finishing her English poem before it gets really freezing.

She pulls the zip on her coat up until it scratches the underneath of her chin, and follows her mother outside, keeping a couple of steps behind her as they make the short walk to Park Road.

Heather's road is nice but Park Road is even nicer. When Heather was little she used to think the houses were mansions. The skip is outside a property that is at least three times the size of their house. There are no lights in the windows and the garden is overgrown, but it's obvious someone has been cutting things back, tidying up.

Mum's not interested in the architecture one bit. Why would she be, when the bright-yellow paint of the skip is calling to her? 'Ooh, look!' she says, getting all excited. 'Can you reach that, Heather? There's a lovely old iron bucket in there.'

'Mum. It's broken.'

'Doesn't matter. I reckon I can fix it.'

Heather stares at the bucket. It's so badly rusted that the bottom has gone thin and papery, almost crumbled away. She tells her mother so, but it doesn't make any difference. In the end she's forced to lean over the edge of the skip and hook it out with her gloved hand. She passes it to her mother.

'Ooh, and what's that underneath?'

Her mother's eyes are really sparkling now. They rove across the skip as if she's just unearthed the contents of Tutankhamun's tomb. She points out items to Heather, and Heather fishes them out, only because it's easier to give in than to stand there arguing in the freezing cold.

Soon her mother's arms are full. She tries to put some of her goodies – a couple of door knobs and a ripped lampshade – in the metal pail, but the heavier items drop through the bottom. Heather sighs.

'Can you reach that chair?' her mother asks hopefully. 'I'd do it myself but…' She waggles her bad foot in explanation.

'Mum, it's old and broken. The leg's hanging half off. Anyway, there's no way you can carry that home with your dodgy ankle.'

Her mum frowns but, miracle of miracles, she shifts her focus to something else. She points, suddenly so excited that she almost drops what she's holding. 'Can you see it, Heather? Can you see it? The vase?'

Heather really doesn't want to spend more time peering into the skip than she has to – it smells – but she does it anyway. Down underneath all the bits of cardboard, metal and dust she can see the neck of a vase. It's translucent cream glass, fading to brown at its top and bottom, with a swirl of painted flowers.

Her mother is almost jumping up and down now. 'I think that might be worth something!'

Heather rolls her eyes. If this is the only thing she's spotted of any value, why is she carting all the other rubbish home? As gratifying as it would be for her mother to find something she could sell and get money for (Heather needs new school shoes, and has done for about a month), Heather knows her mum is never going to actually part with it. Just the *possibility* it's valuable is enough for her.

And even if it is valuable, it won't help in the long run. In fact, it will do the opposite, reinforcing this horrible behaviour, because the one time in a thousand she finds anything nice just makes her sure there are more 'treasures' waiting to be found at the bottom of every dustbin or skip.

'Who knows?' Heather replies. 'But it doesn't matter. There's no way I can reach it.'

Her mother stares hard at the vase, as if she can make it float to the surface by the sheer force of her will, then she turns to her daughter. 'Just hop in and get it for me, will you? You're so light and I'm sure you could stand on that flat bit of metal.'

'No,' Heather says. 'No way.'

Five minutes later Heather's face is flaming as she swings one leg over the cold metal side of the skip. Her mother is looking both tearful, from the argument they've just had in the middle of a very nice street, and triumphant because she got her way yet again. *I hate you,* Heather thinks as she tries to find something solid to put her weight on, and she just about manages to mean it too.

Her mother is a backseat dumpster-diver, it turns out, micromanaging Heather's progress to the right spot by calling out instructions – *Not that way! Put your foot on the edge of that bookcase* – but eventually Heather reaches a place where she can stretch out her arm and brush the top of the vase with her fingertips.

Just as she grips it round the neck and pulls it free, the worst thing ever happens. She hears people coming! They're leaving the house next door. Heather ducks down. She hates even being spotted with her mother on the return journey from one of these expeditions, arms full of junk, but to be caught actually in the skip? Her life would officially be over.

'Oh, my God!' Someone exclaims, followed by a tinkle of appalled laughter. Heather crouches down even more.

'It's legal!' Heather's mum says. 'I'm not stealing. I asked the owner!'

Well, that'd be a first, Heather thinks.

There's more laughter – *at* her mother not with her – because mum doesn't get that the act itself is horrifyingly amusing, not whether she has permission or not.

'So lame!' a younger voice says, and Heather is so surprised she almost loses her balance.

Oh no, oh no, oh no, Heather chants inside her head. *It can't be! Please, no.*

Someone's moving closer, coming to the edge of the skip. There's a part of Heather that's desperate to know for sure, a part that wants to be proved wrong, and maybe that's the bit of her that forgets to keep still, so she loses her balance and has to stand up to steady herself.

She lifts her gaze and stares straight into the eyes of Tia Paine. It doesn't take a genius to work out the house next door belongs to her aunt, and her whole family are there – mum, dad, younger sister – all staring in horror at the urchin that has just risen from the skip.

'Tia?' her mum asks, sounding worried. 'Do you know this person?'

A slow smile creeps across Tia's thin lips. 'No, I don't think so,' she says, locking eyes with Heather and refusing to let her look away. 'I'd never associate with trash.'

Heather drops the vase. It smashes into a million pieces.

CHAPTER THIRTY-FOUR

NOW

Heather rips back the cellophane of the photo album and pulls the image of the woman in the red coat from its gluey backing, tearing the edge of the picture in the process. She holds it up closer to her face and stares at it.

It's her, isn't it? Her heart pounds *yes, yes, yes* in reply.

She can't seem to tear her eyes from it, but the longer she stares, the fainter the thump of confidence in her chest becomes. *Am I just seeing what I want to see?* she asks herself. *Superimposing one memory on another?* After all, until recently her recollection of her early years has always been unreliable, if there at all. Maybe now the truth is out, it isn't setting her free; it's just sending her slowly insane.

But then her head jerks up: Jason. He saw the woman on the pier as well, if only for a moment. She can ask him. She can...

Heather is halfway to the door when she stops. It's 4.12 a.m., hardly the time to be asking him to check out a photo for her, even if it is a life-changing emergency. But that's not the only thing that stops her going upstairs and pounding on his door. It's the fact that she wants to so badly. She's becoming too reliant on him. Too entangled. At the very least, she should wait until morning.

Four hours later she's in her living room, the photograph placed in the middle of her desk, square to the edges, and she's sitting on her office chair, fully dressed and sipping a cup of lukewarm tea. She's been here for the last couple of hours. Waiting.

However, even though she can hear muffled footsteps in the flat above, the bang of a door that she guesses must be the bathroom when she hears the newly fixed pipes sputter and groan, she doesn't go upstairs to see Jason. Somehow she knows that in fifteen minutes or less he'll be jogging down the stairs to see her.

For ten minutes she sips her cold tea and looks at the photograph and then, when the pipes in the ceiling judder and go quiet, she quickly picks it up, tucks it in her handbag, and slips out of the front door.

* * *

Since her car is still sitting uselessly in the driveway, Heather walks into Bromley town centre and catches the first train to Oxted. It's a three-mile walk to Faith's from there, as there's no station in Westerham, but she'd much rather be active than sitting on the one bus that connects the two locations, crawling through the country lanes.

Faith's face is free of make-up when she answers the door, and when she sees Heather standing there she looks puzzled. It's as if, along with her BB cream and mascara, she hasn't had time to apply her sense of seniority either. She looks genuinely concerned to find her sister on her doorstep. 'Heather? Are you okay? Has something happened?'

Heather is clutching the photograph in her left hand. She holds it up squarely in front of her sister's face. 'Do you recognize her?' she asks, knowing she should at least apologize for turning up unannounced, but the question burning on her tongue has hijacked her manners.

Faith's frown deepens. 'I don't think so. Who is she?'

'I think this is the woman who… you know… stole me.'

Faith's eyes almost pop out of her head. She looks at the photo, then blinks and looks at it even harder, shaking her head. 'This is actually her? How do you know?'

Heather peers into the hallway, suddenly feeling the weariness of her trek here on public transport. 'Can I… you know… Can we go inside?'

'Of course! What am I thinking?' She leads Heather through to the large kitchen-diner, where the kids are eating breakfast at the table. They glance up, then both drop their slices of apple and run over to their aunt. Alice looks as if she's going to come in for a hug but she stops just short, looking shy. Barney puts his arms round his aunt's knees and squeezes as he smiles up at her. Heather runs a hesitant hand over his silky hair and, much to her surprise, he doesn't pull away.

'Are you finished with your apple?' Faith asks them. They both nod. 'Then go and watch *Peppa*.'

Alice, sharp as always, replies, 'But you said no more Peppa.'

'Yeah,' Barney chimes in. Heather smiles. She likes their solidarity, the fact her niece and nephew act like teammates rather than opponents.

'Well, I've changed my mind,' Faith says.

Alice frowns. 'But—'

'Do you want to watch Peppa or not?'

They don't need to be asked twice. Both children scurry off in the direction of the living room. When it's quiet again, Faith lays the photograph Heather gave her on the shiny black-speckled granite and they both stare at it.

'Are you sure it's her?' Faith almost whispers.

'I think so. I've been… remembering things.'

Heather didn't think Faith could look any more shocked but she does now. 'What sort of things?'

Heather sees the look of fear in her sister's eyes, the fear that she'll say something awful about what happened to her. 'Nothing much about that time,' she replies and sees her sister visibly relax. 'It's just that I went to Hastings yesterday, just to see if it jogged any memories. I found out that Patricia Waites lived there.'

Faith almost falls off her stool. 'You were going to try and find her? Talk to her? Oh, Heather, I really don't think that's a good idea!'

Heather shakes her head. 'It was an old address, a long shot at best. We knew that when we set off.'

'But still… Don't you think it's better not to go down that route? I mean, it could stir up things you don't want to remember.'

'It already has,' Heather says quietly. 'But I can't give up now.'

Faith nods. She's not happy with this development, Heather knows, always preferring to keep her sister under tabs, but she understands. That's the most Heather had been hoping for when she'd set off this morning.

'Hang on. Where did you get the photo from? I've never seen it before.'

'I found it in one of Mum's old photo albums.'

Faith looks even more confused then, and Heather realizes she's made a mistake. 'But it wasn't in the two you showed me,' Faith says. 'I thought you said that's all that was left.'

Heather makes herself maintain eye contact. 'I lied,' she says simply. 'There's more stuff left. A lot more stuff. I'm sorry. I... I just couldn't face sorting through it all.'

Faith opens her mouth, closes it again, and shakes her head. 'It's okay,' she says. 'I'm upset you lied to me, but under the circumstances... I get it.'

This takes Heather aback. She was expecting much more of a reaction than that. She's not going to say anything, though. She might shock her sister out of this unusually understanding mood.

Faith goes back to studying the photograph. 'But if this was in Mum's album, that means... that means...'

Heather nods. Yup. Faith is just about reaching the point where Heather was when she first found the photograph. She finishes the sentence for her sister. It feels nice to be the one to help for a change. 'It means that our parents knew her. That she was someone who was possibly a friend.'

'Or even a relative!' Faith exclaims. 'After all, Mum always talked about a gaggle of cousins they lost contact with. Maybe there's a reason they became strangers?'

'Maybe,' Heather says, aware she feels oddly calm at the moment. 'I remember this red coat being at the seaside. I always thought it was Kathy, but when I saw that woman standing there at the railings, it was as if everything that had been fuzzy and wrong all these years suddenly came sharply into focus.'

Faith forgets completely about making tea and comes and sits back down. 'What railings?' she says, her voice quite loud now. 'You mean you saw her? *Yesterday?*'

Heather nods, then shakes her head, then shrugs. 'I don't know. I think so. It was the weirdest thing.'

She knows she's not doing a very good job of this, that she's dropping one bombshell after another on her sister, but that's the problem with keeping everything to yourself – she's never really learned how to do this sort of thing properly.

'She saw me too. And then she just... ran.' Heather lets out a long breath. 'We chased her but she just disappeared into the crowds.'

'Oh, my God.' Faith slumps on her stool and stares into space. 'So what do we do now?'

We. That one word is the reason for Heather's journey here. 'I don't know,' she says. 'That's why I knocked on your door this morning.'

Faith stops looking bemused and smiles at her. She knows the silent request Heather is making, and is pleased. It marks new territory between them.

'Thank you for helping,' Heather says softly.

'Thank you for letting me help.' Faith leans across, both of them still sitting on the breakfast stools, and gives her a loose hug. It feels odd. But nice. 'You know it's all I've ever wanted to do, don't you?' she says, her voice cracking a little. She goes very still, and Heather knows her sister is fighting back tears. She doesn't budge until Faith takes a shuddering breath and begins to move again, rubbing Heather's back just once with the flat of her hand.

'I know,' Heather says, and she realizes she does know this. She supposes that on some level she's always known that when the chips are down, Faith is the one person she can count on to be there for her.

All this openness, this vulnerability, gets too much for Heather then and she returns to an upright position on her stool and pulls the photo towards her again, sliding it over the granite counter.

'This was taken outside our house, wasn't it?' Faith says after they've both been staring in silence at the photograph for some time. 'I recognize the big bushy fir tree at the corner of next door's garden.'

Heather nods. 'That's what I thought too.'

'And you say you've been having memories from that time, that going back to Hastings helped jog something?'

'Yes.'

'Then there's only one thing I can think of doing that might help.'

Heather frowns. She's getting that churny feeling in her stomach again.

'We've got to go to where this photograph was taken,' Faith says, sounding much more like her old dictatorial self. 'We're going back to Hawksbury Road.'

CHAPTER THIRTY-FIVE

NOW

Matthew comes to wave Faith and Heather off, the kids climbing all over him as he watches them drive away. Heather is grateful he's been so understanding. As they head north back to Bromley, Faith peppers her sister with questions, which Heather does her best to answer, and then Faith falls silent again, chewing the information over. A few moments later a new enquiry pops out of her mouth. They've covered Hastings and Hawksbury Road, and speculated about the year the photo might have been taken and who the woman might have been, when Faith finds a new avenue for interrogation.

'You know when you were talking about seeing the woman in Hastings?' Faith says as she glances in the mirror then pulls out to overtake a lorry.

'Mm-hmm.'

'You said "we".' Heather doesn't reply. 'You said, "*We* chased her." You weren't on your own, then?'

Heather waits until they've passed the lorry and Faith eases back into the left-hand lane. 'I was with my neighbour. Like I explained earlier, I was having car troubles, so he gave me a lift. That's all.' She keeps looking straight ahead, hoping Faith hasn't noticed the wobble in her voice.

'Neighbour. Hmm.'

'Young? Old?' Faith's got the bit between her teeth now.

'Older than me, but I suppose you'd call him young.'

She glances across and Faith has a smug grin on her face. 'Has this "youngish" guy got a name?'

Heather swallows. 'Jason.' She's looking back at the road again but she can still feel Faith's smile.

'Jason,' Faith repeats as if the key to some great mystery has been handed to her. 'And is he cute?' Heat begins to creep up Heather's neck. Of course, Faith spots it immediately. 'He is!' she says. 'He's cute and you like him!'

'Stop!' Heather says, but for some reason she's smiling too. 'I do not. He just gave me a lift to Hastings on his motorbike, that's all. He was just being a good friend.'

'You went on a motorbike!'

Heather nods. She's quite proud of that.

'You spent an hour pressed up against a man dressed head to toe in leather – there and back! – and you're telling me you're just good friends?'

'Uh-huh.' Heather can feel the heat spreading now. It's reached her cheeks and is climbing steadily.

Faith chuckles. 'A likely story!'

'Oh, shut up!' Heather says, but she's laughing too as she says it. Part of her doesn't mind this teasing. It makes her and Faith seem like real sisters. The atmosphere stays jolly until they pull into the outskirts of Bromley, but when they turn down past Bickley station, only a few minutes away from their destination, they both go quiet.

'I never come this way any more,' Faith says, looking with grim determination at the leafy suburban road full of well-spaced houses. 'Not if I can help it.'

'Me neither.'

They turn down Hawksbury Road and Faith parks opposite their old house. They've begun work on the driveway, Heather notices. When Faith cuts the engine all they can hear is birdsong. They look at each other and open their respective doors, climb out and stand side by side, away from the car so they have a clear view.

'Wow,' Faith says, looking relieved. 'It's changed.'

'Yes.'

Faith pulls the photo from her handbag. Heather had almost forgotten about it. They study it and decide that the woman in the red coat must have been standing in front of the fence between their old house and the house to the right. Faith crosses the road, indicating that Heather should follow, and then makes Heather stand in the same spot as the woman in the photo, so she can estimate where the photographer must have been when it was taken. Faith ends up outside where their front gate had been before the sweeping cobbled drive had been installed. Somehow that seems significant.

They stare at each other for a long time, taking it all in, and then Faith puts the photograph back in her bag. 'Come on,' she says and heads up the driveway.

Heather trots nervously after her. 'W-what are you doing?'

'Taking a look around.' Faith marches up to the curtainless windows and peers inside.

'But you... but we...'

'No one's here. That's what you said on the drive up, didn't you?'

Heather nods. 'Yes, but…'

'It's 10.30 on a Sunday morning, hardly the neighbourhood rush hour. And in this road, two dog walkers and a jogger would constitute gridlock.'

'I don't think…' Heather stops moving. She's giving her sister permission by following her.

Faith stops too, and Heather spots yet another chink in her ever-confident armour. She wonders if those holes were always there and she just couldn't see them before or whether this whole messy situation is causing her sister to crack and change. 'Please, Heather,' she says. 'I need to see the house and garden neat and tidy – rescued. I need to know there's a clean slate.'

Heather's chest deflates. She nods and follows Faith as she sets off again to explore the side of the house. It isn't long before they've opened the gate and are standing in the middle of the newly land-scaped back garden.

Faith smiles. 'Do you remember this tree?' she asks, wandering towards the large horse chestnut near the boundary. It's the only familiar landmark left. 'I used to love collecting the conkers and keeping them in a pile on my windowsill. At least, I did until I couldn't bear to see one more "collection" in the house. Once I turned nine I never did it again. That's sad, isn't it?'

Heather nods. She stares up at the tree. The flowers that stand tall from the end of the branches are gone, having bloomed earlier in the summer, and it's too early to see the spiky pale-green pods that hold the tree's bounty, but as she stares at the twisted bark there's a roaring in her ears. She starts to feel weird again, like she did at the end of the pier, and then the flickering starts in her memory – now, then, now, then – so clear she almost believes she's seeing it with her eyes.

A face smiles at her from above the fence and she steps back, almost stumbling, and covers her mouth with her hand.

'What is it?' Faith comes walking swiftly towards her, turning her head every second or so to see what Heather is looking at. 'What can you see?'

Nothing, Heather thinks. *Nothing that makes sense in this time and place,* anyway. Her hand is still over her mouth and she removes it. 'I think… I think I remembered something,' she tells Faith and is suddenly very glad her sister is here. She wouldn't like to be doing this on her own. Somehow, having Faith here makes her reactions valid, less… crazy.

'What?' Faith looks concerned now, the way she does when she checks the kids' temperatures if they've got a fever.

'Her. Staring over the fence at me. Smiling.'

Faith stares at Heather. Heather can see her brain working hard, dredging through her own memories of that time, evidenced by micro-expressions of confusion, disbelief, and finally shock. 'But that's impossible unless…'

'Unless she lived there,' Heather finishes for her, feeling strangely breathless.

Both sisters race across the back garden of their former home, through the gate and back out onto street. They turn left in unison and run along the pavement, stopping when the fence and shrubs no longer obscure their view.

Once again, in Heather's mind, there are two conflicting versions of reality: a 1930s bungalow with a pretty rose garden, and what stands there now, a sympathetic new-build of much grander proportions. She's not surprised the old house is gone. It always looked out of place nestled amongst the much larger Victorian and Edwardian houses. Her only guess is that the owners of the three-storey, mock-Tudor affair two doors down had at some point in the Fifties sold off a piece of their massive garden to a developer.

Even though the bungalow is gone, she can picture it so clearly: a concrete path that led up to the front door, edged with petunias, pansies and marigolds. Inside the fully glazed front door with the sunburst design, there was a hallway with floral wallpaper and pistachio-coloured carpet that led to a yellow kitchen. She'd always loved the interior of the house. The pastel colours had reminded her of ice cream. It had seemed so bright and cheerful compared to the dirty browns and greys of her own home.

Ice cream.

A memory hits Heather so hard she almost sits down where she is on the pavement.

Mint-choc-chip ice cream. That's what the lady had always given her after she'd skipped up the flowery path and into the yellow kitchen.

Heather gasps, and Faith rushes to her but is unsure of how to help, of what's going on, so she just lays a hand on her sister's shoulder as Heather presses both her palms to the centre of her chest and tries to remember the mechanics of breathing.

Lydia!

'Lydia,' she says out loud, and instantly knows the name is right. She looks at Faith. 'Patricia is Lydia, and Lydia is Patricia. She was our next-door neighbour!'

CHAPTER THIRTY-SIX

TOILET DOOR

Despite this being a 'nice' school, a trip to the girls' loos will confirm that people are people, no matter how much privilege they have. Don't kid yourself that there's any Tennyson or Shakespeare on the back of these toilet doors – it's the same stuff as anywhere else carved into the wood or scrawled across the peeling varnish with permanent marker. There are ten stalls and I know that behind doors number two, five, and nine (it sounds like a game show, doesn't it?) there are comments directed specifically at me. One even has a cartoon. I don't think I've ever read anything so vicious and scathing, but I suppose that's what a grammar-school education will get you these days.

THEN

Heather watches the second hand clunk round the large clock at the front of the class. The bell is going to ring in five minutes. It's now or never. She puts her hand up.

'Yes, what is it?' Mr Salter, her rather fractious history teacher, asks.
'Can I go to the toilet, please, Sir?'

His shoulders slump and he practically rolls his eyes. 'Can't you wait until the end of the lesson, Lucas?'

She shakes her head. 'I really, really need to go.'

'Oh, for goodness' sake. What are you? Three? You can wait.'

Heather blanches. She's going to have to say this. It's the only way. 'But I'm on my period, Sir.'

She's rewarded with a titter from at least half the class. It stings, but she brushes it aside, because it's the lesser of two evils.

Mr Salter sighs. 'If you must…'

Heather doesn't need to be told twice. She scoops up her bag, clutches it to her chest, and scurries from the room without looking back. Just in case someone checks, she heads for the girls' loos down the corridor, and stands just inside the door. She doesn't go into a cubicle. Mostly because she just told Mr Salter a big, fat lie – her period isn't due for another week.

When she thinks it's safe she pokes her head around the door. The corridor is empty. Perfect. She turns in the opposite direction from her classroom and starts to run, out of the door into the playground then, taking a route that means she can't be seen from the modern block full of windows, she weaves in and out of various school buildings until she reaches the sports field, where she dashes across an open piece of grass, praying no one spots her, and dives behind the pavilion.

Heart beating hard, she crouches down, letting her bum sink onto the damp grass as her back presses against the painted bricks. *Phew. Made it.* All she has to do now is wait.

As she sits, panting, she recalls Tia Paine's face in German that afternoon. She kept staring over, eyes narrowed, lips twisted into a smirk, and Heather just knew that this was going to be one of those days where whispering behind her back in class or passing notes around for everyone else to laugh at wasn't going to be enough.

She doesn't know how Tia learned her old nickname, but she has, and now Tia's made it her personal mission to wipe the name of Heather Lucas from the student body's collective memory, so she can replace it with the snappy shortened version she's come up with: *Hobo*.

Tia is into blood sports, bullying being the chief one, and ever since the skip incident four long years ago, Heather has been her favourite quarry. She doesn't know quite what drives the other girl's merciless pursuit of her. It's certainly not jealousy. She has a suspicion it's because she almost fooled Tia, was on the verge of infiltrating her inner circle when she was found out. Whatever the reason, it's relentless.

So when Heather saw that joyously evil glimmer in Tia's eyes across the classroom this afternoon, she knew she needed to do something drastic. Tia and the backing singers, even Claudie, are probably waiting for her at the school gates right now. There is no way she's turning up. She just can't face dealing with a ripped blazer again, or having the contents of her school bag dumped in the dustbin (where trash like her belongs, apparently).

Just as Heather's breath is starting to come normally, she hears footsteps. Instantly she's on her feet, ready to run.

But it isn't a gang of girls that rounds the corner of the pavilion; it's a boy. And not just any boy. Ryan Fellowes, star of the drama club and the hottest boy in Year Ten. If he's surprised at finding Heather there, he doesn't show it. She hugs her school bag to her chest, eyes wide, as he leans nonchalantly back against the wall, pulls a packet of cigarettes out of his blazer pocket, and lights up.

'You don't mind, do you?' he says. Heather is fairly confident he wouldn't stub it out even if she did say she minded, so she shakes her head. He holds the pack out to her. 'Want one?' She shakes her head again. 'You're Heather Lucas, aren't you?'

She stares back at him, too shocked to even nod. Ryan Fellowes knows her name.

He laughs. 'Can you actually talk, or is Tia Paine right and you're a deaf-mute?'

Heather swallows. 'I can talk.' Not fancy, not witty, but it gets her point across.

'She's a total bitch, that one,' Ryan says and takes a long drag on his cigarette. Normally Heather thinks that smoking is disgusting, but it almost looks cool on him. She's fascinated now. How can it be that the two of them are the only ones in the whole year who can see Tia's true colours? Everyone else loves her, and it's got even worse since her uncle got killed off when part of the hospital collapsed on *Casualty*, because then he got a part as one of the minor teachers in the upcoming *Harry Potter* film. The rest of the school treats her like fricking royalty.

Ryan smokes the rest of his cigarette in silence, then stubs it out against the bricks, and puts the butt into a tin that used to contain mints, explaining that he's too clever to leave any evidence behind. He pushes himself away from the wall and prepares to go.

'I'm going to be here again tomorrow,' he says. 'Are you?'

On automatic, Heather almost shakes her head again, but she manages to turn the gesture into a shrug.

One side of his mouth hitches up in a smile. Heather loses sensation in her knees.

'Cool. Well, maybe I'll see you…' And he saunters off, saving her from having to produce an answer.

CHAPTER THIRTY-SEVEN

NOW

Faith and Heather stand on the side of the road, digging up memories for more than half an hour, until a few curious faces appear at windows and an elderly man, who looks as if he might have once been in the military, gives them a pointed look as he marches past. They don't belong here. Not any more. But it's weird because now Heather feels a sense of connection, of ownership, to that blasted house in a way she never has before.

When they get back in the car Faith says she'll take Heather home again, but Heather asks her to drop her off in Bromley town centre instead.

She's not ready to go back to her flat just yet. There are too many things inside her head, things she is afraid she will spill out if given the slightest invitation, and she's not so sure that's wise. She needs to get things right in her own mind before she sees Jason again. It's different with Faith. She was there. For most of the time, anyway. She knows.

But going into town is a mistake. Heather tries to avoid the High Street, keeping to the air-conditioned safety of The Glades instead.

But somehow – possibly because she made the mistake of browsing in Marks & Spencer, which has exits to both the shopping centre and the street – she finds herself standing outside Mothercare.

I'll just go in and have a look, she tells herself. It's Barney's birthday in a couple of weeks, so she needs to find something appropriate for him, and now the Early Learning Centre has relocated inside here, it's the obvious place. She won't look at the clothes and baby stuff. She'll walk right through to the back and stay in the toy area. That should be safe.

She goes to the bit with the realistic-looking plastic animals. She's not convinced they're an exciting present, but Barney loves them with a passion and Faith has given her approval. Heather decides to get five or six – they're not very expensive – and Barney will have enough to open a veritable zoo when he's added them to his collection.

Choosing them actually turns out to be fun. She debates with herself the merits of getting an assorted bunch, lots of different animals, or a family group – like mummy, daddy and baby tigers – and decides she can manage to do both. She picks up two large snow tigers, one prowling, one lying down, and a cute-looking cub with a tiny red tongue sticking out. And then she looks for a few more to make up the assortment. No lions. Barney has plenty of those: a whole pride, practically. But a killer whale would probably go down well, with its stubby plastic teeth and solid mass. She adds a dolphin, just because it seems to be smiling at her, and then hunts for her final choice.

She spots it almost instantly. A jellyfish. It's translucent, with a dull white canopy and neon-pink see-through tentacles underneath. Barney will love it. Who cares that what should be a tiny sea creature is half the size of the killer whale in her other hand? Obviously, when it comes to plastic animals, relative size isn't a concern.

She turns and heads towards the till, pleased with her finds, but then something strange happens. As she's nearing the midpoint of the shop, instead of heading down the wide path between racks of frilly clothes and tiny shoes to pay for her choices, she just keeps going towards the door.

Stop, she tells herself. *Stop!* But her feet don't listen. They just keep moving, even though she knows this is wrong, even though she knows she can't steal Barney's birthday present. If she gives them to him after this, it'll be like making him an accessory. Could a four-year-old even be charged with receiving stolen goods?

'Excuse me!' The voice is loud and clear behind her. Her stride quickens. 'Excuse me, Madam!'

She's almost at the door now, fresh air and freedom taunting her. A hand rests on her shoulder. She turns to find one of the sales assistants – the bossy one with the sharp eyes – looking pink and exasperated. 'Madam... I think you may have forgotten to stop by the till for those items.' She glances down at the plastic jellyfish gripped in Heather's left hand and the assortment of other animals clutched to her midriff with the other.

'Um... But...' Heather stutters. She has no idea how to talk her way out of this one.

Sharp Eyes smiles. It makes her look much nicer. Her gaze dips to Heather's stomach. 'Easily done with "baby brain". when I had my first, I almost burned down the house by trying to cook rice but forgetting to put water in the pan.'

At first Heather can't make sense of what the woman is saying, but when she does a hand flies to her stomach. The sales assistant thinks she's pregnant – or is at least giving her a convenient 'out' – but instead of being cross or embarrassed or grateful, all Heather feels is a stabbing sense of loss that she isn't. Her womb is empty, and she's afraid it will always remain so, that she had her chance and fluffed it.

She realizes the woman is still looking at her, waiting for a response, so she nods and follows her to the till. She's burning with humiliation but also secretly relieved. She couldn't stop herself but this woman intervened and saved her.

'Sorry,' she whispers, as the woman rings the tiger family and sea creatures through the register. 'I... I don't know what I was thinking.'

'No harm done.'

But as Heather leaves the shop, relief starting to crash over her in waves, she's aware of the woman's razor-sharp eyes on her back.

CHAPTER THIRTY-EIGHT

NOW

Someone is ringing the doorbell insistently. Heather pauses the drama series she's watching on TV and jumps up. She's expecting a delivery at some point today. She ordered Barney some story books online that she hopes he'll like. She can't give him the animals. They feel tainted, even though she paid for them. Maybe at Christmas…

She runs into the hallway as Jason comes bounding down the stairs. It makes her heart hiccup. She reaches the front door before him, thanks the delivery guy for her package, and closes the door again. Jason jumps from the last step onto the floor.

'Why did you come down?' she asks, perplexed. 'It was my buzzer he was wearing out.'

He walks towards her and she hugs the cardboard package to herself. 'I haven't seen you for three days and I wanted to see if you're okay.' He exhales. 'Saturday was a bit of a head trip, even for me.'

She nods and squeezes the parcel more tightly. 'I'm okay.'

'Really?'

She smiles at him. 'Really.' And then she sighs. His gentle concern has bulldozed a wall inside her. It's as if, since she spilled everything out to him the other week, the words keep falling out of the hole he made, even when she's not sure she wants to share them. 'I went to see my sister on Sunday. We pieced a little more of the puzzle together.'

'You did?'

She nods then glances towards her open front door. 'Do you want to come in? I'll fill you in.'

He thinks for a moment and then smiles at her. 'I've got a better idea.'

* * *

They jump in Jason's car and he takes her to a nice little pub he knows about half an hour away, in the depths of the countryside. It sits on the edge of the Downs and boasts a terrace with spectacular views of the valley below. Heather doesn't usually like fizzy drinks, but she joins Jason by having a pint of lemonade – the only drink to have at the end of a hot summer's day like this.

She closes her eyes as she sips it and wonders where that conviction came from. Instantly another lost memory flashes up: a picture of her father handing a tumbler of spitting, hissing liquid to her, the blessed coolness as it goes down, the clinking of the ice cubes as she gets near the bottom. She's getting more and more of these memories now. They keep popping into her head at random.

The sunset isn't a showy riot of fiery oranges and purples; just a demure blending of pastel colours at the horizon. Heather tells Jason about the photograph, and about the house in Hawksbury Road and Lydia, as the colourful sky dissolves into a uniform lilac-grey.

'You think this Lydia is definitely the woman you saw on the pier?'

Heather sighs. 'My gut tells me yes, but memory is such a tricky thing…' She scrubs her forehead with her hand, as if trying to clear the dirt from a murky mental window. 'But she said my name, didn't she? She said my name.'

Jason nods. 'It certainly sounded that way, but…' He stares into his half-empty pint glass. 'Maybe she thought you were someone else? There could be any number of reasons…'

'But we were in Hastings, at the same place she took me. All these things keep adding up,' Heather says, feeling surer now. 'It can't just be coincidence.'

When they've finished their drinks, they walk to the end of the pub garden. There's a small playground there with two swings, a slide and some weird contraption for kids to climb on, but it's almost dark now so it's deserted. They stroll to the far side where there's a view over rolling fields, lean on the wooden rail of the fence, and stare out into the twilight.

The sounds of the crowd on the terrace are muffled here, and they're hidden from view by some overgrown shrubs, so Jason leans in and kisses her.

'Every time I tell you something sad or traumatic about my life, you kiss me,' Heather whispers when they pull apart.

'It's not *why* I kiss you.'

Isn't it? thinks Heather. She can't fathom any other reason. He's too much of a knight in shining armour, this one, and she's definitely a damsel in a whole heap of distress. She's not sure he can help himself, despite his protestations to the contrary. And it's horrible timing for her, even though she's been aching for someone to say these kinds of things to her, to look at her this way, for so long. The truth is that she's not ready to get involved with anyone. She's such a mess still.

'What happened with her?' she says suddenly. 'The woman the leathers belonged to.'

Jason sighs. 'Her name was Jodie. She was the sister of my old flatmate, Alex. A couple of years ago she came to stay with us – it was supposed to be temporary, just a couple of weeks until she could get herself sorted out.'

'She was in trouble,' Heather says. It's not a question.

'Yep.' He sighs again. 'She'd split up with her boyfriend. She didn't say much but she gave the clear impression it had been a bit of a toxic relationship: that he'd been controlling, even stealing from her, and that in the end she'd just had to run. But it left her in a bit of a bind financially, which is how she ended up staying with us.'

'And the two of you became an item?'

He nods and gazes off down the valley.

'What was she like?' Part of Heather really doesn't want to know the answer to that question, but another part is fascinated by what Jason finds appealing in a woman.

He shrugs. 'Lively, funny… but vulnerable. I don't know why but she reminded me of a butterfly.'

Heather looks down at her feet. 'You really liked her, then?'

'I was on the verge of asking her to marry me.'

Oh. She hadn't been expecting him to say that. In fact, she wishes he hadn't. How can she compare to this wonderful, vibrant woman he's just described?

She doesn't need to ask the next question because Jason tells her anyway. 'One day some burly-looking guys came knocking at the door. At first, I was going to call the police because I thought they were something to do with her ex, but it turned out she owed their boss money – lots of money.'

'Drugs?' Heather whispers.

He shakes his head. 'Gambling. It seemed Jodie had quite the habit. After that it all came out and suddenly *I* became the controlling one who was cramping her style. She just couldn't see why I was upset she hadn't told me about any of it, about how she'd lied. Those are the worst kind of lies, you know?' he says, looking over at Heather for confirmation. 'Not the fib – or even the whopper – told in the heat of the moment, but the ones that are built slowly, deliberately constructed to obscure the truth.'

Heather's stomach starts to quiver.

Jason laughs softly, shaking his head. 'I started to feel a bit sorry for the ex, realizing there was probably more to that story than I'd cared to know, that maybe it wasn't him she'd been running from after all. I felt like such an idiot. There was the engagement ring, hiding in my sock drawer, and I had no idea who this woman was.'

'She left you?'

'No,' he replies, and his tone hardens. 'I told her she should move out, and when she refused, said this was her brother's flat and she would stay if she wanted to, I packed my stuff and left. That's how I ended up where I am now. It was the first place I found that was suitable.'

Heather nods, because she's not quite sure what to say.

He looks at her intently, leans forward, but doesn't kiss her. 'So that's my story, but it's in the past. I want you to know that, which is why I'm going back to our original topic of conversation. I like you, Heather. *That's* why I want to kiss you. You're kind and imaginative and funny. But if this isn't what you want, we can go back to being friends… neighbours. I can stop kissing you. It's up to you.'

Heather weighs his words for a moment, and then she slides her flattened hands up his chest, loops them round his neck and pulls him closer. 'No,' she says with the barest of breaths. 'Don't stop.'

Stupid, stupid, stupid. But it seems Jason isn't the only one who can't help himself.

* * *

When Heather gets back that evening, she spots the plastic animals she almost stole for Barney, their knobbly shapes clearly visible through a reusable shopping bag hanging from the hooks in her hall.

Bolstered by her lovely night, she takes the bag and walks to her spare bedroom. It's half-sorted now, but boxes and crates still fill one side. She hasn't even dared to touch the chest of drawers up until this point, but now she does, sliding the middle draw out – the one that holds all the stuff she doesn't want to think about – and carefully wedging each plastic animal in the spaces between the other items. It's full to bursting now.

There's no more room for anything else. No more room for this terrible, terrible behaviour in her life. She's got to stop. She's got to. Because if she can conquer this compulsion – this addiction – then she won't have anything to hide from Jason. She won't have anything she needs to lie about, and then maybe there's hope, because she can become the person he already thinks she is. And she'd really, really like to be that woman.

CHAPTER THIRTY-NINE

SUNDRESS

It's yellow, made of cotton, with spaghetti straps and a skirt that flares out a little from the waist. It is bright and optimistic, a perfect representation of all the girlish innocence and hope that fills me this evening. I know it looks good on me. I just don't know how good until it is too late.

THEN

It's Friday evening. Heather hops off the bus near Queen Mary's Hospital and walks along the road until she can see the sloping lawns of Sidcup Place. There's a tree on the brow of the hill. She waits there, nervously adjusting her dress. Ryan has never seen her in anything but school uniform before. She wants him to think she looks nice, and this dress is the nicest thing she owns. Well, her mother owns. She stole it from the hoard this morning.

Heather has been meeting Ryan behind the pavilion after school every day for the last three weeks. He talks to her. Actually, properly talks to her. And he says she makes him laugh. Mostly she does it without meaning to, but sometimes she actually manages to do it on purpose.

Then, this afternoon, he suggested meeting up away from school. She went warm all over when he said that. Heather has always believed that secrets are nasty, dirty things, but this one – her friendship with Ryan Fellowes, hidden from everyone else at Highstead – is delicious. It's left untold because it's too precious to share, not because it's shameful.

She snuck out earlier that evening. Her mother doesn't know she's even left the house. Heather is banking on the fact she'll be too caught up watching eviction night on *Big Brother* to notice she's alone in the house.

She stares out across the valley. The building behind her was probably a lovely house once, but now it's a Brewer's Fayre and the car park has swallowed up what would have been the front garden. However, the rest of the grounds remain: a small formal area and then sloping hills and trees. It's a pity the view is spoiled by the ugly gash of the A20 and the concrete of the Sidcup bypass at the bottom of the hill.

Heather keeps her eyes open but imagines the eyesores away, and then she just keeps going, spinning a wonderful fantasy that'll make this night even more special. She imagines herself and Ryan as characters in a Regency romance, meeting for a secret tryst. It feels daring to think such things, probably because she still can't believe he likes her. But he must like her a bit, mustn't he, otherwise why would he ask her to meet him here?

Ryan arrives, strolling lazily across the grass, a couple of cans of cider dangling from the plastic webbing hooked over his fingers. He smiles and Heather goes hot all over. They walk further away from the road, down the grassy hill and out of sight of both people and cars. She can almost believe her fantasy is real now the traces of civilization are out of sight.

They sit under a drooping tree and Ryan – in a very gentlemanly way, Heather thinks – cracks the first can of cider and hands it to her. They sit there, drinking and talking, until Heather starts to get giggly, and then Ryan moves in closer. 'You know I like you,' he says, and then he leans in and kisses her. Properly kisses her.

Heather whispers, 'I like you too.'

He kisses her again, pulling her closer, and this time his hand comes to rest on her boob. She jerks back at the touch – mostly because she's surprised. She still has her Regency daydream running in her head and, let's face it, it's not what Mr Knightley would have done in the same circumstances. But when he whispers that she needs to relax, she doesn't tell him to stop. This is the ultimate proof that Ryan Fellowes, Highstead heart-throb, actually truly likes her.

Eventually his hand stops kneading her boob and trails its way down her body, under her skirt and up her thigh. It makes everything down there tingle in a nice way, but she's scared too. It's all happening very fast. She expects him to just stroke her thighs, tease a little, so when his hand reaches the spot where the tingling is the fiercest, she gasps.

Ryan takes this as encouragement and keeps going. Heather wants to say something but she's too shocked to make any other noise. This isn't exactly how she thought this would be. She's always imagined it would be more gentle, more romantic, not like the guy is fumbling around as if he's searching for a lost set of keys.

The buzz from the cheap cider is gone now. Heather starts to think about asking him if he'd mind slowing down, maybe even stopping, but the words never leave her mouth because just as she's managed to pluck up enough courage, he leans in and whispers in her ear. 'You're so hot, Heather, so pretty. You feel so good. I just can't help myself with you. You drive me crazy.' And then he kisses down the side of her neck so softly, so tenderly.

Everything changes in that moment. So what if this isn't exactly how she imagined it would be? Maybe it's just that she's new at this. Maybe everyone feels like this the first time they, you know, do stuff. And anyway, it doesn't matter. How Ryan feels about her is what's really important, and he's just told her, maybe not in so many words, that he wants her, that she's special. She reaches up and winds her arms around his neck and kisses him back harder. She is not going to ruin this.

As a result, it's not long before her knickers are lying on the ground near her feet and Ryan is on top of her, grunting. She holds him tight and tries not to mind that her head keeps bumping rhythmically against a tree root. His eyes are closed, his face a mask of concentration. He seems lost inside himself. Heather can't quite believe that it's her making him feel this way. It's quite intoxicating to be the entire focus of someone's attention like this. She even starts to think she might be enjoying it a little.

Even so, as she stares at the sky through the branches above their heads, she wonders how long it's going to be until it's all over and done with.

CHAPTER FORTY

NOW

Heather glances at herself in her dressing-table mirror as she threads a dangly silver earring through the hole in her earlobe. Her hair is brushed and shiny and her eyes are huge, thanks to the careful application of mascara and a little eyeliner. She looks like a different person.

She steps back and takes a look at the whole picture. Her heart flutters a little. She hopes he likes what he sees.

Just as she's reaching for her handbag on the end of the bed, the doorbell rings. She slows her breathing, tells herself to stop being stupid, and goes to answer it. She finds Jason standing there with a bunch of beautiful flowers. Nothing as mundane as uniform roses. This is a riot of colours and textures, and Heather loves them. She blushes. 'Thank you.'

He smiles at her and she blushes again. 'I'll just go and put these in some water and then we can be off.'

After doing so, they walk up the hill into the town centre, taking the shortcut through the park, and end up at one of the Italian restaurants in Bromley North. They walk in the door and as the hostess leads them to their table, Heather stares around at the other diners, many of them young couples sharing a relaxed meal, and she wants to run round the restaurant and high-five them, feeling a sense of camaraderie, of being part of the same club. She's always been the outsider looking in before, the lone diner reading a book and pretending it's fine to be eating solo. But if anyone walks into the restaurant right now, they won't be able to pick her out of the crowd, they won't be able to tell she's the odd one out. She's on a date. She's actually on a date!

She smiles at Jason as they peruse their menus.

'What?' he says, smiling too but looking slightly confused.

Heather glances down at her menu. 'Nothing. Just having a nice time.'

He laughs. 'We've only been here five minutes.'

She shrugs. 'What can I say? I'm easy to please.'

And it's easy to talk to Jason as they work their way through their starters and then begin their main courses. The conversation meanders through pieces of their personal histories – carefully edited on Heather's part – what they studied at university, jobs they've held, movies they've seen and both loved and hated, but as they wait for the waitress to clear their plates Jason gets more serious.

'I've got something to tell you,' he says.

Heather's smile slides from her face. Oh, no. This is it. The bit where he says they ought to be just good friends. She knew this was too good to last. She pulls her features into a blank canvas.

'Well, two things, really. The first is that I've decided to sell the engagement ring I bought for Jodie. I didn't ever give it to her, and I'm never going to. Thinking about your mum and how she held onto stuff that had outlived its usefulness has made me look at my own possessions in a new way.' He shrugs. 'I'm ready to let go, move on, I've realized. I suppose I have you to thank for that.'

Heather smiles nervously. Number one was okay, but number two is still looming...

'The second thing is that I woke up about three o'clock last night, couldn't sleep. I started thinking about you...' Heather flushes foolishly at his admission. 'And then I started thinking about you and that woman, Patricia... Lydia. I couldn't stop thinking about it so I got up, got my laptop out, and put her name in Google again.'

Heather is frowning. She was so sure she was about to get dumped that she can't tell where this is going.

'This time I didn't look for Patricia Waites – I looked for Lydia Waites.'

His words are like a boulder dropping in a still, cold pool. They splash up and drench her, waking her up. Suddenly she is in the moment and everything is crystal-clear. Painfully so.

'You found something?' she whispers.

He nods, then pulls his phone out of his pocket and shows her. The mobile browser is open, revealing a website banner: Haven Women's Mental Health Project. She squints at the screen.

'Scroll down,' Jason tells her. 'To the News section.'

Heather does so, but her fingers feel large and clumsy, like a fist of sausages, and she shoots past the right section of the webpage and has to tap the screen to climb back up to the bit she wants.

Lottery grant awarded... TV celebrity named as new patron... Annual fundraising gala dinner...

Ah, here it is:

Tickets are now available for our gala dinner at the price of £75. Please click the link below should you wish to support us in this way. As well as an excellent dinner at the Palm Court Hotel and an evening of entertainment, we will be holding a silent auction. If you have any items, gifts or services you wish to donate for the auction, please contact Lydia Waites through info@ HWMHproject.org.uk, quoting 'auction' in the subject header.

She looks up at Jason, phone still gripped in her hand, her finger poised to scroll on. 'I know it's not a common name, but do you really think it's her? It could just—'

'Read on,' Jason says seriously. Heather scans the rest of the paragraph. There's nothing more, just details of the hotel the event is being held at. When she reads the address, she actually jerks back in surprise and almost drops Jason's phone.

'Hastings!' she says, a little too loudly, and the couple on the next table turn to look at her. That feeling of being part of the same club has disappeared now. Now she's just a girl making a scene in a public place. 'Hastings?' she repeats more softly. Jason just looks back at her, saying nothing.

'It's too much of a coincidence, isn't it?' she says, knowing she is voicing his thoughts as well as her own.

'There's only one way to find out,' he replies.

* * *

The following Monday, both Jason and Heather take the day off work and travel down to Hastings. They go in her car, now with a replacement battery and showing no hint of having a relapse. This really isn't a motorbike kind of visit.

Heather walks into the registered offices of Haven Women's Mental Health Project at 11.30, while Jason waits outside. A woman is sitting at reception, head bowed as she scribbles on a pad. She has wavy dark hair, a bit like the woman in the photograph, but Heather can't see her face. She walks up to the desk, her pulse drumming. It's stupid. Although it's Lydia that Heather has come here to see, she suddenly feels unprepared.

The woman lifts her head. It's not her.

Heather breathes out again, feeling the double-pronged jab of both relief and disappointment.

'Excuse me?' she says. 'I was wondering if I could speak to Lydia Waites?'

Heather expects the receptionist to smile politely or reach for the phone on her desk, but she does neither of those things. 'What's it about?' she asks, raking her eyes up and down Heather's face and body, measuring her up.

'I… I…' Heather grapples for the speech she rehearsed in her head all the way down in the car. 'I have something I'd like to donate for the silent auction she's organizing. For the fundraising dinner.'

The hardness in the receptionist's eyes dims a little, but not much, and Heather wonders how on earth she got this job. She'd be surprised if the woman didn't scare all but the most robust clients away.

'Oh. Well. That's lovely. What is it you want to donate?'

Heather shuffles on her feet. As much as she's been planning this conversation during the entire hour's drive to Hastings, she hasn't done a very good job of covering all her bases. She hadn't expected an inquisition at the first hurdle.

'I'd rather discuss that with Lydia, if you don't mind.'

The woman straightens her spine and looks down her nose at Heather. She clearly does mind.

'So can I see her?' Heather asks. Her nerves start to prickle. She wants to get this over and done with as quickly as possible.

'She's not here.'

Heather glances towards the row of uncomfortable-looking upholstered chairs against the wall. 'Can you tell me when she'll be back? I don't mind waiting.'

The woman smiles and then plays her trump card. 'Sorry, love. But she doesn't work here.'

'But the website said—'

'She's a volunteer,' the woman says. 'But if you've got something for the auction, you can email this address.' She shoves a colour-ful leaflet about the gala dinner across the desk towards Heather. It's no help at all. Even before Heather picks it up, she can tell it contains exactly the same information that was on the website.

'Is there any way to contact Ms Waites directly? It really is rather urgent. Could you give me her email address or a phone number?'

She was hoping to be able to confront Lydia face to face. She knows she's grasping at straws now. Even if the woman does give her what she wants, the likelihood of Lydia responding if she con-tacts her is probably slim to none.

'Sorry,' the receptionist says, not looking the tiniest bit penitent. 'Data protection and all that. But I can get my manager, if you like? She supervises Lydia when she's in.'

'Oh, no. It's okay...' Heather glances towards the front door, wishing she could just teleport herself to the other side of it and find herself back in the street where Jason is waiting for her. 'I'll just, you know...'

The woman is looking suspicious now. She opens her mouth slightly, as if she's trying to decide whether she should call her manager anyway.

'I'll just use the email, like you said,' Heather replies, then turns and scurries out of there before the woman can say anything else.

She finds Jason perusing the outside menu of a cute little café a few doors down. 'That was quick,' he says when he sees her, but his eyes wander back to the menu while he waits for her answer. Heather decides that maybe her story is better told over a sandwich and a pot of loose-leaf tea.

They choose to sit at a little table in the courtyard garden at the back of the café, and Heather gives Jason a blow-by-blow account of her time in the charity office. 'That Lydia woman is definitely very good at disappearing when she needs to,' Heather says, sighing. 'Here we are again – back at square one.'

Jason stares into the distance as he finishes his sandwich. He swallows before looking at her. 'Maybe not,' he says.

'Have you got another idea?' Heather asks. 'Because, aside from staking out the charity offices for the next month or so, I'm all out.'

He smiles and jabs a finger at the flyer lying on the table. It's the one the receptionist gave Heather. She was still clutching it when they came out here and sat down.

'Did you notice the date?'

Heather looks at the flyer and then meet his eyes. She gets that quivery feeling again.

'It's this weekend. We might not know where Lydia Waites is at this very moment, but we know exactly where she's going to be in six days and nine hours' time.'

CHAPTER FORTY-ONE

NOW

Heather arrives at the Palm Court Hotel that Saturday evening for the Haven Project's gala dinner. She plucks nervously at the hem of the new dress Faith made her buy. When she told her sister of her plans for the weekend, Faith had jumped in the car and frog-marched Heather round Bromley for some late-night shopping. They'd ended up getting a chiffon thing in midnight blue. When she tried it on in the shop, she'd been reassured by the practically Amish neckline, but she hadn't realized it would show quite so much leg when she walked.

She glances at Jason. He looks as he always looks: relaxed, confident, ready for anything life has to throw at him. Heather wishes she felt the same way. Inside she's like a ball of wool that's been mauled by a kitten: all frayed and tangled.

Once she'd booked the tickets, she also had to make good on her bluff and rustle up something to donate to the silent auction. At first she was at a loss, but then she struck gold: Cassandra. Her mother – for once – had been right about one of her treasures: the ringleted horror is worth something even with her busted fingers.

Heather had hoped to drop the doll off during in the week so she could hand it over to Lydia Waites personally, therefore doing away with the need for this whole charade, but the woman was continuing to be elusive, even though Heather had invented a false name to put the donation under. They'd wanted the doll sent to the charity offices, so she'd just packaged it up and taken it to the post office. And now she is here. Scouting. Waiting.

She takes a deep breath as she and Jason enter the lobby. People are milling around, sipping flutes of champagne, dressed in dinner jackets and cocktail dresses. A few women have even gone the whole hog and opted for ballgowns. It's all very fancy. It feels like the first day of school, and Heather knows what a torture school can be. She's very glad Jason's large, warm hand is wrapped around hers.

She inhales sharply as she spots a table on the far side of the lobby. A mop of chestnut curls and piercing blue eyes catch her attention. She scans the rest of the display, realizes these must be the auction items, and stops walking. Jason pulls up short beside her, starts to ask what the matter is, but then follows her gaze and goes quiet. Heather knows she should walk over there and see if Lydia is manning the display – this is what she came for, after all – but some deep, primal sense of self-preservation is telling her to turn and walk the other way. But then a group of people shifts and she gets a glimpse of the volunteer on guard: a starchy-looking man who's seventy if he's a day.

Not Lydia, then.

Does she know? Heather thinks. *On some elemental level, does she sense my net is closing around her, that she'll have to answer for her crimes – not to the police or society, but to me? Her victim.*

'Don't give up hope,' Jason whispers in her ear. 'She has to be here somewhere, even if she's skulking behind the scenes.'

Heather nods, doesn't tear her eyes away from the man as they walk into the ballroom, which earns her a penetrating stare. He straightens as if he's on sentry duty, and then she lets Jason lead her away.

The dinner starts. There's a salad of some kind, and a singer who serenades them through the eating of it, but Heather can't seem to pay attention to anything. When the waiters and waitresses come to clear their plates, she takes the chance to slip to the Ladies. It's right off the foyer near where the auction table has been set up. A perfect excuse.

She hurries along, dress swishing against her legs, and it's only when she's right beside the display that she risks a proper look. What she sees stops her in her tracks.

Finally, it's her. Lydia. Standing there beside the table as if she has a perfect right to be living a normal life, doing normal things. She's not as dressed up as some of the others, only wearing a sparkly top, smart black trousers. and a pair of really ugly shoes. She's busy leafing through a sheaf of papers and doesn't notice Heather at first, but she must sense someone hovering nearby because after a few seconds she stops what she's doing and looks up.

'Oh!' she says. 'It's you.' Bland words that do nothing to convey the utter shock written all over her features.

'Yes,' says Heather. 'It's me. Again.'

Lydia starts shaking her head. Her feet haven't moved, but Heather gets the distinct impression she's backing away. 'I don't think...' she begins.

'Please...' Heather begins. 'I need to talk to you.'

Lydia takes a shaky breath. 'This isn't a good idea.'

Heather takes a step forward and surprises herself with her bold words. 'For you, maybe. Don't be so selfish – you owe me at least this.'

Lydia swallows, then nods. 'Okay.' She looks over her shoulder to a large set of glazed doors that open onto the gardens behind the hotel. 'Maybe somewhere more private?'

Heather nods and they walk silently, side by side, inadvertently matching each other's stride, across the lobby and out onto the paved terrace beyond. When they reach a shadowy section shielded by shrubs, Lydia turns and waits. She doesn't argue, doesn't try to slip away. Heather gets the feeling she's been waiting for this day to come and, now that it has, she's totally resigned herself to her fate.

She doesn't look like a monster, though, standing there with her frizzy dark hair, her sparse make-up, and supermarket-chain clothes. She just looks... normal.

That makes Heather angry. Why should this woman have that luxury? Up until this moment, she's been struggling with how to start, but now the words flow easily from her mouth. 'You stole my childhood from me,' she tells Lydia. 'I want you to know that. What you did changed everything. It ruined my family.'

Lydia looks down. Her shoulders slump forward. 'I'm so very sorry.'

Even though Heather can no longer see her eyes, remorse is radiating from the other woman in thick, grey waves. She knows Lydia feels humiliated and ashamed and guilty, like she's the scrapings of dog's mess on the side of someone's shoe. Just the way Heather has felt for most of her life.

Heather knows she should feel jubilant. She has sought and found, marched out and conquered, and now she's standing face to face with the woman who has eluded her for so long. Not only that, but her quarry is repentant, defeated. However, Heather discovers it's not nearly enough. The whirlwind inside is not dying down. If anything, it's getting worse.

'That's all you can say?' she spits out. 'Sorry?'

There is a small, almost imperceptible bob of Lydia's head. 'If I could change what I did, I would. I didn't mean any harm…'

Heather lets out a loud, barking laugh and Lydia starts to back away. Heather's hand flies out and she grabs the other woman's arm. The action surprises both of them. However, it wasn't just her own lightning reflexes that shock Heather, but the feeling of solid flesh beneath her fingers. For so long this woman has been a phantom, a hazy outline of a memory that was never fully coloured in. Lydia looks up at her, and there is pleading in her eyes.

'I don't think I can give you what you want,' she whispers. 'I want to, but I can't because I don't think anything I can say will ever make it better. That's why I didn't want to talk to you in the first place.'

'Surely that's my call.' Heather waits until Lydia meets her eyes, until there is silent agreement between them, and then she lets go, slowly and deliberately, one finger at a time, knowing the other woman won't leave without her permission.

At that moment, a couple appear at the double doors and stare out at the darkened garden. They probably can't see the two women, facing off like a fox and a scared rabbit in the shadows, but Heather and Lydia don't take any chances. They move farther down the patio, into a corner where wisteria twines over a pergola. The flowers are gone now but the leaves are dense and drooping, needing a good prune. It welcomes them in and hides them well.

Up until this moment Heather has felt powerful, in control, but as the cool night air swirls around her, it dawns on her that she's got this all switched around. She might be the one acting as if she's got a rocket up her backside, and Lydia seems all cowed and meek, but she needs to tread carefully. This woman has what she wants – answers – and if Heather doesn't calm down, she might never mine that treasure. She takes a deep breath. It's time to stop reacting and time to start thinking about which questions Lydia must answer before she disappears into the mist again.

'I remember a lot,' she tells the other woman, for the first time talking to her as if she's another human being, not a monster from a nightmare. 'I remember your yellow kitchen and mint-choc-chip ice cream... I know from the newspaper reports at the time that you... took me to Hastings for a couple of weeks and then I was returned home safe and sound, but it's not the whole story. There are things I don't know that I need to. Please?'

'What like? What do you remember?'

'Not much. I was six. It's all a bit fuzzy, snatches here and there. I have no idea what's real and what my imagination has conjured up since I found out ten weeks ago.'

Lydia gasps. 'You didn't remember at all?'

'No, I didn't remember! And over the last twenty-six years no one in my family saw fit to tell me. That's what a mess we were. That's what you did to us.' She clamps her mouth shut. She didn't mean to say all that. She may have just blown it. 'When it all boils down to it,' she adds quickly, smoothing her tone and lowering her voice, 'there's just one thing I want to know.'

Lydia is quivering, the same way a scared puppy does when it thinks it's about to feel somebody's boot.

'I want to know the truth.'

There's been precious little of that, but it's the blade that can cut through everything else, the thing that will release her tangled knots. The truth will set her free. It has to.

'I want to know why.'

CHAPTER FORTY-TWO

JUMPER

It lies crumpled in a corner of the playground, once elevated to the status of goalpost, but now the single remnant of a game of football, long abandoned. Forgotten. Left behind. I feel sorry for the jumper. I wonder if it's sad, if it knows the fate that awaits it. It will be rained on, trodden on, kicked into the dirt at the edges of the tarmac playground. Eventually it will become nobody's, not even a useful garment any more. Just a piece of nothing, to be thrown away and forgotten.

3 JULY 1992

The squeals and shouts of the after-school bustle have finished. Everyone has gone home. Only Danny Wiseman's jumper and Heather are left behind in the playground. Heather cranes her neck, both hands gripping the handle of her book bag, trying to see if her mummy is running up the road, all flustered and full of *sorrys*, but the street is empty.

A tiny pinprick of rain lands on her arm. Heather was thinking about rain when she was staring at the jumper. She wonders if somehow she made it happen. She's always wanted to be magic, because being magic means you're special. Heather would like to feel special.

Heather decides to wish even harder for rain and almost instantly the drops start to get bigger and fatter. At first she's happy because it seems to be working, but then she realizes it was a stupid thing to do because now she's going to get really, really wet – like the time Faith fell in the stream at Keston Ponds. Inside her head, she commands the rain to stop, but the clouds don't listen. They keep dumping water all over her.

She looks over her shoulder towards the school doors. They're shut now. Her mum says she should always wait for Faith if she's running late (which she is quite a lot, even though they have at least thirty clocks in their house), but Faith has trampolining tonight and she won't be out for ages and ages. Heather doesn't want to wait all that time in the rain, but what else can she do?

After a while, Heather has a thought. Miss Perrins says she's a big girl now that she's six and at school, that it's good for her to have Sponsibility. Heather isn't quite sure what that is, but Miss Perrins has given her the job of washing up the paintbrushes after art, which she likes because the water goes like a rainbow. If Sponsibility is to do with rainbows, Heather thinks she'd like a lot more of it.

But it also means she's big enough to do things by herself, like doing up her own shoes and wiping her own bottom. Heather thinks about this. She also thinks about the fact she knows the way home without anyone having to show her.

Without looking back towards the school building, she sets off across the playground, glancing at the jumper as she passes by it. She shouldn't feel sorry for it, really, because Danny Wiseman called her smelly today. She should be glad it's there getting all soggy and nasty. Besides, he's the one who smells. Every time he comes close it reminds her of old biscuits. Yuck. She turns round and kicks the jumper before continuing on her journey.

She pulls herself taller as she walks through the gates. She doesn't scuff her shoes on the paving slabs, doesn't drag her book bag. Grown-up girls don't do that sort of thing. They walk along feeling all important, like Heather does now.

Crossing the roads is a little bit scary. She tries to use the ones with the green men but not everywhere has them. One time a driver beeps his horn at her and looks very cross, so Heather runs away and hides round the corner until he's gone. It seems like ages before she reaches home – much, much longer than when she walks with Faith or her mum – but eventually she turns into Hawksbury Road.

She's thirsty after all the walking and she needs the toilet, so she runs round to the back of the house and tries the back door, but it won't move. *That's weird,* Heather thinks. *The lock broke ages ago.* It's still raining, so she goes back round to the front of the house and sits under the porch and waits.

She's kind of zoned out, staring at the gate, when someone speaks.

'Hey there, poppet!' She looks up and the nice lady from next door is at the end of the path. 'What are you doing there sitting on the step in the rain?'

Heather shrugs. 'Just waiting. The door won't open and Faith's at trampolining.'

'Where's your mum? Isn't she home?'

'Don't think so.' Heather stands up, but discovers it wasn't a very good idea. She starts to fidget.

'Do you need the toilet?' Lydia asks, watching her dance from foot to foot.

Heather nods.

Lydia holds out her hand. 'Well, why don't you come and use the toilet at my house?'

Heather crosses her legs and tries not to cry. 'I don't think I can hold it in much longer. The back door is stuck and I'm not strong enough to push it open. Our downstairs toilet is right inside. Can you help me?'

Lydia takes her hand and marches a hopping Heather round to the back of the house. The door doesn't move when she pushes it, so she gives it a harder shove. The door opens a crack but springs back. 'There seems to be something in the way,' she says, and gives it another try. She uses her shoulder to push the door, putting her whole weight against it. At first it looks as if nothing is going to move but then suddenly something gives and the door swings wider before getting caught on a fanned stack of *Radio Times.*

The gap is too small for Lydia to get through but it's just the right size for Heather. She squeezes inside, jumping over the piles of paper like one of those mountain goats she saw on the Discovery Channel, and dashes into the downstairs bathroom.

She comes out again feeling much happier and finds Lydia standing on top of the carpet of papers covering the hall floor. She looks frozen, her eyes wide, her mouth loose. Heather wants to poke her to see if she's stuck like that. Maybe the wind changed, just like Aunty Kathy always warned her it would.

Lydia is still for so long that Heather wonders if she magicked her into a statue by accident. Just as she's about to go up and feel if her skin has actually turned cold and smooth, Lydia turns and looks at her. 'Is it... Is it always like this?'

Heather blinks. 'Like what?'

Lydia stares at her hard, as if she's not quite sure Heather is telling the truth. 'Like... this?' She sweeps her hand in a wide circle as she turns. 'All this stuff.'

Heather looks again, more carefully this time. It's just how her house always is: full. Nothing special. Nothing different. But then she remembers Lydia's yellow kitchen and her lovely living room with the sofa with the pink flowers, and she realizes how *not* full Lydia's house is.

'Is your room like this too?' Lydia asks. 'Where do you sleep?'

'I'll show you,' Heather says and takes Lydia's hand to help her. If you're not used to it, walking on top of the stuff can get a bit slippery, and Lydia's old, after all. Heather leads her down the hallway, past the kitchen and into the living room. Lydia makes a funny squeaking noise as she steps inside and covers her mouth with her free hand.

'Over here.' Heather leads Lydia to her corner. Ever since the piles took over her bedroom, she's slept right there. It's an armchair her mother rescued from outside somebody else's house. It's purple, Heather's favourite colour, and the material is a little bit fluffy if she strokes it. It's magic, too, because if you pull a lever, it changes from being a 'sit up properly' seat into a zigzaggy, lie-down kind of seat that's a bit like a bed. Heather's only little, so it's the perfect size for her.

She shows Lydia her favourite pillow and her *Little Mermaid* duvet cover. She also shows Lydia the little knitted angel she gave Heather for Christmas, sitting near the pillow, keeping her safe. Lydia picks it up and begins to cry.

'Don't be sad,' Heather says, hugging her arm. 'Did you miss the dolly? Do you want it back?'

She shakes her head and pulls Heather close. Heather's face gets squished against her dress, but she doesn't mind because it's a nice kind of hug. 'Are you sure you don't want her back?' Heather asks, looking up at her.

Lydia shakes her head, her eyes wet. 'No. I made her for my daughter, but she... She doesn't need it any more. That's why I thought I'd give it to you. You remind me of her.'

Heather smiles. What Lydia said makes her happy. She wishes Lydia's little girl lived next door with her. They could all play together then.

Lydia looks round the room again, shaking her head. At first, her mouth makes the same kind of wobbly shapes Faith's does when she's trying not to cry, but then it flattens into a hard line.

Heather tugs her hand. 'Can we go to your house and have ice cream now?'

Lydia doesn't move. Heather thinks she's gone all statuey again, but then she suddenly looks down at Heather and smiles really, really wide. 'You know what? I think I have a better idea!'

'Better than mint choc chip?'

Lydia nods. 'Do you know what my little girl and I used to like to do after school sometimes? We used to go to the seaside and eat huge cornets full of whippy ice cream and paddle in the sea.'

Heather starts to jump up and down. 'The seaside!' she shouts. 'I *love* the seaside!'

'Then let's go.'

Lydia steers Heather out of the house, pushing from behind. They're going a little bit too fast, like Lydia can't quite wait to be out in the cool, rainy air again, and they slip and slide on the fallen magazines. Outside, it's no longer raining and the sun is peeking out from behind a cloud. Heather starts to get even more excited. The beach is much more fun when it's sunshiny.

They leave Heather's garden and go next door. Lydia tells Heather to wait beside her car while she fetches her lovely red coat, the one with the sticky-out bottom and the big shiny buttons. When she comes back out wearing it, she hands Heather a coat too. It's like those coats the detectives on TV wear, but instead of yukky brown it's pale pink. When she puts it on, the sleeves hang down past her fingers, but Lydia tuts and folds them back, and then they get in her car and drive away.

CHAPTER FORTY-THREE

NOW

A low stone wall surrounds the terrace. Heather sits down on the rough coping. It scrapes against the backs of her legs through her tights. Lydia has finished telling her story and now the only noise is the breeze in the wisteria above their heads.

This is… This is not what she had expected to hear. And yet… There's something about not just the telling but the facts that seem to ring true. It's like déjà vu, that inner knowledge that something is familiar. Known. She has no idea what to think or say about the whole thing and so she latches onto something else Lydia said.

'What happened to your daughter?' Lydia is looking at the floor. Her head jerks up. 'You said she didn't need the angel any more – I still have it, you know. Did she grow up, move out?'

Lydia shakes her head. 'She died,' she replies softly, blankly. 'When she was nine. A brain aneurysm.' Heather watches her as she talks. She is in another place. Another time. 'That's the sort of thing you expect to happen to adults, isn't it, not children? But it can happen to anyone – a defect in a vein since birth, ticking away like a time bomb inside her head…' She pauses, breathes. 'There was nothing anyone could do. It was nobody's fault.'

'But it doesn't always feel that way, does it?' Heather has forgotten the cold stone against her thighs now. Losing a child… Whatever this woman has done, Heather's heart goes out to her for that at least.

'No. It doesn't.' Lydia sighs. 'Anyway, it destroyed my marriage. Within two years we had separated. I couldn't stand to live in Hastings any more, walking past her school every day on the way to the shops, washing up in the kitchen with the back door open, hearing a child laugh and then realizing our garden was empty. So I moved. To Bickley, far enough away but still close to the A21 so I could get in my car and visit her grave if I wanted to, a tarmac lifeline, linking my old life and my new one. Hawksbury Road was supposed to be my fresh start.'

'Is that why you took me there? To Hastings?'

Lydia looks back at her helplessly. 'Maybe. The truth is I really don't know.' She shakes her head again. 'Something inside me just snapped. I thought I was doing better, getting stronger, that I was coping, but I obviously wasn't. And then I saw you inside that house…' Even now her nose wrinkles in disgust. 'That awful, flea-bitten chair where you slept. And all I could think was that lovely, bright, sunny little girls shouldn't have to endure that. They should be laughing and skipping, eating candyfloss and wearing pretty dresses. They should be allowed to be children.

'I thought of how I used to take Natalie to the beach after school sometimes, how much she loved the fresh air and the waves, and I just decided you needed something nice for a change, a treat.' She looks intently at Heather for a few seconds. 'That was all it was supposed to be – an outing. I didn't mean to keep you longer than an afternoon, but at the time I wasn't really thinking properly, about how far away Hastings was, about how your mother might worry. I just knew I had to get you out of that awful, awful place.'

She falls quiet. Heather feels she ought to say something, express at least some kind of understanding, but she can't. Even though her heart is reaching for Lydia, it's too soon, too fresh, and these facts are sitting in her head like hard, wooden blocks – solid and real, yes, but they don't fit. They don't slot in anywhere to make sense. Not yet.

'Why did you run away that day you saw me on the pier?' Heather asks.

'You said it yourself: I did a horrible thing. I ruined your family.' Tears well in Lydia's eyes and she thumps a fist against her breast, providing a percussive beat to her next assertion. 'I know what it's like to lose a child! *I know!* And I still did it to another mother. It's unforgivable! That's why I ran away when I saw you. I thought I was the last person in the world you'd want to come face to face with.'

There's so much swimming around in Heather's head, but something else is just beginning to dawn on her. Something important. 'Lydia?'

She looks up. 'Yes?'

'I know this sounds very obvious. In fact, it's probably going to sound a bit stupid, given what you've just told me, but are you sure my house was messy *before* we went to Hastings?'

Lydia frowns. 'Yes, of course. I would never have—'

Heather stands up, effectively cutting her off. This doesn't make sense. This doesn't make sense at all.

'I'm sorry,' she says, starting to walk away. 'This is all a bit much. I just need to…' And without finishing, she heads for the dark, neatly clipped lawn. Space always helps her think, and here there is lots of it.

Her heels start to sink into the soft ground when she reaches the grass, so she kicks them off, leaving them where they fall, and keeps walking. She doesn't stop until she's in the middle of the vast lawn. Usually, this would be the most exposing place in the garden, but she's far enough away from the hotel that the floodlights can't reach her and the darkness closes in around her like a shield.

When she senses everything and everyone is far enough away, she stops, planting her feet parallel to each other, closes her eyes, and lifts her arms out to the side, reaching, feeling nothing. And then she starts to breathe.

CHAPTER FORTY-FOUR

NOW

Jason finds her there almost ten minutes later, arms by her sides, eyes closed. She is still breathing. *In... out. In... out.* It feels like an accomplishment.

'I was getting worried about you,' he says. 'I even knocked on the door of the Ladies and popped my head in, making some poor woman jump!'

Heather hears this, takes it in. Inside she smiles lightly. She can picture the scene, can logically understand that it must have been amusing, but it doesn't seem relevant to her. It's as if she's inside a thick glass jar, trapped like a butterfly, and the rest of the world is happening 'out there'. She can see it. She can hear its muffled sounds, but she is completely separate.

This is how it has to be at the moment. Even Jason must stay on the other side of the glass because she doesn't know what will happen if she can't maintain this precarious balance. She doesn't want to know.

Jason slides his arms around her from behind. She feels his warmth against her back, but she doesn't sink into him. Not yet.

His mouth is close to her ear, so when he speaks his breath is warm against her neck.

'I saw her – Lydia – walking back inside the hotel. You found her?'

Heather dips her chin slightly and raises it again. It is all that is needed to signal her answer. The more still she stays, the better.

'Are you okay? You seem so calm.' She can hear the worry in his voice, knows he is not fooled.

'She told me everything,' Heather begins. 'It wasn't her fault.'

'What? You mean she wasn't the one who took you?'

'No, she did. But it wasn't… It wasn't like the papers made out.'

She thinks about Lydia losing her child, and not just the promise of a child but a living, breathing thing that could smile at you, call you 'Mummy', put its arms around you and hold you tight. It makes Heather ache so much that she can hardly remain standing.

'She was troubled, hurting. But she was trying to help, trying to take care of me. It just all went horribly, horribly wrong.'

Heather knows about making decisions in the moment, swept away by emotion – love, or what you think is love – and the disastrous consequences that can follow. Memories come then, the whole fortnight, a whole stolen holiday, in less than ten seconds: beaches, warm doughnuts, laughing in the penny arcades and at the crazy golf. Snuggling up at the top of the bed in the evening to read stories. Being tucked in at night. Hot chocolate and strawberry sauce on ice-cream sundaes.

She goes on to tell Jason the whole story, standing there, facing away from him, eyelids still closed. When she's finished, he turns her around and folds her into his arms. This is when she lets go. This is when she opens her eyes, even though all she can see is the too-close fabric of his dinner jacket.

It is as if, when Jason first put his arms around her, a key slid into a lock, and now, with one tiny twist, everything is laid open to him. She has revealed more of herself to him than she has to anyone else in the whole of her life and he hasn't run, he hasn't called her a freak. She feels tears building behind her eyes. They spill over her lower lashes and onto his lapel.

This is it now. She loves him.

The knowledge is both heartbreaking and exhilarating all at once, but Heather is still too numb from her conversation with Lydia to work out which is the overriding emotion. They pull against each other, thankfully, so she seems fairly sane and balanced on the surface.

'In my whole childhood,' Heather says, 'she was the one person who tried to do something to stop the chaos, the mess, and make my life better. Faith did what she could but she was only a child, but why did nobody else do anything? My father? Even though Mum hid the truth from him, it wouldn't have been too hard to guess. I think he just blocked it out, didn't want to face it. Aunt Kathy tried a bit, but then she just gave up. And what about neighbours? Teachers? There must have been signs!' She pulls back a little so she can look him in the eyes. 'Why did no one else care enough to try and do something to save me? Only Lydia. Only her.'

'Yes, but—'

'I know, I know. She did the wrong thing. She probably made things worse in the long run, but for two weeks – *two whole weeks!* – I was properly happy. I cried when they found us and they made me go home again, I remember that now. I was inconsolable for days. It was like putting an animal back in its cage after it's had a taste of freedom. I can't hate her for it any more. I just can't.'

As Heather hears herself say those words, things solidify in her head, and in her heart. She is back at square one again, isn't she? It always comes back to the same thing, and she's just so tired of it. This is all her mother's fault. It was always her mother's fault. How could Heather ever have believed differently?

The rage inside flares up again then, threatening to engulf her. *No wonder her mother hadn't wanted to talk about it for all those years,* Heather thinks. She knew she was guilty. More than that, she didn't want people to know the details because then they'd have to know the reasons why. She'd have to own up to her hoarding, probably get rid of her stuff, and she couldn't do that, could she? Her stuff was more important than anything. Certainly more important than her children, if having one stolen from her couldn't even change anything.

But Heather realizes she can't go down this path now. It is not the place. It is not the time. She takes her anger, packs it into a tight, hot little ball, and hides it away inside herself.

Jason stares out into the darkness. 'What do you want to do now?'

Heather turns to look at him. 'I think we should go back inside. We probably missed most of the main course.'

'You're hungry?'

She shakes her head. 'Not really, but we might as well do what we came here to do: support the charity.'

Jason gives her a look. She knows she's too calm. She knows she's being odd.

'And you're sure you're ready to do this? To go back in there?'

'Yes.' Because what else is there to do? He takes her hand and they walk together across the springy grass back to the terrace, to the hotel and its floodlights. As they go inside, Heather catches a glimpse of her reflection in a glazed door. She stops walking and turns to Jason, pulling her hand free from his. 'I'm just going to take a trip to the Ladies,' she says, indicating her smudged mascara with a wave of her hand, 'and repair some of the damage.'

He nods, watches her walk away for a few seconds, then continues back into the ballroom. Heather goes to the bathroom, deals with her face as best she can, and then she looks at herself in the mirror, takes a shuddering breath, and heads back to join Jason.

Her journey takes her through the lobby again, past the display stand with the items for the auction. Cassandra is standing there, high up as always, casting her beady, haughty eyes over the other offerings as if they are not up to her standard. *Goodbye*, Heather mentally whispers to her. *Good riddance*.

For a moment she thinks she's going to lose her cool. She thinks she's going to reach up, pull the doll down by one shining ringlet and hurl it across the lobby, but she manages to stop herself. She can't rob the charity of the money that has already been bid on the doll. To stop the fire growing in her chest, she deliberately looks away, fixes her gaze on something else, something completely random.

A handbag.

A rather nice handbag, actually. A designer label she recognizes, made from soft red calfskin. She spends a few moments taking in the details – the shape of the clasps and buckles, the stitching on the strap.

It's supposed to be an exercise in distraction. She's not supposed to reach out and touch it, let her fingers close around the handles and grip them firmly. She doesn't mean to lift it off the display table, nor turn and start to walk, not towards the ballroom and back to Jason, but towards the hotel entrance.

Inside her head she screams at herself to stop, but her legs just keep moving.

'Hey!' She hears a voice behind her. 'Hey, you!'

Heather starts running.

CHAPTER FORTY-FIVE

NOW

'Stop!' A hand clamps down on Heather's shoulder, turning her around. 'What do you think you're doing?' It's the receptionist she met the day she went to the Haven Project offices looking for Lydia. She's wearing a hideous lime-green ballgown covered in crystals that clings in all the wrong places.

'I'm… I…' That's the best answer Heather can manage. She doesn't know what she's doing. She tries to break free, ducking down a little to avoid the pressure of the hand on her shoulder, but the woman is too clever, and soon she is joined by a hotel worker from behind the nearby reception desk.

And then more people come: staff, guests from the gala dinner, hotel security… Heather is still gripping the handbag, pulling it into her body as if it's a child that needs protection.

The horrible receptionist yells at the security guard. 'She's trying to steal that! It's for the charity auction!'

Heather shakes her head. 'I… No…'

'I saw her!' a hotel waiter with an empty tray says emphatically. 'I saw her pick it up and run.'

'Madam?' one of the security guards says, looking at her and then looking at the handbag clutched to her chest.

It all gets a bit fuzzy after that. There is shouting, from the receptionist and others too, and she's handed over to the security guards, who march her off to the side of the lobby, peel the handbag from her fingers, then flank her while they wait for someone with more authority to turn up.

Hearing a commotion going on outside, more guests from the dinner start to appear through the open ballroom doors. Very soon a crowd is standing around Heather. It's all too much. She closes her eyes and tries to breathe slowly, but it seems her lungs only want to work in short gasping breaths. She feels the black tide approaching and knows a panic attack is imminent.

No. Not here. Not now.

'Heather?'

It's Jason's voice. Her eyes snap open and she finds him instantly in the crowd. He looks confused, worried even. Heather's eyes lock onto his and she sends him a silent plea: *Help me.*

Jason walks towards a grey-haired man and woman who seem to be in charge, perhaps something to do with the charity. They're deep in conversation with yet another security guard and the nasty receptionist.

'This is ridiculous,' Jason says after he hears a snatch of their conversation. 'This has to be a mistake.'

The receptionist turns on him. 'No mistake! I saw her take it myself.'

Jason shakes his head, and inside Heather something melts just a little bit more. He's standing up for her. Fighting for her. Even though she doesn't deserve it.

Any further discussions are cut short by a pair of police officers edging their way through the crowd. They take charge instantly, escorting Heather off to the manager's office, where the grey-haired couple, the security guards and the receptionist follow. Heather keeps her eyes on Jason as long as she can before a pillar blocks her view and she can't see him any more.

There are more angry words, more explanations, more descriptions. Heather loses track of the speakers, because she sits silently on the chair she has been shown to and stares at the carpet as it all swirls around her.

The last thing she hears clearly is the bizarrely soft tones of the female police officer. 'Heather Lucas, I am arresting you on suspicion of theft. You do not have to say anything. But it may harm your defence…'

CHAPTER FORTY-SIX

NOW

Heather sits on a row of blue plastic chairs that are bolted both to each other and to the floor. Only one other seat is occupied; the hefty policewoman who arrested her is sitting next to her. In front of them a drunken man in his early twenties is swearing at the custody sergeant and being particularly uncooperative.

'Do you want a cup of tea?' PC Calder asks when there is enough of a break in the obscenities to be heard.

Heather shakes her head. The thought of eating or drinking anything makes her feel ill. Besides, she's doing her best to concentrate on the mottled pattern of the vinyl flooring. It's the only thing keeping her sane at the moment.

It feels weird, being asked in a kind voice if she would like a cup of tea, as if she's a visitor in someone's house. She always thought police officers would be dismissive and gruff to those they arrested, but the policewoman has been nice. Motherly, even. But then Heather hasn't given them much reason to get tough with her. They didn't even bother with handcuffs.

It takes ten minutes to get a name and address out of her fellow prisoner, but eventually he is led away and the sergeant indicates that Heather should come forward.

PC Calder reels off the basic details of the arrest: name, time, location, offence. It's only then that the sergeant turns to Heather and starts asking her questions. She answers them mechanically, nodding to confirm her name, supplying her date of birth and address when prompted. No, she doesn't have any medical conditions and she isn't taking any medication. Yes, she's consumed alcohol this evening – half a glass of champagne, maybe two hours ago now – but she hasn't taken any drugs.

She is then instructed to empty her pockets (the dress doesn't have any, so that's easy) and her handbag. She stands there, watching the custody sergeant go through her things, feeling a sense of violation as he picks them up and places them in a clear plastic bag. They take her stilettos away from her, providing her with a pair of plimsolls – laces removed, of course – in their stead. They take her wrap too.

Heather has spent her whole life trying to hide her dark corners from the world, trying to convince everyone she's an honest, productive member of society, and she's done a pretty good job of it, so she can't decide whether she's offended or quietly relieved that these people start with the worst possible assumptions about her then work their way up.

She is asked whether she has been read her rights, whether she understands what was said to her, and if she has any questions, then they offer her the chance to phone someone. She snatches at the opportunity immediately. There's only one person she wants to call. That done, PC Calder leads her away down a corridor to a cell.

When the door clangs closed, she looks around. It's pretty much like you see on television: a concrete bench with a thin blue mattress and a folded blanket, a toilet in the corner, shielded by a partition. There is a light in the centre of the ceiling, but no switch to turn it on or off, and another glass dome, which she supposes to be a camera. She reaches over and pulls the blanket towards her, unfolds it and wraps it around her shoulders. She's shivering, but even with the added warmth from the blanket, she can't seem to stop.

She sits on the bench and shuffles until her back meets the wall, then folds her legs up underneath her, covering herself completely with the blanket so only her head pokes out of the top. The borrowed plimsolls sit on the floor, parallel and empty.

She closes her eyes and wonders what Jason must be thinking. She saw the look on his face as she was led away, bundled into the back of a police car. She heard him arguing with the hotel staff and security guards, even with one of the police officers, saying this had to be a case of mistaken identity, that the Heather Lucas he knows would never do anything like this. She had walked faster then, allowing them to hurry her away to the police station.

Even with her eyes closed, the light on the ceiling is too bright, too bleaching. She concentrates on the feel of the bare wall behind her back, the hardness of the concrete bench through the thin mattress, the sound of her own breath, rhythmic like the waves on the seashore not half a mile away.

Her sense of time slips away, and in its place comes a strange sensation, something she should not be feeling in this moment, in this place – peace. She has been stripped of everything bar the clothes on her back, but for some reason, sitting in this tiny cell, with no choices and no options, this is the freest Heather Lucas has felt in years.

CHAPTER FORTY-SEVEN

KNICKERS

White. Cotton. Marks & Spencer. A bow at the front, which I think is possibly a bit babyish, and lacy elastic round the legs. There's nothing special about these pants. They're part of a multipack of four equally white and unremarkable knickers, so there really shouldn't be anything to make a fuss about.

THEN

When Heather gets off the bus on Monday morning, Ryan is sitting on the wall near the bus stop with his mates. She catches his eye, then puts her head down and walks on, keeping their secret safe. His smile is possessive and it makes her flush from head to toe. She's smiling softly to herself as she walks through the school gates.

Heather's not sure she recognizes herself any more. She's not quite sure who this bold Heather is, the one who does these new and daring things. Even though she got into the shower and scrubbed herself hard when she got home on Friday night, there was a part of her that felt exhilarated too.

She went home that night without anything under her dress. Ryan had tucked her knickers into his pocket, saying the thought of her going home without them made him hot. She can't wait until after school when they've planned to meet behind the pavilion again.

She feels fluttery and excited all day, can't concentrate on her lessons. It doesn't even bother her that Tia Paine is being extra-snarky. Tia just doesn't count any more. And when Heather's secret comes out and other people at school find out that she and Ryan are a couple, 'Hobo' will be a creature of the past. Extinct. Long live Heather Lucas.

As soon as the bell rings, she grabs up her bag and dashes for the pavilion. Even before she can see him, she can feel he's there, waiting for her. She sprints the last part, but when she turns the corner she skids to a halt.

Ryan is there, but so are a lot of other people. Heather frowns. She doesn't get it. This is her and Ryan's spot, their private place. What are they all doing here? Is there a sports practice she doesn't know about?

The surprise wears off and she starts to notice the individual faces. Tia Paine is here with her gang, along with a handful of others from their year. Heather looks at Ryan, hoping he can explain.

He smiles at her and she starts to smile back, knowing that everything is going to be okay, that maybe he's decided they can stop sneaking around, that this is the moment when they're going to tell everyone they're an item, but then he slowly pulls something from his blazer pocket and holds it high in the air. It's only when his arm is at full stretch that Heather works out what is dangling from his fingers.

Her knickers.

'Lost something?' he asks, still smiling, and everybody laughs.

Heather tries to speak, but nothing comes out. Nothing useful anyway.

'Low-down, skanky slut,' Tia Paine says. 'You dropped them for Ryan in record time – and there's the actual proof!'

Heather searches Ryan's face. This has to be a mistake. Tia has tricked him into this somehow.

But then she sees his expression. It's the same as this morning when she walked past him into school, but this time her translation of it is different. It's not passion she sees there, but triumph. Not possessiveness, but ownership. Those things might seem similar but they are actually very, very different. Her eyes fill with tears.

'I don't understand.'

Ryan shrugs. 'It's simple. Tia asked me to do a favour for her – a little acting role – and in return she's going to put in a good word for me with her uncle. There's a chance that he could get me an audition for the next *Harry Potter*.'

Heather tears her eyes from his to look at Tia. 'You…?'

Tia does one of her twisty little smirks. She's so happy she can hardly contain herself. She takes a step towards Heather, towering over her. 'Those kinds of favours are expensive, but it was worth it. He played his part wonderfully well, didn't he? But I reckon we'll have to change your name now. No longer "Hobo". We'll just shorten it to "Ho".'

It all sinks in then. Tia was behind all this? She'd actually planned it, knickers and everything? The truth descends on Heather like one of those booby-trapped ceilings in an Indiana Jones or James Bond movie, the kind that suddenly start pressing downwards, full of knives, crushing and shredding their victims. She turns and runs.

'Don't you want your knickers, freak?' Tia calls after her, a jubilant edge to her tone. 'Your skanky, stinky, hobo knickers?'

Heather wants to lie down right there and die, but she can't so she just keeps running.

CHAPTER FORTY-EIGHT

NOW

Heather is unsure how much time has passed when the cell door clangs again. PC Calder appears and stands at the open door. 'You can leave now,' she says.

Heather looks back at her but doesn't move. She must have heard that wrong.

'The Haven Project has decided not to press charges,' Calder explains. 'So you're free to go.'

It takes Heather a few moments to process this information. All she can hear inside her head is the strident tones of the receptionist: *I saw her do it! Bloody disgrace, nicking from women with problems.* But then she unfolds her legs, which creak and complain at the unexpected movement, stuffs her feet in the borrowed plimsolls, and shrugs the blanket off, leaving it on the bench.

She follows PC Calder out of the cell and back to the custody sergeant's desk, where she is reunited with the plastic bag full of her worldly goods and her heels. She hands the plimsolls back silently and puts her shoes on. Her feet seem to have swollen up in the cell, and the leather pinches as she clip-clops her way out of the back exit of the police station.

'There's somebody waiting for you in the main reception,' Calder says, giving her a kindly smile. 'Just walk out through the car park, turn left, then come back in through the double doors at the front of the building.'

Heather hobbles along the tarmac, clutching the plastic bag to her as if her life depends on it. She rounds the corner and even before she pushes the glass doors open, she can see Jason sitting there. Part of her is dreading seeing him again, the other part just wants to sink against him and sob with relief.

The door squeaks slightly when she opens it, and he looks up. His eyes are dull, as if he was on the verge of nodding off. The moment he sees her, though, he springs to his feet.

'Thank God!' he whispers into her ear as his arms close around her. 'I kept trying to tell them they'd got the wrong person, but they just wouldn't listen! That woman in the green dress – my God! – she was like a dog with a bone. It's just as well Lydia stepped in and spoke to the top people—'

'Lydia?' Heather echoes weakly.

Jason nods. 'I don't know what she said, because she went into the interview room with that other couple, but when they came out again everything was sorted. They didn't look happy exactly, but they've dropped it. That's what they told me, anyway. Is that true?'

'Yes. It's true.'

Jason blows out a breath, runs a hand through his already tousled hair and sits back down on the row of seats. It doesn't escape Heather they're identical to the ones in the custody suite: hard blue plastic, designed to make you as uncomfortable as possible, it seems.

'Thank God that's over,' he mumbles, shaking his head. He looks impossibly handsome, still in his dinner jacket, with his top button undone and his bow tie hanging loose around his neck. He looks up at her. 'What happened exactly? No one would tell me anything. How did they make such an awful mistake in the first place?'

He looks at her expectantly, his eyes full of so much trust that Heather wilts into the seat beside him. Usually she'd find a way to wriggle out, explain, misdirect, but that urge for self-preservation has been completely overridden. She can't do this to him any more. He's all ready to leap on his white charger and defend her honour, but it's actually him that needs protecting. From her.

Sitting in that cell, stripped of everything she had – not just her belongings but her pride, her self-protection, every single mask she wears – has made her realize this is what she has to do. She has to sweep everything clean. She has to be brave enough to do what her mother never could: let everything go, even if it's the thing most precious to her. She takes a deep breath, preparing to launch herself over the edge, like a diver on high rocks.

'You don't know me. You think you do, but you really don't.'

'But—'

'There was no mistake this evening. I took it. I took the hand-bag.'

He looks so confused it almost breaks Heather's heart. 'But how? You must have just...'

Heather shakes her head. 'I meant to. I...' She gulps in some air then carries on. 'I stole it. At least, I tried to. I deserved to be in that cell. I've been lying to you, Jason. I'm not who you think I am.'

He finally stops trying to argue her innocence with her, and his jaw tenses.

At that moment, Faith pushes her way through the front doors.

She looks irritated and scared and confused all at once. She scans the reception area and spots Heather sitting there. Heather stands up.

Faith walks towards her, shaking her head. 'What the hell have you done?' she asks, but there are tears in her eyes. She pulls Heather into a firm hug and holds her there, surrounded. Protected.

When Faith lets go, Heather turns and nods towards Jason.

'This is Jason,' she tells her sister. 'He was with me but not… you know… involved in what happened.'

Jason stands up, frowning. He offers Faith his hand. In the circumstances, it seems oddly formal and Heather finds she wants to laugh. She manages to hold it in, though.

'Hi,' he says. 'You must be Heather's sister. I've heard a lot about you.'

Faith shoots Heather a look, one that says: *This is 'him', isn't it? Not bad.*

But Heather hasn't got time for that. 'Faith's come to get me,' she tells Jason quietly, meeting his eyes.

'But I've been waiting here for hours…'

'I know. Thank you, but I rang Faith from the custody suite. I asked her to come and get me. I'm sorry.'

'But—'

'I need my family,' she explains, feeling steadily more sick as she says each word. 'And like I said, you don't really know me. We don't really know each other.'

She understands that she's being cruel dismissing him this way. He's done nothing but stand by her and believe in her, but she can't risk being nice to him. It might soften things between them and she needs them to be brittle and hard.

'Goodbye, Jason,' she says. 'Thank you.' And then she picks up her plastic bag full of belongings and her wrap and follows Faith back out into the night.

She doesn't look back. Just like the plimsolls, she has to leave him behind. He was only ever borrowed.

CHAPTER FORTY-NINE

NOW

It's almost two o'clock when they reach Faith's house. The sisters enter quietly, leaving their shoes by the front door and padding across the hardwood floor to the conservatory, the room furthest away from the stairs and most likely to keep their conversation from disturbing Faith's sleeping family. Faith makes them both a cup of herbal tea and then goes to root around in the utility room for some alternative clothes for Heather. She returns with a pair of sports leggings and a soft, fleecy top.

'Sorry,' she says. 'I didn't want to risk waking the kids, so you'll have to make do with what's come out of the dryer.'

Heather strips off right there in her sister's conservatory. When she's finished dressing, she curls herself up into one end of the large rattan sofa and prepares herself. Faith, strangely, didn't interrogate Heather on the way back to Westerham. Even more strangely, Heather finds she wants to spill everything out now her sister hasn't tried to prise it from her before she's ready.

She starts with the bare facts: meeting Lydia, their conversation on the terrace, stopping by the auction table when she came back inside. She comes clean to her sister about the remains of their mother's hoard hidden inside her flat, and about her shoplifting habit and the drawer at home stuffed full of contraband. She even tells her about the plastic animals she took when she was shopping for Barney's birthday. Faith's eyes widen, but she doesn't comment until Heather runs out of steam.

'Oh, wow,' she whispers. 'How long has this been going on?'

'Since Mum died. Well, I stole for the first time about two months after that.'

'And always kids' stuff?'

Heather nods. 'I just get this horrible feeling and it builds and builds until I can't stop myself.'

'Oh, sweetheart.' Much to Heather's surprise, instead of telling her off, reprimanding her for breaking one of the Ten Commandments, Faith comes over and hugs her. They stay like that for a minute, silent tears falling down their cheeks, and then they pull apart, snuffling a laugh simultaneously at how attractive they must now look. 'Mum really did a number on you, didn't she?' Faith adds softly. 'I suppose I always knew it was bad, but when you were younger it just seemed like teenage stroppiness, and then I got married and had the kids and I just… I'm so sorry, Heather. I saw but I didn't really see. Not properly. I should have done more.'

Heather shakes her head. 'No, don't take the blame for this. It wasn't your fault.' Somehow, saying these words, even though Heather has always known they were the truth, releases something inside her. It rises up out of her, like a helium-filled balloon, and floats away. 'Mum was always good at passing the buck, making everyone else feel responsible for her mess – literally! – and the truth is it was all down to her.'

Faith punches her arm softly. 'Look at you, talking about feelings and stuff!'

Heather rolls her eyes and they both laugh softly. It reminds her of when she and Faith were younger, the rare times Faith would let her sit on her bed and she'd read her a story because their mother was too busy.

But then Faith gets serious again. 'So, if toys and baby clothes are your "thing", why did you take the handbag?'

Heather shrugs helplessly. 'All I know is that I was trying really hard not to be angry with Mum, just to get through the rest of the evening without exploding into a ball of red-hot lava, and then suddenly the bag was there. I didn't think about it. I didn't choose to do it. I just did it.'

Faith nods. 'If there's anything we should have learned from our childhood, it's that burying emotions never, ever works. Even in a house full of stuff piled so high it almost reached the ceiling, Mum couldn't get away from them.'

Heather takes a sip of her tea. 'You think that's what I was doing?'

'Yes. I do. I think maybe the stealing is somehow connected – in the same way that Mum was driven to "collect", even when she knew it was destroying her family. Even when it ruined her whole life. There was a pay-off somewhere, something that made her feel better.'

'But what inside my warped brain makes stealing things the solution to my problem?'

Faith shrugs and moves back to the opposite end of the sofa so they can look at each other more comfortably. 'I don't know. It doesn't always make sense, though, does it? Mum's problem didn't make sense to anyone, not even her, not on a conscious level.' She ponders for a moment. 'Do you have any idea at all why you're attracted to baby clothes?'

Heather closes her eyes. A gaping hole has just opened up underneath her, one she knew from the moment she started this conversation she was heading towards, but it doesn't make the moment of arrival any less awful.

'Because,' she whispers, keeping her eyes closed. 'Because there's something you don't know. Something that happened when I was fifteen…'

CHAPTER FIFTY

NOW

If Matthew is surprised to find his sister-in-law sprawled half-asleep on the conservatory sofa wearing his wife's clothes the next morning, he doesn't comment. He just goes and makes two cups of tea and then drinks his with her in silence before going to get the kids ready for church. The fact he's getting used to her just popping up unannounced, and usually in a state of crisis, is not a good thing, Heather realizes. It means she is becoming a problem with a capital 'P'. She needs to get a grip on her life, and she needs to do it soon.

Faith takes the unprecedented move of staying home with her sister. While she's flicking through the Sunday papers, she looks over at Heather, who is reading a novel she found on the bathroom windowsill.

'I had no idea you didn't know the house had been bad before the abduction,' Faith says. 'For me, it felt as if it had always been that way.'

Heather nods. It had felt that way for her too. 'It was only when I found that photo with the clear walls that I started to question that assumption,' she says. 'I don't know how to make sense of it.'

Faith shrugs. 'Mum would have these blitzes from time to time. Maybe she'd made an effort just before that picture was taken because Christmas was coming up?'

'Maybe,' Heather says. She supposes they'll never have the answer to that one.

Faith folds the paper she is reading back up neatly. 'I think we should Skype Dad early, before Matthew and the kids get back,' she says. 'I know he doesn't like to talk about it but there are things I'd certainly like to ask him about Mum's hoarding.'

Heather sighs. 'Do you ever talk to him about how it was before you left?'

Faith shakes her head. 'No. After we moved out it became a bit of a no-go area. To be honest, I can't blame him.'

'Neither can I.' It's why Heather hasn't pushed all these years. Christine Lucas broke him too. She broke them all.

'Are you up for it?' Faith asks, looking nervous.

Heather nods. 'You're right. There's stuff we need to know. I'd been trying to keep him out of it – I didn't want to open up those old wounds.'

'Okay,' Faith says, standing up. 'Let's do it.'

Five minutes later they're staring at a slightly pixelated image of their father on Faith's tablet, which is propped up on the dining-room table.

'Hi, girls!' he says, smiling as their stepmother leans in over his shoulder and gives them a little wave.

They wade through the inevitable small talk but before their father ends the call, Heather takes a deep breath and says, 'Can I ask you something, Dad? About Mum?'

The smile falls from his face. Shirley puts a concerned hand on his shoulder. 'I suppose so,' he replies.

'Do you know why she started doing what she did... hoarding? Was there any sense to it at all?'

He sighs.

'I'll leave you to have a chat,' Shirley says, patting his shoulder and exiting discreetly. Moments later Heather hears the sound of a vacuum cleaner in another room.

Their father frowns, thinking. 'I always considered her one of those creative types, you know, a bit disorganized, a bit messy, but it was nothing out of the ordinary when I first knew her.'

Faith leans in. 'When did it start?'

'After you were born,' their father replies. At first I thought she was just nesting, you know, like all new mums do. She kept buying clothes and toys and little helpful gadgets. I could hardly prise her out of Mothercare if we went in on a Saturday afternoon.'

Heather's stomach goes cold. After last night's events, the last thing she wants to think about is the scene of any of her crimes.

'I begged her to slow down – cash was tight, what with her not working and having a new baby in the house – and she always said she would stop, but every day when I got home there'd be something new in the hallway. And then she told me that as a stay-at-home mum, she needed a hobby or two.' He sighs heavily. 'You know what she was like. You could talk to her until you were blue in the face, but you couldn't change her mind.'

'Okay,' Heather says, sorting all the pieces of information into some kind of order in her head. 'So having kids triggered it, but there has to be something more. That need has to have come from somewhere. Is there anything in her past, in her childhood?'

'I really don't know,' their father says. 'The only person who would know that is Kathy.' Faith and Heather exchange a look. 'Is there anything else?' he asks, shifting in his seat, and Heather knows he's dying to change the subject.

'That's enough for now,' she replies. Even if there is more to find out, her brain is too overloaded to deal with it. Before they round off their conversation, Faith promises to call again next week and Heather agrees to think about going out to Spain for a visit. Maybe it would be good to get away? Properly away, that is, not just hiding out at her sister's.

Both sisters head back to the kitchen and Faith makes them a cup of strong coffee. Faith glances up at the clock on the wall. It's only a few minutes until Matthew and the kids are due back, and she's obviously got one last thing she needs to get off her chest before they do. Heather steels herself.

'What you told me last night…'

Heather had suspected the subject wasn't over and done with, but had been hoping her sister's new-found sensitivity might last more than twenty-four hours. Mind you, asking for two miracles in such a short space of time might be too much.

'Yes,' she says lightly.

'I know you probably don't want to hear this – and I know I could ruin everything by saying it again – but I think you need to talk to someone about it. Someone qualified.'

Heather exhales slowly. 'So do I.'

'Really?'

'Yes. I'm reluctant to admit it, you're right – I've been hoarding all the things that have happened, never sorting through how I feel because, well, basically I couldn't remember a lot of it. And what I could remember, I just ignored. As much as I don't like to say it, as much as I don't want to, it's time for a clear-out.'

'I know someone from church. She has her own practice in Biggin Hill. She's properly qualified and everything, and it would be totally confidential. I would only know about what's said in your sessions if you tell me yourself.'

Heather nods. 'Okay.' She trusts her sister's judgement, and it's got to be more reliable than going on the internet and picking someone at random. It's time to sort herself out, once and for all.

CHAPTER FIFTY-ONE

NOW

Heather stays with Faith for the next few days in the lovely guest bedroom. It's got a few more knick-knacks and fussy interior-decorating flourishes than Heather would prefer, but she puts up with them instead of hiding them in the wardrobe and then getting them out again before she leaves, like she did at Christmas.

She borrows Faith's car to get to work, dropping Matthew at the station on the way, so Faith can use his to do the school run. Very quickly they settle into a rhythm. For almost a week she tries to pretend that she's just visiting her sister, that there's no ulterior motive for staying away from her flat, but she can't keep borrowing her sister's clothes. She can't keep pretending.

The thought of going back home nearly prompts another panic attack. Faith has said she can stay as long as she wants. Maybe another week, Heather thinks to herself. She's not kidding herself she can move in permanently. She doesn't want to push this new-found truce with her sister to breaking point.

At six o'clock on Saturday morning, she catches the train back to Orpington then changes for Shortlands. This way she can pick up her car and be a little more independent and not so much of a burden on Faith and Matthew over the next week. It's less than a ten-minute walk from the station to Heather's flat, and her blouse is sticking to her back by the time she reaches the shade of the porch and slides the key into the front door. It's overcast. Muggy. And the air is so still.

She takes care not to make too much noise when she enters the hallway, hoping she can just slip in and out before the other residents wake up. She fumbles with her keys as they slide through her clammy fingers, and it takes three attempts to gain access to her flat. Once inside, she leaves the front door open – a signal to herself this is just a fleeting pit stop and she shouldn't get comfortable, shouldn't allow herself to enjoy the cool tranquillity of her living room – and heads straight for the bedroom.

It's not lost on her that she was doing this only a few weeks ago. Packing. Hiding from Jason. She's more than a little disgusted with herself that she hasn't been able to find a backbone in all that time. But she just needs to find some... stability. Everything is shifting underneath her at the moment, like the pebbles on Hastings beach underfoot. By next weekend hopefully she'll have found something solid to stand on, some truth she can use as her pole star, and then she'll be able to start putting her life back together again.

She's just zipping up her roll-along case when she hears a noise in the hallway. She pivots, still at her bedroom doorway, and sees Jason standing at the threshold of her flat, looking taller and more solid, and also more foreboding than she remembers him.

'You're back,' he says.

Heather swallows. This is harder than she thought it would be. 'What are you doing here?'

'At your front door?' He raises an eyebrow. 'Or do you actually mean, "Up this early when you were trying to sneak in and out without seeing me?"'

'I—'

'Save it,' he says. 'I'm not sure I want to hear another lie.'

Heather's lips quiver and she presses them together to stop them wobbling. She deserved that. But the urge to run and throw herself against him, to feel his strong, solid arms come around her the way they did in the gardens of the Palm Court Hotel, is almost overwhelming. Inside her it feels as if something is ripping.

'I'm sorry,' she whispers. It's the most honest thing she can say to him right now.

'What exactly are you sorry for?' he asks, folding his arms. 'Sorry for getting arrested and then leaving me sitting like a mug in Hastings nick while you swanned off with your sister? Sorry for not even having the guts to contact me for a whole week? For not even letting me know you weren't coming back or if you're alright? Or is it just sorry you can't play the helpless waif who needs a big, strong man to do her detective work for her?' He shakes his head. 'Was that even real?'

Heather winces, not just at his words but at the tone. Caustic. Justified. She'd always told herself that getting close to Jason was a bad idea. There's so much she wants to tell him, but she's afraid if she starts she won't be able to stop. And there are things about her he can never know.

'I'm sorry,' she mumbles again, and is rewarded by a huff of frustrated laughter.

'Well, I suppose I shouldn't have expected anything else.' He shakes his head, looking sober again. 'I'm an open book. I deliberately chose to live my life that way – not spilling it all out there but just not hiding, not holding back. I was so sick of how I grew up, all the lies my dad told, layer upon layer upon layer, and the secrets that went along with that, the secrets he made us keep for him. I thought you understood that.'

'I do,' Heather croaks.

'And then I opened up to you about Jodie, too. God, what a mug I've been.'

Tears well in Heather's eyes and threaten to spill over, but she sniffs them back. It's tearing her apart that she's hurt him, but she can't be an open book like he is, because if Jason ever read the bedtime story that is Heather Lucas, he'd have nightmares for a week. Even now she can't face the fact that he saw her being arrested, that he witnessed possibly the most humiliating moment of her life.

'I suppose I might as well do what I came here to do when I heard you come through the front door, and give you this.' It's only then that Heather notices the long cardboard box by his feet. Her stomach goes cold. *No. It can't be.* 'I bid for it the night of the gala dinner,' he says. 'It was going to be a surprise.'

He picks up the box and hands it to her. She feels sick as she turns it over, dreading what she's going to see, but still hoping that she's wrong, that it's something else.

But no. Cassandra's glossy curls and hard eyes stare triumphantly back at her, as if to say, *You thought it would be easy to escape?* Ha! She almost drops the box and runs. It's only the fact that it would make Jason hate her even more that stops her doing so.

That's the moment when Heather realizes she's got to cut the piece of elastic that keeps pulling her back to this man – the smug curve of Cassandra's peachy lips confirms it – and there's only one way she can think of accomplishing that.

'You want the truth?' she asks him, almost defiantly. 'You want me to be open?'

'Of course.'

Still so sure of himself, Heather thinks, *even though he's got no idea what's coming.*

'Saturday night wasn't the first time I've stolen something,' she tells him.

The surprise on his face would be comical if she wasn't smashing her own heart to pieces in the process, but she's on a roll now, powered by some roaring, deafening need to vomit the truth all over him, and although it's terrible, it's energizing her, feeding its own momentum.

'I've done it before. Look.' She grabs him by the hand, ignoring the warmth of his fingers, and drags him into her flat. It's only the fact she's caught him by surprise that allows her to do it, but she makes good use of her advantage. She flings open the door to her spare bedroom with her free hand, then releases him so she can pull the draw of shame open. She's too wired now, though, and she tugs too hard and both draw and contents tumble onto the floor in a mess of pastel-coloured cuteness.

'I stole *all* of this,' she tells him. '*You want to know who I am? This is who I am! I'm a liar and a thief!*'

Jason is just standing there. Frozen. Stunned. His mouth literally hanging open. And then he blinks, begins to collect himself, and the eyes that have been fixed on the mess on the floor refocus on her. He shakes his head slowly, as if his brain is working so hard on other things that this is the only speed it can manage.

'What an idiot I've been,' he says quietly, and Heather swears she can hear her heart cracking, splintering, inside her chest. Some of the shock begins to wear off, because the anger returns to his expression, narrowing his eyes and twisting his mouth. 'I thought I was falling for you, but I can't have been. You're right – I don't even know you.'

And then he turns and walks away. Heather runs after him. She wants to call him back, wants to tell him it's a mistake, that they can work it out, but she knows that's just wishful thinking. She stops at the threshold of her flat and watches him stomp up the stairs, two at a time, and then slam his door behind him.

Cassandra's box, with its clear cellophane front, is lying on the hall floor, where Heather dropped it when she grabbed Jason's hand. She turns it over to find that the doll landed on her head and now there's a crack, and maybe even a small dent, in her left temple.

She brings the box inside, puts it down on the living-room sofa and then tears it open. She flings the cardboard aside and places the doll very carefully in the middle of the rug, spreading her dress neatly to shake out the folds, fanning her ringlets so they fall around her head like a halo, and then Heather takes her foot, raises it high and brings it smashing down on Cassandra's head. Over and over and over, until her foot is bleeding and there's nothing left but a faceless corpse where her mother's favourite possession used to be.

CHAPTER FIFTY-TWO

NOW

Heather leans on the railings of Hastings pier. Lydia stands beside her and they both stare out across the grey-green waves flecked with white froth.

'Do you know what the weirdest thing about this is?' Heather asks.

Lydia shakes her head. 'No, what?'

'That being here with you *doesn't* feel weird.'

'I'm glad you emailed, but I have to admit I'm a little puzzled as to why you'd want to see me again.'

'To thank you,' Heather says and squints a little. There isn't a patch of blue overhead, but the completeness of the cloud cover somehow makes the sky whiter and brighter. 'For everything you did. They told me how you explained to the charity people that I didn't mean to… that I wasn't feeling… quite myself.'

'It was the least I could do,' Lydia replies solemnly. 'I know you accepted my explanation of what happened all those years ago, that you believe me, and for that I am truly, truly grateful. You have no idea how it's weighed on me.' She stiffens, cuts herself off, as if thinking about herself is a habit she no longer indulges in. 'The truth is, I feel responsible – for everything you accused me of and more. Besides, it didn't take much explaining to the founders of a mental-health charity what had happened to make you do such a thing. If anyone can sympathize with it, they can.'

Heather nods. She doesn't like being thought of in that way – someone with mental-health issues – but she can't run away from it any longer. People who don't struggle with that kind of thing don't do the things she's been doing. 'Well, I appreciate it,' she says. 'That... and the other stuff.'

Lydia turns to look at her fully. 'Other stuff?'

'For being nice to me... when I was little. I'd forgotten a lot of it, but I'm starting to remember more and more.' She looks down, feeling a little shy. 'I always thought of you as a friend.' She risks a look at Lydia. Tears are brimming on her bottom lashes. 'You were kind to me, and you took the time to talk to me, to play with me, when nobody else did.'

Lydia looks down at her feet. Heather can see she is struggling with her emotions. 'I'm glad you remember it that way,' she says eventually, looking up again. They stroll in silence for a while then Lydia says, 'What's happening with that nice young man you were with at the gala?'

Heather shakes her head. 'It's not a thing any more, and even if it was it'd probably fizzle out pretty quickly. My contract is up in a month now and I've got a new job.'

'Oh,' says Lydia. 'Where are you going?'

'Devon, down on the south coast near Dartmouth. There's a house down there, used to belong to a film star – Laura Hastings. Have you heard of her? – and the new owner apparently has some diaries of hers that she wants to do something with, as well as records for a foundation the actress set up to help children. They think my previous job makes me the perfect candidate.'

'Oh. How long will you be gone?'

'A year.'

Lydia nods. 'So you're going to move down there?'

'Yes. There's a lovely little village across the river, apparently. I've already got a house lined up. I'll get to travel to work each day on a tiny little ferry that only holds about ten people. Definitely beats the M25!'

Lydia doesn't laugh at Heather's joke, barely manages a smile.

'I'll come back,' Heather says tentatively. 'And we can email or Facebook or something. I don't want to lose touch.'

Lydia smiles then, and Heather can instantly picture her in her old red coat, her glossy dark curls shining as much as her eyes. It's the first time since she's met this mousy little person that she's seen a glimmer of the woman she remembers.

'That would be lovely,' Lydia says. 'I do Facebook a bit. But don't send me any videos of cats. For some reason, they really irritate me.'

Heather laughs. 'Okay. It's a deal.'

They've reached the end of the pier now and they take a moment deciding where to go. Lydia asks if she wants to do a round of crazy golf, for old times' sake, but Heather isn't quite ready to revisit the place she had that magical afternoon with Jason, the place they went before he kissed her for the first time. She shakes her head and the light fades out of her eyes.

Lydia notices her solemn expression and takes a stab at what might have caused it. 'Are you sure the "thing" with the young man just fizzled out?'

'What do you mean?'

Lydia looks at her kindly. 'I'm no stranger to heartbreak,' she says. 'I know it when I see it.' Heather shakes her head and looks away. 'Running away isn't going to solve anything, you know.'

Heather's throat goes tight. 'Getting a new job isn't running away, it's a necessity. And honestly, I really don't think the relationship is salvageable. Some things you just can't come back from.'

Lydia nods and they start walking along the shore, heading towards the old fishermen's huts on the far eastern end of the beach. 'Okay. I won't badger you about it again.'

'It's alright,' Heather says, and she realizes it really is, that she doesn't mind at all. It's nice having someone to look out for her, to call her out on stuff. She sighs. 'I really ought to go soon. I promised my sister I'd go for dinner. It's my nephew's birthday.'

Lydia nods. 'How old is he?'

Heather smiles. Living with her niece and nephew for a couple of weeks has been nice. She's not so tense around them any more, and Barney sometimes crawls onto her lap without asking in the evenings, as if it's the most natural thing in the world. 'He's four today, and a right little pickle.'

Lydia smiles back, but Heather sees a familiar blankness in her eyes. They walk in silence for a moment, then she asks, 'Do you have a picture of your daughter?'

Lydia nods and pulls her phone out of her bag. They stand in the middle of the pavement while she pulls up a picture that is obviously a scan of an old photograph. The girl is different from how Heather imagined her. She expected to see a carbon copy of herself with the long blonde fringe and the cheeky smile, but instead she sees a miniature version of Lydia, with dark, wavy hair and large, soulful eyes.

'I'm so sorry you lost her,' she tells Lydia. 'I know you must have been a wonderful mother.'

'No, really. I—'

'I won't believe you if you deny it,' Heather says firmly. 'I know, first-hand, how good you are with kids.'

320

Impulsively, she steps in and gives Lydia what she intends to be just a brief hug, but they both cling to each other for an extra few seconds. When they pull away, Lydia looks at her seriously.

'You need to forgive your mum, you know.'

Heather feels all the warmth generated by the unexpected gesture of closeness drain away.

'I don't think I can.'

'I've learned a lot working with Haven,' Lydia says, 'about myself, what drove me to do what I did, but about other people too. She didn't choose to be that way. It's an illness, like depression or OCD or anxiety.' She gives Heather a particularly knowing stare. 'Like stealing things when you don't mean to.'

Heather closes her eyes. She doesn't want to hear this. On some level, she doesn't want to stop blaming her mother, because who else is there to blame? Only herself, and after recent events she hates herself enough already.

'I just… It's a lot to deal with, to process.'

'I didn't say forgiving would be easy, or even that it could be done quickly, but you need to, Heather. Not for her sake, but for yours. Until you let this stuff go, you may never stop dealing with those emotions the wrong way, doing things you really don't want to do.'

'I'll try,' Heather says, looking out towards Beachy Head at the far edge of the bay, but it seems about as genuine as promising she'll jump off the top of the cliffs and fly. She could try, but that doesn't mean it's going to happen. Or even that it's possible.

And then, because she really needs to lighten the mood, she asks, 'Do you want an ice cream?'

Lydia smiles. 'Are you going to have mint choc chip?'

'Only if you're going to have raspberry ripple.'

CHAPTER FIFTY-THREE

NOW

Heather stands at the brow of a hill overlooking the Dart river. When she arrived here in September, there were leaves on the trees and the glow of an Indian summer warming the fields. It's November now, and still beautiful. The naked trees are silhouetted against a slate sky, and the bright colours have bled away, leaving behind a palette of cool blues, greys and mossy greens.

Her lease on the flat hadn't been up until a couple of weeks ago, but she hadn't moved back in after the night of the fundraising dinner. Faith and Matthew had been amazing, letting her stay with them until it was time to start this new job, and supporting her in the aftermath of her arrest. She picks her mobile out of her pocket and dials Faith's number.

'Hey, how are you?' Faith says chirpily as soon as she answers.

'Doing okay,' Heather says. 'Did everything get sorted with the flat? Did Carlton give me my security deposit back?'

'Yep,' Faith says, as if this is no small thing. Heather knows how stingy the man can be. However, she supposes she also knows how feisty her big sister can be, and it gives her a warm feeling to know

Faith has been fighting her corner. 'The flat is cleared and clean, and everything is in the storage facility at the top of Bromley Hill.'

'Thank you,' Heather says again. 'I don't know what I'd have done without you.'

'I was happy to help.'

Heather smiles into the phone. Funnily enough, although it must have been a lot of hard work to move her stuff out of her flat, she knows her sister is telling the truth. But then Heather's thoughts turn to where they always do these days, and her expression becomes more sombre. 'Did you see him?'

There's a pause. 'Yes. He asked about you.'

Heather's eyebrows rise. 'He did?'

'He's angry with you, Heather – and probably with good reason, given the circumstances – but he's not a monster. I think underneath the anger, he still wishes you well.'

Heather lets out a long breath. That, at least, is something. 'What did you tell him?'

'I told him you're doing okay. You are, aren't you? Doing okay?'

'Yes, I think I am. The sessions with the therapist have been... enlightening.'

'And your problem... How's that doing?'

Heather smiles again. Faith is usually so blunt about everything. It's funny to hear her trying to be delicate about the arrest. 'Fine. No more shoplifting.' She's felt the tingle once or twice, but she's been able to walk away. 'It's stunning here, Faith. You'll have to bring the kids down for a visit – maybe in the spring when they'll be able to go crabbing off the pontoon in the village.'

'That sounds like a plan. And talking of plans, I need to ask you about Christmas. How about coming up to us before we go to Dad's so we can catch a plane together?'

Heather thinks for a moment. 'Although I can fly direct from Exeter, I think I might come up and join you. You're flying on the twenty-second, right?'

'Right.'

'Is it okay if I arrive a couple of days before that? I've got a few things I need to do, some loose ends to tie up in that neck of the woods.'

'Of course!' Faith says. Her sister is never happier than when her guest room is occupied, Heather has discovered. 'I'm really looking forward to visiting Dad in Spain. It's the closest thing we've had to a proper family Christmas for decades!'

'I think it will be good for us,' Heather says, carefully sidestepping around the issue that, although she's surprised everyone by agreeing to go this year, she's slightly worried she'll find all those people stuffed together in one small house a little claustrophobic. But this is important to Faith, and she wants to pay her sister back for all she's done for her.

'How's the job going?'

Heather turns to face the house. 'It's interesting. Different. It's not just letters and diaries but movie memorabilia from the old owner's days as a Hollywood A-lister. I'm working with a film historian to try and pin down exactly what all the pieces are and which films they relate to. Her name was Hastings, you know. Laura Hastings. It almost feels like fate that I ended up here.' She shakes her head as she looks at the hard, straight lines of the Georgian architecture. 'I don't know. There's something… healing here.'

'Good,' Faith says softly. 'Good. Anyway, I'll call you tomorrow and give you our flight details.'

Heather smiles. Faith really can't stop trying to mother her, can she? But maybe that's all Faith has ever wanted to do, even if she sometimes goes about it in a brusque and prickly way. 'I love you, Faith,' she says quietly.

Her sister sounds a bit scratchy when she answers. 'I love you too. Now, I'm going to have to run because I've got a lot to organize. Speak soon!'

And then she's gone. Heather puts her phone in her pocket and walks back into the house, where the mobile signal will abruptly and inexplicably die. Out there on the hill is the only place she can seem to call from when she's at work.

She finds her employer, Louise, in the downstairs room that will soon house a display of its former owner's movie memorabilia. 'It's all gone to hell in a handbasket since you stepped outside,' she tells Heather. 'I've just had an email from a journalist wanting comment on the fact Jean Blake's sister has published a "tell-all" biography about her actor brother-in-law, Dominic Blake, saying he and Laura Hastings had an affair, and I'm livid.'

'Did they?'

Louise shakes her head. 'They fell in love, true, but Laura knew his wife was fragile, unstable. She walked away from the man she loved.' She smiles to herself. 'Seems so old-fashioned these days, doesn't it?'

Heather nods and smiles, but inside she's feeling even more sympathy for the woman she's been researching for the last month or two. She understands about walking away, doing the right thing.

'Anyway, our work is even more important now,' Louise says. 'Once we've found all the letters and gone through the diaries, I'm thinking about publishing them. I want to defend Laura's reputation. This vicious money-grabbing sister-in-law was still at boarding school when the alleged affair went on. I think she's making most of it up. She's made Laura out to be a man-eating monster, but there are always two sides to a story and I want to set the record straight.'

'I'd better get back to work, then,' Heather says, smiling. 'It seems we've got a fight on our hands.' But as she ascends the stairs to the old attic where her office is (complete with a cobweb or two, but she's trying not to notice them), she thinks about what Louise has just said, about monsters and other sides, and she realizes she's starting to truly understand what that means.

CHAPTER FIFTY-FOUR

NOW

A couple of days before she's due to fly to Malaga with Faith and her family, Heather makes what should have been a five-hour trip from her new home back to Kent. The roads are crazy with people just like her, people who've finished work for the year and are heading off to visit relatives. It takes her almost eight hours before she arrives on Faith's doorstep and collapses into an armchair.

To make up for the ordeal, her sister presents her, right there where Heather is sitting, with a bowl of beef stew that she's been keeping warm. This is a privilege indeed. Faith never allows anyone to eat anywhere other than at the table. Probably because they were never able to do a normal thing like that when they were growing up. Probably because, in her later days, their mother used to eat, sleep, watch TV, and generally live her life out of her armchair.

The fact that Faith has loosened the rules this way pleases Heather for two reasons: one, she feels her sister has lowered her impossibly high standards where she's concerned and is just treating her like a normal person and, two, Faith doesn't think Heather is a carbon copy of their mother any more. If she'd made that connection, she'd have shooed Heather off to the kitchen table in a jiffy.

Heather is glad of the fortifying meal because she knows she's going to require some supernatural strength to get through the following day. When she's cleared her plate and Matthew has brought her a cup of coffee, she pulls out her phone and sends a text to Jason:

Hi. I know this may be asking a lot, but would it be possible to drop round tomorrow evening? I wouldn't ask, but it's important. Thanks, Heather.

She resists adding an 'x', even though everything in her heart wants to.

She waits. She can almost picture him looking in shock at his phone, shaking his head, laying it on the coffee table and staring at it, weighing up whether she even deserves a reply.

Two hours later she's sitting in bed, her mobile strategically placed face-up on the duvet next to her. She's doing her best to ignore it and finish the novel she's reading instead, but the phone just sits there, disobediently doing nothing. When finally the screen flashes into life, it makes her jump.

Okay. Any time after six. J.

It feels as if there's a hole where the 'x' should be at the end of his text too. She wonders if he almost added it out of habit, then laughs hysterically inside her head at her own lunacy. Of course not. The fact that he's actually replied at all must be making her giddy.

The next evening she drives to Shortlands and parks outside her old house. She sits in the car for more than ten minutes before reaching for the door release. The truth is she doesn't want to go inside. As painful as it's been not seeing him, leaving this conversation unsaid means they're still connected, there's still something hanging between them. What she has to say today will change that forever.

Eventually, she prises herself from her car and walks up the drive. She automatically reaches into her pocket for keys as she approaches the door. Stupid. Faith gave them back for her. She rings the doorbell instead. The door buzzes and she pushes it open and steps into the hallway. It looks exactly the same as it did the last time she was here – the same black-and-white tiled floor, the same unruly potted palm in the corner – but it feels unreal, like a film set.

She climbs the stairs to the first floor, only to discover a miserable-looking guy dressed head to foot in black waiting at Jason's open door. She's never seen him before in her life. 'Yes?' he snaps.

'I-I'm looking for Jason,' she says.

'Downstairs,' he says and slams the door in her face.

Oh, thinks Heather as she stands there absorbing the information. Downstairs. In her old flat. *That's going to be… interesting*.

Instead of going back outside to press the right buzzer, she just knocks on the door of the ground-floor flat. A few seconds later a dark shape appears behind the partially glazed door, and then it opens and she's staring into Jason's eyes.

He doesn't smile, doesn't say 'Hi', just steps aside so she can pass him. Not sure where to go, she heads for the living room. The first thing that strikes her is how full it seems, with more furniture, more technology, more stuff in general.

Jason sees her looking. 'Do you want to sit down?'

Heather shakes her head. Even though it might be the polite thing to do, she's not sure she could sit still while she says what she has to say. She would dearly love to stand in the centre of the room, as she always used to when she was feeling het up, but there's a coffee table in the way. She chooses the biggest empty piece of floor, in front of the French doors, and stands there, one hand clasped painfully in the other as she tries to work out how to begin.

'I owe you an apology,' she tells him as he perches against the arm of the sofa, crosses his arms, and looks at her. There's no hiding, no misdirection now. She's using her new-found skill of being open, telling the truth about herself, but instead of wielding it to wound, as she did the last time she saw him, she hopes she can mend a little of what she tore. 'I'm really sorry for everything I put you through. It wasn't planned, wasn't calculated, but that doesn't make it any better.'

He nods but remains silent.

'And I owe you an explanation – you probably don't want to hear it. I wouldn't if I were you – but I'd like to give you one. If you'll let me?'

He doesn't say anything for a moment, but then replies, 'Okay.'

Heather breathes for a moment. *In… out. In… out.* And then she launches straight in. 'I started stealing after my mother died. Always baby clothes and toys. I didn't know why at the time. I didn't even want to. It just… happened.'

She checks his expression. He's looking predictably incredulous.

'I know, I know. It sounds like a cop-out.' She takes another hurried breath and carries on before she runs out of nerve. 'You know about my mother's hoarding, how I grew up, but there's stuff I didn't tell anyone, secrets I buried and never dealt with.'

She sees his eyes narrow at the word 'secrets' and she looks down at her feet. It was probably the wrong thing to say, but it's too late to change that now. The only thing she can do is carry on. 'I only even told Faith recently.'

She inhales. Time to stop being a coward. If she's going to say the rest, if she's going to tell him her most awful, shameful secret, the one that she's been running away from since she was a teenager, she needs to be looking at him. She lifts her head, makes sure she has eye contact and carries on.

'When I was fifteen, I got pregnant.'

CHAPTER FIFTY-FIVE

BABY SHOES

*They're tiny. I can sit both of them side by side in the palm
of my hand. They're made of lilac corduroy with a spray of
tiny purple flowers embroidered on the top. I sit on my bed
and stare at them. I have something growing inside me that
might one day fit into these, walk around in these. I am horrified and awestruck in equal measures.*

THEN

Heather's mother yells up the stairs for her. 'Heather? I need to talk
to you. Come down here!'

Typical, Heather thinks. *I always have to go to her, never the
other way round.* Her mother is so selfish.

She puts the little shoes down on her bed and stands up. She
found them in a plastic bag in the bathroom and she's fascinated
with them. Perhaps they belonged to her or Faith once upon a time?
Of course, they might just have been a result of one of her mum's
shopping splurges. She really has no idea.

Before Heather leaves the room, she picks the shoes up again and tucks them carefully under her pillow. Her mother doesn't know she's got these, and Heather doesn't know how she'd feel about it if she did. Better to just let it be one more secret stacked up alongside all the others.

As she heads out onto the landing, she catches her reflection in the mirror. She's wearing a baggyish T-shirt, so she pulls it up and inspects her stomach. She's done this at least once a day ever since she found out. There's a tiny bulge there now. Her skirt was getting tight before, but not so much that anyone could guess. She could have just gorged herself on cakes or chips or mint-choc-chip ice cream.

She's known for exactly six weeks now. Her mum has known for three. She caught Heather throwing up four mornings in a row and put two and two together. Seeing as she spends most of her life checked out and on planet *stuff*, Heather's quite pissed off that this was the moment her mother actually started to pay attention.

Her mum was alright at first, although she made Heather take another test, even though Heather told her she'd taken the bus to Lewisham and bought one there, where nobody knows her, that she followed the instructions, did it all properly. But now Mum has got over the shock, she's started nagging.

'Heather!' she yells again.

Heather sighs. This is probably her gearing up for another round. She pulls her top back down and negotiates the stairs. Only half of each tread is visible because her mother has started using the edges as a bookshelf again. There are at least ten volumes piled on every step.

She finds her mum in the living room, of course, sitting on her corner of the sofa. The shopping channel is blaring away on the TV.

'There you are,' she says. 'Now, we need to make an appointment to go and see the doctor to get all of this sorted out.'

Heather frowns. 'You said it would be my choice. I haven't made up my mind yet.' She knows she's been dithering but, for once, she has some control over her life, her future. Once she's made her decision, that'll be gone.

Her mother gives her an exasperated look. 'I know, but you're almost eleven weeks. We can't wait much longer.'

Heather stares back at her. She knows this. Of course she knows this. It's all she's been thinking about. She doesn't want to be one of those girls: just another teenager down the High Street with a pram. She has plans to go to university, to get away from this crap hole for good. She knows what her mother is trying to push her into doing makes logical sense, but it's just…

Her hand drifts to her stomach and she splays her fingers against the hint of a bump there. When she first found out she was horrified. One day, she actually leaned over the wall of the bridge next to Bickley station. *Would it hurt if I climbed up and stood there*, she thought to herself, *if I let myself fall? Would I flutter down like a leaf and just melt away or would I land with a sickening smack and still be alive when the wheels of the carriages tore over the top of me?* It really scared her, because it took close to ten minutes before she could make herself stop staring at the tracks and walk home.

At least she didn't have to face everyone at school. She hasn't been back since the incident behind the pavilion. How could she? She just refused to go in.

Her mum was livid at first, but when she found out the real reason, she continued to moan but didn't insist. Heather's hoping she'll be able to switch schools in the autumn. It's that or dropping out altogether because she's not going back to Highstead. And her mother can't make her, either, because who can she call? No one. She's not going to report her own daughter for truancy. That would mean someone from the school might come round to the house.

And then Dad would find out too. Something Heather fears almost as much as her mum does. She doesn't want him to look at her and think his Sweetpea has turned into a knicker-dropping ho. She wants to keep being his little girl.

'What if I want to keep it?' she asks her mother suddenly, her thoughts flinging themselves out of her head and off her tongue without warning. As much as she was gutted when she first realized she was pregnant, she's got used to the idea now. It's amazing to think she's growing something inside her, something alive. Something that will be cute and smiley and love her back no matter what.

Her mother's so shocked at her outburst that she turns the TV off, which has to be something, because it's bargain hour. She stands up. 'Don't be ridiculous, Heather! You're too young. You've haven't even taken your GCSEs, for goodness' sake! Just think for a change, will you? After all, you've got your whole life ahead of you.'

Heather has thought all of these things herself, but she's angry at her mother for saying this, because it's becoming clearer with each passing day that she's not thinking about her daughter's best interests, only her own. She doesn't want doctors or midwives or social workers involved because that would endanger her precious *stuff*.

'You said it was my choice!' Heather yells back at her. 'That means I get to pick, not that the right choice is the same as your choice because that's no choice at all!'

Heather turns and runs from the room before her mum can say anything else, but instead of dashing back upstairs and slamming her door, she heads out of the front door and down the road. She walks and walks until she starts to feel hungry, which means feeling queasy too these days. She remembers that there are some digestives in the kitchen which will deal with the sicky feeling quite nicely.

I'm keeping it, Heather thinks as she turns and heads back home. *I've come to my decision. There.*

She doesn't care how this baby was made or how much of a rat its father is, she will love it. It is something that is truly hers and hers alone, something her mother can't lose or trash or bury.

She feels almost peaceful for a few brief minutes, but as she nears the house she begins to feel chilly, as if clouds have moved in overhead, even though the sun is shining and the sky is blue.

When she reaches the gate, she stops and stares at the house. Not the way you do when you've lived somewhere for years – the present reality mixed in and blurred with a million memories of how it used to be – but the way someone standing there for the first time would see it.

Heather doesn't need to walk up to the front door and open it to look inside. She can pull up a mental snapshot of each and every room, of just how cluttered and filthy and messy it is.

How can I? she thinks, the cold feeling in her stomach growing. *How can I introduce a child I know I would love, even given my young age, to all this chaos?* She knows exactly how toxic it is, exactly how much the poor kid would get screwed up even if she tried to be the best mother in the universe.

She has no choice, does she? Not really. Because her mother has already made it for her. She did it years ago, after Dad and Faith left, when she decided to start filling the house up again even though Heather begged and cried and pleaded with her not to.

Heather opens the gate and her body feels like lead. She drags herself up the path. It's a horrible thing to acknowledge, because it makes her feel so small and worthless, but she has to face the fact that her mum has never done what's best for her children. In that moment, as Heather pushes the front door open and returns into the gloom and the stale smells, she decides she is brave enough to be different. She is not, and never will be, like her mother.

Heather feels numb as she returns to the living room and finds her mum staring at the blank television screen.

'Okay,' she says. 'Take me to the doctor. Let's make whatever appointments we need to make.'

Her mum leaps up, all smiles and kisses now, and she hugs Heather, rocks her like she's her little girl again. Heather lets her even though she wants to vomit all down her back – not because of the morning sickness, but because of the awful, twisting unfairness of it all – but as her mother rocks her to and fro she's thinking, *I hate you. You stole this from me, and I will never, ever forgive you for this, not for the rest of your life and certainly not for the rest of mine.*

CHAPTER FIFTY-SIX

NOW

Heather finishes her story. Jason listened patiently, if stony-faced.

'You think this is why you took things?' he says eventually.

Heather nods. 'Faith keeps speculating as to whether I'm trying to nurture my inner child because of our horrible upbringing, but I don't think that's it. After it was done... gone... my mum and I didn't ever talk about it again. I never told her how I felt – how devastated and angry I was – and then I was furious with her for bailing out on me before I had the chance. It wasn't long after that it all started.'

'But now you've stopped?' he asks, not entirely confidently, it has to be said.

'Yes. I hope so.' Heather looks at the floor again. Keeping eye contact has been exhausting. She feels as if she might be fading away. 'I don't want to do it. I never wanted to do it. But all the stuff with Lydia... The abduction... It was enough to send it all spiralling out of control. I'm glad it did, though, because it meant I finally had to deal with it.' She turns to stare out of the windows into the garden. 'My mother buried her "stuff" with *actual* stuff. I stupidly thought that because my physical space was so different to hers, that my mental space was too. Seems I was wrong. Seems there was a lot I wasn't facing, but I am now. Or at least I'm trying to.'

Jason is reflected in the glass. She sees him stand up behind her. 'Good.'

'Lydia told me I needed to forgive my mother,' Heather says, finding it easier to look at Reflection Jason than the real one. 'I think she's right. It's the only way to fully put the past behind me. I struggled with that for a bit, until I realized it wasn't the same as saying what she did was okay.'

He moves closer, until he's standing just behind her. They're not actually looking into each other's eyes because it's just ghostly reflections superimposed onto the dark garden, but Heather still feels something spear her through the chest when she sees the concern in his expression.

'You've actually forgiven her for this? For what you've just told me?'

The questions just keep on coming, don't they? It feels a bit like an interrogation, and just as uncomfortable as facing that sergeant in Hastings police station, but she understands the need for it. There was so much she didn't tell him.

'I've forgiven her for a lot. Looking at my own issues... compulsions... and talking through them with someone who has a professional understanding of them, has helped me see her differently. I'm finding that the more I can understand, the more I can let go. But not this. Not yet.' She shrugs and feels tears threaten. 'I'm trying,' she adds hoarsely and blinks the now-blurry version of Jason away.

Don't cry. Not now. Don't cry.

She turns around again. One last thing to say, and then she can go and collapse in her car and sob. 'So... That's why I'm glad you let me explain myself to you. I was hoping that if you understood, even just a little bit, that *you* might be able to forgive *me*?'

He rubs a hand over his face, shows the first chink of emotion. It looks as if he wants to step forward, to reach out and touch her, but he doesn't. It gives her the tiniest bit of hope.

'I would like to be your friend again,' she says hoarsely. 'One day, anyway.'

He sighs. 'I am your friend, Heather. You just… You know… It was a lot to deal with. Still is.'

She nods. 'I get that. I really do.'

Just friends, then. Maybe. Nothing more.

It's more than she deserves, she knows, but she still feels like curling into a ball and crying, right there in the middle of Jason's living-room floor. Instead, she straightens her spine, looks at him, and does her best to smile.

'Okay. Good. Thank you, Jason. That's all I wanted to say. I won't take up any more of your time.'

CHAPTER FIFTY-SEVEN

NOW

'You've been ever so quiet since you got back from seeing Jason,' Faith says later that evening after dinner.

Heather shrugs. She knows. She wasn't ready to share about it straight away, and she appreciates her sister's patience in bringing it up.

'I did what I went there to do,' she says blankly. 'I *think* it helped.'

'But not in the way you wanted it to?'

'No.'

Faith sighs. 'I wish I could say it'll all work out, but I really don't know that. What I do know is that you were incredibly brave to go.'

'It wasn't that brave. I should have gone months ago.'

'But you told him, you know, *everything*?'

Heather nods.

'I wish I'd known,' Faith says wistfully. 'But that was the summer after my A levels. I was all full of getting ready for uni, letting off steam with my friends...'

'I wish I'd told you,' Heather echoes, realizing now that Faith, although she had been even more blunt and spiky in those days, would have had her back.

'You must have been so scared,' Faith says.

'Yes,' Heather replies quietly, staring out into the garden, but she can't see any of the shrubs and trees through the glass, just her own pale face staring back at her. 'And although Mum was there with me all the time, I felt very alone too.' She turns to look at Faith. 'She was just kind of powering through it. I could tell that once it was all over she was just going to shut the lid on it and pretend it had never happened. I wanted to feel that way too, but there were so many mixed emotions. I knew it was a choice I had to make, but it wasn't one I wanted to make. But it was what it was. I'm learning to deal with that.'

Faith nods. 'There'll be other chances in the future.'

'You really think so?'

'I do. I know things didn't work out with you know who, but you're in a much better place than you were a year ago. When you're ready, you'll meet someone, I just know it.'

Heather wishes she could believe her sister, but she's not convinced. A tear slides from her eye and Faith hands her a tissue. 'Thanks,' Heather snuffles as she mops her face. It's such a relief not to get the lecture she knows she deserves, that she just starts crying harder.

But the next morning, as she sets off to Gatwick with Faith and her brood, she determines to dry her tears and concentrate on having the best Christmas the Lucas family have had in years.

They take a taxi to Nerja and arrive at their father's whitewashed house in a modern development, feeling tired and gritty. Their dad hugs them while Shirley bustles round, offering everyone drinks.

That evening after they've put the two strung-out kids to bed, Faith and Heather sit down with their father and have a long talk, and Heather tells him everything, even the secret she's kept from everyone for more than fifteen years. He sits back in his chair looking pale and shell-shocked, and then he hugs both sisters in turn, holding on a little longer than normal, before they retire for the night.

The next day, Shirley is like a wind-up toy, running this direction and that – chopping, frying, tidying, and plumping – but she shoos the sisters away when they offer to help, saying they're supposed to be on holiday. Why don't they go to the swimming pool in the centre of the development? The kids will love it and there will be more than a few British families for them to make friends with.

So that's what they do. Matthew affixes armbands to his kids and splashes around with them in the pool, while Heather and Faith lie on sun loungers, sipping ice-cold drinks. As the afternoon wears on, they graduate to sangria, which is probably a mistake.

Heather sighs. 'Do you know that I caught Shirley "tidying up" all the cutlery before dinner last night? I'd laid it nicely, but it obviously wasn't good enough for her because when I walked past the dining room ten minutes later she was readjusting it all. When it comes to Christmas lunch, I wouldn't be surprised if she gets out of those measuring rods out they use for state dinners at Buckingham Palace. She probably keeps one tucked up her sleeve, just in case!'

Faith chuckles from behind her sunglasses. 'She is a bit OCD, isn't she?'

'A bit? I swear, if she plumps one more cushion, I'm going to scream!'

'Driving you nuts?' Faith asks.

'Yes!'

'Because she won't accept help from anyone and, even though she invited us here, you can't help feeling that she's secretly fretting we keep messing up her stuff?'

'Yes!' Heather says again, more emphatically.

Faith arches an eyebrow and gives her a slow, knowing smile. 'Welcome to my world,' she says drily.

Heather sits up so fast she almost spills her sangria down her front. 'I am not like that! I am not!'

Faith just chuckles.

'I'm not, am I?' Heather repeats, sounding a little less sure of herself.

'Maybe not exactly the same, but I can see parallels.'

Heather finishes her drink while she absorbs this information. 'You think I'm being too tough on her?'

'A little. She's a bit high-maintenance, yes, but she adores Dad and she's got a heart of gold underneath those marigolds. I'm just saying you should give her more of a chance. You've never really got to know her.'

'You think I might end up like that if I don't mend my ways?' Heather asks, half smiling, half serious.

'Oh, almost certainly,' Faith says, closing her eyes and sinking into the sun lounger. 'I happen to know for a fact Santa's put a pair of bright-pink rubber gloves in your Christmas stocking.'

'He has not!'

Faith just smiles, and Heather starts to get worried. She knows Matthew and Faith have done stockings for everyone, not just for the kids.

'Oh, shut up and drink your sangria!' Heather directs at her smug-looking sister, but she's also smiling. She pretends to ignore Faith and settles down to read her novel for another twenty minutes. When she's starting to feel a little bit sleepy from the combination of reading and alcohol, she puts her book down and turns to Faith, who doesn't seem to have moved a millimetre since their last exchange.

'In this new-found spirit of Lucas-family honesty, I think I ought to come clean and tell you that Lydia came down to visit me at the end of November.'

That gets her sister's attention. Faith pushes her sunglasses back on her head and sits up.

'Lydia? Isn't that a bit weird?'

Heather exhales. On the face of it, she supposes it is a bit weird, but she and Lydia have kept in contact. For some reason, Lydia feels like family now, even after what happened all those years ago. Or maybe even because of it.

'She lives in a horrible little bedsit in Hastings, Faith. You should see it! And she has no one. Mainly because I think she's been punishing herself all these years for doing what she did.'

Faith snorts. It seems her forgiving mood only extends as far as the boundaries of her family at the moment. 'Maybe she should.'

'Stand down, Mamma-Bear Faith,' Heather retorts, which earns her another eyebrow-raise. 'If I can get past it, so can you. Anyway, Lydia fell in love with South Devon. I'm deliberating over whether I should encourage her to move there, maybe even see if I can talk to Louise about getting her a job locally. I think it's the fresh start she needs.'

'I get why you wanted to see her again, to say thanks for what she did with the police and all that, but I'm not sure I get why you want to stay in touch long term,' Faith says. 'Like I said... it's weird.'

It makes perfect sense to Heather, so she pauses for a moment and tries to reformulate her argument in a way her sister can digest.

'Helping Lydia will help me too,' she explains, 'because I don't think I can let go of it all if she can't. Does that make sense?'

'Almost,' Faith says grudgingly.

'She's nice. Heart of gold underneath all that guilt and self-loathing. Maybe *you* ought to give *her* a chance?'

It looks very much as if Faith is searching hard for a witty comeback, but eventually she gives in and says, 'Touché! Nicely played, little sister.'

'Does that mean I'm the winner and you're the amateur?' Heather says with a mischievous glint in her eye.

Faith plants both feet on the floor, and Heather knows any second now she's going to need to run.

'No way!' her sister shouts, flinging off her sunglasses and leaping to her feet in one smooth motion.

Heather is fast, but not fast enough. Twenty seconds later, both are in the pool, much to the delight of the armbanded children watching them from the shallow end. Who actually got the better of whom will probably be a point of discussion until next year's Christmas dinner.

* * *

There's a lull in the storm of Christmas lunch preparations, and it's during this quiet period, when Shirley is treating herself to a well-earned buck's fizz, that Heather's father finds her and leads her onto the balcony for a chat.

He shakes his head. 'I've been thinking about what you and Faith told me yesterday. Obviously, after you'd left Hawksbury Road for good to go to university, I found out Christine had gone back to her old ways, but I don't think I realized that it got so bad so quickly after I left. Especially for you.' He sighs heavily. 'Heather, I'm so sorry I didn't ask more questions.'

He has that haunted look in his eyes again, a look that he hasn't worn for years. Not since he met Shirley, really, Heather realizes.

'Dad. You couldn't have known. I lied to you – so many times. I got very, very good at covering my tracks.'

'But I knew how loyal you were to your mother. I should have come round to check for myself, but I just... I just...' He trails off, and he doesn't need to finish his sentence. Heather knows exactly what he was going to say. He couldn't face it. And she can't condemn him for that. For many years, she found that house impossible to face too. It's what it did. It might have looked pretty with its elegant proportions and high ceilings, but that house ate people up and spat them out.

'I should have paid more attention, Heather. I let you down when you needed me most,' he says and there's a hollow tone in his voice. 'I'm so sorry, Sweetpea. Can you ever forgive me?'

'Oh, Dad.' Heather can't bear to see his eyes glisten like that. She knows he's talking about the grandchild that could have been. 'Of course I do. We were all victims of the hoarding. Even Mum.'

She wraps her arms around him and pulls him close. There's nothing else they need to say.

'We'd better go and see if Shirley needs a hand,' Heather says finally.

He just chuckles. 'Good luck with that.'

When they go back into the house, Heather is shocked to see Alice and Barney laying the table. She looks at Faith, who is 'supervising' them from across the open-plan living space with a glass of prosecco. 'She cracked,' Faith says, raising her glass to her sister. 'The kids were so overexcited that she practically begged me to keep them occupied.'

'Done!' Alice squeals as she throws down the last fork. 'Can we open another present now? Can we, Mummy? Please, please, *please?*'

'Okay,' Faith says, and points to two small packages that seem to be ready and waiting for them near the Christmas tree. The two children run over and rip the paper to shreds.

Heather looks at the table. It's an utter disaster. There are knives and forks in the wrong places, the plates aren't evenly spaced, and Alice's version of arranging the napkins 'nicely' is to dump them in the middle of the table and run. Heather starts adjusting, tweaking. Lining things up the way Shirley likes them. Faith is right. She's spent her whole life waiting for her sister to give her a break over stuff like this, so maybe it's time to pay it forward.

When her stepmother arrives from the kitchen with a couple of bowls of homemade cranberry sauce, she almost drops them in surprise. The table looks perfect. She looks first at the table, then at the two kids, and then back at the table, frowning.

Heather goes over to Shirley, takes the sauce dishes from her and places them in exactly the right spot on the table. Before her stepmother walks away, Heather leans in and gives her a peck on the cheek.

'Thank you for doing all of this for us,' she says. 'We really appreciate it. And I know how hard it can be having people in your home.'

CHAPTER FIFTY-EIGHT

NOW

Faith invites Heather to stay on with them in Westerham when they return to England on 28 December, saying it'd be miserable spending New Year's Eve in a tiny cottage all on her own. The idea of a quiet evening ushering in the new year quite appealed to Heather – she's got a lot to say goodbye to from the old year before it disappears – but she's done some thinking while she's been away and there are a few things she wants to do before she heads back down to Devon and her new life, so she decides to take her sister up on her offer.

She gets up early the next morning and goes to the facility where the rest of her belongings are stored, pulls up the shutter on her unit, and stares at all the stuff there. She's been nervous about doing this – really, she's been putting it off since September – but she doesn't feel anything as she stands at the entrance and scans the locker full of boxes. No waves of panic, no urge to run. Maybe it's because it's out of context now it's neither in the house on Hawksbury Road nor in that dreaded spare room, but she hopes it's more than that.

She spends the whole day going through each and every container. It's weird, these things just don't seem connected to her any more. She can lift them up, categorize and sort them just as she does the documents and items that are part of her daily work. She can see them for what they are now, not for what they represent.

She takes two runs to the council dump and three runs to various charity shops, then comes back again to sort the last few containers. At the bottom of the last one she finds an envelope. She's about to screw it up and throw it away, but something makes her look inside.

Lying there, looking slightly tarnished and in need of a good clean, is her mother's engagement ring. She lifts it out and looks at it. She remembers the story her mother used to tell her and Faith, when they begged and begged and begged to hear it again, of how their dad had proposed. She remembers how her mother had smiled when she used to tell them the story, how she'd look all misty-eyed and then hug her girls hard. Heather slips the ring onto her own finger. The memory attached to this object is a happy one, an important one, no matter how her parents' marriage turned out.

That accomplished, she crushes the last cardboard box, takes the one crate of things she's keeping from all that stuff, locks the storage unit again, then hands the keys to the man at the desk and walks away.

* * *

Heather wakes up on New Year's Eve feeling strangely energetic. A walk is needed, she decides, brisk and long, and full of bracing country air. She grabs her scarf from the hooks near the front door then goes in search of her phone. She could swear she left it plugged in and charging on the kitchen counter last night but now it's nowhere to be seen.

'Alice? Barney?' Heather yells and moments later two angelic-looking children come skidding into the kitchen. 'Have either of you seen my phone?' Barney shakes his head. 'How about you, Alice?'

'I think I saw Mummy with it,' she says, blinking innocently at her aunt.

Heather frowns. Alice has form for nabbing people's phones and playing any game she can find on them. 'Are you sure you don't mean, "I had it and Mummy took it away from me"?' The look of affront on her niece's face almost makes Heather laugh, but she manages to hold it in.

She finds Faith in the bathroom, giving the toilet a good scrub. 'Alice said you had my phone?'

Faith goes still, toilet brush poised. She stands up and turns around. 'Um,' she says.

'I wondered if you'd had to rescue it from her?'

Faith's face breaks into a wide and unexpected smile. 'Oh...yes! I did.' She pulls it from her back pocket and hands it over. 'You know what she's like,' she says and then quickly turns her attention back to the toilet, plunging the brush under the waterline and scrubbing furiously.

Heather stares at her phone. She frowns, then looks back at her sister. 'Anyway, I'm thinking of going for a walk? Possibly to Chartwell. I know the house is closed, but the gardens will be open. Want to come?'

Faith stands up abruptly, the toilet brush dripping on her nice clean floor. 'Oh!' she says, then repeats herself. 'Oh.'

'"Oh", what?'

'Um, it's just that...' She waves her hand, indicating the toilet.

'I've got this to finish and then we're having roast beef with all the trimmings for lunch. Can you hang on until this afternoon? We could go for a stroll across the fields instead. I'm always worried Barney's going to dig something up in those lovely gardens and we'll be banned from the National Trust for life.'

Heather chuckles. 'Okay, but I think I'll just go and get a breath of fresh air now anyway, and then I'll come back and help you with lunch.' It's grey and misty outside, but it's promising to be a glorious, bright winter's day with a crisp blue sky and a milky-white sun and she's just itching to get out there. 'See you in a bit!' she says, and then she's out the bathroom door and down the stairs, ignoring Faith's pleas to just hang on a minute.

* * *

Heather spends a blissful half an hour walking round the fringes of the village and returns to her sister's house ready to down the largest and hottest cup of tea known to mankind. She's taken some amazing pictures on her phone of the frosty hedges, and she's scrolling through them as she turns into Faith's driveway, eager to show off her photographic prowess, but when she sees who's standing there on the gravel, her heart stops.

There's a tall man dressed in leathers, standing beside a motorbike. A Harley. *Don't be stupid*, she tells herself. *You're just seeing what you want to see.* But then the rider unstraps his helmet and takes it off, and it's him. It's Jason.

Heather's mobile phone hits the gravel beside her feet.

She's still fumbling to pick it up when he arrives next to her. She straightens, phone all gritty and dusty in her hand, flushing, stuttering.

'Hi,' he says.

'Hi.' She stares into his face. *It is really him, isn't it? She's not hallucinating?* 'What are you doing here?'

'I came to see you.'

She knows he's standing in front of her so, logically, his words make sense. But, at the same time, they really, really don't. 'W-why?'

He sighs heavily. 'I went on a date last night. I was trying to move on.'

Heather takes a moment. He went on a date last night, but he's here to see her this morning? That also makes no sense. It's as if, ever since she turned the corner into Faith's driveway, reality has gone a little loopy. 'You did?'

'Yeah.' Jason stares blankly for a moment, obviously replaying the previous evening's date in his head. It just makes Heather's stomach churn all the harder. 'She was nice,' he adds wearily. 'It was fine. We had a good time, but… '

'But…?' she echoes.

'But this morning I found myself getting on my bike and heading for Westerham.'

Heather shakes her head. A moment ago, her mind was feeling fresh and energised and clear, but now it's full of cobwebs and fuzz. 'But how did you know I'd be… ?' she trails off as she notices her sister's face pressed up against the lounge window. It all starts dropping into place – the phone, the stalling tactics when she said she wanted to go out. 'Faith,' she mutters.

He nods. 'She thought maybe we had some unfinished business.'

'And do we?' she asks. 'Have unfinished business?'

He sighs and nods again.

Heather can imagine the woman he took out to dinner last night. She can imagine them sitting in a restaurant, Jason flashing his smile, the woman smiling back, looking at him from under her lashes. She's got a good job and lots of friends. She's witty and confident and sleek. 'I still don't get it,' she tells him. 'Why would you pick a freak like me over someone nice, someone normal?'

He gives her a wonky smile. 'You're not a freak, Heather. You're just someone who went through a really tough time.' He steps closer. Heather can't tear her eyes away from his. 'And we're all a bit messed up in our own way. Nobody's perfect. But it took guts to come and say what you said to me. I thought about it for days afterwards, couldn't get it out of my head.' He reaches forward and touches her face, his eyes full of emotion. 'I'm so sorry that happened to you...'

Heather doesn't know quite what to say to that, so she doesn't say anything. There's a dangerous stinging at the top of her nose. 'But I lied to you. You hate it when people lie to you.'

'I told myself that, but...' he shrugs '...here I am, because it occurred to me that honesty isn't just about what you say or don't say. Sometimes it's about being vulnerable, about being completely honest about who you are – and you did that quite spectacularly the morning you came to talk to me.'

As much as his words are making Heather fly inside, she rubs her forehead, trying to smooth her jumbled thoughts out. 'What does that mean? What are you saying?' She's starting to feel a bit dizzy.

He takes her hand away from her head and holds it, looks into her eyes. 'I'm saying that I'd like you to give me another chance. I think we could be a good fit, Heather, despite everything that went on.' And then he leans in and kisses her. Heather lets go of her last shreds of disbelief, winds her arms around his neck and kisses him back. He understands, you see. He understands that she ripped herself open for him, bared all. There are no secrets or lies left to unearth.

There's a small whoop of joy from the vicinity of the living room window. Heather smiles against Jason's lips. Oh, her meddling sister…

Jason smiles too, then pulls away. He walks over to his motorcycle and opens the lock box on the back. Inside is his spare helmet and leathers. 'Want to go for a ride?'

'But Faith's cooking a big meal for later.' Heather glances over to the house.

Faith has opened a window and is leaning through it, grinning like a loon. 'Sod the Sunday dinner!' she calls out cheerfully, not even caring that the kids might be listening, then gives her sister a thumbs-up.

Heather laughs, runs over to the open window and shoves her coat into Faith's open arms, then she quickly slips the leathers on and fastens the helmet on her head.

'Have you had breakfast yet?' he asks, and Heather realizes that in her desire to get out and walking in the fresh air this morning, she completely forgot to eat. She shakes her head and he smiles. 'Fancy a sausage butty?'

Heather's not sure whether to laugh or cry. 'That sounds perfect.'

After she's climbed on behind him, he looks over his shoulder and revs the engine. 'Got everything you need?'

Heather hadn't even got her phone, which is with Faith, inside her coat pocket. She leans against him and presses her cheek against the warm leather of his jacket. 'Yes.' She's got everything she needs. Right here, right now.

The engine rumbles into life. She holds on tight and closes her eyes.

CHAPTER FIFTY-NINE

NOW

Heather is due to drive back down to Devon the day after the New Year's Day, but she has a couple of pit stops to make before she gets truly on her way. First, she and Faith drive to Beckenham crematorium. They park their respective cars and start to stroll through the well-tended gardens, each clutching a bouquet. It's been raining but has stopped now, leaving the tarmac paths shiny and the first flowers of the year beginning to broadcast their scent.

'So... you and Jason,' Faith says.

Heather smiles. 'Me and Jason,' she echoes, feeling a warm, quivery feeling in her stomach. He'd brought her back to Faith's after their breakfast the other morning, and her sister had insisted he stay for roast beef. She'd even pushed lunchtime back until mid-afternoon so they wouldn't be too full to enjoy it. And then she'd waved them off on his bike when Heather had hinted she'd like some more time alone with him.

They'd gone back to Jason's flat and spent New Year's Eve quietly, drinking red wine, curled up on the sofa, talking. And not talking. It had felt good to clear the air completely before the chimes signalling the New Year had rung.

'What now?' Faith asks. 'Isn't it going to be a bit difficult having a long-distance relationship?'

'It's only five hours away,' Heather says, 'not even that on a good day.' She grins. 'And he has transport…'

Faith smiles back. 'That he does.'

'Besides, I'm only there for another nine months, and I feel I'm readier than I've ever been for a relationship, but it still might be a good idea to take things slowly.'

'I'm happy for you,' Faith says, smiling.

'I'm happy for me too,' Heather replies and tucks her arm in her sister's. 'Come on. I think I'm ready to do what we came here to do.' It's not much further to the memorial garden where their mother's ashes are buried, marked by a small plaque. The sisters reach the spot and stand there in silence for maybe five minutes.

Faith lays her flowers first, a bunch of clean, white lilies, and Heather steps back under a small yew tree as her sister does so. She can hear Faith mumbling a few words and, as much as they came to do this together, this moment is private.

As she waits, Heather touches the diamond solitaire on her right hand, searching for a connection to its former owner and finding it. When Faith stands up, Heather takes her turn, reaching down to lay a collection of yolk-coloured sunflowers – their mother's favourite – in front of the plaque. She brushes the polished granite with the tips of her fingers, feels the relief of the words 'Beloved Mother'.

'I'm sorry it wasn't different,' she whispers. 'For all of us. Rest in peace, Mum.'

CHAPTER SIXTY

NOW

Heather has one more task to accomplish after she and Faith hug and go their separate ways. She drives to Hawksbury Road, where she parks opposite her old house.

After a few moments she gets out of the car, lifting a wicker basket filled with goodies – good-quality teabags and coffee, some all-butter shortbread and chocolate-chip cookies, a bottle of wine, and a couple of candles – and walks across the road.

However, when she gets closer, she hesitates. She didn't think anyone would be here so close to the holidays, but a removals van is parked outside. She had intended just to leave it on the doorstep and slip away. She starts to turn back towards her car, but then she pauses. Maybe she can. There's lots of movement, lots of noise and bustle. It would be easy to just creep up to the porch and away again without being spotted.

Shifting the handle of the wicker basket more securely onto her arm, she holds her head up, tries to look as if she belongs there, and crosses the road. She makes it up the drive and is almost at the front door before someone notices her.

'Hi, can I help you?' a woman in her forties with immaculate highlights asks.

Heather swallows. 'I didn't realize you were moving in today. I just bought a—'

She is interrupted by two girls with long blonde hair, about primary-school age, bundling past her and arguing about who is going to have the biggest bedroom. Their mother shushes them and then turns back to Heather.

'Sorry, what were you saying?'

Heather hands the basket over. 'It's just a "happy new home" gift. Just a few things for the house.'

The woman beams at her. 'How lovely! Are you one of our new neighbours?'

Heather smiles. 'Sort of. I just wanted to say I hope you're happy here. It's a wonderful house. I always knew that with a little bit of love and attention it could be the perfect family home.'

'That's very kind of you to say. Would you like to come in for a cup of tea? It's a bit chaotic, but…'

Heather's tempted because she's terribly nosy to see what they've done to the interior, but she shakes her head. 'Thank you, but no. I've got to run.' And she smiles, turns away and walks down the drive, then climbs into her car and leaves Hawksbury Road for the very last time.

Acknowledgements

Huge thanks to my editor, Anna Baggaley, who was so enthusiastic when I pitched the idea for this story that I hardly stopped to think how different it was from some of my other books and so I just dived straight in and started writing. It took a bit of trial and error to get some of the story elements right, but I'm very thankful for her bird's-eye view of the story when was so close to it that I couldn't see which path was the right one to take. Massive thanks also to Lisa Milton and the wonderful, dynamic team at HQ. I'm very grateful that I have a home where I am free freedom to explore the stories that excite me.

I would like to thank Colin Gale, archivist at Bethlem Museum of the Mind, for taking time to talk to me and answering all my questions about his fascinating job, even though much of the detail hit the cutting room floor, so to speak, in the editing process.

As always, I need to thank my fellow authors who cheer me on through the writing process – I surely wouldn't get through it without you ladies! All my love to Donna Alward, Susan Wilson, Heidi Rice, Daisy Cummins and Iona Grey. Thanks too to the readers who contact me to let me know how much they enjoy my stories – you honestly don't know how much that tweet or Facebook message or email means! When I'm down in the writing dumps and think I've lost the ability to reach 'The End', you shine a light on my path.

Many thanks, too, to my husband, Andy, for sharing his passion and knowledge about probate genealogy, and to both him and my daughters, Siân and Rose, for enduring endless episodes of "Hoarders", all in the name of research, and for putting up with my sudden and unexpected need to de-clutter our house while I was writing *The Memory Collector*. I didn't anticipate how much writing about other people and their 'stuff' would affect my attitude to my own belongings and I'm very grateful for all the help with charity shop runs and trips to the dump and for not locking me in the cupboard under the stairs when I asked, for the hundredth time, "But do you really *need* it?"!

And, finally, all honour to my God and Saviour for being the master storyteller. I would not be where I am today without your strength, love and inspiration.

ONE PLACE. MANY STORIES

Bold, innovative and
empowering publishing.

FOLLOW US ON:

@HQStories